D1639476

000000931708

A TAINT IN THE BLOOD

According to the police, Victoria Bannister's two boys were in a drugged stupor when their mother set fire to the house. Their lives were insured for a million apiece. Now, three decades too late, her daughter wants Kate Shugak to prove Victoria Bannister's innocence. The case is as cold as they come. But when her client is killed Kate has to wonder why – with Victoria behind bars – the people in this family are still dying...

A TAINT IN THE BLOOD

A TAINT IN
THE BLOOD

by

Dana Stabenow

Magna Large Print Books
Long Preston, North Yorkshire,
BD23 4ND, England.

British Library Cataloguing in Publication Data.

Stabenow, Dana
    A taint in the blood.

    A catalogue record of this book is
    available from the British Library

    ISBN   978-0-7505-3966-1

First published in Great Britain in 2013 by Head of Zeus Ltd.

Copyright © Dana Stabenow, 2004

Cover illustration © Karina Simonson by arrangement with
Arcangel Images

The moral right of Dana Stabenow to be identified as the author of
this work has been asserted in accordance with the Copyright,
Designs and Patents Act, 1988

Published in Large Print 2014 by arrangement with
Head of Zeus Ltd.

All Rights reserved. No part of this publication may be reproduced,
stored in a retrieval system, or transmitted in any form or by any
means, electronic, mechanical, photocopying, recording or otherwise
without the prior permission of the Copyright owner.

Magna Large Print is an imprint of Library Magna Books Ltd.

Printed and bound in Great Britain by
T.J. (International) Ltd., Cornwall, PL28 8RW

This is a work of fiction. All characters, organizations, and events portrayed in this novel are either products of the author's imagination or are used fictitiously.

For
Janice Weiss,
the real head of women's education at
Hiland Mountain Correctional Facility,
who is making a difference every day

All the rings and the relics encrusted with sin
– And the taint in a blood that was running too
   thin.

– 'Sale,' Theodore Roethke

CHAPTER 1

'I'll get it,' Kate said, and fetched the Crisco forthwith.

Auntie Vi eyed her. 'Your auntie not that old, Katya.'

'I know, Auntie,' Kate said. 'But I was closer.'

She had, in fact, been in the next room at the time, but Auntie Vi, exercising monumental, not to mention unnatural, restraint, forbore to comment.

'I can do that,' Kate said, taking the scraper out of Old Sam's hand. The *Freya* was in dry dock, where her hull had been drying out above the high-tide line in preparation for a new coat of copper paint.

Old Sam took the scraper back. 'I can do it myself.'

'I know, but I can help,' Kate said, reaching for the scraper again.

Old Sam warded her off. 'Yeah, and the next thing I'll be listening to you whine about getting the goddamn copper paint outta your hair. Now you get outta mine, girl.'

'I can do that,' Kate told Bernie, and took the bar rag out of his hand.

'You know that's what I do,' Bernie said, watching her with a wary eye.

'I know, but I'm here,' Kate said, chasing an

elusive drop of beer.

'You certainly are,' Bernie said, and went to pour himself a beer, an event almost unheard of in the annals of the Roadhouse, then sat down at a table, an event unparalleled in memory of man.

'Oh, shut up,' she told Harvey Meganack at the July board meeting. 'You know Billy's right. Any moron knows there's no way the shareholders are going to vote to open up Iqaluk to drilling anyway.'

Harvey's face turned a dark and unbecoming red.

There was a collective suck of indrawn air around the conference table in the Niniltna Native Association's boardroom, followed by a thud as the forelegs of Billy Mike's chair hit the floor. 'You know, Kate,' he said, 'I really appreciate you dropping by.'

He propelled her to her feet and frog-marched her to the door.

'I was just trying to–'

'Come back anytime,' he said, closing the door in her face.

'That's nice of you, Kate,' Ruthe Bauman said, looking askance at the cord of wood stacked next to the back door of her cabin. 'It'll go real well with the five cords I already ordered from Darryl Totemoff.'

'You can never have too much firewood,' Kate said.

Ruthe looked down into Kate's earnest face. 'No,' she said, 'I suppose you can't.'

'Give her to me,' Kate said, stretching out her arms.

Bobby glared. 'I can diaper my own damn daughter!' he bellowed. 'What the hell's got into you, Shugak, the Red Cross? Jesus!'

Hurt, Kate said, 'I just wanted to help.'

'Well, stop it!' Bobby said. He rolled his chair over to Katya's changing table. Katya stared at Kate over his shoulder, blue eyes blinking at Kate from beneath a corkscrew assortment of black curls.

Kate went to stand next to Dinah. 'I could dry those dishes for you,' she said in a small voice.

'You can wash them, dry them, and put them away if you want,' Dinah said amiably.

Brightening, Kate took the sponge and waded in.

'What in hell is going on with that broad?' Bobby demanded of his wife, soul mate, and chosen partner in life when the sound of Kate's truck had faded across the Squaw Candy Creek bridge. 'I can't lift a hand in my own goddamn house! For crissake, Dinah, I'm not some cripple!'

'I know,' Dinah said soothingly. In fact, he was missing both his legs below the knee, souvenir of a land mine in Vietnam, but it wasn't as if it slowed him down much. Or at all.

Bobby settled Katya into her crib for her afternoon nap. Katya, infuriatingly, stuck her thumb in her mouth and her butt up in the air, gave a deep, satisfied burp, and promptly fell asleep. 'She never does that for me,' Dinah said enviously.

But Bobby was not to be distracted. 'So what's wrong with her?'

15

Dinah deduced correctly that he wasn't speaking of their daughter. His face – taut black skin stretched over high cheekbones, a broad brow, and a very firm chin – bore an anxious expression, which didn't become him, mostly because she'd never seen it before. Her heart melted, and she subsided gracefully into the lap that there was enough left of his legs to make. 'I think it's her house.'

He was honestly bewildered. 'Her house?'

'The one the Park built for her. I think she feels like she owes us.'

He still didn't get it, but he was calming down. He tucked a strand of white-blond hair behind her ear. 'Why us?'

'Not just us us,' Dinah said. 'Everybody in the Park us. Everyone who had a hand in the construction and the furnishing thereof anyway. And the purchase of materials for.'

'Oh, sure,' Bobby said after a moment. 'I get it. Her cabin burns down and the Park rats build her a new one, so she turns herself into a one-woman version of the Salvation Army, with a little Jimmy Carter thrown in?'

'All summer long,' Dinah said, nodding her head. 'Billy Mike told me he had to throw her out of an NNA meeting before things escalated into a shooting war.'

Dinah was happy when Bobby grinned and then threw back his head and laughed out loud. 'I'd like to have been a fly on the wall that day.'

'Yeah, Billy said Kate kept insisting on telling the truth, out loud and in front of God and everybody. Said it took him a month to calm the

16

board down to where he could get a decent vote out of them.'

Bobby shook his head. 'How long do you think she's going to keep this up?'

'I don't know. Edna told me Kate got her and Bernie a counselor so they could work on their marriage. Annie Mike says Kate's been calling in favors all the way up to the state supreme court to help out with Vanessa's adoption.' Dinah paused, and said with a straight face, 'I hear tell she took Keith and Oscar fishing for reds down at the aunties' fish camp.'

Bobby stared at her with an expression as close to awe as his face could humanly manage. 'You gotta be shittin' me, Cookman.'

Dinah shook her head, grave as a judge. 'I shit you not, Clark. She camped out with them, and then she took them into Cordova, where she treated them to breakfast at the Coho Café.'

Bobby whooped so loudly this time that Katya grumbled and wiggled her butt. There were actual tears of mirth in Bobby's eyes. 'Did they hit on any of the fishermen?'

'Not that I've heard.'

He wiped his eyes. 'She's gonna help the whole friggin' Park into an early grave is what she's gonna do.'

Dinah grinned. 'If someone doesn't help her there first. I also hear tell that she was sitting in on one of the aunties' quilting bees at the Road-house the other night.'

There was a moment of dumbstruck disbelief. Bobby's jaw might even have dropped.

'She sewed the quilt they were working on to

her jeans.'

This time, his whoop was so loud, Katya did wake up.

'Okay,' Old Sam said. He took a deep, calming breath and removed the boat hook from Kate's hand.

'But Uncle–'

'Go to the galley,' he said. 'Write fish tickets.'

'But–'

'Go. Now.'

Old Sam didn't sound calm that often, and when he did, it always presaged a force 10 storm. Johnny held on to his pew with both hands, watching with wide eyes as Kate obeyed orders, and spent the rest of the sunny August afternoon stuck at the galley table, writing fish tickets for fishermen who were always absolutely certain that they had delivered half a dozen more reds than Old Sam had counted when they were transferring them to the *Freya's* hold. Even Mutt deserted her, preferring the open air on the bow to the claustrophobic confines of the galley. Miserable, Kate didn't blame her.

When the period ended and the last fisherman cast off, Old Sam fired up the engine and they left Alaganik Bay for the cannery in Cordova. Johnny hid out in the chart room, nose stuck assiduously in a beat-up paperback copy of Zenna Henderson's *Pilgrimage*. They could have used a Presence on the *Freya*, was what he was thinking.

Old Sam didn't say a word to Kate the whole way, even when she brought his lunch to the bridge. It was a corned beef sandwich, too, with

18

lots of mayo and mustard and a layer of lettuce thick enough to choke a horse, served on home-made sourdough bread, his favorite sandwich in the whole entire world.

Still in silence, they delivered their fish, took on fuel, and found their slip in the boat harbor. Shitting Seagull waved from the harbormaster's shack and disappeared, leaving Kate to wonder why he hadn't come down to say hi like he always did. She had a bit of walrus tusk that she'd scored from Ray in Bering, part of a gift package she'd received from the Chevak family. She should probably head on out to Bering sometime soon, come to think of it, see if Stephanie was the youngest astronaut in NASA yet, and if she wasn't, to sit down and help her figure out a career path to get her there.

In the meantime, the walrus tusk would go to Gull, who carved ivory whenever he got his hands on some, and sold the results through a gift shop in Anchorage. If they hadn't already been presold to Andromedans who'd stopped in town on a joyride from the Great Spiral Nebula. Kate pulled the last knot tight and climbed the ladder to the wheelhouse.

'Hold it,' Old Sam said. He was still sitting in the captain's chair, tilted back against the bulkhead.

She paused. 'What's up, Uncle?'

He cranked his head around the door into the chart room. 'You?'

'Me?' Johnny said.

'You. Uptown. Go visit your girlfriend.'

'I don't have a girlfriend,' Johnny said.

'Find one.'

Johnny delayed long enough to mark the page in his book, and vanished.

Old Sam pointed at a stool. 'You,' he said to Kate. 'Sit.'

She sat. 'What?' she said. She craned her neck to see Johnny hotfooting it down the float toward the harbormaster's shack. Probably going to ask Gull what alien ships were moored in transient parking this week. Last time they were there, it had been Cetaceans. Or maybe a bureaucrat from the Council of Planets on a regular inspection, driving Gull nuts with demands for colder water to cool the drives. She kind of lost track of Gull's hallucinations after a couple of trips into town.

'You've got to get a grip, Katya,' Old Sam said.

The lack of the usual bombast and profanity, plus the use of her family name, pulled her gaze back to the old man. Honestly bewildered, she said, 'A grip on what, Uncle?'

'You're gonna mother us to death, whether we want you to or not,' he said. 'And mostly we don't.'

'I – what?'

'So we built you a house,' he told her. 'Ain't nothing we wouldn't have done for any of us in the same situation, specially if there was a kid involved. I know, I know,' he said, holding up a hand to ward off her protestations, 'you always pay your debts. It's one of the qualities that makes you a marginally acceptable human being.'

Overwhelmed by this unaccustomed amount of praise heaped all at once upon her head, Kate remained silent.

'The thing you don't get,' he said, fixing her with a stern and piercing eye, 'is that you don't

20

owe us squat. Shut up.'

Kate closed her mouth.

'One of our own lost her home. We, her family, friends, and neighbors, replaced it with a couple days' labor and, when it comes down to it, very little cost to ourselves.'

'The house kit – the materials had to cost a lot,' she said immediately.

'Most of it was donated,' he said. He paused, the wrinkles on his face creasing and uncreasing as he fought an internal struggle. 'The fact is, for whatever misguided reasons of their own, a lotta people in the state think they owe you, and most of 'em were willing to kick in to get you under a roof again. Not to mention that it's good politics for people who do business in the Bush to be nice to a Shugak from the Park.'

There was a long, weighty silence. Everything he'd said was true, and, what was worse, Kate knew it. Still.

'What?' he said.

She couldn't help herself, she actually squirmed. 'I hate owing anyone, Uncle,' she blurted out. 'I hate it. Especially those people who helped out because I'm Emaa's granddaughter.'

'Yeah, well, suck it up,' he said, unimpressed. 'Stop trying to run everyone's life and start taking care of your own, including that boy of yours.'

She looked up quickly. 'Is Johnny in trouble?'

He said unblushingly, 'What fourteen-going on fifteen-year-old isn't in trouble? I'm telling you to start minding your own business instead of everyone else's. Starting right now, with mine. I ain't yet so goddamn decrepit I can't pew my

21

own goddamn fish.'

Kate turned as red as Harvey Meganack. 'I'm sorry, Uncle,' she said in a small voice.

'You sure are,' he said, and cackled when her eyes narrowed. 'Now I'm writing up my tender summary like I always do, and so far as I know, I ain't yet lost the ability to perform long division. You got it?'

'I got it, Uncle,' she said, and slunk aft to her stateroom, changed into clean clothes, and slipped down to the float to hotfoot it up to the harbormaster's shack, where Gull was regaling Johnny with an account of the eating habits of the Magelleni. They liked their food still trying to get away, it appeared. Neither of them seemed exactly overjoyed to see her, and after a few moments, she went uptown, where the streets seemed to be markedly empty in every direction she turned.

She looked down at Mutt, who looked back, ears up, tail waving slightly. Mutt didn't look that intimidating. Well, as unintimidating as a 140-pound half husky, half wolf could look. Couldn't be her clearing the streets.

Kate was forced to admit, if only to herself, that Old Sam might have a point.

She thought of the two-bedroom, two-bathroom home, now outfitted with electricity and running water, sitting where her cabin had been, before a murderer had set it on fire, hoping she was inside. The cedar prefab house was so new it made her teeth hurt, so clean she was afraid to let Mutt get hair on the rug, so large she imagined an echo when she spoke.

Well, okay, maybe it didn't echo. But it sure as

22

hell was big compared to what she was used to, with all the room in the world for her newly adopted son, Johnny, an orphan of his father's death and his mother's neglect.

She climbed the hill past the old high school and found a spot to sit and look at the view, narrow Orca Inlet, Hawkins Island, Hinchinbrook Island, outlined in orange and red and hot pink by the setting sun. To the east, tiny Mummy Island stood out in bold relief; to the west, the passage to Prince William Sound. It was beautiful, but suddenly she longed for her own place in the world, the clearing filled with a semicircle of buildings surrounded by wildflowers and diamond willow and spruce and alder and birch. Mutt sat next to her, leaning against her side, a warm, solid, reassuring weight. Kate knotted a hand in Mutt's ruff and felt three months of tension begin to gear down, one ratchet at a time.

Three notes sounded in the still evening air, a pure descending scale. She cocked her head to hear them better when they repeated.

'Okay, Emaa,' she said softly in reply. 'Time to go home.'

She'd see out the red season, but after that, it was back to the homestead. If it was an unfamiliar roof, a roof lacking in any family history whatsoever, at least it was hers.

Besides, she thought, getting to her feet, it was more than time to continue her bedevilment of Sgt. Jim Chopin.

She smiled. It was more a baring of teeth than an expression of amusement, and if Jim had seen it, the marrow would have chilled in his bones.

23

Oh yes. Kate Shugak had plans for Jim.

The red run petered out the third week of August and George Perry flew into Mudhole Smith Airport to fly Kate and Johnny back to the Park. He was very businesslike, cutting short Kate's attempts at conversation on the ground and becoming totally absorbed in the controls of the Cessna once they were in the air. He'd even been perfunctory with Mutt, who seldom met a man she didn't like. Finally, Kate said, 'It's okay, George. You can relax.'

She was riding shotgun, and she could feel him stiffen next to her. 'I don't know what you mean.'

'Sure you do,' she said. 'I'm done trying to reorganize Chugach Air Taxi. Although I do think you should call Jake Baird over to Bethel. He's got some ideas he could pass along. But' – this as he began to stiffen again – 'I'm done trying to do it for you. I promise. It's your business, hands off.'

'Seriously?'

'Seriously.' She took a deep breath. It was never easy for Kate Shugak to admit she'd been in the wrong, especially when she wasn't absolutely sure she had been. 'I got a little off there for a while. It freaked me out, you guys building that house for me and all. I felt like I had to pay you back.'

'All of us, all at once,' he said. He glanced at her. 'Is it true you went to one of Marge Moonin's Tupperware parties?'

'Oh hell,' she said, and had to laugh. 'I hosted one in my new house.'

When he stopped laughing he said, 'I would have paid good money to have seen that.'

'If I'd known that, I would have charged admission,' she said, and the rest of the flight went much more smoothly, both in the air and inside the cabin.

On the ground in Niniltna, she endorsed her paycheck from Old Sam and handed it to George, who would take it to the bank in Ahtna. 'Half in savings, half in cash,' she said.

He stuffed the check into a random pocket. 'Okay. You going to be back in town anytime soon?'

She shook her head. 'Just to get the rug rat registered for school and that's not until next week. If you see Auntie Vi, give her the cash. If not, just hang on to it.'

'Okay.' He took a chance. 'Good to have you back in your body, Shugak.'

She laughed. 'Good to be back in it, Perry. Later.'

The red Chevy pickup was parked next to George's hangar. She and Johnny tossed their duffels into the back. Mutt jumped in next to them with a joyous bark, tail wagging furiously. The engine started on the first try.

Kate grinned at Johnny. 'It's good to be home.'

He grinned back. 'Yeah. I like Cordova, but...'

She nodded. 'It's a city.'

He nodded. 'Too many people.'

'Two thousand and more,' she said, nodding.

They both shuddered. Mutt barked encouragement from the back, and Kate put the truck in gear and they started the last leg home.

The gravel road from Niniltna was rough, the remnants of an old railroad bed graded every spring by the state and then left to fend for itself until the following year. Every now and then a remnant of its former life surfaced as a railroad spike in someone's tire. The tracks the spikes had held together had been pulled up by the owners of the Kanuyag Copper Mine, the rapidly decaying ruins of which lay four miles beyond Niniltna. The ties had long since been scavenged by Park rats and used to surface access roads, fence gardens, and serve as the foundation for more than one house.

It was going on sunset when they turned onto the game trail that led to Kate's homestead. It was a little wider and less rough than it had once been, due to all the traffic down it the previous May, but the indefatigable alders were coming back fast and now whispered at the windows of the truck as it went by. Kate saw the steep, neatly shingled roof of the new house first, and the late-evening sunshine made the river of windows down the front gleam a bright gold, repeating the warm blond surface of the shaped cedar logs and glinting off the railing surrounding the deck that ran all the way around the house. The sight of it seemed to soften the jagged peaks of the Quilak Mountains rearing up behind it.

Kate was so mesmerized by the sight that she nearly rear-ended the royal purple Cadillac Escalade parked square in the middle of the clearing, equidistant from the half dozen buildings that formed a semicircle around the edge. She slammed on the brakes and she, Mutt, and Johnny all pitched forward.

The view was not further improved by the sight

of the woman sitting on the deck.

Johnny swore beneath his breath.

Kate swore out loud.

'Who is she?' Johnny said, sounding as surly as Kate felt.

'I don't know,' she said, and slammed out of the truck.

'Kate Shugak?' the woman said, rising to her feet as Kate all but stamped up the stairs.

'Who's asking?' Kate said, not caring how unfriendly she sounded.

'Charlotte Muravieff,' the woman said without a blink. 'It's nice to meet you, finally. I've heard a lot about you.'

She was a woman in her mid-forties and her face had that carefully tended look that only the rich can achieve. Her hair was as bright a gold as the sun setting on the windows behind her, and her eyebrows had been dyed to match. She was elegantly, almost painfully thin, and she wore what Nordstrom probably considered proper for one of the few outings that wouldn't include a trip to the spa – khakis tailored to fit well, but not so tight as to be called vulgar, a hand-knit sweater of 100 percent cotton over a button-down shirt of the softest linen, the shirt one exquisite shade of blue darker than the sweater, and perfectly knotted brown leather half boots, polished until they reflected the setting sun as well as the house's windows. The bootlaces might even have been ironed. Kate didn't recognize the couturier, but the whole ensemble reeked of a platinum card with no credit limit and no expiration date.

Kate took the hand automatically. The nails

27

were well-shaped ovals, gleaming beneath a coating of pearlized polish. Kate was made aware of the rough calluses and ragged hangnails on her own hands, which accounted for at least some of the pugnacity displayed in the jut of her chin. 'Charlotte Bannister Muravieff?'

The woman nodded, and looked at Johnny over Kate's shoulder and gave him a dazzling smile. 'You must be Johnny Morgan.'

Both Kate and Johnny bristled at this unearned assumption of familiarity. Muravieff saw it and, in an obvious attempt to forestall an immediate eviction, said to Kate, 'Could I speak to you privately?'

Kate had had a very long summer, most of which, yes, had been of her own making, but still. She wanted a long, hot shower in her brand-new bathroom. She wanted to make moose stew in her brand-new kitchen. She wanted to curl up with a good book in her brand-new armchair, and she wanted to turn in early for a long, uninterrupted night's sleep on her brand-new bed in her brand-new loft. She had determined to have all these things, while at the same time quelling the uneasy conscience that told her she hadn't earned them, didn't deserve them, and didn't really own them, and that was, in fact, the root of most of her actions over the past three months.

In consequence, her voice might have been a trifle brusque. 'For what purpose?'

Muravieff looked at Johnny. He folded his arms and met her gaze with a hard stare. Muravieff looked back at Kate and found no softening there.

She took a deep breath, and let it out with a

long, defeated sigh. The 'to the manor born' pose vanished, leaving behind a middle-aged woman whose expensive clothes, authentic jewelry, and makeup by Clinique could not disguise an exhaustion that seemed as if it had been accumulating not just over the day but over decades. Though the wounds were not visible, she looked beaten, emotionally, spiritually, and physically.

'I want you to get my mother out of jail,' she said.

CHAPTER 2

Johnny was in the shower in the three-quarter bathroom downstairs, and from the sound of things he wasn't coming out anytime soon. Proscribed by the unwritten law of Park hospitality from booting out even an uninvited guest without offering them refreshment first, Kate had made a pot of coffee and unearthed a package of very stale Oreo cookies. She punched holes in her last can of evaporated milk, filled the sugar bowl with the last grains from the bag, and added both items to the growing list stuck to the refrigerator door.

The refrigerator door. It was still hard to believe that those three words had any real meaning to her life. She would still order groceries twice a year, spring and fall, but now she could get a half-gallon container of half-and-half, and if it didn't last a month, at least it wouldn't go sour before she used it up.

She paused in the act of pouring Muravieff's coffee. Maybe she should get a freezer. She had a back porch with an overhang now, not to mention an exterior plug-in. No more climbing the ice-encrusted pole ladder to the cache in the dead of winter when she wanted roast moose for dinner. Wow. She sat down quickly, before her legs gave out, and poured her own coffee.

It took both of Charlotte Bannister Muravieff's frail wrists to lift the heavy porcelain mug, which looked like it had been hacked out of the side of a bathtub. She took a cautious sip and, it appeared to Kate, by force of will refrained from wincing. Kate liked her coffee strong enough to smelt iron. She took Muravieff's mug and emptied half of it into the sink. She'd had a sink before, so that wasn't as big a thrill as opening her refrigerator door or listening to the shower. She wondered if the propane tanks would hold out, and if there was some way she could cut off fuel to the hot-water heater before that happened. Preferably while Johnny was still in the shower with the water on full.

Meanwhile, the silence around the table began to grow heavy. Kate shoved the half-full mug toward Muravieff again. 'Try it with some milk.'

'Thank you,' Muravieff said in a faint voice, and stirred in three spoons full of sugar, as well. Her impeccably plucked brow smoothed out after the next sip, and she even went so far as to pick up a cookie. When Kate cleared the table after Muravieff left, the cookie was still there, nibbled around the edges to the frosting and no

30

further. You can never be too rich or too thin, some divorcée had once said, and Muravieff seemed to be taking the dictum to heart. The rich only listened to the other rich.

Kate hooked a toe beneath one of the four matching dining chairs that surrounded her table like the advance troops for an upscale interior decorator and crossed her feet on the seat. She had her shoes off, she told herself, and it was her damn house. 'Ms. Muravieff–'

'Charlotte, please.'

'Okay, Charlotte, and I'm Kate. You want me to get your mother out of jail. I'm guessing she's been convicted of a crime, as opposed to just having been arrested?'

'Yes.'

'What was she convicted of?'

Charlotte hesitated, licked suddenly dry lips, and said in a low voice, 'Murder.'

With difficulty, Kate refrained from rolling her eyes. 'Who did she kill?'

'She didn't kill anyone.'

Kate realized that she was dealing with someone who actually believed in the benefit of the doubt. 'Okay, who didn't she kill?'

Again, Charlotte hesitated. She dropped her eyes to the mug clamped between her thin fingers. This time when she spoke, her voice was so low that Kate couldn't hear her. 'I beg your pardon?'

Charlotte raised her eyes. They were her best feature, large, gray-green, and thickly lashed. The gold of her hair made a nice frame for them. Probably Charlotte's stylist had already pointed this out to her, so Kate didn't. 'My brother,'

Charlotte said finally.

Kate stared. 'I beg your pardon?'

'My mother was convicted of killing my brother.'

Kate absorbed this in silence for a moment. Okay, even she had to admit that this was a bit out of the ordinary. If anything, it made her even less inclined to listen to Charlotte's sob story, but the other woman was still drinking Kate's coffee, so she said, 'How?'

'They said she burned down the house with him in it.'

Arson, Kate thought. One of the easiest crimes to detect, given the current state of forensic technology. It was next to impossible to hide even the most minuscule remnants of a timer, no matter how unsophisticated, from an experienced arson detective with a good lab tech behind him, to say nothing of the dogs trained to sniff out accelerants. 'How did they decide it was her?'

Now that the worst of the story was out, Charlotte was eager to speak. 'It was mostly circumstantial. She lived in the house with us, she'd just taken out insurance policies on all our lives–'

'All?' Kate said.

'All three of us.'

'There was a third child?'

'Yes, my other brother, Oliver.'

'Where was he?'

'He was in the house, too.'

'But he survived.'

'Yes. He got hurt getting out, but he survived.'

'Where were you?'

'I was with my mother. We were coming home from my uncle's house. There was a party that went on a little late.' Charlotte paused. It was obvious that the memories were painful. 'When we pulled into the driveway, the house was already on fire. And then Oliver fell out of one of the upstairs windows.'

Kate was forcibly reminded of the night the previous May when she had driven into her clearing and found her cabin on fire. The cabin her father had built for her mother, the cabin in which she had been conceived and born, the cabin where she had lived most of her life following their deaths. Johnny had been camping at the Lost Wife Mine, or she could have come home to something far more horrible than a pile of smoldering embers. In spite of herself, she sympathized with the pain she saw in Charlotte's eyes. 'Was he badly injured?'

'Yes. His right leg shattered on impact. He still limps.' Charlotte's voice was stronger now, the words coming as if by rote, as if she had said them too many times before. 'It wasn't until the next day, when the firemen were able to go into the ruins, that they found William's body. We were hoping he'd slept over at a friend's house and just hadn't heard about the fire at home.'

'One thing I don't understand,' Kate said. 'You're not exactly a kid, and I'm assuming your brothers aren't, either. What are you all doing still living with your mom?'

Charlotte looked surprised. 'Oh, we aren't.'

'Well then, I really don't understand,' Kate said. 'Were you all home on a visit? Did this happen over the holidays, or what?'

'Oh, no,' Charlotte said, 'it was in the spring.'

'This last spring? April, May?'

'Oh, not this spring. The fire and my brother's death happened thirty-one years ago.'

Charlotte said it in such an offhand way that it took a moment for her words to sink in. They caught Kate with her mug halfway to her mouth. 'You,' she said finally, 'have got to be kidding me.'

'No,' Charlotte said, her lips firm now, her mouth a straight, determined line. 'I'm not kidding. She didn't do it, she has served thirty years for a crime she did not commit, and I want you to get her out of jail.'

'Thirty years,' Kate said.

'Almost thirty-one,' Charlotte said.

'Oh,' Kate said, 'almost thirty-one. Of course, that changes things completely.' She knocked back the rest of her coffee, ignoring the scalding slide down her throat, and blinked the resulting tears away. She got to her feet. 'I'm sorry, Ms. Muravieff. I can't help you.'

Charlotte wouldn't get up. 'You have to. I've asked everyone else. You're the only one left.'

How flattering, Kate thought sourly. What, she was now the patron saint of lost causes? 'Who gave you my name?' she said.

Charlotte looked up, hope kindling in her eyes. 'An attorney.'

Kate was immediately suspicious. 'Which attorney?'

'Brendan McCord.'

Kate took a deep and, she hoped, unobtrusive breath. 'Did he,' she said through her teeth. If this was some kind of joke, there wasn't going to be enough left of Brendan McCord, Esq., to feed to a parakeet.

On the other hand, Brendan had helped a great deal on her last case. If this was payback, she owed him. She took another deep breath, not bothering to hide this one. 'Did you tell him you were coming to me?'

Charlotte nodded, beginning to tear up.

'What did he say, exactly?'

Charlotte produced a delicate lace handker-chief and caught each individual tear before it damaged her makeup. She folded it neatly and put it back in her pocket. 'He said that you were expensive but that you were the best in the state.'

Well. At least Brendan wasn't sending her charity cases. Still, her shower – always supposing she ever got a chance at the hot water – and her books and her bed were no less inviting than they had been half an hour before.

'Oh,' Charlotte said, 'and he also said that you owed him one.'

Son of a bitch. There wasn't going to be enough left of Brendan McCord to feed a goddamn earthworm.

Charlotte looked at her uncertainly. 'Are you all right? Your face looks kind of red.'

'Me?' Kate said. 'I'm fine. Peachy.' Just because she owed Brendan McCord one – well, several – oh hell, probably a baker's dozen – didn't mean she was giving up without a fight. 'Did Brendan happen to mention just how expensive I am?'

Before Charlotte could answer Johnny came out of the bathroom in clean sweats, rosy, tousled and damp. He looked cheerful until he saw that Charlotte was still there.

35

'Is there any hot water left?' Kate said.

'Sure,' he said, and vanished into his bedroom. The door shut most definitely behind him.

There was a brief silence, broken by Charlotte. 'I was thinking that you could look at the evidence. Maybe with all this new DNA technology, there would be some way of proving she didn't do it.'

'Ms. Muravieff–'

'Charlotte, please.'

'Charlotte,' Kate said, 'your mother's been in jail for thirty years. We haven't been a state much longer than that. Back then the Alaskan judicial system was still figuring out how to find its own ass without even a flashlight, much less two hands. Besides, we're not talking about a cold case here. Your mother was tried and convicted. They'd have had no reason to keep whatever physical evidence they had in your mother's case. It'll be long gone.'

'Well, then, witnesses,' Charlotte said.

Kate didn't know if this was loyalty or stubbornness speaking, but she admired both, which kept her response more civil than it might have been. 'Same goes,' she said. 'Thirty years. Some of them are bound to be dead, or just unfindable.'

'But Brendan says you're the best,' Charlotte said stubbornly.

Exasperated, Kate said, 'Why did you wait thirty years to do this?'

'She's dying,' Charlotte said.

There was a long pause. 'I see,' Kate said at last. 'What does she have?'

The tears began to flow again. The handkerchief reappeared. 'Uterine cancer.' She met Kate's eyes.

'I don't want her dying in prison. I won't let that happen.' Charlotte rummaged in her genuine-leather day pack and pulled out a checkbook. She scribbled Kate's name, an amount, and a signature, and ripped it out and handed it to Kate.

The amount of zeros made Kate a little dizzy.

'That amount again when you get my mother out,' Charlotte said. 'Plus expenses, of course.'

Kate put the check down on the table between them and pushed it across to Charlotte. She didn't bother asking if Charlotte had that much money. She said as gently as she knew how, 'This is a waste of your money and my time.'

'She didn't do it,' Charlotte said, pushing the check back.

'Even if she didn't,' Kate said, 'even if someone else did it, and even if he or she were alive for me to find, it would be a miracle if I picked up a trail this old and this cold.' She pushed the check back at Charlotte.

'She didn't *do* it,' Charlotte said, shoving the check back so hard that it slid across the table into Kate's lap.

Johnny slammed out of his bedroom and rummaged in the kitchen cupboards for food. Fortunately, Top Ramen kept well. He started a pot of water boiling and got down the sesame oil, which also held up under benign neglect.

He was fourteen, and in spite of an avowed determination to quit school as soon as he was legally old enough to do so, Kate was equally determined that he was going to at least get a GED and learn some kind of trade before he embraced Park rathood permanently. Besides, he was showing signs of serious interest in wildlife biology, serving what amounted to an apprenticeship in the middle of one of the most prolific wildlife areas in the world, with expert supervision from people like Park ranger Dan O'Brien, geologist Millicent Nebeker McClanahan, and self-taught naturalist Ruthe Bauman. Kate nourished the faint hope that Johnny might change his mind about college. And college cost money.

She looked at the obstinate lines of Charlotte's expression and reflected that she found herself doing a lot of things she never used to do before she became a mom.

She swore to herself. 'All right,' she said, and crumpled the check in a fist and jammed it into a pocket. 'You've got yourself a private investigator.'

The lines of Charlotte's face eased. She was wise enough to display no triumph. 'Thank you, Kate.'

'Don't thank me,' Kate said, 'please.'

Charlotte stood up. 'Thank you for the coffee, then.' She hesitated. 'Do you need help with a place to stay in Anchorage?'

'I have a place,' Kate said, aware that Johnny had gone motionless behind her.

'Oh. Good.' Almost timidly, Charlotte added, 'When can I expect to hear from you?'

Kate stood up and started walking her out. 'I just got home. I'll need a day or two to get things arranged.'

Involuntarily, Charlotte looked over her shoulder at Johnny. 'Ah.'

'Yes.'

38

'Of course,' Charlotte said, producing keys to unlock the monster SUV, which she would never have gotten down the trail had Mac Devlin not opened the way for the house-raising the previous May. Leaving Kate's homestead open to every itinerant petitioner with a tale of woe.

Who locked their car in the Park?

Charlotte climbed in and started the engine. Kate walked to her door, and the electric window slid down silently.

'Do you want to get your mother out of jail because she's innocent,' Kate said, 'or because she's dying?'

Charlotte's lips trembled. 'Both.'

The Cadillac reversed smoothly, swung wide in a circle, and vanished up the trail. Mac Devlin had cut quite a swath through Kate's section of the Park with his D-6, but not quite wide enough for two cars to pass each other, so Alaska state trooper Jim Chopin had to pull over to wait for Charlotte to pass.

This was good, because it allowed Kate a few extra moments to collect the elements of her vamp persona and fix them firmly in place.

Dump her, would he?

Oh, she didn't think so.

CHAPTER 3

Mutt, of course, bounced up to the white Blazer with the state trooper's seal on the door, generating enough energy with her tail to open a portal into the fourth dimension. Kate strolled after her, and Jim, fending off Mutt's attentions with an absent pat, watched her approach with a reluctantly fascinated eye.

Kate was only five feet tall. She didn't have enough leg to be able to stroll toward him with that much sexual menace. Nevertheless, he felt himself taking an involuntary step back, at which he was thwarted by his vehicle. He swallowed hard and, unable to do anything else, watched her come toward him.

It was true Kate Shugak was only five feet tall. It was true that taken individually her features – high, flat cheekbones, narrow hazel eyes that slanted up just a hint and that were sometimes brown and sometimes almost green and some-times gray, a wide, full-lipped mouth, pale gold skin with an olive tint that tanned easily to a warm honey color – were nothing that would excite a Paris designer into hiring her as a model for his next show. Her hair, thick and short and impossibly black, trimmed to her ears and swept back from a broad brow by an impatient hand, was nothing a trendy New York stylist couldn't improve upon with a hacksaw. Her clothes, white

T-shirt, faded jeans, a worn brown leather belt, thin white ankle socks, black-and-white tennis shoes, were so unself-consciously nondescript as to be almost characterless.

The scar, a thin rope of pale, knotted skin that bisected her throat almost literally from ear to ear, could not by any stretch of the imagination be called arousing. If anything, one look at that, one listen to the rusted voice that throat produced ought to have a sensible man beating feet in the opposite direction at once, if not sooner.

Instead, when she smiled at him, a wide, knowing smile that revealed a set of healthy white teeth whose incisors seemed to him to be noticeably longer than they had been the last time he'd seen them, he had an inexplicable desire to fall to his knees and bare his throat and let her suck right out of him the last drop of any bodily fluid he had on offer.

Maybe it was the way her hips moved beneath the denim, or the way the knit fabric outlined her breasts, or the way her hands curled slightly at her sides, as if in anticipation. Maybe it was the way she moved, a smooth, confident fusion of muscle and bone that did a good job of hiding the strength, the quickness, and the agility latent beneath.

He'd known other women who exuded sex. He'd known other women who had been able to slay men with a single smile.

Kate smiled at him now. 'Hey, Jim,' she said, and the two words ran like a rasp right up his spine to the base of his skull.

He'd just never known one like this. Everything

41

he had was at attention. He cleared his throat. Hormones. He was male, she was female. He'd react the same way to any woman. 'Kate.'

He was helpless to stop the single syllable from sounding like a plea, and he watched her smile widen. Desperately, he sought for something to say. 'I haven't seen you around the Park lately.'

She laughed, a low, intimate sound in the increasing dusk. A strand of hair fell into her face and she tucked it behind an ear, holding his eyes all the while. 'Is that what you came to tell me?' She took a step closer. 'Have you been missing me?'

'No,' he said, 'no, not at all. I've been too busy to miss anybody.'

'Really? What with?'

He tried to think of something noteworthy he'd accomplished over the summer. 'Oh. Well. You know. Claim jumping. Fishing behind the markers. Hunting out of season. Rape, robbery, murder. The usual.'

She didn't move. She didn't look away from him, either. He started to sweat. It was getting harder and harder to remember why he'd walked away from her last May, why he'd announced an end to his ongoing pursuit, why he'd renounced his goal of getting her into his bed.

It was something about love – he remembered that much. Well, he didn't love her, and he wasn't going to, wasn't going to get anywhere near it, or her, damn it.

Johnny Morgan, elbows on the railing, watched from the deck. It was pitiful, was what it was. Here was this tiny little woman, couldn't weigh

120 pounds wringing wet, facing down this big, strong, good-looking guy, an Alaska state trooper no less, a man accustomed to command, a man who hunted down criminals and brought them to justice, a man to whom Park rats of every age, culture, and occupation looked to to lay down the law of the land. He had to be at least six two, although the Mountie hat he used to wear had made him look even taller than that, and he had to weigh two hundred pounds easy, although the bristling arsenal of badges and guns and epaulets and handcuffs and nightsticks added heft. He was good-looking, too, with heavy dark blond hair, piercing blue eyes, and strong features – jaw, cheekbones, nose. He didn't look like a wimp, and if half of the Park gossip Johnny had heard was true, he'd had a ton of girlfriends. He just wasn't a needy kind of guy.

Kate glided another step forward, moving in a way that reminded Johnny irresistibly of a large, powerful cat. Jim looked like cat food, inches away from leaping into his vehicle and roaring off.

Wimp, definitely.

An object lesson was what his teacher, Ms. Doogan, would have called it. No way was he ever going to fall into that honey trap, which was what Old Sam Dementieff called it. The irresistible force meeting the not-quite-immovable object was what Bobby Clark called it.

He shook his head, half in pity for a fellow man, half in shame, and went back inside. It was just too painful to watch.

Just for the hell of it, just because she could, just because her mere presence affected Jim Chopin in a manner that she had to admit she found deeply satisfying, Kate took another step forward, bringing her into physical contact. She could feel his badge, his belt, what she thought might – or might not – be his gun pressing against her. She smiled up at him and purposely dropped her voice to a whisper. 'How can I ... help you, Sergeant Chopin?'

'Knock it off,' he said through clenched teeth.

She blinked innocently at him. 'Knock what off?' She ran one finger down the buttons of his shirt.

He caught her hand before she could start messing with his belt buckle. 'Damn it, Shugak, knock it off.' He shoved past her and found a safe, Kate-free place in the exact center of the clearing, free of corners into which she could back him.

No law she couldn't stalk him, however, pacing after him with that slow, deliberate, unmistakably predatory stride. Her hair gleamed in the last rays of the setting sun like the coat of a healthy, proud animal reveling in her prime. 'Hot for this time of year, isn't it?' she said. She pulled the tail of her T-shirt free and knotted the hem beneath her breasts, leaving a good six inches of smooth, taut, golden-skinned midriff exposed.

Jim thanked God her jeans weren't low-riders. He wasn't sure he had a spine that would stand up to the seductive power of Kate's belly button.

He also felt slightly shell-shocked. It wasn't that no one had ever seduced him before, usually with his active and enthusiastic cooperation, it was just that he'd had no idea that Kate Shugak could turn it on like this. She was always so sensible, so matter-of-fact, so businesslike. Not to mention

44

hostile, antagonistic, and downright bitchy. It had been clear from the beginning that if she let a man into her life, it would be on her terms, and now, suddenly, she was revealing a secret identity, the Circe inside the Shugak.

He wondered if Jack Morgan had known of this secret identity. If Jack had, it would explain his willingness to cleave only unto her, even to serve out an eighteen-month hiatus in their relationship, waiting for her to come back to him.

Lucky, lucky bastard, he thought, not for the first time, and then pulled himself together. He wasn't getting sucked into that, no matter how much – yes, he'd admit it – no matter how much he wanted her. It was just sex; that was all. Nobody ever died because they didn't get laid. And it wasn't like there was no one else he could go to for aid if such were the case. Laurel Meganack, for example. She'd batted enough eyelash his way to start a small tornado.

That was a plan. If there was anyone who could drive the ghost of Kate Shugak out of his mental attic, Laurel was the girl most likely.

With commendable resolution he ignored the little voice in his head that told him it had already been tried. The summer was strewn with the corpses of women who had heard on the Bush telegraph that Chopper Jim Chopin was once again open for business. The problem was that none of them seemed to hold his interest past 'Hello.'

He spoke abruptly, hoping to divert her attention. 'Have you talked to Dan lately?'

This would be Dan O'Brien, chief ranger for

45

the Park, avowed Park rat, and longtime friend of Kate's.

She didn't exactly cease and desist in giving off pheromones, but he did sense a certain alertness that hadn't been there the second before. 'Somebody's been trapping brown bears,' he said, his voice still sounding hoarse to his own ears.

'Have they,' Kate said, letting her eyes linger on his lower lip. She touched her own with her tongue.

He took a deep breath. 'Yes, they have. Dan has found a dozen carcasses all over the Park. He says whoever it is is using cable snares.'

Kate abandoned her vamp stance for a moment. 'Gutted?'

'Yeah.'

'Gallbladders removed?'

'Yeah.'

She swore.

'Yeah,' he said.

'You know who it is,' she said.

'Of course I know who it is,' he said, annoyed. 'So do you, and so does Dan. Knowing and proving are two different things, as you also know very well.'

She smiled at him again. 'You want me to help you prove it, or you want me to stop it? Which are also two very different things.'

'If we never had this conversation, I want you to stop it,' he said. 'If we did, I need evidence.'

'Why don't you find some?'

'I could,' he said, his jaw tight. 'If I wanted to track down a judge who is most probably pulling kings out of a river somewhere in the Bush on the other side of the state at the moment. I could put together some kind of probable cause and get him to issue a warrant. And then of course I'd have to go out and serve it, and do a search, and make a list of all the property taken into evidence, and photograph the scene before and after, and put him under arrest, and transport him to Tok, because they still haven't shipped the goddamn bars in for the cells in my brand-new Niniltna post, and all this would take me probably two days!'

His voice had been rising steadily throughout this peroration. He glared at her.

Kate laughed. It even sounded like genuine humor, as opposed to a come-on. 'Okay, I'll talk to him. Now, you can do something for me.'

He stiffened. 'What?' he said warily.

She laughed again, and the siren was back. 'Relax,' she said, still laughing, 'I need a trial transcript.'

He was hugely relieved and at the same time bitterly disappointed. 'Give me a name.'

'Victoria Pilz Bannister Muravieff.'

'Got a date?'

'How about a year? Count back thirty years.'

He stared at her. 'Jesus, Shugak, we were barely a state thirty years back.'

'And I don't want microfiche, I want it printed out on paper. I don't think they were doing tapes back then, but who knows. I want a transcript, something I can read.'

'It'll cost you.'

'Not me. My client.'

'You've got a client?'

She nodded. 'I'm headed into Anchorage in a

couple of days.'

He couldn't stop himself from saying, 'How long you going to be gone?'

She smiled. Oh yeah, the siren was most definitely back. 'Just long enough for you to miss me some more.'

Suddenly, the real Jim Chopin stood up. He stepped forward and bent down until the brim of his cap nearly touched her forehead. 'I already do.'

In real life, this was Kate Shugak's cue to back off, to give ground, usually with dignity, sometimes in a hurry, and always with attitude.

She didn't move. She didn't even blush. Instead, she leaned into him until the brim of his cap did touch her forehead, and said huskily, 'There's a cure for that.'

The mouse roared and he was outbluffed into an undignified retreat. 'Yes. Well. I'll get to work on that file. You get to work on our alleged poacher.'

'I want that file by tomorrow,' she said, raising her voice as he started the engine.

He raised a hand in acknowledgment without looking around.

She watched him vanish into the trees at the edge of the clearing. Who knew chasing Jim Chopin would be so much fun?

She climbed the stairs and went into the living room. Johnny looked up from the couch and scowled at her. She halted in midstride. 'Does it bug you?'

'What?'

'Jim and me.' She didn't elaborate, but Johnny was going on fifteen and extremely intelligent.

48

'There is no Jim and you.'

She grinned. 'Not yet.'

His frown deepened. 'He's not good enough for you.'

'Absolutely not,' she said cheerfully. 'No one is.'

'What about Dad?'

She sat down next to him and looped an arm around his neck. 'He almost made the grade.'

The frown eased. 'Only almost?'

'Well,' she said. 'I really am something, after all.'

He was forced to laugh. 'You sure are,' he said, and protested the headlock and the noogie she gave him.

'We'll drive into town tomorrow, get you registered for school.'

He was not displeased by this news, as Vanessa Cox was in town, living with her adoptive parents, Annie and Billy Mike. 'You gonna get that woman's mom out of jail?'

Kate felt for the check crumpled in her pocket. 'I'm going to try. I don't hold out a lot of hope that I'm going to succeed.'

'You'll do it,' Johnny said with boundless faith. 'You always do.'

That earned him another noogie, and he squealed and wrestled free. 'Where am I staying while you're gone?'

'I figured Auntie Vi's. She's got the room, and it's close enough for you to walk to school.'

'Okay.'

She gave him a suspicious look which he met with a bland stare. 'I think it stinks that your love life is better than mine,' she said.

He blushed beet red, and she laughed.

Bright and early the next morning, they climbed into the cherry red pickup and lurched back up the twenty-five miles of road into Niniltna. The road ran through the heart of the Park, 20 million mostly pristine acres extending from the Canadian border on the east to Prince William Sound in the south to the TransAlaska Pipeline in the west to the Glenn Highway in the north. Plus maybe a little extra all the way around. It was sparsely populated, the biggest town being Ahtna, which technically wasn't even in the Park but which was the market town for everyone who lived there – Park rats, rangers, hunters, trappers, fishermen, farmers, mostly Native and Anglo, living in tiny villages at the confluences of rivers, on land homesteaded by great- and great-great-grandfathers when the federal government strove to justify the expenditure of $7.2 million to purchase Alaska from Russia by offering incentives to Outsiders in the form of free land. This free land was far north of the fifty-three, but it was free, and in spite of the frosty latitude, a few thousand took the feds up on it. A few thousand more stayed on after the gold rush in 1898, and a few thousand more stayed on after World War II, and a couple of hundred thousand more after oil was discovered at Prudhoe Bay. Most of them stayed around long enough to put in their twenty and then decamped with their pensions to Arizona and Hawaii.

Fortunately, Kate thought as the truck lunged into a pothole and lunged out again, most of the six hundred thousand plus people living in Alaska today didn't live in the Park. Nope, most of them lived in Anchorage.

Oh. Wait. She was going to Anchorage.

The sun always seemed to shine when she had to leave the Park. The Quilaks loomed less menacingly on the eastern horizon, the spruce, aspen, birch, cottonwood, alder, and willow never seemed more lush and profligate, everywhere she looked an eagle or a raven or a Canada goose was taking wing. Which reminded her: She needed a new shotgun; she'd look around for one in Anchorage. Moose with their sides bulging from a summer's browse ambled across the road looking like a filled freezer. A freezer being something else she could get in Anchorage.

She thought of the last time her meat cache had been knocked over, and the labor that had been required to put it back up again. To the uninitiated, it might look like Kate was turning her back on decades of tradition, but it wasn't disloyalty. It was progress. Her father had always been for progress. At least she thought so, being as how he'd died when she was seven, and while she had many memories of her father, that wasn't necessarily one of them.

A freezer. What would Emaa have said?

Kate hoped her grandmother would have hated it. She hoped Emaa would have said disapprovingly, 'A cache was good enough for your father, Katya, and it was good enough for me.' But even though she hoped it, she wouldn't have bet on it since Emaa's house had been the first one in the village wired for electricity.

She laughed suddenly.

'What?' Johnny said.

'Just promise me you'll never become a professional againster,' Kate told him.

He gaped at her. 'A what?'

'Never mind,' she said, and they pulled into the schoolyard.

They emerged an hour later with a fistful of papers, which Kate immediately consigned to the glove compartment. 'Or a school administrator,' she said, and they drove to Auntie Vi's and knocked on the kitchen door.

Auntie Vi opened the door and promptly closed it again.

Kate sighed. 'Auntie, open up. I promise not to cock anything or wash anything or fix anything.' She eyed the porch roof. 'Or take a paintbrush to your soffits,' she said in a much lower voice.

The door opened again. 'What you here for, then?'

Kate nodded at Johnny, duffle in hand. 'I need a place to park the kid for a week or so.'

An arm reached out, snagged Johnny by the collar, and hauled him into the house. The door closed firmly behind him.

'Thanks, Auntie,' Kate said to the door.

Mutt was already in Johnny's seat when Kate got back to the truck. 'At least you still love me,' Kate told her.

'Woof,' Mutt said consolingly, and Kate drove to the airstrip. George was gone, and so was the Cessna. Okay, it was another twenty miles to the Roadhouse. When she walked in, Bernie hid the bar rag.

'It's okay,' Kate said, 'I'm looking for information, not Mr. Clean.'

'And no more counselors. I'm not sharing with anybody else how I feel. Is that clear?'

'It's clear.'

'I don't want to hear any more about that goddamn house, either,' he said menacingly, or as menacing as Bernie Koslowski, the mildest of the race of mild-mannered ex-hippie draft dodger-saloonkeeper-basketball coaches could get. 'We built it. You're living in it. Deal with it.'

Kate patted the air with her hands. 'I come in peace for all bear kind.'

He examined her suspiciously, and when she made no sudden moves toward the push broom, he relaxed, sort of. 'Bear kind?'

'Has Kurt Pletnikoff been in lately?'

Bernie shrugged. 'As much as anyone during fishing season.'

'Has he been keeping out-of-town company?'

'Come on, Kate,' he said. 'You know I don't like to gossip about my customers behind their backs.'

'I promise you, Bernie,' she said, 'you're going to have a lot more customers of the federal kind if you don't help me now. And they won't be as polite and refined as I am.'

He snorted. 'More business for the bar.'

'Not from the locals, if Kurt continues to decimate the bear population.'

'Who says he is?'

'No one,' Kate admitted. 'But according to Jim Chopin, there are degallbladdered bear carcasses all over the Park. And we all know what that means.'

Bernie would rather by far be on Kurt Pletnikoff's bad side than Kate's. She never forgot and she never forgave, and she was related to half of his customers and had in one way or another helped out most of the other half. Besides, Kurt's tab was at five hundred and counting, and Bernie wasn't in the business of loaning money. 'Kurt was in here a week ago.'

'Alone?'

'He had company, looked to be of the Asian persuasion. One man, late fifties, I'd say. He had plenty of hair, but it was all gray.' Bernie smoothed back a nonexistent hairline that ended in a long gray ponytail tied back with a strip of leather.

'You know him?'

'Never seen him before.'

'He speak English, or have an accent if he did?'

Bernie shook his head. 'Kurt did all the talking.'

'How long were they here?'

'One drink, couple of beers. They didn't finish them.' Bernie looked mildly annoyed. 'Alaskan Amber, too. I hate pouring good beer down the sink.'

'You notice anything else? Anything change hands?'

Bernie shook his head again. 'Not in the bar.'

'Okay. Thanks, Bernie.'

'No problem. You didn't bring the wolf in to say hi?'

Kate grinned. 'She's chasing geese.'

Bernie swore. 'Not Edna's geese, not again, Kate.'

Kate relented. 'She's in the cab.'

Bernie looked relieved. 'Thank god I won't have to stop my wife from rioting in the streets.' He plucked a package of beef jerky out of a jar on the bar. 'For the wolf.'

'Thanks.'

From the Roadhouse, Kate drove back to Niniltna and the airstrip, and this time she managed to arrive at the same time George Perry touched down. He was in the act of removing his headphones when he saw her. 'Oh crap,' he said, 'what now?' He headed immediately for the 1966 Ford Econoline van – held together by faith, dirt, and duct tape – which served as ground support for Chugach Air Taxi's air-freight business. He backed it around to the Cessna and began unloading boxes from the one and stacking them in the back of the other.

Normally, Kate would have given him a hand, but over the past twenty-four hours she had been made humiliatingly aware that she might have overdone it in the gratitude department. 'Have you done any business with Kurt Pletnikoff lately?' she said to George's determinedly turned back.

'Nope,' he said, tossing a box into the back of the Econoline with a fine disregard for the FRAGILE sticker on its side.

'Has he met any flights lately – say flights with unknown passengers of Asian origin on board?'

George paused. 'Maybe.'

'Did he or didn't he?'

'He might have,' George said.

Kate gritted her teeth. She wasn't a patient person, but she was on probation and she knew it. 'When might he have?'

George gave a characteristic little wiggle, something between a shrug and the Shimmy. 'An Asian gentleman could have flown in last Tuesday.'

'And could he have said why he was here?'

George shook his head.

'Did he have you call a ride?' There wasn't what you could call a cab in Niniltna, but George did have the names of people from the village who had vehicles and were willing to rent themselves out by the mile.

He shook his head.

'When did he leave?'

'That evening.'

'Did you notice if he was carrying something out that he didn't carry in?'

'Maybe a duffel bag.'

'How big?'

'Basketball-size. Maybe a little bigger. Had handles. Dark blue. Had a logo on it.'

'What logo?'

George screwed up his face. 'Can't remember. Some sports team maybe. Not the Kings.'

As in the Kanuyaq Kings, the local high school team, and very likely the only team logo George could recognize on sight. He was dutiful in his devotion to the hometown boys, but he wasn't the biggest sports fan. 'And this was last Tuesday?'

George nodded.

'Okay,' she said. She started to thank him, then caught his eye, and thought better of it. 'I need a ride into town,' she said instead.

'When?'

'Tomorrow morning.'

He thought for a moment before giving a short

nod. 'I can do that, if you don't mind early.'

'I don't mind early. Seven?'

He nodded again. 'Don't be late. I've got to be back here in time to bring the Grosdidier brothers home from Alaganik.'

'You can fit them all into one plane?'

He grinned, the most natural expression he'd shown her all summer. 'I packs 'em tight,' he said, adding, 'Don't tell the FAA.'

She drove up to the Niniltna Native Association headquarters, a prefabricated building beneath a metal roof that positively sang in the rain and to which even the heaviest snowfall did not stick, to the imminent danger of those walking into and out of the building through the set of double doors centered most precisely beneath its eaves. It looked as if someone had let Auntie Balasha off the chain because the side of the building facing the road was engulfed in flowers of every size and hue, from nasturtiums at the road's edge to delphiniums tethered to stakes brushing the first-floor windowsills. It was a riot of color right across the spectrum, and it made the building look as if it housed something other than the organization that oversaw and administered the moneys and lands Kate's tribe had received as a result of the Alaska Native Claims Settlement Act of 1971.

Billy, chief of said tribe, looked up from his desk when Kate walked in, and, it must be said, paled at the sight of her. Kate, weary of this reaction, held up a hand. 'It's all right, Billy. You get to help me this time.'

He failed to hide his relief. 'What do you need, Kate?'

Billy Mike's face used to be as round as his body, and his smile at least as broad. He was thinner now, paler, too, and there was a bruised look in his eyes that had not been there before and that hurt Kate to see. It was only three months since he'd lost his youngest son, Dandy, and Billy and his wife, Annie, were both still grieving. They had taken in another child, a fourteen-year-old named Vanessa Cox, who was Johnny Morgan's boon companion and who, Kate greatly feared, was rapidly becoming rather more than that. This was in addition to the Korean baby they had adopted when Annie began to suffer from empty nest syndrome, not to mention the six children who had grown up, gone to school, and, instead of moving back home, had stayed in Anchorage, where there were jobs and bars and cable television, and who were proving remarkably dilatory in providing the Mikes with the grandchildren both of them were vociferous about wanting.

That Billy and Annie didn't blame Kate for Dandy's death was a mystery for which she would be eternally grateful. That they had opened their home and hearts to Vanessa, the killer's child, was even more extraordinary, but it was a fact that Vanessa, orphaned when both her parents had been killed in a car crash Outside and then shipped to Alaska to live with her nearest relatives, was looking more like a kid and less like a prematurely aged old woman than she had since she arrived in the Park the year before.

'I'm looking for Kurt Pletnikoff,' Kate said. 'He's not in the same old cabin out on Fool's Gold Creek, is he?'

Billy shook his head. 'He moved. He came into some money when his father died. The father evidently couldn't figure out anybody better to leave it to. Kurt bought Luba Hardt's property off Black Water Road and built himself a house. Sort of.'

'I didn't know that,' Kate said. 'Did Luba move out of the Park?'

'No, she just got thirsty, and Kurt happened to be standing next to her at the Roadhouse with a fistful of his daddy's cash when she did.'

'Where's she living now?'

'Last I heard, she was on the street in Anchorage. I got George to put the word out at Bean's Café and the Brother Francis Shelter that when she wants to come home, we'll foot the bill.'

'I'm going to Anchorage myself tomorrow or the next day,' Kate said. 'I'll look around.'

Billy nodded. 'Appreciate it. Why do you want to know where Kurt is?'

Kate looked at him and raised an eyebrow.

He waved her off. 'Yeah, I know, ask a dumb question. Don't kill him, okay?'

'No promises,' Kate said, and left.

Kurt Pletnikoff's home, if you could call it that, had been built on an elevated foundation of cement blocks around a frame of two-by-fours in a space in the middle of a thick stand of tall, heavy spruce that blocked out the sun. It was a gloomy little clearing, but neat, the wood stacked and the trash picked up.

The steps to the front and only door were made of more two-by-fours, in which there were a lot of nail pops to catch at the soles of Kate's shoes. The building shook slightly when she knocked on the door. 'Kurt?'

There was no answer.

She knocked again. 'Kurt Pletnikoff? It's Kate Shugak.' Still no answer. She tried the handle. It was unlocked. She peered inside.

It was one room, about the size of her former cabin, with neither the loft nor the charm. The inside was even less prepossessing than the outside. A narrow iron cot with a thin mattress stood beneath the only window, a couple of green army blankets smoothed across it. A broken-down couch stood on one side of an oil stove made from a fifty-five-gallon drum. On the other side of the stove stood a table made of an old door, with two-by-fours for legs. There was a pile of magazines, nothing too sophisticated – *Guns & Ammo, Sports Illustrated, Penthouse*. A cupboard minus the doors had been screwed to one wall and was filled with canned and dry goods. A bag of apples, the top knotted off, sat on top of a bag of dog food.

The floor was clean, and a big galvanized garbage can sat next to the cupboard. A bowl, a spoon, and a mug were upended on a dish towel spread next to the apples.

Kate touched the bowl. A drop of water coalesced on her fingertip. She felt rather than heard motion behind her, and she stepped quickly to the left, dropping to the floor in a shoulder roll and regaining her feet in the same movement. She picked up the chair and brought the seat down on the head of the man who had been sneaking up behind her, not hard enough to knock him out, just hard enough to get his attention.

'Ouch!' the man yelled. He grabbed his head.

'Hi, Kurt,' Kate said, and put the chair down. It had been a while, and it pleased her to know that she still had the moves. Especially after she'd gotten blindsided by that shovel in May, an event she still couldn't think of without a certain amount of shame. Mutt, galloping up to the door, her tongue lolling out to one side, surveyed the situation with an expert eye, gave a short congratulatory bark, and went back to sniffing out the moose cow and calf who had left such an intriguing scent trail crisscrossing the yard around the cabin. She wasn't all that hungry, but like Kate she liked to know that she still got game.

Fifteen minutes later, Kurt was sitting on the bed and Kate was sitting on the chair. Two mugs of steaming chamomile tea – Kurt was into herbal teas – sat on the table, along with a box of sugar and a spoon.

'Did you have to hit me so hard?' Kurt said plaintively, rubbing the crown of his head with a careful hand. 'I mean, Jesus, Kate.'

'Did you have to shoot half a dozen bears just for their gallbladders?' Kate said. 'I mean, Jesus, Kurt. Where are they, by the way?'

'I worked hard for those bladders, Kate. You can't just–'

'Yeah, I can. Where are they?' When Kurt looked stubborn, Kate surveyed the cabin. 'Well,' she said, 'it's not much, but it's home, and I have to say I like your housekeeping. Be a shame if I had to start tearing it apart.'

Kurt muttered something. 'I beg your pardon?'

61

Kate said, and sipped her tea. 'This is pretty good tea. I'll have to get some for myself.'

He stretched out one shaking hand for the other mug. She waited until he'd gotten on the outside of the better part of it. 'Come on, Kurt,' she said with a patient, even kindly air, 'I'm giving you a choice. I can either take them in or I can take you in.'

He looked up from his mug, hope in his eye as he fixed on the one relevant point in her dialogue. 'You're not taking me in?'

'Not if I don't have to,' she said. She let the pleasant smile on her face fade. 'Not this time. You pull this again, Kurt, and it's federal prison for you – no passing go, no collecting two hundred dollars.'

He looked back into his tea. 'I'm broke, Kate,' he said in a low voice.

'We're all broke,' she said, 'so what else is new? Being broke is part of living in the Park. You want to get rich, move to Anchorage and get yourself a job with the state.'

'You should talk,' he muttered. 'You've got a brand-new house you don't even have to–'

'Stop right there, Kurt.' Kate took another sip of tea. It really was quite good, soothing the instinctive embarrassment that threatened to overwhelm her at his words. He was right. With a house like that, she was nowhere near as broke as he was. She forced herself to speak evenly. 'My house has nothing to do with you shooting bears to harvest their gallbladders and sell them on the black market. It's illegal, and you know it. It's harmful to maintaining a viable population of grizzlies in the Park, and you know that, too. And if you don't understand that if you do this again Jim Chopin is going to have to take you into protective custody so that Dan O'Brian won't feed your ass to those same grizzlies, you're too stupid to live.'

He remained silent, head down.

'Where are they?' Kate said. 'And don't make me ask again.'

They were in a game bag secreted beneath a loose floorboard. They smelled pretty ripe.

Kurt watched her, glowering. She paused in the doorway, game bag in hand. 'I don't want to have to come back out here, Kurt.'

He maintained a surly silence. He wasn't holding his head anymore, but he looked a little green. Nausea was a frequent companion to blunt-force head trauma, as Kate knew only too well, and she decided to leave him to it.

As she drove out of the clearing, she had a sinking feeling that it wouldn't be her last visit to Kurt's cabin.

CHAPTER 4

She spent that night at home, putting together a bag for Anchorage and reading the file Jim had handed her when she stopped by the trooper post in Niniltna with the bladders. His attitude amused her (a sort of 'Here's what you wanted, now don't let the door hit you in the ass on your way out' kind of thing), but she didn't have time to ride him, so she let it go with a knowing smile, which she knew full well annoyed the hell out of him.

The file was thick, the pages yellow and frayed, and the text in IBM Selectric typescript, with multiple errors fixed with X's or whiteout. She couldn't remember the last time she'd seen a court document that wasn't a computer printout, if ever. Jim had even managed to acquire a copy of the police file, probably as a means of avoiding her asking him for it.

She read steadily, cover to cover on both files, and was done before the lengthening shadows crept across the floor and she looked up to see the jagged blue-white peaks of the Quilak Mountains rearing up on the eastern horizon like destriers charging into battle, teeth bared, manes flying. Beneath their poised hooves, the Step dropped off abruptly to glacial moraine, which gave way to a long, wide valley crisscrossed by eight hundred miles of Kanuyaq River and attendant tributaries draining southward to Prince William Sound.

She sat there for a moment, just looking. It was still a source of amazement that she could sit on a couch in her own living room and without moving look up and out on such an incredible vista. 'I am the luckiest person in the world,' she said out loud.

Kate Shugak wasn't an especially humble person. She had a good opinion of her own intelligence and capabilities, and there was very little she had set out to do in life that she had not accomplished. She thought of the man she'd caught in the act of torturing a child as a prerequisite to murdering her, and she fingered the scar at her throat. She had killed him with his own knife, after he'd marked her for life. She'd saved the child, though, and what was a scar compared to the life of a child? It wasn't the only time she had killed. The fact did not weigh heavily upon her. In each case, she had been defending herself or someone else. She had no regrets, and the only nightmares she had involved the children she hadn't been able to save.

She was comfortable with who she was and what she had done to get there. Mostly, she did things for people. Most of the time, it helped, enough of the time it earned her a living, and she was comfortable with that, too.

She was, she admitted to herself, uncomfortable with being done for. The Park had come together as one unit, ranger and developer, subsistence and sport and commercial fisherman, lumberjack and tree-hugger, wildlife biologist and hunter, Native and white, all to build her, little old Kate Shugak, her own house. She still had trouble believing it. Old Sam had helped her to a vague understanding, but she feared she would never feel worthy of it.

She turned and looked at the living room, into which all of her former cabin could have fit with room to spare, never mind the kitchen, the bedrooms, the bathrooms. It still felt odd to have separate rooms for things, and doors into them.

'Okay,' she said out loud. 'I guess I got you by doing what it is that I do, and I guess if I want to earn it out, I keep doing what it is I do.'

Mutt had mastered the art of opening the door

on the first try, and she came in in time to hear the last of Kate's announcement. She cocked a quizzical ear in Kate's direction, received no enlightenment, and flopped down on the sheepskin in front of the couch with a sigh whose satisfaction might have had something to do with the tuft of parka squirrel fur adhering to her muzzle. 'Been up on the hill again, have you, girl?' Kate said.

She made herself a cup of tea, seasoned liberally with honey, which was also low in the container, and she added that to her Costco list for town. She curled up with the tea and the two files again, leafing through them at random this time, pausing here and there to reread a section.

Whether the fire had been set in Victoria Muravieff's house was not at issue. Traces of a trail of gasoline led from the fireplace in the living room downstairs to two different sets of drapes hanging at two windows on either side of the fireplace. It was a typically amateur attempt to hide arson, trying to simulate a wood fire in the fireplace sparking out of control and consuming the house. Kate was no arson investigator, but even she knew that it had been a long time since one had fallen for that trick.

She looked at the picture of the house in the police file. It was big and rectangular, with two stories and what had been a white paint job with pale green trim. She knew less than nothing about burn patterns, but from the smoke and char marks on the exterior of the house, it looked like the fire had started on the first floor and worked its way upstairs. A window on the extreme left of the second floor was open. The rest of the windows were broken, jagged pieces of glass still evident in the frames. What had been a nice yard had been trampled into a muddy mire.

William Muravieff, seventeen, had been asleep in an upstairs bedroom – probably not the room with the open window – when the fire had broken out. He'd been asleep, and according to the coroner's report – Alaska had still had coroners back then – he had never woken up.

Oliver Muravieff, sixteen, had. He had managed to grope his way to the window, open it, and more or less fall out, landing awkwardly on his right leg, which had fractured in half a dozen places, which led to a charge of assault with intent. With the first-degree murder charge, and another for attempted murder, the assault charge was only gravy for the prosecutor.

The good news for Kate's new client was that there was no physical evidence linking Victoria Pilz Bannister Muravieff with the crime.

The bad news was that there was a lot of circumstantial evidence pointing straight at her like a road sign at a crossroads with a choice of only one destination. Victoria lived in the house. The gas in the can in her garage was a chemical match for the traces of gas found in the living room. She had fought with William over how much time he was spending playing basketball, as opposed to doing his homework.

Kate snorted over that last piece of 'evidence.' Like there was a parent out there who hadn't fought with their teenager over something.

Both boys had been drugged with scopolamine. The coroner had gone on at length about the derivations of this substance (the nightshade family – chiefly from henbane). It acted by interfering with the transmission of nerve impulses. The symptoms were dilated pupils, rapid heartbeat, and dry skin, mouth, and respiratory passages. An overdose could cause delirium, delusions, paralysis, and stupor. It was found in a lot of nonprescription sedatives, one of which just happened to be found in Victoria's medicine cabinet.

More damning was the insurance policy – for a cool $1 million – she had taken out the week before on William. However, she had taken out insurance policies on Oliver and Charlotte as well, and Charlotte had been with her mother when William was killed.

Kate went back to the trial transcript. Certainly, Victoria hadn't had the most vigorous defense, but it didn't necessarily look incompetent, either. She made a note of the attorney's name, one Henry Cowell. He was probably retired, but if he was still alive, the bar association would have his address. A talk with him might prove useful.

On the whole, despite her disdain for circumstantial evidence – like every law-enforcement professional, she wanted to find the perp standing over the body, smoking gun in hand – she was inclined to believe that the jury had come to the only possible verdict. Victoria was guilty of filicide, one of those wonderful clinical terms dreamed up by shrinks to put a bearable distance between the act and the description thereof. It was what it was, the murder of a child by its parent.

The death of a child by itself was traumatic enough. Parents were not supposed to outlive their children, it was unnatural. A child's death guaranteed the mutual sympathy and terror of parents everywhere. The deliberate taking of a child's life by a parent invoked a horror akin to what one might feel at a display of cannibalism.

What was that old Greek yarn, something about a husband seducing his wife's sister and, in revenge, the wife killing their sons and feeding them to him? It would be pretty to think that such things happened only in ancient legend. Kate knew the truth, and it wasn't pretty, not at all.

Mothers, who committed less than 13 percent of all violent crimes, committed 50 percent of filicides. Children under the age of five were the most at risk.

Kate looked back at the file. William had been seventeen. Not even close to the profile.

Filicide was usually characterized by a display of great violence – beating, shaking, stabbing, suffocation, poisoning – with little or no advance planning. And there was always postpartum psychosis, which the statistics said struck only one mother in five hundred, but which Kate had recent cause to know could sometimes lead a mother to a serial killing of her own children immediately after birth. The last time Kate had looked at the FBI stats, the experts had a mother, killing a child in America every two or three days.

There were far too many ways to kill children. It happened when an exhausted mother shook a baby to make it stop crying and instead shook it to death. It happened when a fourteen-year-old got pregnant and stuffed her newborn into a garbage can. It happened when a wife tried to leave an abusive husband and, in retaliation, the husband killed all three kids, the wife, and then himself. It happened when whatever filter the parent had screwed to her lens allowed her to see the child as a threat, and it happened when that filter let her believe the best thing she could do for the child was kill it.

Kate had had coffee with a fireman awhile back, and he had told her that there was a feeling among arson investigators that filicide by fire, despite going undetected too often and being underreported more often than that, was increasing at an alarming rate. All too frequently, the fireman had said, the natural sympathy one feels for parents who have lost their children led investigators to overlook evidence that might give rise to the suspicion that the fire that took the child's life might have been deliberately set. Most of the victims were young, he'd told her, and again she considered the age of the victim and the intended victim in this case. William had been seventeen, Oliver sixteen.

Sometimes, the children had been shot or smothered, and the fire set to cover the evidence. Sometimes, the escape routes were blocked – doors jammed, windows nailed shut.

Kate rummaged around for the picture of the Muravieff home. The photo showed the top-floor window was still wide open, one side of the curtain hanging outside, maybe because of the wind. Or, if it were Oliver's bedroom, because of his swan dive to escape the smoke.

She wondered how hard Victoria had tried to get the boys out. She went back to the trial transcript, and surfaced a little while later with no clear answer to her question. The defense had laid out a timetable that showed where Victoria and her daughter, Charlotte, had been that evening – at a fund-raiser at her brother Erland's for one of the gubernatorial candidates. The man had subsequently lost the election. It cheered Kate to know that the rich and famous could be just as bad at picking politicians as she was.

But she was straying from the point. Victoria and Charlotte had gone to Victoria's brother's house early that afternoon to help with the preparations. Kate found that odd. Didn't the Bannisters and the Pilzes have serfs to do that stuff for them? She had a hard time imagining Charlotte Muravieff with a vacuum cleaner in hand. She and her mother were probably needed to spread pâté made from salmon that had never seen a commercial net. On ladyfingers, no doubt. Not that Kate had ever seen a ladyfinger in real life, but she was very well read, and they ate ladyfingers and cucumber and watercress a lot in English novels. None of it sounded very appetizing.

Again, she was straying from the point. Victoria and Charlotte had remained at Victoria's brother's house until the party was over. Everyone who had been interviewed agreed the party broke up at 10:00 P.M. Victoria and Charlotte had arrived home a little after eleven. Victoria's brother's house was in Turnagain. Victoria had lived in the valley north of Anchorage, on five acres near Bodenburg Butte, maybe an hour away by car, which fit.

When had the fire been set? The trial transcript

71

didn't say. Kate found that odd, and one, if not the only, point for her side. If the defense attorney could have demonstrated that the fire might have started while Victoria was on the road or even still at her brother's, he could have given the jury reasonable doubt as to opportunity. Alternatively, if the prosecution could have made a case for the fire in the fireplace taking as many hours to travel the gas paths across the carpet to the curtains as it took Victoria and Charlotte to drive to the party, plus the length of the party itself, that would have significantly improved the state's case.

Usually the parents in such cases were in their twenties and thirties. Victoria was thirty-six the year the fire had burned down her house and killed her son.

Still, the various inconsistencies didn't necessarily mean anything. Serial killers were all supposed to be skinny little twenty-five-year-old white guys with no beards, usually preying on young women in their teens and twenties. And yet four months ago, Kate had helped apprehend a sixty-year-old white woman, definitely on the plump side, who was a card-carrying member of the Republican Party, who had killed five of her own children before they learned how to focus their eyes. There were no hard-and-fast rules for this kind of crime, only percentages and statistics that sometimes helped nudge the investigator in the right direction.

One thing Kate didn't understand was how Victoria Pilz Bannister Muravieff had managed to run out of money to the extent that she had to resort to murder, and filicide at that, to replenish her share of the family coffers known to all to be overflowing. That also was not in the trial transcript. Evidently, the prosecuting attorney and the jury both felt that the lure of six zeros was enough, no matter how rich you already were.

The other thing she didn't understand was where Mr. Muravieff was. He hadn't even been called as a witness at the trial.

The third thing she didn't understand, which probably had nothing to do with the case, was what the lily white clan of Pilzes and Bannisters were doing allying themselves with somebody named Muravieff. What made this interesting was that the marriage would have taken place years before the Alaska Native Claims Settlement Act gave Alaska Natives land and money in exchange for a right-of-way down the middle of Alaska to build the TransAlaska Pipeline. Land and money equal power in Western society, and Alaska Natives had had very little of any of the three prior to ANCSA.

In the cities and in the state overall, the power structure was built on white blood, American mostly, with contributions from stampeders from all over the world, including Scandinavians looking for free land in a place physically similar to their peninsulas, and Russians escaping the Revolution.

Like every other student at the University of Alaska required to take History 341 to graduate, Kate Shugak knew all about the Pilzes and the Bannisters. Hermann Pilz had been a German mining engineer who had come north with the Klondike stampede and stayed to start the first coal mine in Kachemak Bay, which had led to a timely investment in the Alaska Steamship Line, which evolved into a shipping company that specialized in getting freight to every community in Alaska not on the road system. Since most of the communities were not on the road system, the formation of an airline was initiated out of necessity. For a while, the Pilz name had been painted on virtually anything that moved in and out of the Alaskan Bush. Now everything was owned and managed by various holding companies that had pieces large and small of various other essential Alaskan businesses, such as grocery businesses.

Which led to the Bannisters. Isaiah Bannister had been attached to Lt. Henry Allen's army expedition in 1885 up the Kanuyaq River to the Tanana, down it to the Yukon, up it to the Koyukuk, back down to the Unalakleet-Yukon portage, and on down to St. Michael. He survived the mosquitoes and the bears and left the navy to form a company to import supplies, edible and otherwise, into Alaska. The Arctic Trading Company now owned the largest chain of grocery stores and supermarkets in the state, and Safeway and Kroger's had both been rumored to be sniffing around about a possible buyout.

Isaiah Bannister, well-established in Alaska by 1898 (it wasn't the stampeders who got rich; it was the people who sold them food and supplies), had bankrolled Hermann Pilz's Kachemak Coal Company. Hermann had reciprocated, in what was generally held to be a tit-for-tat kind of deal, by marrying Isaiah Bannister's thirty-nine-year-old spinster daughter, his lone ewe lamb, who

74

rejoiced in the name of Calliope. Calliope had surprised everyone by bearing a son a year for five years, raising them to be good men and true, and outliving her much-younger husband by twenty-seven years.

The Muravieffs, on the other hand, didn't come from anywhere, they were Alaskan-born and -bred, with a little Norwegian and a lot of Russian thrown in. There was another story, one not in the history books, something about a Muravieff maiden and Capt. James Cook, but that was only talk late at night around the fire, and not around Muravieff fires, either. The Muravieff ancestor of choice was Mikhael Muraviev, a Russian ex-patriate who patrolled the coast of Alaska from Ketchikan to Barrow as captain of a Coast Guard cutter and who left descendants in nearly every port. Pre-modern Alaska Natives admired and respected procreation in any form. The more kids you had young, particularly male kids, the better you ate when you got old.

In short, Victoria Pilz Bannister Muravieff was Alaskan history walking around on two legs, even if those legs currently languished in the Hiland Mountain Correctional Facility in Eagle River.

Kate could practically smell the trial judge's horror at Victoria's crime and his unswerving conviction that she was guilty. He sustained all but one objection by the prosecution and none by the defense, although the defense didn't make that many. When the jury returned a guilty verdict, the judge issued a life sentence without leaving the bench, and said for the record that he was sorry Alaska didn't have a death penalty, because that was what true justice demanded and Victoria deserved.

The list of witnesses called to testify during the trial read like a *Who's Who* of the previous hundred years of Alaskan history. Kate read through the names, torn between a natural reluctance to stir up that much shit and an even more natural delight at the prospect. She thought Victoria was most likely guilty as hell, but she figured Victoria's daughter had a bunch of money she was going to give away to someone to tilt at this windmill, and it might as well be Kate.

Besides, given that someone had tried to burn her own cabin down around her ears not four months before, the case kind of resonated with her.

She filled a duffel bag with clean clothes, set her alarm, and turned in for the night.

CHAPTER 5

George touched down at Merrill Field just before 10:00 A.M. Mutt gave him a loving farewell with the rough end of her tongue, which he pretended to hate. 'When do you want to come back?' he said, tossing her duffel into the back of the cab he'd called for fifteen minutes out.

'I don't know,' Kate said.

'One of the long jobs?'

'I'm dotting the *i*'s and crossing the *t*'s of a thirty-year-old case. I figure it'll take me twenty-four hours, if that. I'll stretch it out a little for the sake of the fee, but not much.'

George pulled a small, extremely tattered spiral notebook that had served, or something very like it, as Chugach Air Taxi's reservation system for as long as Kate had known him. It was as covered in airplane grease as George was. 'This is the twenty-third, so okay, I'll put you down for a return on the twenty-eighth. I've got the Bingleys coming out with their kids for school shopping that morning.'

'Sounds good.' He was lifting off the end of runway 24 as the cab went through the light at sixth and Karluk. Mutt recognized the Cessna and gave a farewell bark, which frightened the taxi driver, a middle-aged Russian emigrant who had been prepared to admire Kate until he got a load of her bodyguard.

Fifteen minutes later, they were deposited on the doorstep of one of a row of town houses lining the north shore of Westchester Lagoon. Kate unlocked the door and they went in. It was a barn of a place, three stories, including the garage. The kitchen, dining room, living room, a small room meant to be a den, and a three-quarter bath were on the second floor, the third floor given over to more bedrooms and bathrooms. Kate tossed her duffel onto the couch, turned on the refrigerator, and checked the phone for a dial tone. There was one, and she turned on the answering machine.

The Subaru Forester in the garage needed a wash but it started just fine. The first stop was an Anchorage branch of Last Frontier Bank, just to make sure Charlotte's check was good. It was,

77

and the cashier's reaction to all those zeros had Kate, momentarily forgetting her own response, toying with the idea of applying for a loan. She remembered in time that she didn't need to buy anything her checking account couldn't cover and got the hell out of there.

Hiland Mountain Correctional Facility housed women convicts and male sex offenders, which Kate had never understood. She'd been in and out of the place often when she'd worked for Jack, but a new governor had been elected since then and all the faces were new, including the fresh-faced young woman riding the desk out front, who hadn't been lied to by enough cons to have lost her innocence. She frowned prettily at Kate. 'You want to see Victoria Muravieff?'

'Yes, Officer.'

The young woman, whose badge was difficult to sort out from all the other patches and shields adorning her bountiful bosom but whose name Kate thought might be T. Offerut, looked Kate over. Kate tolerated the examination of her attire – her usual jeans, T-shirt, and tennis shoes, no coat because it was in the blisteringly high seventies – with what passed for her for equanimity.

The young woman realized that the frown was producing an unsightly line across her forehead, smoothed it away with one hand, and turned the frown into a smile. 'Of course, you must be the one from UAA,' she said, as if that and that alone would explain the jeans.

Kate didn't deny it.

'May I see some identification, please?'

Kate produced her driver's license, was deemed

to be who she really was, and was permitted entry. When the door closed behind her with a solid thud, she had the same reaction she always did: an overwhelming wave of claustrophobia, which was not alleviated by the wall of windows that lined one side of the large room to which she had been admitted and which looked out on a spectacular view of the Chugach Mountains. The worst part of Kate's job with the district attorney had been having to enter various correctional facilities around the state voluntarily to interview perps. She'd hated it then, and she hated it now. She took a deep breath, trying to fill her lungs with fresh air that wasn't there.

The room was filled with long tables and plastic bucket chairs, and there were a couple of kids running around, obviously on visits to their mothers, who were hunched over tables, talking either to their mothers or their lawyers. At another table, a group of women were laboring over some arts and crafts project. A couple of them were in bright orange jumpsuits, which meant that they had misbehaved in some way on the inside, which could mean anything from petty theft to assault. A majority of them were Native and black, big surprise.

Kate was ushered to a chair at the end of one table and told firmly to wait there. She sat. Lunch was being cooked somewhere – burgers, at a guess – and her stomach growled.

'Kate Shugak?'

She looked up and saw a woman standing in front of her. The last time Kate had seen her, Kate had been seated in the witness chair and she had been at the defendant's table next to a public defender who was trying to impeach Kate's testimony. Kate searched her memory and dredged up a name and, with a little more effort, a case file. 'Myra Hartsock,' she said. Child endangerment, fourth offense, and the judge had taken away her children and evidently thrown enough jail time at her to keep her in Hiland for six years.

'Are you here to see me?' Myra said.

'No,' Kate said.

'I'm sober now.'

'I see that.'

'And I'm straight. I been straight for four, going on five years now.'

'Good for you.'

Myra hesitated, hands clenched on the edge of her tray. 'My kids,' she said. 'I see them sometimes.'

'Really.'

Myra nodded. 'My mother brings them here to visit me.'

'Good for her.'

'I read to them, and we play games.'

'Good for you.'

Myra gestured with her head. 'I've been working in the prison greenhouse. My case officer says she thinks she can place me in a job pretty easy when I get out.'

'Good for her.'

Myra took a deep breath. 'Because I'm coming up for parole in seven months.'

'Really?'

'You could speak for me at my hearing.'

'I could,' Kate agreed.

Myra's look of hope faded. 'But you won't.'

'No.'

Myra bared her teeth. 'Bitch.'

'Backatcha,' Kate said.

Myra started to cry. 'Why won't you help me?'

'Because your kids come first for me,' Kate said, 'like they should have with you. Reading to them and playing games with them one or twice a month doesn't make up for the fact that Andy had to learn how to write left-handed because you broke his right hand in so many places that he can't even brush his teeth with it, and that Kay will probably be in therapy for the rest of her life because you sold her for money you used to buy booze and drugs.'

'I was a drunk and a junkie back then!' Myra said, her voice rising. 'I told you – I don't do that anymore!'

'You don't in this adult day-care center of yours,' Kate said. 'Doesn't mean you won't when you get out again. Best thing that can happen to your kids is for you to be away from them as long as possible. If I had my druthers it'd be forever.'

'Let's move it along, Myra, shall we?' a guard said, coming up behind her.

He took her arm. She yanked free, glared at Kate, and stomped off.

Kate could feel the eyes on her from all over the room. Oh yeah, it was old home week for her here at Hiland Mountain, a regular felons reunion. A few minutes later, the officer returned, Victoria Pilz Bannister Muravieff in tow.

She didn't look anything at all like Kate had imagined she would. For one thing, she didn't look ill, and for another, she didn't look sixty-seven. She was a tall woman with a thick head of gray hair cut bluntly to a determined jawline and parted over her right eye. Her brow was broad, her eyebrows arched, her nose so high-bridged as to be almost hooked, which it probably would be eventually, her mouth full and firm. She was wearing street clothes, a faded pink T-shirt tucked into a pair of button-front Levi's, and tennis shoes with Velcro fasteners.

She moved with a brisk step, her shoulders square, no hint of osteoporosis about her. Her cheeks were pink, her wrinkles confined for the most part to the corners of her eyes and mouth, beneath her chin, and on the backs of her hands. Her eyes were dark blue and direct, fixing Kate with a puzzled stare. 'You aren't Caroline.'

Kate got up and offered her hand. 'No, I'm Kate Shugak.'

Victoria took it automatically in a strong, cool grip, one firm pump and release. 'I'm sorry. Have we met?'

'No,' Kate said.

The older woman looked at the table and then at the floor next to Kate's chair. 'Didn't you bring them?'

'Bring what?'

'The GED workbooks,' the older woman said impatiently.

'I didn't know I was supposed to,' Kate said.

Victoria Pilz Bannister Muravieff put her hands on her hips and looked down her nose at Kate. 'How the devil am I supposed to teach my class without workbooks? Listen, Ms. Shugak, if this is another end run by the university around my program, I have told you people before that I won't–'

'I don't work for the university,' Kate said.

Victoria halted. 'Then who the hell are you?'

'I told you. Kate Shugak.'

Victoria tapped her foot. 'Is that supposed to mean something to me?' Her eyes narrowed. 'Wait a minute. Any relation to Ekaterina Shugak?'

'My grandmother.'

'I see.' A brief pause. 'I knew her.'

'Everyone did,' Kate said. There was a sick feeling rising in the pit of her stomach. 'Have you talked to your daughter lately?'

All trace of expression wiped itself from Victoria's face. Her eyes narrowed and her mouth settled into a thin line. 'What's Charlotte got to do with this?'

'She hired me,' Kate said.

Victoria folded her arms. 'To do what?'

'To look into your case.'

'What case?'

The sick feeling intensified. 'The case that put you in here, Ms. Muravieff. The murder of your son.'

The tapping foot had stilled, but the older woman's shoulders were so tight, Kate thought they might break off if someone tapped them. From the corner of her eye, Kate could see people turning to look at them, and she could hear conversations dropping off one by one into an expectant silence. Into it, Kate said, 'Your daughter thinks you were wrongly convicted, Ms. Muravieff, and she hired me to prove it. I'd like to ask you some questions, if I may. First, I'll need–'

83

'You may not,' the other woman said in a taut voice.

Kate, thrown off her stride, said blankly, 'I beg your pardon?'

'Tell Charlotte I fired you,' the other woman said. And with that, she marched off.

Kate watched her go, not a little mystified, and recollected herself only when one of the officers started to move toward her. She held up a hand and headed for the door.

She dropped the visitor badge off at the desk. As she was going out, another woman was coming in with a large box. Kate held the door for her, and as it closed behind her, she heard the fresh-faced young guard say, 'Caroline, hey. I thought you weren't coming. I thought you'd sent someone else today.'

Kate kept going. Mutt was sunbathing on the hood of the Forester. 'Let's go,' Kate told her. She started the engine and drove out of the parking lot. About a mile down the road, she pulled a U-turn and drove back up the hill and into the parking lot, this time pulling into a space about two rows down and ten spaces over.

Mutt gave her a quizzical look. 'To confuse anyone inside who's monitoring the cameras on the roof,' Kate said, pointing them out.

Mutt looked pointedly at the door. Kate leaned over to open it up and Mutt got back up on the hood.

The sun beat down. Kate rolled down first her window, then the one on the passenger side, then the two back windows. She kicked herself for not bringing a book, and cleaned out the glove compartment in lieu of reading. There was the car manual, a near-empty box of Wash 'n Dries, a handful of lemon drops, a Reese's Cup that was silver with age but which Kate ate anyway, and a comb with a few strands of short, dark, curly hair caught in its teeth. She touched them gently. How strange that something grown by a man dead for almost two years could feel so alive.

Kate had read in various places how scientists were mapping the human chromosome down to the last molecule, and how it might be possible in the future to reconstruct a human being from the DNA in a strand of hair. They wouldn't have the same life experience, of course, the same memories. The all new and improved Jack Morgan wouldn't necessarily like Jimmy Buffett, for example, and Jimmy Buffett had been responsible for bringing Jack and Kate together.

She became aware that she could no longer see the hair or the comb for the tears in her eyes. She blinked them away and put the comb back in the glove compartment.

The sun beat down some more. Mutt rolled onto her back, paws in the air in a disgusting display of abandon. Kate considered starting the engine just to see how high Mutt could jump from a prone position.

An hour passed. The woman Kate had passed in the doorway came out and went to her car, a beige Toyota Camry that looked, if possible, even more beige beneath an unregarded layer of mud and dust. Kate opened the door of the Subaru. Mutt jumped as if someone had given her a nudge with a cattle prod and then slid down from the hood in an ignominious heap. She leaped to her feet and pretended that she had meant to do that.

Kate approached the woman as she was about to get in her car. 'Excuse me?'

The woman looked over her shoulder. 'Yes? May I help you?'

'My name is Kate Shugak.'

The woman looked puzzled. 'I'm sorry. Have we met?'

Twice in one day. If this kept up, Kate was going to get an inferiority complex. 'No. I've been retained by Victoria Muravieff's daughter to look into her case.'

The woman looked more puzzled. 'What case?'

Kate sighed. 'Listen, I'm fresh off a plane and I'm hot, and I'm hungry and I'm thirsty. Have you – what was your name?'

'Caroline Landry,' the woman said, and then looked as if she wished she hadn't.

'So, Caroline, have you had lunch?'

Caroline Landry hesitated, clearly trying to decide if Kate was dangerous or not. 'No.'

'Great. You like Mexican food?'

They found a table at Garcia's in Eagle River. 'I'll buy,' Kate said, absorbed in the menu.

'I'll buy my own, thanks,' Caroline Landry said.

'It's an expense,' Kate said.

'For what job?'

'Charlotte Muravieff has retained me to look into her mother's murder conviction,' Kate said.

Landry was still staring at Kate with her mouth slightly open when the waiter arrived. Kate ordered tostaditos to start and fajitas for the main course. Landry's mouth relaxed into a smile. 'You are hungry,' she said.

'Don't get a lot of Mexican food in Niniltna,' Kate said. 'I'm making up for lost time.'

'Tostada salad,' Landry told the waiter, 'and something tells me I'm going to need a margarita.'

The waiter, a slim young man with a hopeful smile, looked at Kate. She shook her head. 'Water's fine. If you could bring me a couple of wedges of lime, that would be good.'

The margarita came and, surprise, so did the lime, and in her head Kate ratcheted up the tip. Landry took a long swallow of her drink. 'Oh yeah,' she said, putting it down, 'that hits the spot. Okay, what do you want to know?'

'Anything you can tell me, Ms. Landry.'

'Caroline.'

'Kate. You know Victoria Muravieff. She thought I'd come in your place today.'

'Yes,' Caroline said. 'I work with her.'

'Work with her?'

Caroline raised an eyebrow. 'Yes, work with her. Victoria runs the education department at Hiland.'

'A prisoner runs the education department?'

'Pretty much. The governor cut the budget a couple of years back, so the Department of Corrections had to cut fripperies like education. At this point, it's pretty much up to the prisoners to drum up interest and funding from local groups and agencies if they want anything in the way of programming out there.'

'How's that working?' Kate said.

'Pretty good, actually,' Caroline said. 'A local computer supply store funded a course in Microsoft certification. A local cellist started a chamber orchestra with chairs underwritten by the Trial Lawyers Association.'

Kate laughed. 'A natural.'

Caroline smiled. 'It seems so. At any rate, there's a waiting list to get in.'

'Do they perform?'

'Yes, in-house. They're agitating to perform outside the facility, but the director hasn't been beaten into submission quite yet. Another woman comes out every three weeks to teach classes in bead art, with supplies donated by the Bead Society, which puts on a show every year of inmate art. They call it Con Art.'

'You're kidding me.'

'Nope. They got a write-up in the paper and a story on television, and now they've got so many submissions that they think they're going to have to start jurying it.'

'Are they selling?'

Caroline nodded. 'Oh yeah, check out the gift shop the next time you're there. And then there's the greenhouse. They make a lot of hanging baskets and start a lot of vegetables, and sell them, too. Victoria's working on some of the master gardeners in town to start a master gardener's program at the prison.'

'And you were bringing GED workbooks in.'

'Yeah. We've got so many inmates wanting to make up for time lost in their real lives that we've pretty much got a class going nonstop. It's hard for some of them to finish because they're not in for long enough.' She realized the humor of that last observation at the same time Kate did, and this time they both laughed. Lunch arrived, and Kate inhaled the aroma of charred beef with vast satisfaction.

When she'd gotten on the right side of most of it, she said, 'Who's "we"?' When Caroline gave her a blank look, she said, 'You said "we've pretty much got a class going nonstop." You and who else?'

'I thought I said,' Caroline said with some surprise. 'It's all Victoria. None of this would be happening without her.'

According to Caroline Landry, Victoria Muravieff had been committed to Hiland Mountain Correctional Facility the day the verdict had been returned in her trial, some thirty years before, with a B.A. in education already in her pocket. 'She was a bookkeeper before...' Caroline hesitated. 'Well, she was a bookkeeper. She enrolled in a correspondence course for her BA practically the day she arrived, and after that she went for her master's. I think she got the first in eighteen months and the second a year later.' She smiled. 'I've read her thesis. "Teaching on the Inside: Why Prisons Need Schools."'

'Yeah?' Kate said, suspending her construction of the perfect fajita for a moment. 'How bad was it?'

'It wasn't bad at all,' Caroline said sharply. 'It was even published, and I understand it's a reference work for prisons across the nation.'

'My mistake,' Kate said, and went back to building her fajita. She'd read a lot of dissertations turned into books, enough to know that most academics can't write worth shit, but she wasn't being paid to interrupt the flow of information with

89

literary criticism.

Mollified by Kate's compliance, Caroline said, 'After that, she got the head of the education department out here at that time to take her on as her assistant. Trustee, in prisonspeak. She's...' Caroline hesitated again. 'Do you know who she is? Her family?'

Kate nodded.

'Well, she's managed to bribe, seduce, or coerce all of them and all of their friends into donating something in the way of money or books over the past thirty years. The education program here is privately funded; it wouldn't exist without her. And the people she has helped – my God, you wouldn't believe some of the stories, women who have never had any decent role models or positive reinforcement in their lives.' She paused. 'One time, Victoria was reading some student essays out loud. Some of these essays were so bad they'd make a first grader blush, but Victoria has this way of making even the most hopeless people believe they can achieve something. After class, one of the women came forward and said to Victoria, "Nobody ever told me I could do anything before." I wanted to cry. That woman' – Caroline pointed her fork at Kate – 'that woman went on to get her GED, and when she got out, she had twelve college credits. She went onto complete a degree in accounting.'

'What'd she do to put her in jail in the first place?'

A brief pause. 'Check kiting,' Caroline said a little reluctantly. She met Kate's eyes and they both laughed again.

'You like her,' Kate said. 'Victoria.'

'I revere her,' Caroline said.

'Ah, but would you want her to move in next door to you when she gets out?'

Caroline flushed and she played with her food. 'Do you think there's a chance that you'll get her out?'

'You think she should be out?'

There was a brief silence while Caroline stared out the window that looked out on the parking lot. 'Her crime was horrific. I have a son. I can't imagine–'

'You think she did it, then?' Kate said, surprised.

Caroline met her eyes. 'She's never denied it. She pled not guilty at her trial, but that's the last time she said she didn't do it to anyone, so far as I know.'

Kate raised an eyebrow.

'Okay,' Caroline said, 'I looked up the trial after I started working with her. I wanted to know who I was dealing with. She's never denied doing it to me,' she repeated.

'Did you ask?'

'Once, yes, when I was new to the program, when I didn't know who she was. I learned afterward that it's best not to know what they've done. It's easier to work with them when you don't know.' She hesitated. 'It was hard,' she said in a low voice, 'hard to come back to work with her after I'd read the newspaper accounts of the trial.'

I'll bet, Kate thought, remembering some of the women she'd been responsible for putting away. She wouldn't have worked with any of them at gunpoint, starting with Myra Hartsock. 'What did she say? When you asked if she'd done it?'

'She said, "The jury thought so."'

'That's all?'

'That's all.'

Kate contemplated this for a moment. 'Do you think she did it? Do you think she killed her son for the insurance money?'

'Everybody in prison is innocent,' Caroline said, 'to hear them tell it.'

Kate nodded. 'I know. I've spent a fair amount of time putting people in them. They're all as pure as the driven snow.'

Caroline turned the now-empty margarita glass between her fingers. 'But Victoria...'

'Yes?'

Caroline shoved her glass to one side and leaned forward. 'Listen, Kate, Victoria Muravieff has been a phenomenal force at that prison. It's practically an adjunct institution for the University of Alaska. I'm the liaison between the two, my job is predicated on there being an education department at Hiland, and the education department is there only because Victoria is.'

'You'll lose your job if I get her out, is that what you're saying?'

Caroline flushed again. 'No, of course not.' She sat back. 'Well, yes, but that's not what I meant. I'm just saying – look, if I'd met Victoria on the outside, I would have been proud to call her my friend. Guilty, innocent, I don't know. She's made a real difference every day she's been in that place. It's not too much to say that she has literally changed lives. She has given hope to people who never knew before what that word meant. Much less how to spell it.'

'You make her sound like some kind of saint.'

'That's nothing,' Caroline said a little sadly. 'The inmates? They think she's a god.'

CHAPTER 6

Kate walked into Brendan's office to be scooped off her feet, tossed in the air, and roundly kissed. She heard cheering from the hallway. 'Put me down, you lummox,' she said.

Brendan sighed and let her slip to the floor. ''Twas ever thus,' he said sadly. 'I require large amounts of food to get over the lack of self-esteem your rejection has forced upon me.'

Kate handed him a take-out carton. He opened it and pursed his lips in a long, reverent whistle. 'Steak and shrimp fajitas, my favorite. I'm kissing you again, Shugak, I swear.'

'Shut up and eat your lunch.'

He settled behind his desk and tucked in. She sat in a chair opposite and regarded him with affection.

He was a big man with sandy hair, blue eyes, and a face as chronically red as his grin was wide. He was an assistant district attorney for the state, and while it was true he had no chance of ever becoming DA, due to an undiplomatic endorsement of the sitting governor's opponent in the last election with a television camera pointed his way, it was also true he had no ambition to do or be anything other than what he was. 'I like putting the bad guys away,' he'd told Kate once. 'Gives me the warm fuzzies. And it makes me feel like I'd've had a shot at Grace Van Owen.' He liked the legal system, too, its intricacies and nit-picking and arcane rituals. Kate remembered that he thought British attorneys were one up on American attorneys in that they got to wear wigs. 'Ever seen those in the movies?' he'd said. 'Makes 'em all look like Sam'l Pepys.'

'Where is the wolf?' he said with his mouth full.

'I made her wait in the car. I was afraid she might be competition for the fajitas, and you'd have to take her out.' She grinned at him. 'You owe me, McCord.'

'The hell you say,' Brendan said, and chucked a manila envelope at her.

Inside were a list of names and addresses, both business and home.

'It's the witness list from the Muravieff trial – who's still around, and where,' Brendan said.

Kate met his eyes and dropped her voice an octave. 'I have never wanted you more,' she said.

He flung back his head, roaring with laughter. She waited for it to subside. 'What do you think?'

He gave her his wide and uncomplicated trademark grin. 'She's in jail, isn't she?'

'Come on, Brendan.'

'I haven't read the file, just the witness list. You want my professional opinion?'

'Always.'

'You're going to put an eye out, you keep fluttering your eyelashes at me that way,' he said.

'Okay, all right, I'll read it. You at Jack's?'

She nodded.

'Johnny?'

'With Auntie Vi. I don't know how long this case is going to take, and school starts in a couple of weeks.'

Brendan dropped his eyes and shook his head.

'Why are you smiling?' Kate said.

'You really think you've got a chance of getting her out?'

Kate remembered the stubborn line of Charlotte's mouth. 'I'm being paid to think so.'

'Ah.' There was a wealth of understanding in the one word. 'I'll look at the trial transcript. I just had a case settle, so I can squeeze a half hour into my schedule.'

'And on a Saturday, too,' Kate said. 'Thanks, Brendan.'

He cocked an eyebrow. 'How grateful are you?'

She laughed, and watched him dribble steak juice down the front of his polyester suit (Sears, on sale), but it sort of matched the dull brown color, not to mention the – what was it, oatmeal? – he'd left there at breakfast that morning. 'One more thing,' she said.

'What?'

'Could you find out if the investigating officer is still around?'

'What's his name?'

'Charles Baltzo. Sgt. Charles Baltzo.'

'Sure, why not, since it looks like I'm working for you instead of the state this week anyway.'

'Brendan–'

He laughed. 'Lighten up, Shugak. That was a

95

joke.' He burped behind a napkin and sat back. 'So what else you got on the agenda?'

'I talked to Victoria today.'

'Yeah? And?'

'And she fired me.'

He stared at her. 'You're kidding me.'

'But it didn't take, since she wasn't the one who hired me.'

'Interesting, this is,' he said. 'And unexpected.'

'Stop talking like Yoda. Do you know anything about Victoria Muravieff, Brendan? Like what she's been doing in prison for the last thirty years?'

'Sure. She's even been written up in the paper a couple of times. According to the local editorial writers, she's a cross between Socrates and Anne Sullivan.'

'And that doesn't impress you?'

'I don't have to tell you how easy it is to be the good guy in prison, Kate,' he said. 'No drugs, no booze, no men to fight over, no kids to drive you crazy. She's an intelligent woman with, evidently, a strong drive to succeed. She's in prison, I might add, because she succeeded at murder.'

'She got caught.'

'I said she was intelligent. I didn't say she was smart enough to get away with murder. Very few people are.'

Kate sighed.

'Ah hell, Kate,' he said. 'If it was easy, everybody'd be doing it.'

On the way home, Kate stopped in at City Market to load up on groceries, and, as was her deplorable wont when she was in Anchorage, she overdid it on the fresh fruit and vegetable front.

It was hard to be in the produce section of any Anchorage grocery store with a lot of money in the bank. She consoled herself with the thought that the back of George's Cessna was large and that she could take home whatever was left over at the end of the job.

She made herself an enormous fruit salad with Auntie Vi's special sweet dressing made from mayonnaise, white vinegar, and honey. She ate it at the dining room table, next to the window overlooking the lagoon, watching walkers, joggers, bladers, and bikers on the bike trail that ran next to the water's edge. When she was done, she looked at Mutt and said, 'Let's go scare some of those sissy city dogs.'

They walked around the lagoon and through the tunnel beneath the railroad tracks that led to the coastal trail. It was a beautiful evening, clear, with a warm breeze, which was strong enough to keep the bugs off but light enough not to dissipate the rich aroma rising up off the massed *Rosa rugosa* bushes crowding the fence. Mutt trotted next to her, looking down her lupine nose at the dogs going in the other direction, who had to be kept on leashes and still lunged out to the ends of them, barking hysterically at anything that moved. When a pair of Dobermans got especially yappy, she snapped her teeth together, just once. It sounded like the cock of a pistol. They shut up. If they'd had tails, they would have tucked them between their legs. Their owner, clinging desperately to the other end of their leashes, glared at Kate.

'She's like that around dogs with no manners,' Kate told him.

They went over a bridge that crossed a creek whose mud banks were exposed by low tide. Where the creek's current debouched into the inlet, the white backs of beluga whales gleamed against the grayish brown water. Eating on the salmon fixing to head upstream to spawn, Kate thought, and raised her eyes to the horizon, where the block of Foraker and the arc of Denali stood out in white relief against the deep blue sky. It was a beautiful day, and she was in a comfortable house in a great Anchorage neighborhood, a house that was paid for, but she couldn't help wondering if it was as beautiful a day in another and much less crowded neighborhood two hundred miles to the northeast.

There was an answer for that. The sooner she got the job done, the sooner she could go home.

'Go ahead,' she said to Mutt, and like an arrow loosed from a bow, Mutt leaped the boulders piled against the bank, landed on the strip of sand below, and streaked off, not in pursuit of anything – she knew better than that in town – but just indulging in a nice little minimarathon to stretch her legs. She was going to be hungry later on, and she wasn't going to be happy with the dog food Kate had bought at the store.

Kate started walking again, hands in her pockets, a frown on her face. A fat woman with frizzy blond hair who was doing something that looked like slow-motion karate saw the frown and lost her balance.

Kate was having difficulty reconciling the woman who had burned down her home to kill her sons in order to get the insurance money with

Saint Victoria of Hiland Mountain Correctional Facility. She wondered if perhaps Victoria had had a habit – drugs or alcohol maybe. It happened in the best of families, and a substance-abuse problem all too frequently led to other problems, which often included bankruptcy. It could have been one way Victoria, even with her moneyed background, could have wound up desperate enough for funds that she'd committed filicide. Kate added another to the list of questions she was accumulating for Charlotte.

A short rise through a thick growth of birch trees and the trail opened out into a fenced playing field where what looked like a hundred ten-year-olds swarmed around a soccer ball. Two benches were bolted to the pavement at the edge of a cliff. On one of the benches, a young couple in bike pants and helmets sat with their legs up on the crossbars of their bicycles, glowing with sweat and gulping down water from bottles that matched their bikes.

Kate went to the edge of the cliff and shouted, 'Mutt! Come!' and sat down on the other bench. There was a short silence from the young couple, followed by a concerned murmur when Mutt came galloping up the cliff a few moments later, her tongue flopping out of the side of her mouth. She skidded to a halt in front of Kate and set her teeth in the hem of Kate's jeans.

'Knock it off,' Kate said, but Mutt kept tugging until she pulled Kate off the bench. Mutt leaped away and crouched down, her tail wagging furiously.

'Uh, are you okay?' the man asked.

'I'm fine,' Kate said, shaking with laughter. She got to her feet. 'Okay,' she told Mutt, 'you wanna play, let's play.'

Mutt gave a joyous bark and headed for the cliff. She was halfway down the narrow, twisty little trail before Kate hit the edge. Mutt sprinted the rest of the way and waited for Kate at the bottom. Fortunately, the tide was out, exposing the narrow strip of sand between the cliff and the vast expanse of glacial silt that made up the mud flats of the northern reaches of Cook Inlet. 'Okay,' Kate said menacingly, 'let's see what you got.'

They roughhoused up and down the beach for thirty minutes, until Mutt's coat and Kate's hair were filled with sand. Other dogs and owners appeared and then disappeared as quickly. The couple on the bench came to the fence to watch the crazy woman running with her wolf, and soon they were joined by others. The light started to go, and Kate woke up to the fact that the sun was beginning to set. She suspected she'd have bruises the next day, but she felt good anyway, loose and ready for action. 'Not that there's going to be any action,' she told Mutt.

She labored back up the cliff to the trail, where the crowd had dispersed, and they headed for home.

Victoria Pilz Bannister Muravieff had looked straight as an arrow when Kate had met her that day, but that didn't mean anything. Some of the pleasantest people Kate had met had been in prison, where confinement had separated them from their drug of choice and they were sober and straight for the first time in their lives. Prison

100

was detox at its simplest.

Myra Hartsock, case in point.

Back at the town house, she showered and put on one of Jack's blue shirts, the tail of which hit her knees, and a pair of his thick wool socks. She'd just come back downstairs for a snack and to find a movie to watch when the doorbell rang. She looked at the clock on the bookcase, a solid dark green jade cutout of Alaska, the numbers pegged out in gold nuggets and a small plaque beneath announcing 'John "Jack" Morgan, Investigator of the Year,' presented by the Anchorage Police Department. She remembered that year, and the case that had precipitated the award.

The doorbell rang again. Mutt raised her head and gave Kate a questioning look. It was almost 10:00 P.M. 'All right,' Kate told her, 'I'll answer it, but I'm not in the mood for wrestling with Brendan.'

She looked through the sidelight and a smile started at the corners of her mouth. She opened the door and pulled it wide. 'Well, hey. Jim.'

Jim glared down at her. 'Where is he?'

'Where's who?' Kate said, running her eyes over him and taking her time about it. It really was worth the effort; even on days when she hadn't been able to stand the sight of him, Jim Chopin was, well, just this short of magnificent, especially suited up in his state trooper's uniform. 'Come on in,' she said.

He hesitated. Her smile broadened. She pulled the door wider and raised one eyebrow ever so slightly.

It was obvious she had little on beneath the oversized man's shirt. Jim might actually have blushed, but he shouldered by her before she could be certain and closed the door firmly behind him before Kate could show off that length of bare leg to anyone else. Mutt hurtled out of the living room, reared up to place both paws on Jim's shoulders, and gave him the tongue bath of his life.

He couldn't help but laugh. 'All right, Mutt. All right, damn it, knock it off. Jeeze.' He wiped his face in the crook of his arm and looked down at her gazing up at him adoringly, tongue lolling out of one side of her mouth, tail wagging hard enough to achieve liftoff. 'You'd think we hadn't howdied in a month.'

'Absence makes the heart grow fonder,' Kate said, and watched him try to pretend that he'd forgotten she was standing there. 'What can I do for you, Jim?' She let her eyes linger on his mouth. It was wide and firm and she already knew he could kiss.

With a fascination he couldn't help, he let his eyes roam, too. Then he remembered why he was there and said in a gruff voice, 'Where's Kurt Pletnikoff?'

She blinked. 'Kurt?'

'You heard me. I know he came to town. George said he followed you in today.'

'What?'

'Where is he?'

Her eyes narrowed. 'What do you want with him anyway? I told you I'd stop him poaching bears for bladders, and I did.'

'Oh, really? That must be why Dan called me this morning and said he'd found another carcass.'

'What?' she said again, smile vanishing. 'Where?'

He pulled off his cap and smacked it against his thigh. 'Just below the Step, if you can believe that. Jesus, the nerve of this guy, shooting a bear that close to the ranger station. If Dan had caught him at it, I'd be working a homicide investigation right now. Anyway, that's it. Kurt's going down. Where is he?'

'He didn't shoot it,' she said. 'Not that bear anyway.'

'How do you know?'

She thought back to the man she had confronted in the cabin the day before. 'I just know.'

Jim rolled his eyes. 'Well, that's it, then. I'm totally convinced. I'll head on back to the Park and find out who really did it.'

'Kurt's not why you're here,' she said softly.

'What? What are you talking about?'

'You're the one who followed me to town, not Kurt.'

They were still standing in the entryway. He was a step, two at the most, from the front porch, ten feet from the door of his borrowed truck, thirty feet from the street and escape. He turned his head a fraction of an inch at a time and found her looking at him. He'd never been able to determine the color of her eyes. Sometimes they were hazel, sometimes brown, sometimes even green. Now, they just looked dark, a little slumberous, and far too knowing.

He was suddenly and acutely aware of how alone they were in this house, how far they were from the Park and all the prying eyes and listening ears that helped him keep his balance on the tightrope of his libido. At the moment, his safety net of Auntie Vi and Auntie Joy and Auntie Balasha and Old Sam and Bernie and Bobby and Dinah was two hundred miles away.

A small plane buzzed far overhead. Outside, light was fading from the sky, and stars not seen for four months were winking into existence to preen themselves in the still mirror of the lagoon. Inside, the silence was still and heavy with expectation.

'Kate,' he said, or tried to say. His tongue felt thick.

A slow smile curled lips that looked fuller and redder than they had a moment before. 'Jim,' she said, softly mocking. She stepped forward, and in spite of the red lights and the sirens going off in his head, he couldn't stop himself. He leaned down into her kiss.

Skin on skin, that's all it was, the light touch of her breath on his cheek, the faint smell of soap and shampoo and sweat and wood smoke that was uniquely Kate Shugak. He couldn't help that, either. He reveled in it, in fact, but then he caught himself and pulled back. 'I don't want to do this,' he said, his voice sounding weak in his own ears.

'Don't you?' she said, eyelids drooping, voice husky. 'Okay.'

He didn't move.

Still with that damn knowing smile on her face, she let her eyes slip down over him again. He could feel her gaze like a touch. He couldn't breathe inside his shirt. It was too tight, his pants were too tight, and his tie was knotted too tightly around his neck. His hand came up to loosen it.

'Don't,' she said.

'Why not?' was all he could think of to say.

'So I can do this.' She knotted a hand in the tie and used it to lead him up the stairs.

He looked down and saw his feet moving of their own volition. Their footsteps were muffled by the plush blue carpet on the stairs. It seemed forever before they got to the bedroom, which had what looked like an acre of bed in it, and at the same time he saw the journey in flashbacks, still shots, the heel of her thick white socks a little worn, the blue flannel caressing her ass. Her hair was damp and finger-combed, the ends drying in slight curls against her neck.

He halted in the center of the room and stood, dumbstruck, as she stripped leisurely out of her clothes, keeping her eyes on his face as a slight smile played around the corners of her mouth. She reached for his belt, and he might have made some kind of protest, one last plea for leniency, but by then she had swung him around and pushed him so that he landed on his back on the bed, and she was over him, and on him, and in him, and he gave himself up to the woman and to the night.

He woke up alone, splayed out like a starfish and about the same temperature. He was back on the bed, thank God, although the mattress had slid partway off the box springs. The pillows were gone. He turned his head and saw them piled in front of a chair, and remembered how they'd gotten there. The blanket was jammed between the edge of the mattress and the bed frame, the fitted sheet had popped its corners and clumped up into a ball, and all he had covering him was the top sheet, which appeared to be tangled around his left leg. He didn't have the energy to reach for it, so he lay there, goose-pimpled and numb, mostly because he wasn't sure he could move and he was afraid to find out.

He knew he must have slept at some point during the night, but for the life of him he couldn't remember when he'd had the time. Kate had been like a force of nature, overwhelming, relentless, inexorable. 'Here,' she'd said, and dutifully he'd gone there. 'Harder,' she'd said, and obediently he had stroked or sucked or thrust harder. 'Again,' she had said, and the good soldier had done as he was told. There had been no escape, even if he'd been inclined toward it, which parts of him most definitely weren't. He looked down to see if anything remained between his legs. He was immensely relieved to find that there was, although he wasn't certain there was any fluid left in his body.

He'd done it. He'd spent the night with Kate Shugak, the one thing he had been avoiding all summer long. He stared at the ceiling and watched the storm clouds gather.

Kate Shugak was a serial monogamist. That worked for some people, and she was one of them, but that group didn't include him. It was the one thing he knew absolutely. A relationship to him meant sex and a lot of it, along with a lesser amount of lazy affection, which he was more than willing to provide so long as it didn't take a lot of emotional work on his part. He didn't want anything to do with love. *Love,* Jesus, there was a word to frighten the living hell out of you. Love led to things like marriage and children and growing old together, not to mention spousal abuse and infanticide and murder. He'd responded to his share of domestic disturbances, he knew all he needed to know about love and marriage. He'd never told a woman he loved her, and he never would, and he sure as hell wasn't starting with the woman who had shared this bed with him, no way, no how. The very thought of it sent a chill right down his spine. Even if he couldn't feel his spine at the moment.

It wasn't like he couldn't have walked out at any moment last night. There were a couple of times at least that he'd been pretty sure she was asleep. Plus, he was fourteen inches taller than she was and outweighed her by at least eighty pounds. She couldn't have made him stay even if she'd been awake. He had stayed because he wanted to, and he had made love to her because he wanted it, but it was what it was, one night, and that's all it was. Any attempt on her part to make more of it would be rebuffed, kindly, yes – he didn't want to hurt anyone's feelings – but firmly. He was still his own man, he still had ownership of his own soul, and his heart was not now, nor ever had been, in danger.

The rich aroma of fresh coffee drifted into the room. It was more than mortal man could resist. Groaning, he pulled himself to the edge of the bed and let his legs slip to the floor. Some help from the bedpost and he was vertical again. Something squished beneath his bare foot. It was a used condom.

'Oh crap.' He peeled it off and limped into the bathroom. He checked his crotch again in the mirror just to be sure – one cock, two balls, yep, all present and accounted for. He even felt himself up to make sure they weren't a mirage. He turned the shower on as hot as he could stand it and got in.

He arrived in the kitchen damp but resolute.

It was empty.

'Kate?' he said. There was no answer. 'Kate?' he said again, raising his voice.

No answer, and no Mutt, either.

He opened the door to the garage. The Subaru was gone.

There was coffee in the automatic coffeemaker, a clean mug on the counter beside it. There was also a note on the table.

He eyed it with foreboding. It was probably some mash note, saying how wonderful they'd been together and telling him that she'd gone out to buy the ingredients for an elaborate breakfast, which he would be expected to eat massively and praise effusively, and over which he would be required to hold her hand and make cow eyes.

With reluctance, he reached for the note. It read:

Half-and-half in the fridge.
I had a good time.
Thanks, Kate

CHAPTER 7

After a hearty breakfast of bacon and eggs, Kate found the pay phone at the Hogg Brothers and called Charlotte. Charlotte didn't want to talk on the phone – who knew why – so Kate got directions and hopped in the car. Mutt looked at her, tail wagging expectantly, and Kate unfolded the napkin holding the rest of her bacon. 'Don't tell me I never sacrifice for you,' she told her.

Charlotte lived in a big house, of course, on Hillside, naturally, as high up as you could go and not be in Chugach State Park, it went without saying. Kate had been on Hillside before, and that she had not been carted back down in an ambulance wasn't the fault of the person she had come to see. Her attitude increased with the altitude, and by the time she was knocking at Charlotte's door, she had formulated an entire scenario about Charlotte Bannister Muravieff and her life and times.

Charlotte destroyed the first stereotype by answering her own door, and the second by answering it dressed in ragged gray sweats, although she was as meticulously made up as she had been when she had come to see Kate in the Park. 'Please come in,' she said, standing back and motioning to Kate.

'Where did you stay?' Kate said. 'I never thought to ask.'

'Where did I stay where?' Charlotte asked.

'In the Park. When you came to see me.'

Charlotte's brow cleared. 'Oh, I didn't stay. I drove on home.'

It was sixty miles of pitted gravel just to Ahtna, and another three hundred highway miles to Anchorage, and Charlotte had left Kate's homestead at sunset. 'Did you drive there that day from Anchorage?'

'Of course.'

Kate never understood why anyone would choose to drive instead of fly, and Charlotte had to have enough money to charter her own plane. The rich really were different.

She followed Charlotte into about the biggest living room she'd ever seen, filled with light from the bank of southwest-facing windows that filled one wall. The floors were wood, the walls invisible beneath a layer of paintings, not prints, all by local artists of the very first rank, and the furniture a rich teal leather that looked as comfortable as it did classy. There were a few sheepskin rugs tossed here and there, an entertainment center with a shelf full of CDs and DVDs, and a wall full of books. There went the third stereotype – that the rich don't read. It annoyed Kate. She wanted Charlotte to be a part of the Great Washed, the ones with more money than brains, the ones who inherited and thus never had to scramble around for the rent, the ones who said. 'Let them eat cake' without ever having been short of bread. In Kate's mind, Charlotte belonged to that group of people who put twenty-four-karat-gold faucets in their bathrooms, who embraced prenuptial agreements and liposuction as sacrosanct and who regarded taxes as something someone else paid.

However, she, Kate Shugak, had an unimpeachable work ethic, and she, Kate Shugak, would fulfill her contract, thereby separating an exemplar of the Great Washed from some of that lovely, filthy lucre by that most legitimate of means, work for hire, a concept of which the Great Washed had no working – pardon the expression – knowledge.

Suffused with a righteous sense of superiority, she sat down on the indicated chair and said without preamble, 'Your mother fired me.'

Charlotte looked a little startled, but she rallied. 'Would you like some coffee?'

'Thank you,' Kate said, inclining her head a regal inch or thereabouts, 'no. I went to see your mother yesterday, and she was not enthusiastic about you reopening her case. Let me repeat: She fired me.'

'She can't fire you,' Charlotte said, 'she didn't hire you.'

'Yeah, well, as I told you from the outset, this whole endeavor is a long shot at best. Victoria not talking to me is not shortening the odds.'

'I told you she wouldn't,' a voice said.

Kate looked around and saw another woman standing at the bottom of a flight of stairs. She was pudgy in form and pugnacious in manner, with a short mop of tight gray curls and a jaw like a bulldog. She wore an elegant three-piece suit, charcoal with a faint pinstripe, the hem of the skirt hitting directly at midknee. The cream-colored blouse was tied beneath her chin in a soft bow. Her eyes were brown, and they narrowed as

111

they stared at Kate.

'Kate Shugak, allow me to introduce to you to Emily Gessner.'

Emily strode forward, the very high heels of her very narrow Italian shoes making a strong staccato statement against the wood floor. Kate saw Charlotte wince.

'Kate,' Emily said, and went to stand in back of Charlotte, placing one hand on her shoulder.

'Emily,' Kate said.

'Emily's my attorney,' Charlotte said.

Emily rolled her eyes. 'And her partner,' she said.

'You're an attorney, too?' Kate said to Charlotte.

Emily huffed out an impatient sigh. 'That's life partner.'

She didn't add 'you moron,' but Kate could tell the temptation was almost too great to resist. 'Congratulations,' Kate said.

Emily, prepared for shock and disgust, blinked a little. Pressing her advantage, Kate said, 'What did you tell Charlotte?'

Emily rallied. 'I told her Victoria wouldn't talk to you.'

'You know her?'

Emily shrugged. 'We've never met, but Charlotte's told me a lot.'

'What kind of law do you practice?' Kate said.

'Criminal.'

'Are you a litigator?'

Emily's smile showed all her teeth. For a moment she looked like Mutt in a bad mood.

'And in your professional opinion, do I have a

112

hope in hell of getting Victoria a get-out-of-jail-free card?'

Emily opened her mouth to reply, but Charlotte beat her to it. 'It doesn't matter what Emily thinks. It's what I want that matters.'

Kate sighed. 'Look, Charlotte–'

'You don't have to talk to my mother,' Charlotte said.

'What about the witnesses who testified at the trial?'

'Most of them testified for the prosecution,' Kate said.

'Then most of them were lying,' Charlotte said.

Kate thought over the list of witnesses she had compiled from the trial transcript. 'You realize who some of these people are?'

'What,' Emily said, 'you afraid of rocking the establishment boat?'

'No,' Kate said, 'I'm making sure Charlotte isn't.'

'I want my mother out of jail,' Charlotte said flatly. 'There is no way she'd try to kill my brothers. She didn't do it, and now she's dying, and I won't let her die in there.'

'I have to say that Victoria didn't look all that ill to me,' Kate said.

With jerky movements, Charlotte rose and walked over to a desk to extract a file. She almost threw it at Kate.

Kate opened it up. It was a medical report confirming Victoria's cancer.

'They'll let me take her out for the operation, but she's going to have to go through chemo and radiation and she's going to require some long-term care, and even then those toadies down at the hospital don't think she has much of a chance. I don't care how much it costs or whose toes you step on, I want her out of that place as soon as possible. Are you out of money yet? I can get my checkbook.' She half-rose.

'I've barely cashed the first check, Charlotte.'

Charlotte settled back onto the couch, sitting at its extreme edge, her back rigidly straight. Emily suddenly looked less pugnacious and more worried. 'Charlotte–' Emily said.

'I want her *out*,' Charlotte said without looking around at her partner.

Emily met Kate's eyes. 'All right, Charlotte, we'll get her out. Won't we, Kate?'

'Based on the trial transcript and the police report, I don't think we're going to be able to prove that she didn't do it,' Kate said, 'So, Charlotte, if your mom didn't do it, who did?'

Charlotte slumped, her face dropping into her hands. 'I don't know,' she said, her voice muffled. 'Don't you think I've asked myself that question over and over again? Who sets out to murder two teenage boys? And why only the boys? Why not me, too?'

'Were you always supposed to go with your mother that day?'

'Yes, it was a fund-raiser for Mr. Stafford, and Mom always helped Uncle Erland when he put one of those on.'

'Too cheap to pay for catering,' Emily said to Kate.

Charlotte reddened but didn't deny it. 'It had been planned for a month.'

'And everyone knew you'd be there.'

'Yes. Mom paid me. It was part of my allowance to do stuff like that.' She paused. 'And I liked doing it. It's what I do now.'

Kate looked at Emily. 'Cater,' Emily said. 'At least now her uncle has to pay her for it.'

'Where is your surviving brother?'

'Oliver? He lives here in town.'

'Is he in the book?'

'He's my partner,' Emily said.

Kate looked at her, brow raised.

Emily rolled her eyes. 'My law partner,' she said.

'He's an attorney?'

'Yes,' Charlotte said.

'A criminal attorney?' Kate said.

'Yes.'

Kate climbed into the Subaru and thought for a moment. It was a little past 10:00 A.M. Emily had promised to make an appointment for Kate to speak to Oliver, but that probably wouldn't pan out today. Emily had wanted Kate's cell phone number, and Kate had to admit that it would have been handy to have had one.

She could go home and make a start on the list of names and phone numbers Brendan had given her.

Instead, she drove to Bean's Café, a warehouse on Third Avenue that had been converted into a soup kitchen, and inquired after Luba Hardt. A slender dark-haired woman with a calm, pretty face knew the name and told her that Luba had been in the previous Monday for lunch. The bad news was Luba looked like she was living on the street. The good news was Luba didn't look like she'd been strung out on anything. 'She mention a location?'

'Who are you?' the woman said.

'I'm from Niniltna, Luba's village,' Kate said. 'Her family heard I was coming to Anchorage and asked me to look around for her.'

'What family?'

'Billy Mike.'

The woman's face cleared. 'Sure, I know Billy. Heap big chief.'

Kate smiled. 'You know him, all right. But about Luba?'

The woman shook her head. 'I'm sorry. If they find a safe place to stay, they don't usually talk about it, for fear someone is going to hear and move in on them.'

On the way out, Kate examined the faces of the people standing around, smoking and talking, all waiting for the doors to open for lunch. More than half of them were Alaska Native, mostly Aleut and Athabascan and Yupiq, from the looks of them, with maybe a few Inupiaq thrown in. Kate had an urge to cram them all into the back of the car and truck them out to Merrill and put them on planes back to their villages.

One familiar face popped out at her and she halted. 'Kurt?' she said, disbelieving.

After some argument, she bundled him into the car and took him to the Bone. A redheaded waitress in a crisp white apron with a name tag that read HEIDI pinned to it bustled up and gave

116

them their pick of booths.

'My treat,' Kate said, and Kurt ordered as much deep-fried chicken as you could fit in one basket. She drank coffee while he ate. He sat back when he was done and looked around like it hadn't quite registered where he was until then. Heidi brought him coffee and smiled blindingly down at him, and he watched her walk away with appreciation, although Kate couldn't be sure whether it was Heidi or the fried chicken that inspired it.

Kate looked out the window. The Subaru was parked right in front. Mutt was nowhere to be seen. Probably draped over the backseat, snoozing. Kate owed her a good run.

Mutt had greeted Kurt with enthusiasm, which gave Kate pause. Mutt's built-in bullshit detector was second only to her own. Kate might have to readjust her ideas about Kurt. 'So,' she said. 'Kurt.'

He braced himself, both hands curled around his cup of coffee. 'Kate.'

'What are you doing in town?'

He shrugged. 'What you told me to do.' She looked blank, and he said, 'Look for a legitimate job in Anchorage if I couldn't find one in Niniltna.'

'That was only two days ago,' she said. 'I didn't mean you had to do something immediately.'

He shrugged again. 'You confiscated my bank account.' He didn't sound accusatory, merely factual. 'Fishing's over, and I never was much of a trapper, and anyway, Dan O'Brien's got the Park pretty much locked up for trapping, at least for this year. Didn't have a dime to get me through a

117

winter in the Bush. Figured I'd give Anchorage a try.' His smile was wan. 'Bigger selection of women in town anyway.'

'And first thing you wind up at Bean's?'

He nodded. 'For lunch. Sometimes people come down there looking for day labor. I figured it was worth a shot. Plus, I really don't have any money.'

'Have you signed up at Job Service?'

He nodded. 'I went straight there from Merrill.'

'And?'

'They're not hopeful. The seasonal work's just about over for the year, and I don't know Microsoft Word, whatever the hell that is.' He drank coffee. 'I'll check with contractors, see if anyone's got anything going. I hammer a pretty straight nail.'

She felt guilty, although she shouldn't have, and she knew it. He'd been poaching bears, and endangering a species while he was at it. He'd been violating the wanton-waste law by taking only the bladders, leaving the meat and the pelt for carrion, a Class A misdemeanor. By statute, he could have been fined $2,500 and jailed for a week, no suspension or reduction in sentence allowed. Not to mention the thirteen hundred dollars he'd be ordered to pay as restitution to the state for the unlawful taking of a grizzly bear. Some people were just too dumb to live.

The question was, Was Kurt one of them? She regarded him over the rim of her coffee cup, thinking about Mutt's greeting. 'Have you got a place to stay?'

'Yeah. Buddy of mine's got a house in Spenard. He's letting me sleep on his floor until I get on my feet.'

Spoke well for a man that he had friends, especially solvent friends. She made up her mind and put down the cup. 'I've got a job for you,' she said.

'What?'

'I'm on another job myself, but while I'm here, Billy Mike wants me to look for Luba Hardt. That's what I was doing down at Bean's.'

He reddened. She pretended not to notice. 'Take a day or two, find her for me. I'll pay you, what, eight bucks an hour, plus those expenses incurred on the job for which you provide a receipt.'

'Why eight bucks?'

Her turn to shrug. 'Rounded up from minimum wage. You want the job?'

'Ten bucks an hour.'

She thought of the check she'd deposited in her account the day before. 'Nine,' she said. She was willing to go to ten, but she wasn't going to say so. Kurt had taken the easy way out from high school on. Kate wasn't going to help perpetuate his stereotype if she could help it. Let him work for his pay, starting with bargaining for an hourly wage. And she could always give him a bonus if he did good.

He looked irresolute. 'How do I find her?'

'Beats the hell out of me. She was a drinking buddy of yours in Niniltna, so chances are you'll know better than I do where to find her in Anchorage.' He reddened again, and Kate relented enough to say, 'Bean's told me she was there for lunch on Monday.'

'So I should hang out there and wait for her to show up again?'

'I was thinking you could be a little more proactive than that, Kurt,' Kate said dryly. 'Ask around. I know she has friends in town, and I know you do, too.'

'Nine dollars an hour,' he said.

She scribbled the phone number of the town house on a napkin. 'Call me when you find her. Remember to keep track of your hours as well as your receipts.' She pulled out a wad of cash, counted out five hundred dollars, shoved it and the check in his direction, and stood up. 'You can start with this one.'

She'd called Axenia before she left the house that morning and left a message on her cousin's answering machine. She checked Jack's answering machine from a pay phone and found no response.

Fine, she'd earned some personal time. She drove out to Costco and spent an hour loading up two carts with dry and canned goods, and made arrangements to have them palleted and sent to a warehouse in Ahtna that shipped into the Park. There was a woman at a kiosk selling cell phones, and Kate lingered in front of it, reading the literature and asking questions long enough for the woman to become a little impatient. In the end, the two rebates tipped the balance (she would actually make fifty dollars on the purchase) and Kate walked back to the car with a brand-new phone, which probably wouldn't work from the Park. 'Money corrupts,' she told Mutt severely, 'and too much money corrupts absolutely.'

Mutt raised one bored eyebrow. Mutt wasn't into shopping.

She drove to Twice Told Tales and spent another, much more halcyon hour browsing through the store, the resulting pile large enough to require three boxes. Kate, reaching for a book on a high shelf, couldn't hold back a small moan. 'Are you all right?' Rachel said.

'I'm fine. Sore is all. Must have overdone the exercise yesterday,' Kate said blandly, and if Rachel saw the little smile on her face, she was tactful enough not to say so.

The total due made Kate wince and Rachel smile. Kate paid extra to have most of the books mailed book rate to her post office box in Niniltna, keeping out half a dozen to read while she was in town, including two biographies, one of Shakespeare and one of Douglas Bader, the legless flying ace of World War II. Kate's reading habits were nothing if not eclectic.

Rachel tipped her off to a good antique store and Kate returned home just after four o'clock, the gloating owner of five Wagner cast-iron skillets, each one a different size, and one glass lid that didn't fit any of them. The cast-iron pots and pans she had inherited from her parents had been lost in the fire, and she was determined to replace them all. Apart from the sentiment, she didn't really know how to cook in anything else.

The car Jim had parked in the drive yesterday evening was gone. Good.

She smiled to herself and went upstairs to change the sheets. When she was done, she stood for a moment looking down at the bed.

Everything she'd demanded of him, he had given. She remembered some of what he'd given and felt a wave of heat begin deep and low and spread up and out. She looked down and saw that her nipples had beaded against the fabric of her T-shirt, and she laughed out loud. The man had talent. More than that, he had consideration, not to mention courage. Most men would have been afraid to give that much. Too many men were afraid of strong women. Too many men were afraid of her.

Jim didn't get it yet, but he was a smart man and he would eventually. In the meantime, she didn't mind torturing him a little. She wondered how long it would take him to find an excuse to come back. Probably he had enough strength of will to stay away for a day or two, and there was always the job, which could call him away at any moment. As long as people kept misbehaving on the front page of the *Anchorage Daily News,* they were both in business.

Which reminded her of her own job. She looked at her watch. It was 4:30 P.M. Her stomach growled. Intensive shopping burned up bacon and eggs fast, and she'd missed lunch. Still, her body felt tender in various places, and she delayed dinner to run a hot bath. Showers were all very well, but a hot bath was good for what ailed you.

She crawled in and closed her eyes, dozing until the water cooled. One of the great things about coming to Anchorage was having a hot bath at Jack's, all over wet, submerged up to her nostrils like a hippopotamus, her hair spreading out around her head in a floating fan.

But she had an honest-to-god bathroom in the Park now, two of them, in fact, and one even had its own tub. The realization made her a little wistful. Who was it who had said that joy was sharper when it was conditional? Oh, right. That renowned American philosopher Travis McGee, although in a much different context. Regardless, he was right. Life was made precious by the prospect of death. Baths in Anchorage had been made precious by the lack of baths in the Park. No more.

She ran more hot water into the tub and inched back down into it with a voluptuous groan. She remembered feeling like this when she and Jack had been apart for a long time, exhausted and aching in every muscle and very pleased with herself.

She thought about that. She had slept with Jim Chopin in the same bed in which she had spent many nights with Jack Morgan. She felt no shame, no sense of betrayal; in fact, if she listened closely, she thought she might hear Jack applauding, although the voyeuristic implications of that weren't very attractive.

'I miss you, you son of a bitch,' she said out loud. 'But I'm moving on.' A lone tear slid down her cheek, and she let herself slip beneath the water, allowing the curative power of heat to melt away, at least for a while, her aches and pains and guilt at being so vibrantly alive beneath sun, moon, and stars when Jack was so cold and so dead in the dark, dank ground.

She toweled off her melancholy and slipped into a pair of clean underwear and another of Jack's blue plaid flannel shirts, of which he appeared to have had approximately two dozen, rolling the sleeves up to her elbow. Thick gray socks completed her ensemble, and she surveyed the result in the mirror, not without satisfaction. Who knew this outfit could be so seductive? Besides, high sixties or not, Anchorage was heading into fall, termination dust would be on the mountains with the next hard rain, and the nights were beginning to tend toward chilly.

She went back downstairs, opened the two-inch-thick New York strip she'd bought at City Market, dredged it in olive oil, and rolled it in a combination of herbs and garlic powder. She turned the oven on, set it for 350 degrees, put the steak in, and set the timer for an hour. A bunch of spinach in a pot with a few tablespoons of water at the bottom of it for when the steak came out of the oven and dinner would be served.

She curled up on the living room sofa with the telephone and the witness list Brendan had given her. Reminding herself to find a way of thanking him that didn't include actual coitus, she dialed the first name on the list.

She hung up the phone when the timer went off an hour later. The steak was perfect, done to a pale pink on the inside, the oil having crisped the herbs to a nice crust. The spinach went limp five minutes after she turned on the burner and she tossed it with some red wine vinegar. She sat down at the table with a glass of apple juice and ate slowly, relishing every mouthful, as she reviewed the phone calls.

There were twenty names on Brendan's list. Kate suspected the round number was due to

Brendan's decision to stop, rather than to the actual number of witnesses. Eight of the names were marked 'Deceased' and a date of death was noted beside each, and many of the voices Kate spoke to were definitely older.

'It was all so long ago,' one woman had said fretfully. 'I can barely remember what I was doing last month, let alone thirty years ago.'

'I'm headed out of town indefinitely,' one man had told her before hanging up.

'Kate Shugak?' a determinedly sultry voice had said. 'Ekaterina's grand-daughter? Your grand-mother and I were very good friends; we sat on several boards together. How lovely to speak to you, dear. Perhaps you'd like to come over for dinner one evening while you're in town. My hus-band would love to meet you. He's done some work for the Raven Corporation. He's an attorney, you know.'

One woman hung up on her. Kate checked the name for future reference. Another said strongly, 'I still can't believe Victoria could do something so horrible as to kill her own child. I don't even want to think about it, much less describe it all over again to some stranger,' and then she hung up. Kate checked that name, too. Memories strong enough to provide either reaction were worth further investigation.

One man had said sharply, 'Does Erland know about this?'

Erland was Victoria's brother. 'I don't know, sir. I've been retained by his niece, Charlotte.'

There was a moment of electric silence. 'What the hell does she think she's playing at? Erland is

125

not going to be happy about this.'

And then he hung up on her.

Kate remembered Victoria's anger at her appearance and wondered if Charlotte had told anyone in her family what she was doing.

The phone rang as she was finishing dinner. It was Emily. 'Can you come down to our offices at four-thirty P.M.?'

'Tomorrow?' Kate said, eyes going to the clock.

'Yes. Oliver has said he can see you for half an hour.'

'I'll be there,' Kate said.

Emily gave her the address and Kate hung up.

CHAPTER 8

Oliver kept her waiting in his outer office, during which she had ample time to admire the gray walls, the maroon carpet, the teak furniture, and the abstract art. She didn't admire it, actually, but she had time to.

Emily didn't come out to greet her. The receptionist, a woman in her late thirties who had artfully arranged hair and was wearing a trim black suit that must have cost most of three months' salary, was seated at a large desk with a pile of what Kate instantly recognized as court documents. Occasionally, the phone would ring and the receptionist, whose nameplate announced her to be one Miss Belinda Bracey, would answer it in mellifluous tones. Every now and then, she would look at Kate and smile. Kate would smile back. Now and then, the sound of footsteps came from that part of the office suite at whose entrance Miss Bracey was standing guard, and the sound of voices in muted conversation.

It went like that for fifteen minutes, until the outer door opened and Oliver Muravieff stepped into the room wearing a suit that cost even more than Miss Bracey's. He had a slim cane, ebony, with brass fittings, which he leaned upon heavily. The brass was only marginally shinier than his shoes, which matched his suit perfectly. His thick black hair grew straight back from his forehead, ending at a recently trimmed line just above his collar.

Maybe Oliver Muravieff and Associates had a personal shopper on staff.

In spite of the window dressing, Muravieff brought the aura of a street fighter into the room with him. He was maybe five four, five five, and thick from the neck down. He worked out with weights, Kate would bet money on it, to such effect that his biceps pushed his arms out from his sides like an ape's. Making up for the gimpy leg, Bobby Clark would say. Muravieff moved well, belying his bulk with purpose and strength, if not with grace, his step quick and firm, his movements deft and sure.

Instinctively, Kate slid forward on the couch and pulled her feet in so that her weight would be over them if she had to move fast. The movement caught the corner of Muravieff's eye and he turned to look at her. His face was square and blunt-featured. He had a long nose with a flat bridge, heavy black brows, and deep-set brown eyes. His gaze was steady and assessing, and he was smart enough not to dismiss her on first sight, even if she was wearing jeans.

'This is Ms. Shugak, Mr. Muravieff,' Miss Bracey said in a low murmur, and dropped her voice even further to add, 'Your four-thirty.'

'Your four-forty-five now,' Kate said, and smiled.

There was a brief silence. 'Of course,' Muravieff said smoothly. 'I'm Oliver Muravieff, Ms. Shugak.' He walked past the receptionist's desk and opened a door in the wall. 'Will you come with me to my office?'

Kate followed him through the door, down a hallway, and through an office with three women in it typing at computers, one of whom pursued him into his office with a document for his signature.

'Have a seat,' Muravieff said, nodding at the chair sitting on one side of a vast expanse of teak. He signed the document and shed his jacket, handing both to the woman. 'May I offer you some coffee, Ms. Shugak?'

'Certainly,' Kate said. 'Cream and sugar, please,' she said to the woman.

'Black,' Muravieff said. 'Thanks, Nancy.'

Nancy went out, soft-footed. 'I apologize for being so late,' Muravieff said. 'I was held up in court.'

'That's quite all right,' Kate said, and wondered at the sudden graciousness of her grammar.

'Shugak,' Muravieff said. 'Any relation to Ekaterina?'

'Why, yes,' Kate said.

'I believe my mother may have known her.'

'So she tells me,' Kate said.

An awkward silence fell, broken by Nancy coming back with the coffee, served on a silver tray in porcelain cups and saucers, with a matching sugar bowl and creamer. Kate doctored her coffee, Muravieff didn't, and they both settled back in their chairs. Muravieff barely sipped his before placing it to one side. 'So, Ms. Shugak,' he said, 'how may I help you?'

'Your sister, Charlotte, has hired me to look into your mother's case.'

Muravieff's expression didn't change. 'So Emily has informed me. It was not a wise decision on Charlotte's part.'

'Why is that?'

'Because my mother has no case, Ms. Shugak. She was tried, convicted, and sentenced to life in prison.'

'Your sister believes otherwise,' Kate said. 'She believes your mother was wrongly convicted, and she wants me to find the evidence necessary to prove it.'

His eyes went flat, and for the first time Kate saw the pit bull lurking inside every decent trial attorney. 'Charlotte is mistaken. My mother even admitted doing it.'

'Your mother admitted her guilt?' Kate said.

Oliver nodded. 'Yes.'

'When? There is no mention of it in the court records.'

'Privately, to us, after she was convicted and she knew lying wouldn't keep her out of jail.'

'To "us"? Meaning Charlotte and yourself?'

129

'Yes. They took us in to say good-bye to her after the verdict. She told us then. So you can see for yourself, Ms. Shugak, my sister has sent you on a fool's errand.'

'That's something you will need to take up with your sister,' Kate said, setting her cup and saucer down. 'May I ask you some questions?'

'I don't want to talk about that time.'

'It was thirty years ago.'

'It was yesterday,' Muravieff said.

A brief silence. 'Well then, did your mother say why she did it?' Kate said.

'What does that matter? She killed her own son. She would have killed me. She admitted as much to me, face-to-face, the last time I saw her.'

'You haven't seen her since?' Kate said.

'She tried to kill me,' he said. 'She told me so. Why would I want to see her ever again?'

Kate regarded him in silence. He met her gaze steadily. 'The prosecution held that your mother tried to kill you both for the insurance money.'

'Yes.'

'Was she really so in need of money?'

'I suppose she was.'

'A Bannister? Out of money?'

He said nothing.

'Charlotte told me that you and she went to live with your uncle afterward.'

'Yes.'

'He or your grandparents couldn't have helped your mother financially, whatever trouble she might have been in?'

'Look, Miss Shugak,' he said, 'I don't know what her problem was. All I know is what she said. You worked for the DA for five and a half years. You certainly know the difference.'

'I do,' she said. And wasn't it interesting that he knew of her previous employment. 'Did you know your mother has cancer?'

He stared at her. 'No,' he said finally. 'I didn't know that.'

Nancy tapped at the door. 'Mr. Muravieff, I'm sorry to interrupt, but Mr. Ellefson is on line two.'

'Not a problem,' Kate said. 'Mr. Muravieff and I are done here. Thank you for your time, Mr. Muravieff. May I call if I have any further questions?'

'Certainly,' he said, and handed her a card.

Interesting, she thought as she walked out of the building, that Oliver's chosen profession was that of a defense lawyer, a job designed to get criminals off. An Alexander Ellefson had been the second story on last night's ten o'clock news, something regarding a little disagreement he'd had in the parking lot of a local bar, involving three other men and a .38 Special.

She got home to a blinking red light on the answering machine, her first this time in town. She pushed the button, smiling a little, expecting some heavy breathing and a few rude remarks from Brendan.

'Yes, this is a message for Kate Shugak,' a pleasant female voice said. 'Ms. Shugak, this is Rosemary Watson, secretary to Erland Bannister. Mr. Bannister is having a party tomorrow evening at his home in Turnagain, and he wonders if you

131

might like to attend. Seven o'clock, drinks and hors d'oeuvres – oh, and semiformal dress, please.' Directions were given and the message ended.

Kate stared at the answering machine. It sat on the kitchen counter, squat, black, and unrevealing. She played the message again. Rosemary Watson repeated herself.

'Christ,' Kate said.

She went into the kitchen, filled a glass with ice, and poured a Diet 7UP over it. She took it into the living room and curled up on the window seat to watch the joggers go by.

Erland Bannister. Victoria's brother, the president and CEO of Pilz Mining and Exploration, PME Corporation after the postbankruptcy restructuring. He hadn't been president when Victoria went to jail, but he had been on the way up.

She remembered the response of the man on Brendan's witness list: 'Does Erland know about this?' She had the feeling that if Erland hadn't known about her investigation into Victoria's thirty-year-old case he did now.

She went upstairs and climbed back into Jack's shirt and socks. She went back downstairs and stood looking into the refrigerator for a while, as if it might hold the secrets to the universe, which refrigerators sometimes do. She wandered back out into the living room and ran a finger down the spines of the video library.

On impulse, she called Brendan. 'What are you doing home on a Monday night?' she said when he answered. 'On any night, for that matter?'

'Pining away by the phone, waiting for you to

132

call,' he replied promptly.

'You like tequila, don't you?'

He was amused. 'Sure, why? You want to get me drunk and take advantage of me?'

'There are a few bottles rattling around in the cupboards over here. One of them is a bottle of something called *añejo*. You want it?'

'I'll be right there.'

He was, in fifteen minutes flat, and Kate fetched the bottle from the kitchen, along with a glass. He immediately slammed back a shot. 'All right,' he said, looking impressed. He offered her the glass. 'Your turn.'

She shook her head.

'Right, I forgot, you don't drink. Darn, now I don't have to share this bottle.'

She laughed. 'I've been calling the numbers on your list.'

He leaned back into the easy chair, a big man comfortable with his size, and let his eyes run up the expanse of smooth skin between the bunched top of the thick socks to the tail of the blue plaid shirt. 'What about them?'

She smiled. Flirting was the thing Brendan McCord knew best how to do, next to litigation.

'The response has been' – she hesitated – 'mixed.'

'Getting hung up on by the elite?' Brendan asked.

'How did you guess?'

'Yeah, well, hang on to your hat, because I've got some more bad news for you.'

'Great.'

'The investigating officer is dead.'

Kate searched her memory. 'Sgt. Charles Baltzo?'

'Yeah.'

'Damn,' Kate said with real feeling. 'Do you know of anybody else who was around at the time of the murder? Someone who might know something about the case?' She added, 'Who is actually alive?'

'I can see where alive would be good,' Brendan said gravely.

'Also, is Henry Cowell still practicing in Anchorage?' He raised an interrogatory eyebrow. 'Victoria's defense attorney. I looked in the phone book. He's not there.'

He thought. 'I don't know the name.'

'Could you find out where he is?'

He poured himself another shot. 'What's it worth to you?'

She raised an eyebrow. 'I figured you got your payment in advance.'

He looked at the bottle and opened his mouth, and the doorbell sounded.

Kate's pulse scrambled. 'Excuse me,' she said, and went to the door.

Jim Chopin was on the doorstep, his face like a thundercloud. It seemed that Kate had credited him with more self-control than he actually had.

'Jim,' she said, unable to keep a grin from spreading across her face. 'How nice to see you again. What's—'

He stepped inside, shoved her against the wall, and kissed her hard.

'Who is it, Kate?' Brendan said from the living room.

Jim raised his head. 'Who the hell is that?' He stalked into the living room, hands knotted into fists. Kate pulled herself together and followed.

Jim looked from Brendan, shot glass in hand, taking his leisure in the easy chair, to Kate standing next to him in Jack's shirt and socks and apparently very little else. He looked back at Brendan and said, 'Get out.'

Brendan thought about that for a little longer than Jim thought strictly necessary. He moved, but Kate grabbed his arm. 'Thanks for coming over, Brendan,' she said. 'Let me know what you find out. I'll be here.'

Brendan saw the barely repressed glee in her eye and threw in the towel, at least for tonight. 'All right, don't shoot. I'm gone.'

He lumbered outside. The door had barely shut behind him when Jim turned and tossed Kate up into his arms. He took the stairs two at a time.

'Ooooooh,' she said, 'I feel just like Scarlett O'Hara.'

'Shut up,' he said.

He woke up alone again.

'Son of a *bitch*,' he said.

While Jim was jerking on his pants, full of a fine, righteous wrath, the source of which he did not bother to identify, Kate and Mutt were out for a run on the coastal trail. She didn't run as a habit, but at home simple maintenance around the homestead kept her fit. In town, she took her exercise where she found it. Considerate of Jack to buy a house so close to the coastal trail.

She was feeling much more limber this morning – the benefits of regular sex on the various muscle groups were not to be denied – and she ran smoothly, stretching her legs out in front of her, carrying her arms at midtorso, breathing deeply in and out, with no hint of labor. It was another day of unbroken sunshine, Susitna and Denali and Foraker were on her right, and she felt good. Hell, she felt great, every cell in her body was singing. Mutt, loping next to her, tongue lolling out of the side of her mouth, legs and haunches moving like pistons, looked not unhappy herself. Mutt knew how to live in the moment, to savor it, not to fear or try to second-guess the future. Kate decided that Mutt had a lot to teach her, and picked up the pace.

They trotted down a hill and around a curve, and a park bench appeared. It was occupied.

There were two boys, one lying on the bench, the other beneath it. Both were asleep. Two bikes lay on their sides on the grass nearby.

The boys looked to be about ten and twelve, respectively. Kate slowed to a halt and stood looking down at them. Their eyelashes stood out darkly against their cheeks and their faces were smooth and innocent enough to break her heart.

She could think of a number of scenarios that would result in the boys sleeping on a bench next to the coastal trail, chief among them trouble at home, a fight between parents maybe, resulting in the boys getting out of the house until it was all over.

There was also the possibility they had not left their home voluntarily, that they could have been thrown out. Or had run from punishment, or abuse.

She found herself reluctant to disturb them. At least in sleep, there was respite from whatever troubled them awake.

But she was equally incapable of just walking away. 'Hey,' she said.

Neither boy stirred.

She raised her voice. *'Hey.'*

The boy on the bench moved, groaned, and opened his eyes. It took him a minute to focus. When he did, he sat up abruptly, accidentally kicking his companion, who banged his head against the bottom of the bench when he sat up.

'Ouch!' He rubbed his head.

His brother – the resemblance was obvious around the eyes and the way the hair grew stiffly from the hairline – risked taking his eyes off Kate for a moment. 'You okay, Kevin?'

Kevin rubbed his head. 'Yeah. I'm all right. Who's she, Jordan?'

'Nobody.' Jordan got up and headed for his bike. 'Come on, Kevin. Let's go.'

'Where you going?' Kate said.

'None of your business,' he said shortly.

'You're right,' she said, which at least surprised him enough to halt forward motion. 'But I could give you some breakfast, if you're interested.'

He looked at her, frowning. Kevin rolled out from beneath the bench and brushed ineffectively at the leaves adhering to his clothes. 'I'm hungry, Jordan,' he said plaintively.

'We don't know her, Kevin,' Jordan said. 'She could be some kind of weirdo.'

'Right again,' Kate said, noticing that Jordan wasn't automatically making for home. 'How about this? You follow me to my house. You stay outside, and I'll bring the food out.'

'You'll call the cops is what you'll do.'

She met his eyes squarely. 'Not unless and until you give me permission to,' she said.

With the timing and tact of a seasoned diplomat, Mutt trotted over and shoved her nose under Jordan's hand. Her tail whapped vigorously against Kevin's knee.

Even Jordan smiled.

Jim was still at the town house when Kate and entourage arrived. He stood glaring at her from the front door. She almost lost the boys when they saw his uniform shirt. 'He's a trooper from the Bush, he doesn't know from Anchorage,' she said quickly.

They didn't run, but they looked ready to.

'Who're they?' Jim said as she leapt the steps to the minuscule front porch.

'Friends,' Kate said, 'hungry friends.' She turned. 'Come in or park it on the lawn, your choice.'

In the end, the four of them sat down to breakfast together – eggs scrambled with cheese, onions, garlic, and green chilies, served on tortillas with salsa and sour cream. The boys had cocoa and she and Jim had coffee.

I'm going to have to buy more eggs, she thought as she watched the boys, their heads bent over their plates. Hungry as they were, they ate neatly. Someone had been teaching them manners. That wasn't always a good thing, in her experience.

She looked at Jim. She saw him look at the boys. He opened his mouth, and she caught his eyes and shook her head once from side to side.

He closed his mouth again.

She wondered why he was still here. She wondered if he was ready to cave. Probably not, she thought. Probably just pissed off to wake up alone for a second time. Probably thought waking up alone the morning after was the sole province of women.

She got up to get the coffeepot, and paused next to Jim to refill his mug. She took her time over it, leaning in, ensuring as much body contact as possible.

He wrapped his hand around one of her thighs, and for a split second she didn't know if that hand was going to slide up or shove away. It shoved, and she went with it, moving around the table to refill her own mug and replace the coffeepot. Neither of the boys, faces still in their plates, noticed anything. She slid into her seat, her eyes mocking. Jim looked very tense around the jawline. She smiled at him. His hand tightened around his mug. She hoped he wouldn't throw it at her, as she didn't know what the boys were running from and she didn't want them to run from her house, too.

They cleaned their plates and then cleared the table. 'I guess we better go,' Jordan said.

Kevin looked forlorn, but he nodded obediently.

Jim looked at Kate.

She pushed back from the table and draped a knee over one arm of the chair. 'Where you going to go?' she said to the older boy.

'Home,' he said.

Kevin raised his head to give his brother a quick, alarmed glance.

Kate nodded. 'Think things will have calmed down since you left?'

'They always do,' he said, his eyes bleak.

Drinkers, she thought. They'll have sobered up by now. And it's chronic enough for the boys to know the routine. 'You live off the trail?'

The boys exchanged a glance. 'Sort of.'

Not even close to it, she thought. 'I'd like to give you a ride home.'

'No,' Jordan said immediately.

Jim opened his mouth. Kate closed it with another look. 'Guys, you did good. When things got bad, you left, you found a place to sleep, and you found a nonweirdo to feed you breakfast. You did good, but you were lucky, too. I'd just as soon you don't have to be lucky again.'

'We do okay,' Jordan said.

Kevin said nothing, pale of face, standing very close to his brother.

'I bet you do,' Kate said. 'But you don't have to do it alone.'

Kevin plucked at his brother's sleeve. 'Jordan—'

Jordan looked down at the pleading face of his little brother and all the fight went out of him.

Their home was a trailer in Spenard, a good three miles from the coastal trail. Their mother came to the door after Kate pounded on it for a while. The smell of spilled booze and stale cigarettes was strong enough to rock Kate back a step.

140

The woman, short-waisted and thick through the middle, looked to be at least part Aleut, something Kate had suspected from the first time she had seen the boys.

She blinked at her sons. 'Kevin? Jordan? What are you doing up already?' She saw Kate. 'And who is this woman?'

When Kate got back to the town house, Jim was still there. 'You're still here,' she said, brushing by him in the doorway.

'We've got to talk,' he said, following her into the kitchen.

'Really?' She poured the last of the coffee. 'I wouldn't wish the home those boys are living in on a dog.'

Mutt looked reproachful, or as reproachful as she could pressed up next to Jim, tail wagging with delight.

'Call DFYS.'

Kate pressed her lips together. 'They aren't starving, and nobody's hit them. Yet. I had a conversation with their mother. Might have scared her some. I'll keep tabs.'

Diverted momentarily from his mission, Jim said, 'You can't save everyone, Kate.'

'What was it you wanted to talk to me about?' she said.

'You know damn well what about,' he said. He kept himself well to the other side of the room, out of her reach.

She cleared her face of all traces of a grin before turning. 'I must be a little slow this morning,' she said, leaning against the counter, hands cradling

141

her mug. She smiled at him through the steam rising up off the surface of the coffee. 'Explain it to me.'

He stared at her in fulminating silence for a charged moment, then finally blurted, 'Those damn boys, for one thing! Are you out of your mind, bringing them home like that? You should have called DFYS the instant you walked in the door!'

'No, I shouldn't,' she said equably. 'Is that all?'

It was like throwing gas on an open fire, she noticed and waited hopefully, thinking she might be tossed over his shoulder and hauled back upstairs. To her disappointment, Jim managed to rein in his temper. That couldn't be good for his blood pressure. She drained the mug and put it in the sink. 'Well, I've got work to do, and I'm sure you do, too, back in the Park. I won't keep you.'

He found himself being ushered from the house. One moment he was in the kitchen, full of legitimate fury, and the next he was on the sidewalk, looking up at her framed in the doorway, with no clear idea of how he got there.

'Kate,' he said.

'Yes, Jim?' she said.

He opened his mouth and closed it, several times.

He looked so bewildered that she relented, if only a little. 'Isn't this how you wanted it?' she said.

'What?' he said.

'Isn't this how you wanted it?' she repeated. 'Straight sex with no complications – when it's over we go our separate ways, no harm, no foul?'

'Sounds good to me,' the man next door said, retrieving the newspaper from his front step.

'You mind your own goddamn business,' Jim told him.

The man, grinning, vanished back inside.

When Jim turned back, Kate had closed the door in his face.

CHAPTER 9

Kate was still chuckling at the memory of Jim's baffled expression, when the phone rang.

'Is that lucky bastard gone, or is he standing there ready to come up here and rain all over my sorry-ass parade once he knows it's me?' Brendan McCord said.

'He's gone,' Kate said.

'Good,' Brendan said. 'Henry Cowell no longer practices law in the state of Alaska.'

'Did he retire?'

'I don't know.'

'Did he move?'

'I don't know.'

'Did he die?'

'I don't know.'

'Brendan–'

'Kate, this guy seems to have just vanished off the map.'

'When?' Kate said.

There was a brief silence. 'According to the records, he represented no clients, or at least no

Alaskan clients, after he rested his case for Victoria Pilz Bannister Muravieff.'

'Victoria's case was his last case?'

'You're a little slow on the uptake this morning, Shugak,' Brendan said. 'That's what happens when you've been up all night, I guess.'

'Brendan,' Kate said, unheeding, 'don't you think it's interesting that Victoria's attorney vanishes right after her trial is over?'

She could hear the amusement in his voice. 'Boy, you're desperate, aren't you, Shugak? Like massive amounts of somebodies hightailing it out of Alaska and leaving no forwarding address is a new thing.'

He was right, and she was a little deflated. 'Yeah. Well, if you do stumble across some mention of him, let me know.'

'Wilco,' he said cheerfully.

'And you were going to BOTLF a cop who might have been around at that time, too, don't forget.'

'How about Morris Maxwell, a cop on the force at the time,' he said, 'although I'm still working on what it's worth to me.'

Kate took a deep breath. 'Brendan, at this moment I could lick whipped cream off your butt. Where do I find him?'

'Oooooooh, Shugak, you – pardon the expression – silvertongued devil you,' he said. 'The Pioneer Home between I and L. And Kate, no guarantees on what he is or isn't going to remember. The guy's like a hundred and nine.'

The phone was barely back in its cradle when it rang again.

'It's me, Kate,' Kurt Pletnikoff said. 'I found her.'

Luba Hardt was in the hospital with multiple contusions, a cracked rib and, the medical staff informed them, a raging case of withdrawal. So much for the Bean's Café assessment of Luba's condition. Not only was she not talking, she wasn't focusing very well. She didn't respond to Kate's questions, and after a moment Kate went into the hall. 'Where did you find her?' she said to Kurt.

'In the trees between Third Avenue and the railroad yards,' Kurt said. 'A bunch of street people have built themselves shelters there.'

'Was anyone else there?'

He shook his head.

A big man in the one-tone black of the Anchorage Police Department approached. 'Shugak,' he said.

'O'Leary,' she said.

'Long time no see,' he said, his tone indicating it hadn't been long enough. 'You know the vic?'

Kate nodded. 'She's from Niniltna.'

O'Leary eyed Kurt. 'And this is?'

'Kurt Pletnikoff. He was looking for her, at my request.'

O'Leary nodded, holding Kurt's eyes. 'I see.'

'I didn't do this,' Kurt said.

'Who said you did?' O'Leary said.

'I'll vouch for Kurt,' Kate said. 'He works for me.'

Kurt's expression was wooden, but O'Leary knew something was off. 'Oh yeah?' Sandy eye-

145

brows didn't quite disappear into the receding hairline that O'Leary hid with his uniform cap. Kate had never seen him without it.

'Really,' Kate said.

'I thought you worked alone.'

Kate shrugged. 'You thought wrong.' She threw a little attitude into her tone, too, as if to say, Nothing new. And by the way, back off, mother-fucker.

O'Leary nodded. 'Got a number?' he said to Kurt.

Before Kurt could answer, Kate gave O'Leary hers. 'We'll come down to the cop shop tomorrow for statements.'

O'Leary's turn to shrug. 'I've got everything I need.'

Safely in the parking lot, Kurt said, 'What's with him?'

'We've got history,' Kate said. 'Plus, I don't think O'Leary thinks Natives are really necessary. Especially not Native women.'

'Necessary to what?'

'Life, liberty, and the pursuit of happiness.' She turned to face him. 'You did good, Kurt.'

He looked glum. 'I wish I could have found her before she got hurt.'

'Me, too, but at least she didn't lie out for three days and die of exposure. You found her. That's what I hired you for. How hard was it to find her?'

He shook his head. 'Not that hard. I walked all over downtown, talked to the guys who hang out on the grass in front of the visitors' center, went into all the Fourth Avenue bars, described Luba, asked if they'd seen her. She's been living on the

146

streets since she got to town, I think. Eventually, I found someone who told me a couple of places she might be. I found her the third place I went.'

Kate nodded. 'How much did it cost?'

He pulled out a small wire notebook and thumbed through it. 'About a hundred fifty bucks' worth of cheap beer, and a hamburger.'

Kate nodded again. 'How did you like it? The job, I mean. How did you like doing it?'

He thought about it. 'It was okay,' he said in a surprised tone of voice. 'All I had to do was be halfway civil, buy a few drinks here, a six-pack there, and people were ready to talk.'

'Not everyone has the ability to listen,' Kate said. It took him a minute to realize that she'd paid him a compliment. When he did, he blushed like a teenager. 'How would you like another job?'

He looked at her. 'Same wages?'

She nodded, hiding a smile. 'First thing, though, you buy yourself some new clothes. Get a decent sports jacket, a couple of pairs of slacks, some good shoes.'

He looked appalled. 'Jesus, Kate. Do I have to?'

She sighed. 'Yeah. Look, go to Nordstrom. Go up to the second floor and ask for a salesperson named Alana. Tell her Kate Shugak sent you in for a businessman's makeover. She'll get you out-fitted.' Whether you want to be or not, she thought. She gave him an assessing glance. 'Tell her I said you need a haircut, too. Second thing, I want you to go to a print shop and get a business card made up.'

Still terrified by the prospect of his makeover, Kurt said weakly, 'A business card? What do I put on it?'

Kate thought. 'Your name, with my phone number beneath it. Wait, I'll go with you. I know a print shop, and I know what I want the card to look like.'

'I don't know what the hell I need a card for.'

'The people you're going to be talking to on this job will expect a card. It's part of the costume.'

'The costume for what?'

'I want you to find someone for me,' she said. 'We'll have to rent you a car, too, come to think of it.'

'Who do you want me to find?'

'Someone who disappeared thirty years ago.'

'America's Mounties, that's what they used to call us,' Morris Maxwell told Kate.

They were in the Pioneer Home, a big brick state-run old folks home on I Street. Morris Maxwell was a shrunken giant, pretty much confined to a wheelchair – 'I can walk,' he told her, 'I just choose not to' – shoulders stooped, hair completely gone from a wrinkled liver-spotted scalp, but there was a bright gleam in his eyes and he was quick to grin. He insisted she wheel him from his room into the common room so he could show all the other old geezers that he had a good-looking woman visiting him. Now they were sitting at a table over cups of weak coffee that no amount of sugar or creamer would improve.

'Alaska's Mounties,' he repeated, 'that was us, the territorial police. TPs, they called us. Weren't that many of us. I remember figuring once that if you divided the square miles of Alaska by the

148

number of state cops we had back then, each of us was responsible for eight thousand eight hundred and eighty-five square miles.' He cocked an eyebrow, and she looked suitably impressed.

'I was a pilot, so they assigned me to the Bush. I got forty-three hours in the air my first week.'

'What was it like?' Kate said.

'What was it like? *What was it like?* I'll tell you what it was like. It was eating corned beef out of a can for three days straight when you were weathered in in Tooksook Bay, and the weather running you out of corned beef and you having to eat fermented seal instead. It was taking a rolled-up magazine with you when you went outside to take a crap to beat the dogs off your ass in McGrath. It was having to be nice to every living soul no matter how much of an asshole they were or what god-awful thing they'd done in Nome, just so you wouldn't get into a fight and mess up your uniform, which cost two hundred dollars, and the state sure as hell wasn't paying for a replacement.'

Kate, entranced by and a little envious of this portrait of frontier law enforcement, said, 'Tell me more.'

He tossed back his head and let out a cackle of laughter, and for a moment she saw him for the vibrant man he had been, instead of the shriveled-up hulk he was now. Just so would she be in fifty years.

'Can you get around without that chair?' Kate said.

His gaze sharpened. 'Why?'

She jerked her head. 'If you can, let's blow this

pop stand for a while.'

She took him to Club Paris for one of their justifiably famous steaks, and there was nothing wrong with Max's appetite, or his teeth. Under the influence of his second martini, he began to wax even more eloquent about times gone by. He had a gift for storytelling, and after a while the bartender stopped even pretending to polish the section of the bar closest to their table. The waitress just pulled up a chair. She wasn't the only one.

Max had severe opinions on the topic of American presidents for whom he had worked security detail. 'Eisenhower was a gentleman. Johnson was an asshole.' This led to reminiscing on the subject of statehood, which came in while he was a TP. 'Some of the villages we went into, we were the only representatives of any government, state or federal, those folks had ever seen. I'd fly into a village, wearing my full uniform, and give a talk at the school on the new state and pass around my cuffs and my empty revolver. Most of them had never seen a revolver before, although they all had rifles and shotguns. Then I'd do it all over again for the village council that night. I remember one time – where was that? Chuathbaluk? Tuluksak? No, farther north, maybe Point Lay or St. Mary's – I was the first they knew Alaska had become a state.'

He'd had some experience in giving medical care, too. 'I stopped counting the babies I delivered after I got to ten. Of course that kind of thing could rebound on you – if you knew how to deliver babies, they were apt to think you could do other things, like splint a broken bone or dig

150

out a bullet.' He finished off his martini and the bartender had a third in front of him in sixty seconds flat.

'We didn't have a state penitentiary back then, and the state rented cells from the feds. Cost about ninety-eight dollars a day to put up state felons in federal prisons, which was probably why everybody's sentences were so short. We never sent Natives up for longer than five years, they just didn't survive being jailed. Some of them didn't survive the five years.' He looked at Kate. 'You're Native.'

Kate nodded. 'Aleut. Mostly.'

'Never got that far south.'

'I'm from Niniltna,' she said.

'Niniltna, Niniltna... Oh yeah, sin city for the Kanuyaq Copper Mine.'

'That's the one.'

'How'd Aleuts wind up that far away from the water?'

'World War Two.'

'Huh. I remember I had to fly up to Niniltna one time to investigate an arson case. It was breakup. Lot of arson during breakup – everybody needs a start-up check in the spring. Still like that?'

'Pretty much.'

'Who's the cop up there nowadays?'

'Jim Chopin.'

Max shook his head. 'Never heard of him,' he said, 'a Johnny-come-lately, eh?'

'I'll say,' Kate said, but he was already off on his adventures in Barrow, where the Naval Arctic Research Laboratory just east of the village made

151

the cardinal error of letting lumber sit around in a pile in the open. 'Just a few boards at a time,' Max said, 'that's all, but pretty soon the pile was gone, and the next time I flew into Anaktuvuk Pass, about a hundred miles southeast, I noticed a brand-new addition on somebody's house. The navy guys decided to chalk it up to experience. They locked up their lumber after that, though. The invention of the snow machine really opened things up for people living in the Bush, I'll say that for it.'

After about two hours of this, during which time Max never repeated a tall tale, Kate had to forcibly remind herself why she was there. The staff had to begin setting up for the dinner crowd and Max and Kate were left alone.

He cocked an eyebrow in her direction. 'I'm guessing you didn't haul this old carcass out on the town for the pleasure of listening to me yammer on, as delightful as I know that must be.'

She grinned. 'You guessed right.'

'So?'

'So. You remember the Victoria Bannister Muravieff case?'

He looked at the ceiling through narrowed eyes. Kate could almost hear the card index flipping forward to the M's. She wondered why they put these old cops out to pasture, the sharp ones like Max, walking, talking repositories of decades of Alaskan criminal history. They knew which oil company had bribed the sitting governor with subsidized travel in return for favorable exploration legislation, they knew which banker had bankrupted which local Native corporation with

152

bad business practices, they knew where all the bodies of the strippers and hookers shot by the serial killer were buried. It was all there, available for the price of asking the question. And maybe a couple martinis. It seemed like such a waste.

'Muravieff,' Max said, 'Muravieff. Thirty-one years ago. A house burned down in Bodenburg Butte in the valley. A seventeen-year-old boy was home, died from smoke inhalation. Turned out the mom had taken out a large life-insurance policy on him a few months before. She was convicted. Got life.'

Kate looked at him with real respect. 'I'm impressed.'

He preened a little.

'Did you work the case?'

He shook his head. 'Nope. Heard the shop talk about it, of course, and we were a lot smaller force in those days, so what one trooper knew, pretty much all of us did.'

It was the closest thing she was going to get to an impartial eyewitness account. To say that Kate was excited was an understatement. 'Tell me everything you remember,' she said.

'Tell me why you want to know,' he countered.

'Victoria's still in jail, out at Hiland Mountain. Her daughter hired me to get her out before she dies, which is looking sooner rather than later because Victoria's got cancer.'

'No parole after thirty years?' he said, frowning. 'That doesn't sound right.'

'I've read the trial transcript. The judge was horrified that she'd killed her own son for money. He didn't want Victoria to get out of jail, ever.'

'Which judge?'

Kate closed her eyes, the better to visualize the transcript. 'Kelly? Kennedy? Kiddle, that was it, Judge James Kiddle.'

'Oh yeah,' he said, a nasty smile spreading across his face, 'old Jim Kiddle. We loved cases coming before old Jim. He never met a perp he liked.'

'Is he still around?'

Max shook his head. 'He retired about seventeen years ago, when the grandchildren got old enough to enjoy. Three years ago, he took his grandson white-water rafting on the Russian River and fell out of the raft.' Max shook his head. 'Damn shame, that. Man was a monument to law enforcement.' He reflected. 'Of course, he was eighty-four at the time. At least he went out doing something fun.'

It was the only reference he'd made all day to his own situation. 'Do you have family?' Kate said, her voice carefully devoid of sympathy.

'Nah. Well, an ex-wife, who stuck it out up here for all of five minutes before she hightailed it back Outside.' His face softened. 'It was my fault. She was new into the country, wasn't used to the cold or the dark, and I was gone a lot. She thought she was getting a husband, and what she got instead was missing in action. I don't blame her for leaving.' He dismissed the subject with a wave of the hand. 'About your case.' He paused, eyes narrowing. 'It was a different place back then, a different time. You need to understand that going in.

'Weren't but fifty thousand people in the whole state. Everybody knew everybody else – we were all on a first-name basis, made no difference if

154

you were digging ditches or running an airline. Best thing about a frontier society is that it's wide open to everybody. Course, that never lasts long. Civilization is an insidious thing. You ever hear of Lazarus Long?'

'Sure,' Kate said. 'Robert Heinlein character, lived forever.'

Max's smile was approving. 'Lazarus Long said that when a place gets crowded enough to require IDs, it's time to go elsewhere.'

'You think it's time to go elsewhere from Alaska?' Kate said.

He cackled. 'I'm about to any minute now.'

Kate laughed with him, even if it did feel a little macabre. 'Still,' he said, 'even on the Alaska frontier there were the high-muckety-mucks, like there always are, people who get things done or get lucky, usually both. This woman – what was her name again?'

'Victoria.'

'That's right, Queen Victoria. We called her that,' he said in answer to her look, 'Queen Victoria. You couldn't see the crown when they brought her into the station, but she held her head like it was there, and she sure as hell looked down her nose like it was there. In court, too, from what I hear. Yeah, Queen Victoria was a daughter of two families who made it big in the north, part of the Alaska aristocracy, at least before ANCSA came along and the Natives started elbowing for room at the top. The Pilzes made their money in coal, the Bannisters in supplies, and then they merged by marriage, and it was like the whole state was served up on a plate to their offspring. There isn't a pie baked in Alaska they don't get a slice of.' He cocked that eyebrow. 'You talk to any of them yet?'

'Her daughter, Charlotte, who hired me. Her surviving son, Oliver. And Victoria. Sort of.'

'And I suppose she says she didn't do it.'

'She's not saying anything at all. She fired me.'

It was the first time all day she'd seen him look surprised. 'You're kidding me.'

'Nope. Turns out her daughter didn't tell her she'd hired me to begin with, and Victoria wasn't happy when she found out. I went out to Hiland to talk to her and she fired me.'

'Then what are you doing here listening to me yammer on?' He drained the current martini. 'Not that I'm complaining.'

'Her daughter pointed out that since she was the one who hired me, she was the only who could fire me.'

'Huh,' he said, and looked around for the bartender. 'I have to say, that may be the first time I've ever heard of a perp not declaring their innocence every hour on the hour, of every day they're on the inside.'

'Me, too,' Kate said. 'Will you tell me what you remember about the case?'

'Do I get a consultant's fee?'

Kate grinned and pointed at the new martini that had materialized in front of him.

He cackled, throwing his head back, and again Kate could see the man that he had been. She wondered about the ex, if she was still alive. He hadn't mentioned children.

'Thirty years ago,' Max said, taking an appreciative sip of martini, the unending supply of which did not appear to be affecting him in the slightest. He spoke clearly, without hesitation, from memory, and as he spoke, a young woman walked past on the sidewalk outside the window. She was wearing a black leather jacket hung with chains, racing gloves with the knuckles studded with silver, and black eye shadow and lipstick. Paper clips climbed the curve of her ear, which led the eye upward to the spiked purple hair moussed to stand straight up from her scalp. In the space of two strides, she morphed into a slim young woman with straight light brown hair hanging to her waist, round glasses perched on the end of her nose, a blue-flowered dress gathered just beneath her waist and falling to feet, clad in Birkenstock clogs. Nickleback was superceded by Paul Revere and the Raiders, crack and AIDS was yet to be heard of, the United States was still in Vietnam, and the final report of the Church hearings was three years away.

In Alaska, ANCSA was barely a year old, plans for the TransAlaska Pipeline were going full bore, and in two years little Molly Hootch of Emmonak would file a lawsuit that would force the state of Alaska to build her and her one thousand coplaintiffs schools in their villages so they wouldn't have to leave home to get an education.

'We'll start with the crime,' Max said, 'because that's where we always start. First I heard of it was reading the story in the *Anchorage Times* that morning. House burned down in the valley. Seventeen-year-old boy died in the fire. His brother, though injured, survived. His mother and sister were somewhere else and came home just in time to see the younger brother swan-dive out of his upstairs bedroom window. There was a lot of sympathy for the family. The funeral was like a Who's Who of Alaska. I think the governor came, and I know both senators and our congressman did.'

'Was the husband there?'

'Who?'

'Eugene Muravieff, Victoria's husband and the dead boy's father. Was he there?'

Max rubbed his nose. 'No.'

He let the single syllable lie there and gather dust.

'What?' Kate said.

Max shook his head. 'Who's telling this story? All right, then, let me tell it.'

The investigation turned up signs of arson right away, 'like it always does,' Max said. 'I know the jails aren't filled with smart people, but I think arsonists have to be some of the dumbest of the bunch. You get a halfway-bright investigator with a decent lab backing him up, you're always going to know if it's arson. But all the arsonist is thinking about is getting on a plane to Hawaii with the insurance check in his pocket.' He shook his head. 'Nature's optimist, that's an arsonist, every time. Well, except when they're firebugs.'

'Pyromaniacs,' Kate said.

'That's what I said, firebugs,' Max said.

So they found an accelerant, Max said, in this case gasoline, which the lab identified as being the same gas that was in Victoria's car.

'Did the car have a locking gas cap?' Kate said.

'A what?' Max said.

'Never mind,' Kate said, 'keep talking.'

'Troopers were doing the investigating, because Butte didn't have a police force and the city limits didn't even include Eagle River at that time. I was in the office the day they found out about the insurance policies Victoria Muravieff had taken out on her children.'

'What did you think?'

Max snorted. 'What do you think I thought? I thought the same thing the investigating officer thought. I thought two million dollars was a hell of a motive for murder. So they brought her in.'

'She didn't confess.'

'She didn't say much of anything at all. She called her brother and he got her an attorney. Then we went to court and she went to jail.'

'What about her husband?'

'That would be Eugene,' Max said. He seemed to savor the name.

'Eugene Muravieff,' Kate said.

'Ah yes, Eugene. You know the Muravieffs.'

'We've howdied at the AFN convention, but I don't think you could say we've shook,' Kate said.

Max nodded. 'Think their shit don't stink.'

'I wouldn't put it quite like that,' Kate lied.

Max barked out a laugh and conjured up another martini. His eye had lost none of its keenness, his words none of their bite. Amazing. 'From what I heard as the investigation went back then, Victoria and Eugene had a relationship that looked from the outside more like an armed truce than it did a marriage.'

'Unfriendly, were they?'

Max stroked his chin. 'Wouldn't say that, exactly. You ever read up on the Civil War?'

'A little,' Kate said. 'You can't avoid it.'

Max snorted. 'Know what you mean. They're still fighting that war in the South. Anyway, used to be a hobby of mine, and I remember one of the things I read about was that in the middle of a battle – maybe it'd be Christmas, or maybe it wouldn't even be a holiday – they'd call a truce, say for twenty-four hours. And for that twenty-four hours, brothers on opposing sides would step out into the no man's land between the lines and call out messages to each other, news about the family and friends, who was still living, who'd died. And then the truce would be over and they'd go back to killing each other. That was Victoria and Eugene's marriage, no man's land, with the occasional truce and some communication, but mostly shooting and a lot of blood.'

'What was the trouble?' Kate said. The Muravieff family was a pretty uptight bunch, born-again Christians, going back to the first Baptist minister to arrive in Sitka willing to go up against the local Russian Orthodox priest. Of course, Eugene Muravieff could have suffered from PK syndrome. The PK stood for 'preacher's kid.' In high school, Kate had watched the daughter of the pastor of the Niniltna Little Chapel go from singing soprano in the choir to cooing seductively at the varsity basketball team. She dropped out of school suddenly in the middle of her senior year and was not seen in Niniltna again. Her parents said that she had won a scholarship to a private school whose graduates were guaranteed admis-

160

sion to the Ivy League, and they left the following June when the pastor's contract with the chapel was up.

At the keggers in the dorms at UAF, it was the same thing; the heartiest partiers were always the kids from the most straitlaced backgrounds. Yeah, she could see a guy like Eugene turning into a rounder, something a WASP like Victoria Bannister couldn't and wouldn't put up with.

'What do you think was the problem,' Max said, heavy on the sarcasm.

Kate readjusted her ideas. 'Because she was white and he was Native?'

Max looked at her, not without pity. 'You're awful young, aren't you?'

'Thirty-five,' Kate said. She had to admire how he had put her on the defensive.

'Then you should clean the wax out of your ears when your elders are talking,' Max said, not without relish. 'You think because Natives got land and money now that they always did. Back when Victoria married Eugene, ANCSA was barely a twinkle in Willie Hensley's eye. Anybody who was anybody in the state was white, and white didn't share power with Natives, didn't socialize with Natives, and white sure as hell didn't marry Native. In particular, the Bannisters and Pilzes didn't marry Native. This would be mostly in the big towns,' he added parenthetically. 'In the villages, it was different.'

'No white women in the villages,' Kate said.

'Bingo,' he said, firing a gnarled finger at her. The bartender, listening in, took that as a sign and brought over another martini, and, for the first

161

time all afternoon, refreshed Kate's club soda.

'Alaska had been a state for less than ten years when Victoria told her parents she was marrying Eugene. Some people still had 'No Dogs or Natives' signs in their store windows. The Bannisters would never have gone that far – they needed the customers, and Alaska Natives spent as much money on groceries as anyone else – but the no-no was there for anyone to see. Except Victoria evidently didn't.'

'How did they meet?'

'Beats me.'

'Three kids,' she said. 'They were married for a while.'

'Yeah,' Max said. 'Surprising, when you think of the pressure they must have been under.'

'Her parents support the marriage?'

'In public, I never heard different.'

'His parents?'

'Same thing. Gossip had it that they weren't any happier about the marriage than the bride's family was, being as how Eugene was a bona fide war hero who could have done a lot better for himself than a daughter of someone who wouldn't sit next to an Eskimo in a movie theater because they smelled. But one thing the two families had in common was the ability to keep family conflict private. Who knows what went on behind closed doors. I'm just surprised Muravieff didn't bail sooner.'

'Why didn't they divorce right away?'

Max rolled his eyes. 'You didn't divorce back then, Shugak, especially if you were a Bannister or a Muravieff. Bannisters were old-line Catholics and the Muravieffs were born-again Christians trying to live down their Native heritage. What?' This as Kate frowned.

'I still don't see how you get race as a contributory factor in the breakdown of the marriage.'

'You sound like a social worker,' Max said. 'And you don't see it because you don't know the whole story.'

'Why am I buying martinis by the keg for you, old man,' Kate said in mock indignation, 'if you're not telling me everything?'

Max grinned. 'Well, hell, girl, I figured it was 'cause you were falling madly in love with me and willing to put up with just about anything so you could jump my bones.'

Kate grinned back. She liked this quintessential Alaskan old fart. He reminded her of Old Sam Dementieff. 'Good guess.'

Max went into a paroxysm of choking laughter, which Kate was afraid was going to carry him off before she could get him back to the Pioneer Home and life support. 'Where were you thirty years ago, woman?' he gasped out finally.

'Right here, just in kindergarten,' Kate said, and that set him off again. She waited, and when he had recovered himself by getting on the outside of some more of his martini, she said, 'You were talking about race, and what it had to do with Victoria and Eugene Muravieff's marriage.'

'Yeah,' he said, setting the martini glass down with a satisfied smack of his lips. 'Basically, Eugene wanted a job with Pilz Mining and Exploration, and they wouldn't have him.'

'Why not?'

'They said it was because he didn't have a mining degree.'

'Did he?'

'Nope.' Max shook his head. 'Erland, Victoria's brother, didn't, either, but his father handpicked him to run the company. He started as gofer to the manager of the Skyscraper Mine and worked his way up. All Eugene wanted was the same chance.'

'And they wouldn't give it to him.'

'Nope.'

'Because he was Native.'

'Yup. Course they didn't say that.' Max reflected. 'Or maybe they did. Wasn't a lot of call for PC back then.'

'So Eugene bailed on the marriage.'

'Yeah. Dumb.'

'Why dumb?' Kate said. Her sympathy was, not unnaturally, all with Eugene.

'Dumb because he had a good thing there, by all accounts. Up till then, he had a good wife, three kids, a paying job with the Bannisters. Man was a bona fide war hero in Korea, came home with a couple of medals. You'd think he would have had more grit than to fall down a bottle.'

'Is that what happened?'

Max nodded. 'Yeah. He started screwing around on her, and they fought.'

'It got physical?'

Max nodded again. 'One night, he came home drunk and started another fight. Victoria had had enough, and she shoved him into a radiator. He was unconscious when the ambulance arrived. He moved out after that and after the trial he disappeared.'

'Disappeared?' Kate said.

'Of course,' Max said, 'nobody was looking that hard for him.'

Kate wondered about that. The Muravieffs didn't sound like a family that gave up on its kids, no matter how badly they behaved. In particular, they would want to keep the bad ones around to remind them to repent of their sins and as an object lesson for any other offspring who threatened to get out of line. And what about Eugene's own children? 'The defense attorney has vanished, too.'

'Oh yeah?'

'Right after the trial.'

'Really,' Max said thoughtfully. 'Well, maybe he went hunting and a bear ate him.'

'Maybe.'

'Been known to happen.'

Kate nodded. 'A time or two.'

'Or he could have just got a wild hair and hit the Alcan with a blonde and a case of beer.'

'Yeah.'

'That's been known to happen, too.'

'More than once,' Kate said.

'But still,' Max said. 'Interesting.'

'Mmmm.'

'They could both have taken off with the same blonde,' Max said.

Kate smiled. 'And shared the beer?'

'Does seem a little unlikely, doesn't it?'

Kate signaled for the bill. 'One more thing. What happened to Victoria after Eugene split?'

'She took a job with her brother, Erland, at Pilz Mining and Exploration, which by then had

165

mining concerns all over the state and had moved their base of operations from Homer to Anchorage.'

'What did she do?'

'She was a bookkeeper,' Max said. 'It was that or wait tables down at the Lucky Wishbone. What else could a woman with no schooling and no experience but marriage do back then?'

CHAPTER 10

After Kate dropped Max off, she spent ten sweaty minutes figuring out how to dial out on her new cell phone. She was not helped in this by Mutt, who was intrigued by the sounds it made when the keys were pressed, which sounded a little like ptarmigan talking among themselves. Eventually, woman triumphed over machine and Charlotte answered on the second ring. 'Do you remember the make and model of the car your mother was driving the year your brother died?'

There was a brief silence. 'No,' Charlotte said.

'Is there someone who would?'

'Why do you want to know?'

'I want to know if it had a locking gas cap.'

'Just a minute, I'll go out in the garage and check.'

Charlotte put the phone down before Kate could say anything, which was all right since Kate was speechless. When Charlotte picked up the phone again, Kate said, 'You've still got the car your mother was driving before she went to jail?'

'It still runs,' Charlotte said, 'why wouldn't I? It doesn't have a locking gas cap. I'm not sure they were even making locking gas caps back then.'

'Me, either,' Kate said. 'One more thing, Charlotte. Have you heard from your mother's attorney since the trial?'

'Henry?' Charlotte's voice changed. 'No, I certainly have not.'

'You didn't like him?'

'If he'd done his job, my mother wouldn't be in jail.'

'I see,' Kate said. This was not an atypical response from someone whose attorney had failed to earn his client an acquittal. 'So you haven't heard from him.'

'He would know better than to call me. I told him what I thought of him in court the day the verdict came in.'

'And you haven't seen him since?'

'No. And I returned anything I got in the mail with his address on it.'

'You got mail from him?'

'Bills,' Charlotte said. 'Like I would pay them after he got my mother put in jail.'

'How do you know they were bills if you didn't open them?'

'What else would they be?' Charlotte said.

'Okay,' Kate said, repressing a sigh. 'Thanks, Charlotte.'

'Wait,' Charlotte said, 'does this mean you've found something?'

'A few somethings,' Kate said, 'but nothing to convince a judge that Victoria didn't set that fire.'

'Oh,' said Charlotte. She rallied. 'But you'll keep looking.'

'That's what you're paying me for,' Kate said.

'Until you find something to get her out.'

Kate said nothing.

In a forlorn whisper Charlotte, said, 'Because I want her *out*.'

The outfit was still hanging in Jack's closet, although Kate had to do a little excavation to find it. Jack had poked a hole in the bottom of the trash bag for the hook of the hanger and tied the bag in a knot at the bottom. She hesitated before untying the knot. It was silly, but Jack had tied that knot with his own hands. She thought about tearing the bag open from the top, but that seemed even sillier. What was she going to do, save the garbage bag so she could save the knot? She could just hear Jack, and the thought made her smile.

The jacket was short, single-breasted, with a V neck that revealed a discreetly sexy cleavage. It was covered with bright red sequins, which glittered in the light. The pants were black silk, with a single stripe of lighter black silk running in a trim line down the outer seam of both legs. She rummaged around the closet and found the shoes tucked into their original box.

Jack had bought her this outfit nearly three years before, in order to infiltrate a party Ekaterina was throwing at the Hotel Captain Cook for the Raven Corporation shareholders during the annual Alaska Federation of Natives convention. They'd been investigating a double homicide at the time. Kate, brutally rebuffed when she had suggested they go as servers in white shirts, black pants, and comfortable shoes, had been coerced into Nordstrom entirely against her will, and then into a glorified barbershop to have her hair done, also entirely against her will.

A grin stole slowly across her face. It had been worth it to see the expression on Jack's face when the first group of men had caught sight of her in all her glory. She'd cleaned up pretty well.

In a drawer of the dresser she found the diaphanous lingerie that Jack had taken such pleasure in selecting, and she slipped into it. The jacket, worn alone, felt heavy against her skin. The tuxedo pants, by comparison, felt barely there.

She looked in the mirror. Her hair, cut short to the nape, was brushed straight back from her forehead. For the hell of it, she wetted it down and parted it high up on the right. She looked like Victor/Victoria. She ruffled it up again. No jewelry, because she didn't own any and wouldn't have worn it if she had. Her feet hadn't changed any in the intervening years and she stood an inch taller in the shoes.

She surveyed herself in the mirror. 'Okay,' she said.

Mutt whined.

'Yeah, yeah, heard it all before,' Kate told her. 'You coming?'

They headed for Turnagain.

At Minnesota, she pulled off into the Texaco station and got out her cell phone. She managed to dial the number without yelling out the window for help, but it was a close call.

'Yeah,' Brendan said.

'It's Kate, Brendan.'

'Yeah,' Brendan said, drawing it out, and Kate could imagine him leaning back in his chair and putting his feet up, a grin spreading across his face. 'Light of my life, heart of my heart, sexiest thing walking around town on two legs. What can I do for you? Apart from the obvious.'

'I got invited to this party,' she said.

'Really? Need an escort?'

'No. Especially not you.'

He laughed, and she realized how that had sounded. 'No, I meant I don't want to use you yet.'

He laughed harder.

'Damn it!' she said, half laughing, half exasperated. 'I don't want anyone to know I have an in at the DA's, not yet.'

'Could be deeper in,' he said.

'Down, boy,' she said.

'Too late,' he said.

'Will you please behave? I'm going to Erland Bannister's for a cocktail party.'

Dead silence.

'Brendan?'

'Why?' he said finally. All humor had left his voice.

'He invited me.'

'Erland invited you?'

'Yes.'

Another silence. 'Again I ask the question. Why?'

'He's my client's uncle.'

Another silence, followed by, 'I don't think that's a good-enough reason, Kate.'

'I don't, either,' she said. A big shiny black Ford

170

Explorer pulled into the pumps. It had a bumper sticker that read I'M TOO POOR TO VOTE REPUBLICAN. Kate doubted that, given what bumper that sticker was on.

'If you don't need an escort, why did you call?' Brendan said.

'I don't know.' She hesitated. It sounded ridiculous, now that she came to put it into words. 'I was thinking someone should know where I was.'

He didn't laugh. 'So noted. Kate?'

'What?'

A brief, taut silence. 'Park for a quick exit.'

'I always do,' she said. 'Brendan, at the party, what should I watch out for?'

'Assholes.'

She laughed, and started out again for Turnagain with a lighter heart.

The Turnagain neighborhood had been one of the first residential suburbs of Anchorage and one of the hardest hit during the 1964 earthquake, magnitude 9.2 on the Richter scale. Half of it fell into Turnagain Arm and the other half just fell apart. Frantic to keep people in the state following the earthquake, the city traded home owners in the area for property up on what was now Hillside, the west-facing slopes of the Chugach Mountains, where now, if you didn't have five thousand square feet beneath one roof, including the indoor swimming pool and the marijuana grow, you weren't shit. For example, Charlotte Bannister Muravieff lived on Hillside.

Of course, twenty years later waterfront property again began looking good to people with short memories and a greedy turn of mind, and the previous owners of property below the Turnagain Bluff successfully challenged the city for title to that property. Now, the rich and powerful were building mansions on what was essentially in midquake quicksand, and since Alaska sat on the northern edge of the Ring of Fire and experienced literally at least one earthquake per day, the future was ripe with the possibility of violent death, not to mention potential litigation. 'Ah, Alaska,' Kate said out loud, threading the Subaru down the switchback. 'The land of opportunity, and of opportunists.'

Mutt yipped agreement. 'What do you know about it?' Kate asked her as they emerged from the trees to a vast parking lot in back of a house the size of the Hyatt Regency Maui. The view was superb, though, a gentle slope of green grass down to the coastal trail, after which the land gave way to mud flats and Knik Arm. It was a lovely evening, and the Knik was placid as a pond. On the far side of the water, Susitna, the sleeping lady, lay in peaceful repose, and beyond her Foraker and Denali scratched at the sky.

'Might be worth it,' Kate said after a few moments' judicial study, 'might just be worth living with the constant prospect of imminent death to have this view.'

This from a woman who hated to get her feet wet on a hunt. Mutt gave this observation the credulity it deserved, shoving past Kate when she opened the door. Kate left a window open for her and didn't bother locking the car.

The front door of the mansion was actually two, reached by a wide set of stairs that spilled to either side in graceful arcs around a carefully tended grouping of flowers arranged by hue and height. Sidelights and a fanlight let a gentle interior glow leach through, and Kate could hear the sound of many voices and the tinkling of glasses. She supposed it might sound inviting to some.

She looked down at Mutt. 'Want to come in?'

Mutt bared her teeth.

'Okay, try not to get into too much trouble,' Kate said, and at a hand signal Mutt was off the porch and into the underbrush like an arrow from a bow.

Someone cleared his throat. Kate looked around and beheld a young man in what looked like a bellhop's uniform, an ingratiating smile on his face. 'May I park your car?' he said.

'It's already parked,' Kate said, and headed up the steps.

He nipped ahead of her and opened the door. She eyed him suspiciously. His smile stayed in place. The door remained open. 'Thanks,' she said after a moment.

She went in, and the gates of mercy closed behind her.

The room was large, the biggest private room she'd been in, with floor-to-ceiling windows framing the spectacular view and hardwood floors polished to a shine bright enough to hurt your eyes. Not that Kate could admire either the view or the shine, because the room was jammed with what seemed to her appalled eyes like simply hundreds of people. Most of the men were in suits.

173

Most of the women were in black, with the only variables the depth of the neckline and the height of the hemline. There was a lot of loud jewelry flashing from ears and wrists, and everybody had big hair, even the men. There was an occasional black face and a few more Native ones, but this could not be construed in any way by even the most nearsighted viewer as a multicultural gathering. Kate could feel her skin getting darker by the second.

They were all talking at the tops of their voices. The resulting roar sounded like a 747 on takeoff. It took a few moments for Kate's ears to accustom themselves to the cacophony.

'Excuse me? Mr. Mayor, I'm so glad to have this opportunity to shake your hand and tell you what a fine job I think you're doing for the city. You've got my vote all the way.'

'That's great. I'm not the mayor, but I'll be sure to tell him when I see him.'

'Down to there and up to here. She couldn't be more obvious if she was wearing her own billboard.'

'That's not what they taught us at Harvard.' Modest laugh. 'I'm sorry, I went to Harvard. MBA. With honors.'

'I believe you mentioned that already. Seven or eight times.'

'Erland was telling me the other day that he's bidding on the leases opening up in the Beaufort next year.'

'He thinks the tax breaks are getting through, then?'

'–and now he's going for full custody, and how

he can ask for that with a straight face with that bimbo he's got living in his brand-new house–'

'Sounds like you could use an attorney. Mine took Phil to the cleaners for me. I've got his card here somewhere–'

'It's buried so deep in committee it'll never see daylight again.'

'Who sits on that committee? Maybe Erland'll make a few calls.'

'Harvard, schmarvard. Wharton's the place you want your kids to go to if you want them to learn anything about making money.' Modest laugh. 'Class of 'eighty-eight. I'll make a few calls for you.'

'The union is just going to have to suck it up. The state can't foot the entire insurance bill. People are going to have to ante up their share. I'm telling you, it's not an option. If they don't like it, they can get a job in the private sector.'

'The legislature makes one move on the permanent fund and Jay is going to rise up out of Lake Clark like Saint George coming after the dragon.'

'I keep thinking if we just explain to people, educate them–'

'We've been sucking at the federal tit since Seward bought Alaska from Russia. We don't know how to do anything else.'

'Erland says all we have to do is cut the fat out of the budget.'

'So we got a granite countertop and, would you believe it, they've put it in three times and they've broken it every single time.'

'Sounds like you could use a better contractor.

Let me give you my card.'

'I come from Seldovia. There used to be five goddamn canneries in Seldovia when I was growing up. You know where the name comes from? *Seldevoy*. Russian word, means herring town. No goddamn herring in Seldovia anymore. Not much goddamn salmon left, either. We used to be able to pull goddamn king crab right out of Seldovia Bay. They aren't even in the Kachemak anymore. What, you never read the book *Cod?*'

'Yeah, but that was the Atlantic.'

'The Pacific's just another ocean. I'm telling you, we need to go to a thousand-mile limit and start arming the goddamn Coast Guard with cannons so they can sink a few of those goddamn fish processors. And I ain't talking about just the foreign processors, either, 'cause the American processors are just as bad, if not goddamn worse.'

'Well, as long as I can pull a king salmon out of the Kenai, I'm happy.'

'Global warming's a myth.'

'Right, and so's the Pribilofs remaining ice-free year-round, and golfing in Palmer in January.'

'They were acting like they were at a slumber party, instead of prosecuting a rape-murder, with the victim's family right there in the courtroom. I sent the DA an E-mail and told her so.'

'What'd she say?'

'The usual – the media blew it all out of proportion, it wasn't really that bad, Anchorage DAs are held to a high standard, yakety-yak.'

'Erland went to school with her, didn't he? Maybe you should talk to him about it.'

Glasses clinked, people put pinkish blobs of

something into their mouths and kept talking around the blobs, and the air was thick with cigarette and cigar smoke. Kate's sinuses gave a single vicious throb, and instinctively she made as if to turn back to the door, everything in her telling her to escape from this hellhole before she saw someone she knew.

'Kate!'

Inches from a clean getaway, she took courage in hand and turned back to face the room. 'Oh,' she said a little weakly. 'Hi, Pete.'

Pete Heiman elbowed through the crowd and stood grinning at her. 'Couldn't believe my eyes when you walked in. What the hell are you doing here?'

'I was invited,' she said, trying to talk without breathing.

'Really? You know Erland?'

She shook her head. Not breathing wasn't working, so she tried to breathe through her mouth instead. 'His niece.'

'Charlotte?'

'Yeah.'

'Well, hell, small world.' He was still grinning. He looked her over. 'You clean up pretty damn good, Katie.'

'Pete? Nobody calls me Katie.'

'I know. It kinda puts me in a class by myself, don't it?'

He pretended to preen, and she had to laugh.

Pete Heiman was the legislative senator (for life, some people had started saying after the last election) from Kate's district, her mouthpiece in Juneau and like Max one of the original Alaskan

177

old farts. He'd played pinochle with Abel and fished for salmon alongside Old Sam and swung a pick, if only for a photo op during an election swing, next to Mac Devlin. His politics were conservative but erratic; he was a member of the Republican party, but he voted against the majority in Juneau often enough to keep his liberal and Libertarian constituents happy, and he'd managed to weasel his way through the subsistence issue without having to take a firm stand in one camp or another. He was pro-choice, which always surprised the hell out of Kate, until she remembered that he was a longtime friend of Auntie Vi. Kate had a feeling that Auntie Vi had something on Pete, but she'd yet to find out what.

'Want a drink?' he said.

'Sure.'

'Come on.' He grabbed her hand and towed her through the crowd, nodding and smiling with that practiced politician's charm to clear a path. There was a bar with a smiling bartender, who seemed genuinely disappointed to pour her only a glass of club soda with a twist of lime.

'Want something to eat?' Pete said. 'What am I saying, you always want something to eat,' and he towed her forthwith to a buffet laden with shrimp, crab, salmon, and halibut, six different kinds of cheese, a dozen different kinds of crackers, chips and dips, and a dazzling display of Godiva chocolates.

Kate took one look and said, 'Why are the plates so small?'

Pete eyed the column of shrimp leaning like the tower of Pisa from the tiny saucer held in Kate's hand and said, 'Couldn't tell you.' He turned to survey the crowd. 'Eat up. There are some people I'd like you to meet.'

'Some people' turned out to be every second person in the joint. Kate gulped her food – the pink blobs turned out to be cheese puffs, which didn't explain why they were pink – and endured handshakes that ranged from the limp noodle to the damp rag to the hearty grip to the bone crusher, and smiles that ranged from tight-lipped to a vast expanse of synthetic enamel, from the ingratiating to the predatory.

The women were impressed by her outfit, less so by her hair and lack of makeup, and greeted her with suspicion, if not outright hostility. Whose man was she there to take? Red was a power color. Whose attention would she usurp? The men wondered if she was Pete's protégée or his new girlfriend, or both, and what that might mean in the next legislative session in terms of lobbying. Would she be long-term or short? If long-term, how much influence would she wield over Pete's vote? Would she drink on their tab, or would her favor be more labor intensive to acquire? Would they have to sleep with her? Would she sleep with them? Some were clearly hoping for the latter.

One woman, a slender, hard-faced blonde, who wore a black blazer over a black silk shell, white leggings, and black boots with four-inch heels that buckled over the instep, looked Kate up and down and drawled, 'Cute outfit honey. Your mother pick that out for you?'

'Sondra–' Pete said, or started to.

'That's all right, Pete,' Kate said, and smiled at

Sondra. 'Not my mother, my man.' She ran one teasing finger down the buttons of the glittering red jacket and back up again to trace the neckline. 'He liked the idea of ... buttons.' She gave the man hovering at Sondra's elbow a languishing glance and ran her tongue slowly over her lower lip.

The man inhaled part of his drink and started to cough, spraying green liquid of some kind over Sondra's leggings. Sondra swore. 'You moron!' She brushed ineffectually at her leggings and glared at Kate.

Pete threw back his head and roared with laughter.

'Um,' the man said, his eyes watering a little, 'I'm Greg Nowaka. And you are–'

The woman transferred the glare from Kate to him.

Still laughing, Pete waved him off. 'Way out of your league, buddy boy. Run, run for your life.'

He towed Kate away as she said to the woman over her shoulder, 'Did you practice that nostril flare in the mirror? It's kinda cool, makes you look like you're about to charge a red cape.'

'Jesus, Shugak, enough already.' When they had achieved what Pete considered to be a safe distance, he stopped to grin down at her. 'Where'd you learn to do that? I figured I was shepherding a lamb through the wolf pack, but I'm thinking now I got that backward.'

'When in Rome,' Kate said, and wondered how soon she could get the hell out of there.

A touch on the shoulder stopped her. She turned to see Charlotte, Emily at her elbow. Emily looked at Kate with the first expression of approval Kate had yet seen. Charlotte was even smiling. 'Thanks,' Charlotte said.

'For what?' Kate said.

Charlotte looked over her shoulder. 'Hi, Pete.'

'Hi, sweetie.' Pete kissed her cheek and then Emily's. 'How you doing?'

Charlotte's smile widened. 'Better now.'

Pete laughed. 'I bet.' He grinned down at Kate.

Kate, mystified, was about to inquire as to what had just happened, when Charlotte said, 'Let me introduce you to my aunt.' She nodded to Pete, who stepped back. Charlotte led Kate to a chair tucked into a corner next to the windows. 'Aunt Alice?'

The woman seated in the chair wore a sleeveless scoop-necked mauve linen sheath and was chatting animatedly with a well-dressed, smooth-featured man twenty years her junior, who looked like he was trying not to appear bored. She looked around at Charlotte's greeting. Her hair had been artfully streaked, her large gray eyes were exquisitely made up, her fingernails were polished the same shade as her toenails, displayed in elegant sandals with delicate straps. Her collarbone was a knife edge above the neckline of her dress, her arms about the width of a piece of spaghetti, and there was something wrong with her face. The skin was very smooth and very taut, but it seemed to be pulling her lips open to show the fleshy inner lips inside. It tugged at the corners of her eyes and eyebrows, narrowing the eyes and elongating the brows. Kate wondered if perhaps Alice was recovering from burns of some kind. She'd seen burn victims grow just that kind of new skin.

181

'Aunt Alice, I'd like you to meet Kate Shugak.'

Aunt Alice extended a hand, the back of which was mottled with age spots. 'How do you do, Ms. Shugak.'

Kate accepted the hand and wondered if she was expected to kiss it. 'Kate, please,' she said.

Alice gave a perfunctory smile and said to the bored-looking man, 'Alvin, meet Kate Shugak.'

Alvin took Kate's hand. 'How nice to meet you.' His eyes traveled down her throat. 'Hmm.' He raised one hand and, before she could step out of reach, traced her scar with impersonal fingers. 'Who's your surgeon?'

'I beg your pardon?'

'Your plastic surgeon, who is he? Never mind. Whoever he is, he ought to be shot. Here.' Alvin produced a business card. 'Give me a call. We'll set up an appointment.' He took her chin in cool, impersonal hands and turned her face from side to side, and Kate was so dumbfounded at the uninvited familiarity that she let him. 'How old are you?'

'Thirty-five,' Kate said.

'Hmm,' he said again. 'Not much else to be done there, at least not yet. In another twenty years, we'll probably have to do some work on those eyes.'

'What's wrong with my eyes?' Kate said, and then she pulled herself together. 'There's nothing wrong with my eyes. Who the hell are you anyway?'

Alvin produced a wide smile of practiced charm. 'I'm sorry. I'm Alvin Bishop. I'm a plastic surgeon.' The mirthless smile widened. 'Beautiful faces are us.'

'I've already got one, thanks,' Kate said smartly, and looked down at Alice. She understood the face now, although she would never understand the impetus behind the edifice. She had to work at keeping the pity out of her own (already beautiful) face.

'And how do you know my niece?' Alice said brightly.

Before Kate could reply, a booming male voice said, 'And who do we have here?'

Kate peered up through the steadily thickening haze at what appeared to be quite the tallest man she'd ever met in her life.

The man stooped to kiss the cheek Alice presented. 'Have I told you tonight how lovely you look, dear?' He dismissed the plastic surgeon with a look that stopped just short of insult. Dr. Alvin Bishop faded into the crowd, Kate catching a look of relief on his face as he went.

'Just fine, dear,' she replied. 'This is Kate Shugak, a friend of Charlotte's.'

He straightened. 'Is it. Well now.' His eyes ran over Kate assessingly, and Kate got that instant vibe that every woman gets when a man is interested. Her own eyes narrowed a little.

He was a big man, long-limbed, rangy. She knew him to be in his late sixties or early seventies, but he looked twenty years younger. His face was long, the nose and chin very strong, his eyes blue and intent. His smile was more charming than Alvin's, but there was power in it, and the arrogance that comes with power. Erland Bannister would be a man whose every move, from

the wink and the slap on the back to the unfriendly takeover of a rival corporation, would be
calculated for a specific effect. He looked like a
man who got what he wanted when he wanted it
and not a second later.

He was dressed more casually than anyone in
the room, in slacks and a well-worn gray tweed
sport jacket over an Oxford shirt open at the
neck. Kate was reminded of a story about
Napoleon's coronation, when he made all his
generals wear gold braid while he wore a simple
soldier's uniform. Make everyone dress up and
then dress down yourself. Yet another example of
his power, a small one, but telling.

An arm snaked through Erland's and a voice
purred, 'Erland, darling, who's your little friend?'

The blonde in the green-stained leggings was
back, looking at Kate as if she'd crawled out from
under a rock. Next to Kate, Charlotte stiffened.
Alice's smile looked even more rigid, and it
wasn't just her latest face-lift. Suddenly, Kate
understood the subtext of the little scene a few
minutes before. She looked at Alice. Fitzgerald
was right: The rich really were different. But
Hemingway was righter; the only difference was
they had more money, which they could spend
on more dumb things. It occurred to Kate for the
first time that there were advantages to being
broke for most of your life.

She looked back at the blonde and examined
her face with interest. 'You must be a patient of
Alvin's, too,' she said, putting as much innocence
into her wide eyes as she could muster.

The blonde went a dull red. She opened her

184

mouth, but whatever bile had been about to spew out was forestalled when Erland patted her hand. 'Why, you've met.'

'Not formally,' Kate said with her biggest smile.

'Well, then, allow me to introduce you. Sondra Blair, this is Kate Shugak. Sondra, you know my wife, Alice, and my niece, Charlotte, already.'

There was something in Erland's voice that alerted Sondra. Her hostility vanished, to be replaced by an oozing enchantment, which fooled no one it was aimed at. 'Of course. How do you do? Alice, Charlotte, lovely to see you again.'

'And Emily,' Charlotte said in a tight voice.

'And Emily, of course,' Erland said with no less charm.

'So nice to meet you, Emily,' Sondra said, stifling a yawn. 'And you, too, uh, Kaley, wasn't it?'

Kate laughed in her face.

There was a startled silence. Charlotte couldn't repress a smile. Emily chuckled. Alice woke up from cryosleep and looked at Kate as if Kate were her last hope of heaven.

Erland grinned down at Kate. 'Feisty little thing, aren't you? Let me buy you a drink.' He let Sondra's arm fall and slipped a firm hand beneath Kate's elbow.

Sondra looked livid.

'Uncle Erland–' Charlotte said.

'Now, Charlotte, you just relax. I won't eat her.' He smiled down at Kate. 'Unless she asks me to. Nicely.'

Again, Kate felt that jolt. She didn't think any woman under the age of eighty wouldn't have. It put her even more on her guard. Men like Erland

Bannister didn't come on to a woman without an ulterior motive, and it wasn't just because he was bowled over by her manifest charms.

The dull look was back on Alice's face as they left. Charlotte opened her mouth as if to say something, then shut it again, worried eyes meeting Kate's, as if trying to impart a message of some urgency. Whatever it was, Kate didn't get it.

The crowd parted for Erland as it never would for Pete, and if people had been curious about Kate on Pete's arm, they were doubly interested to see her on Erland's. A brief electric silence would fall at their approach, succeeded by a buzz of comment and speculation after they had passed. 'It's like a fishbowl in here,' Kate said.

Erland smiled down at her. 'I know. People will gossip about their superiors.'

'Why are they here, if you hold them in such contempt?'

He didn't bother denying it. 'I find them useful.'

'All of them?'

He shrugged. 'Most of them. Some come with their very own Kato Kaelins, and they have to be fed and watered along with the rest of the cattle, but it's the price I pay to get their masters in the door.' He didn't bother lowering his voice, she noticed. He paused next to the bar and smiled down at her. 'What can I get you?'

'Club soda, with a twist of lime.'

He didn't try to talk her into anything stronger, which she appreciated. He got a scotch and water for himself and led her to a plush love seat tucked into a bow window. A couple seated there were

186

dismissed with the same ease and finesse with which Erland had dismissed Alvin, had cut through the crowd, and had gone to the head of the line at the bar. Kate took the corner with the view; Erland took the corner with the view of Kate and crossed his legs so that a richly polished loafer touched one of hers. She let it stay there, for the moment.

'You're not quite what I expected,' he said, watching her over the rim of his glass.

'What did you expect?' she said, sipping her club soda.

He smiled. 'A little less city, a little more Bush?'

She smiled back. 'Sorry to disappoint you.'

'I'm not disappointed.' He let his eyes wander over her. 'No, indeed.'

'Why am I here?' she said. Kate didn't do subtle.

'I knew your grandmother,' Erland said.

'Everyone did,' Kate said. 'How did you know I was in town?'

He swallowed scotch. 'Word gets around.'

'What word?'

He smiled again. It came easily to him, and it lent him charisma. He would have found that out early on. He would have put it to work for him, the way he was putting it to work for him now. 'A friend called. Said you'd been making inquiries about my sister's case.'

The man she had called from Brendan's list who had refused to talk to her. 'Charlotte didn't tell you,' Kate said in a neutral voice.

His smile faded. 'No,' he said, a hint of sadness in his voice. 'We're not as close as I'd like.'

'Have you talked to Victoria?'

He shook his head. 'Not in thirty years.'

'Not since she went inside?'

'No.'

'Why?' Kate said baldly. 'She's right up the road, twenty minutes door-to-door.'

He shrugged helplessly, which Kate didn't buy for a New York minute. 'She refuses to speak to any of us.'

'Why?'

'I don't know. Guilt, I suppose.'

'So you think she's guilty.'

His eyes were very blue and very intent. 'She didn't deny it. She didn't even take the stand in her own defense.'

Kate nodded. 'I know. I've read the trial transcript.'

Someone approached the couch. Kate looked up to see Oliver Muravieff leaning on his cane.

'Oliver,' Erland said, getting to his feet and extending a hand.

It was grasped warmly. 'Uncle Erland,' Oliver Muravieff said. He looked down at Kate. 'Ms. Shugak.'

'You're late, boy.' Erland clapped him on the shoulder. 'Let me get you a drink.'

Kate watched him go thoughtfully. She didn't expect Erland Bannister fetched drinks for just anybody. She looked at Oliver. What did Erland want from his nephew that he would wait on him?

He took his uncle's place. 'What do you think of the party?'

'Interesting,' Kate said.

Oliver gave a short laugh. 'That's what you say when you see a painting you hate. "Interesting."'

She didn't contradict him. 'Why are you here?'

He shrugged. 'Uncle Erland asked me.'

'And you come when he calls.'

She was being deliberately offensive, but he smiled. It was an oddly grim expression, having little to do with amusement. 'Yes,' he said, 'I do, and so does everyone else here.'

'Oliver,' a voice said, and Kate looked up, to behold a man with more and bigger teeth than JFK, all of them switched on. Looking into that smile was like staring through a dark night into headlights turned on bright.

'How the hell are you?' Smiley Face said, beaming down at both of them, and without waiting for a reply, he added 'Who's your friend?'

Oliver's face took on an even more dour cast. 'Kate Shugak, Bruce Abbott.'

'Ah,' Bruce Abbott said, nodding wisely. 'Ekaterina Shugak's granddaughter. I heard your speech at AFN a couple of years back. Rousing, I thought.'

'You didn't think I went over the top on the fish farming,' Kate said, sitting up and looking anxious.

He extended a hand and she put hers into it, which allowed him to pat it reassuringly. 'Certainly not. We must protect our wild stock at all cost if we are to maintain the reputation for quality Alaska salmon enjoys. Not to mention a healthful subsistence lifestyle for the Native peoples.' He affected a shudder. 'Nasty stuff anyway, farmed salmon. Dry, they have to dye it pink, diseased, tasteless. Your points were well taken.'

Interesting, Kate thought, especially since her impromptu speech had begun with a story about a moose kill and she hadn't said a word about farmed fish. She beamed a smile at him that rivaled the brilliance of his own. Oliver made a sound in the back of his throat and stood up. 'Take my seat, Bruce. I need a drink.'

He walked away before Bruce could answer. 'May I?' Bruce said.

'Certainly,' Kate said, patting her hair and maybe fluttering her eyelashes a little. What the hell, give ol' Bruce a thrill while she figured out what the hell the governor's chief of staff had to say to little old Kate Shugak from the Park. 'We've met before, you know,' she said in breathless, confiding accents. She leaned forward and looked at him with wide, admiring eyes, or what she was hoping might be a close approximation thereof.

He looked astounded. 'No,' he said in a tone of flattering disbelief. He gave her the once-over and flashed his teeth again. 'I'm sure I would remember if we had.'

He'd been in some kind of supervisory position with the Department of Corrections at the Cook Inlet Pretrial Facility, back in the days when Kate used to be an investigator for the Anchorage district attorney. She had never liked the glad-handing, brownnosing little prick from the first time she'd watched him oil his way out of responsibility for the prisoner suicide that had happened on his watch. It had never been made officially known, but the employee grapevine said that he'd had his feet up on his desk, reading the newspaper instead of watching the monitors in the mods, one of which was trained on the suicide's cell. The dead guy had been put on a suicide watch, too, so it wasn't like Bruce Abbott wouldn't have known the guy was at risk.

Kate decided that now was not the time to remind Bruce Abbott of past misdeeds. She smiled instead.

Under the influence of those admiring eyes, Bruce puffed out his chest and started dropping names. Every sentence began 'The governor said to me' or 'And then I said to the governor' and all of their conversations were liberally sprinkled with references to the political high and mighty, both state and federal. Any local contacts, it went without saying, were dismissed as being too paltry even to mention.

Kate threw in a couple of bright-eyed 'Reallys!' and one 'Fascinating!' and stifled a yawn, but his acute political instincts told Bruce he was losing his audience. He switched on his smile again. 'You're being spoken of in high places, Kate. I may call you Kate?'

Something told her that what Bruce Abbott said next would turn out to be why she had been invited to this party. 'Really,' she said. 'I can't imagine what anyone in the governor's office might have to say about little old me.'

His eyes narrowed fractionally, and for a moment she thought she might have overdone it. But his smile switched on again, brighter than ever, accompanied this time by a fruity chuckle. 'Oh, I didn't mean to mislead you, Kate. Not necessarily the governor's office, but certainly at high levels.'

'Really,' she said for what felt like the seventeenth time. The secret to a successful interrogation was to make the suspect do all of the talking. She would not ask what 'they' had been saying about her. Besides, Bruce was dying to tell her, and why should she thwart him, poor man?

Realizing she was about to doze off with her eyes wide open, she pulled herself together.

'Yes, you have been mentioned as quite the little up-and-comer,' Bruce said.

'Have I?' Kate said. 'Really, I can't imagine why. As you know, Bruce, I'm not in politics myself.'

'Not everyone can be,' he said earnestly, 'some just don't have the gift for it. But we need you out here, too.' A gesture encompassed the greater part of the Great Unwashed, of which Kate presumed he meant she was a voting member. Not that she'd voted for his boss, but she didn't find it necessary to say so at this very moment. She batted her eyelids again. Her eyes were drying out from trying to keep them open.

Bruce smiled and patted her hand again. 'Yes, being Ekaterina Shugak's granddaughter, well, that certainly puts you first on any list.'

'I'm on a list?' Kate said, suddenly wide awake.

He beamed his teeth at her. 'Of course you are,' he said warmly, 'and first on it, like I said.'

'For what?' Kate said, and kicked herself for asking.

He smoothed the lapel of his jacket. 'As I'm sure you know, the Alaska state troopers are opening a new post in Niniltna. You live there, I believe?'

'I do,' Kate said.

'And of course you used to be an investigator for the Anchorage district attorney.'

'I did,' she said.

He smiled some more. 'The Department of Public Safety is thinking of assigning a VPSO to Niniltna.'

She stiffened, enough so that he noticed. 'Are they?' she said. The words were bitten off more than spoken.

'Indeed, yes,' he said, looking a bit bewildered, clearly not expecting hostility as a reaction to his good news.

He was easy to read. Jobs of any kind were scarce in the Alaskan Bush. Surely she knew what this meant? A monthly salary, in a village with only two others, the trooper and the postmaster. Medical insurance, workman's comp, a retirement plan. He couldn't understand her lack of enthusiasm, or for that matter the complete absence of overwhelming gratitude that he had come to expect from these little chats. The current governor of Alaska was a past master at the art of patronage, and Bruce Abbott the designated dispenser thereof. It was a job he clearly enjoyed, and now Kate was ruining it for him.

She took pity on him, in spite of the anger building beneath her breastbone. He was just a go-fer, after all, a yes-man, a beck-and-call boy who only implemented the decisions made by the people in authority. He would never wield that authority himself, but credit where credit was due, he would never want to. He was a round peg in a thoroughly round hole, he'd found his niche, and he knew it. 'I appreciate the thought, Bruce, but I really wouldn't be the right person for the job.'

Bruce didn't just look disappointed, he looked aghast. It might have been the first time anyone had ever turned down the governor's offer of a job. 'But – but the salary. The – the benefits,' he said, actually stuttering. 'Oh, if you're worried about the time it would take you to go through the academy in Sitka to qualify, I've been instructed to tell you that in your case, because of your training – we've been told you did a year at Quantico right after taking your degree in social justice from UAF – and your experience on the job – your record is, hell, it's flawless – well, after all that, the state would be willing to waive the academy requirement. We don't have that many people of your caliber available, Kate.'

She almost lost her temper. Almost, but not quite. She was here on a fact-finding mission, not to indulge her evil twin. She rose to her feet and plastered a false smile on her face. 'I'm sorry, Bruce.'

'But we like to recruit VPSOs locally whenever we can!' He stood up. 'You're Alaskan-born and -bred, Kate, and what's more, you live in the very place you'll be posted in!'

She forbore from pointing out that that wasn't always a good thing in the Bush. All too often when the village public safety officers arrested someone, either they were related to the perp or the rest of the village was. It was frequently an argument for arresting no one, no matter how severe the crime. 'There are a lot of people who would like and would be suited for the Niniltna VPSO job.' She wondered at the near panic she saw on his face, but not enough to relent. 'I'm sorry,' she repeated, and headed for the door.

By the time she got there, Erland Bannister had returned to the love seat and was standing in close consultation with Bruce Abbott. Oliver was with them, a little apart, a frown on his face as he watched her slip out the door.

CHAPTER 11

Kate's temper was not improved when she got home and found Jim Chopin waiting on her doorstep. Repressing a wish that he'd been in the driveway, so she could run over him, she drove into the garage. She slammed out of the Subaru and stormed into the town house, steaming down on the front door like Patton's Third Army. She yanked it open and bellowed, 'How dare you! How *dare* you!'

Amazingly, he didn't hear her, having apparently been struck deaf at the sight of her in party clothes. His expression one of dumb fascination, his eyes followed the V of the jacket's neckline to the soft hint of cleavage. He swallowed audibly and opened his mouth, but nothing came out.

'Did you do it?' she said fiercely. 'Answer me!'

'Do what?' he croaked.

'Pull strings at the Department of Public Safety to get me the VPSO job!'

He blinked. 'Huh?'

'The job that would have me working as your

second number in the Park, you moron!' She poked him in the chest. 'Did you try to get me that job?'

Mutt, observing all this from a safe distance, turned tail and vanished into the den, where she intended to remain until the decibel level fell.

Jim pulled off his hat, as if it had suddenly become too tight for his head. 'I don't know what the hell you're talking about, Kate.' He dared to look at her again, knowing it was a mistake. He shouldn't look. If he looked, he'd want to touch, and that wasn't why he was here. Damn it.

He hadn't told her, and she hadn't asked, that he was still in town because he'd been called to testify at a trial involving the bust of a marijuana grow in the Valley he'd been TDY'd to the previous summer. And this under protest and only because the arresting officer scheduled to testify – a man he'd been assisting at the time – had been called Outside because of a death in the family. And now here he was, on the doorstep of this town house tonight, and pretty damn late it was, and where the hell had she been at this hour dressed like that?

Didn't matter. He was here to make it clear to Kate Shugak once and for all that there was no relationship of any kind going on between the two of them, not even sex. Not even 'sex with no complications – when it's over, we go our separate ways, no harm, no foul.' Nope, not even that.

The jacket, made of some rich fabric that clung to every curve, the whispering black silk of the tuxedo pants tailored in so masculine a fashion that when worn by a woman they were nothing more or less than a blatant invitation to get her out of them. Which he suddenly knew he was going to do, given half the chance.

He ran a finger around the inside of his collar. Okay. He'd tell her it was over in the morning.

She stamped back into the house, pausing only to kick off her shoes. Jim followed her inside, watching her very fine ass move inside the black silk, and closed the door behind them.

'God, my feet,' she said, leaning a hand against the wall and raising one foot to rub at it.

He eyed the shoes. They had a barely discernible heel. 'Sit,' he said, and steered her into the living room. She sank into the easy chair with a sigh, and he sat on the coffee table and lifted her feet into his lap. He began to knead them.

'Oh.' Her head fell back against the chair. 'Yesssss.'

He'd heard that sound before, just not in this context. He had to shift a little where he was sitting. He cleared his throat. 'Where did you go in that getup?'

She opened her eyes and looked down at herself. 'Not bad, huh?'

'It's fucking spectacular and you know it.'

She looked up, startled at the grim sound of his voice. He didn't look happy, either. She sniffed the arm of the jacket and made a face. 'Ick. Everybody was smoking like a chimney. I'll have to wash my hair.'

'Where were you?' he said again. He'd been thumping on the door once every hour since 7:30 P.M. He arrested stalkers for less egregious behavior. The thought did not please him.

197

'At a party.'

'I deduced that from the camouflage. Whose party?'

'Erland Bannister's.'

His hands stilled. 'You're kidding me.'

'Nope. Big-ass house down on the flats below the Turnagain Bluff.' She wriggled her feet suggestively and he started massaging them again. 'Oh yeaaah.'

She moaned and he wanted to cry.

'I was scared to death there was going to be an earthquake the whole time I was there,' she said, 'and that we were all going to fall into Cook Inlet.'

Disregarding this, he said, 'Who was there?'

'Anyone who is anyone in Alaskan power politics.' She reflected. 'Well, most of them. Seemed to be a contingent or two missing.'

'Like maybe from the nonwhite races?' Jim said.

'How did you guess.'

It wasn't a question, and he didn't bother answering it. 'Why did you go?'

'Because Erland invited me.'

'How did you come to meet Erland Bannister? Did his sister introduce you?'

'No,' Kate said, 'I have it on the best authority that Erland and Victoria haven't spoken since she went inside.'

'Thirty years?' Jim said. 'What, she's been cast off by her family?' He reflected. 'Yeah, well, she killed their nephew, their grandson, their cousin. I can see it. I wouldn't feel all that kindly toward her myself in that situation.'

It occurred to Kate that she had not thus far

discussed in depth her current job with Jim. 'No, I think it was her choice. She's cut herself off completely from her family. I hear she still talks to friends, however, hitting them up for money to fund the school she's running out at Hiland Mountain.'

'She runs a prison school?'

Kate nodded, and told him about it, and about the case.

'No wonder,' Jim said when she finished.

'No wonder what?'

'You've got that thing about teachers.'

This brought back memories of the week she'd spent picking morel mushrooms in the north of the Park, and of the teacher who had been killed there. She still grieved for him. But she said, 'Doesn't mean I think she's innocent.'

He raised an eyebrow but forbore to comment. 'So if Victoria didn't introduce you, how did you wangle an invitation to Erland's party?'

'He invited me,' Kate repeated thoughtfully.

'How did he know to call you?'

'Brendan gave me a list of the names of witnesses at Victoria's trial.' Jim scowled. Kate ignored it. 'I started calling them, and one guy sounded really upset and wanted to know if Erland knew what Charlotte was doing, reopening her mother's case. I think he called Erland, and Erland called me.'

'Why?'

'Good question.'

'Why were you yelling at me?'

Warmth was spreading up from her feet through her body, and her mind was starting to wander from the case. 'Oh. Because I thought you might have pulled some strings to get me the VPSO's job at the new trooper post in Niniltna.'

'Why the hell would I want to do that?'

She fluttered her eyelashes. It had seemed to work at the party.

His hands were warm and firm on her feet. The caress contrasted with the rise in the volume of his voice. 'Why the hell would I want you around even more than you already are?'

She could have asked him what he was doing at the town house this evening, with her feet in his lap. Instead, she just smiled. 'But I'm thinking now that there was something else going on there.'

He did his level best to resist the come-hither in her smile. 'What?'

'Bruce Abbott was the one who made the offer.'

'Jesus. You really were flying high tonight, Kate, the governor's right-hand man.'

Kate snorted. 'Yeah. Real high. This guy doesn't have a thought in his head that the governor didn't put there.'

'It's how he earns his salary.'

'Well, he didn't earn it tonight.' She paused. 'There was an implication – nothing overt, just a hint – that if I didn't return home immediately, the job would go to someone else.'

'What? Bullshit. The department hasn't even posted the job specs yet.'

'That's another thing. He said that my attendance at the trooper academy in Sitka would be waived because of my prior education and experience.'

'What! Over my dead body! We want more than glorified security guards to back us up in the villages, Kate. VPSOs have to be trained in procedure, case preparation, and firearms, at the very minimum.'

'Don't shoot the messenger, Chopin. I'm just reporting here.'

'Besides,' he said, 'no offense, Shugak, but you're not exactly known for following the rules.'

She grinned. 'I admit, not my strong point.'

'Strong point, my ass. You never met a rule of evidence you liked.'

'And the courts are so picky about that "fruit of the poisoned tree" stuff.'

'I don't think you even know what *Miranda* means.'

'If someone wants to talk, why wouldn't I listen?' she said wide-eyed.

'I could never be absolutely sure I could make a case with you working for me.'

'Probably not.'

But she caught perps, they both thought, and both had to bite back a smile.

There was a brief silence. 'It was a bribe,' Jim said on a note of discovery.

'Indeed it was,' Kate said.

'What for?'

'I don't know.' She let one foot slip down from his hands and let it rest in the notch between his legs.

He stilled. 'Kate?' It came out like a croak.

She leaned forward and smiled into his eyes. 'I've got to get out of these smelly clothes.' She nuzzled him, her nose against his nose, her lips against his lips, a gesture of warmth and tenderness that should have scared the hell out of him. 'They've got all these' – she fluttered a hand – 'buttons.'

He swallowed hard. 'I noticed,' he said hoarsely.

'Mmmm. I don't know if I can manage all of them on my own. I might need a little' – she ran her tongue around the curl of his ear – 'help.'

She might just as well have led him up the stairs by his dick. It was doing all his thinking for him anyway.

The next morning, there were three boys waiting on the doorstep. 'Okay,' Kate told Kevin, 'you're beginning to overgraze your range.'

'Hello,' the third boy said, and stuck out his hand. 'I'm Garrett Hyde.'

Kate shook it. 'How do you do,' she said, going formal on instinct. 'I'm Kate Shugak.'

Garrett was Jordan's age and had straight blond hair neatly cut and direct brown eyes.

'I was about to start breakfast.' She stood back from the door. 'Would you like to join us?'

Garrett didn't budge. 'I'm not supposed to go into strange people's houses.'

'I'm Kevin and Jordan's friend,' Kate said. 'But don't come in if it feels wrong.' She walked away from the open door and went into the kitchen.

Breakfast this morning was oatmeal with raisins and brown sugar and sourdough toast dripping with butter. Kevin and Jordan ate like horses, with Garrett eating just as much, only not as quickly. Afterward, Kevin disappeared into the living room with Mutt, and shortly thereafter the

202

television could be heard.

Jordan, who was helping Garrett load the dishwasher with the breakfast dishes, paused and looked at Kate. 'He likes Barney,' he said, and rolled his eyes.

'What are you going to do,' Kate said.

Jordan half-smiled.

Garrett looked at Jordan and said, 'Okay.'

'The Garrett Hyde seal of approval?' Kate said.

He flushed. 'We go to the same school. They're friends of mine. We look out for each other.'

'Good to have friends,' Kate said, 'understood. Were you out together all night last night?'

He shook his head. 'We had a sleepover at my house.'

Kate was relieved. 'Good.'

He hesitated. 'Do you think you can help them? Their mom...' His voice trailed off.

'I'll try,' Kate said.

'Okay,' Garrett said again.

Kate raised her voice. 'Kevin, in here for a minute.'

He came back into the kitchen and looked at her with wary eyes. 'Relax,' she said, 'I haven't called DFYS. Yet.'

Their faces closed up.

'Guys,' she said, 'come on. It's good you found a bolt-hole, but it's temporary. It won't be long before I go home. What are you going to do then?'

'I'll look out for them,' Garrett said immediately.

In a voice carefully devoid of ridicule, Kate said, 'How?'

'I'll take them home with me.'

'Your parents up for two more kids in the house?'

She saw the answer on his face. More important, she saw it on Kevin's and Jordan's faces, too. 'It's okay,' Jordan said. Kevin looked at him, and he dropped his eyes. 'Most of the time.'

Kate felt a touch on her arm and looked down to see that Kevin had drawn close, his small, pleading face raised imploringly to hers. 'Don't make us leave our mom,' he whispered. 'Please don't.'

'What are you going to do?' Jim said when the door closed behind them.

'I don't know yet,' Kate said, rubbing her face with both hands. 'But something.'

Jim looked as if the struggle to remain silent was difficult.

Kate drove to the library, wondering what to do about them. Jim was right. She should call DFYS and let them sort it out.

Two things stopped her. One, she had taken control over where she would live when she was in kindergarten, meeting and beating her grandmother's determination that Kate live with her in town. Two, she remembered Abel, the surrogate father Emaa had found for Kate when Kate refused to leave the homestead. He was the one who had found her there when Emaa was frantically scouring the Park for her missing granddaughter. Abel had respected Kate's act of self-determination enough not to manhandle her over to his cabin.

Kate felt that if she manhandled Kevin and

Jordan's future, she would somehow be demonstrating a lack of respect for her foster father, another crusty Alaskan old fart who believed absolutely in independence and self-reliance. She couldn't do that. Not yet, at any rate.

Not to mention that young Garrett had left her with the distinct impression that he expected better of her than that.

She pulled into the library parking lot and found a space in the first row, facing the fountain, the same row she always parked in when she came to the library, so she could find the car again. On impulse, she got out her cell phone and after three tries managed to dial Auntie Vi's cell phone number. She wondered what color Auntie Vi's phone was today. The last time she'd seen it, it had been lime green. The time before that, it had been cherry red.

Auntie Vi answered. 'It's me, Auntie,' Kate said. 'Is Johnny there?'

'Hey, Kate,' Johnny said, trying to be cool but clearly delighted that she had called home just to talk to him.

They chatted for a while, Kate telling him about her overworked bullshit detector at last night's party and Johnny grilling her about her shopping list at Costco to make sure she didn't forget the important things, like batteries and bags of chips.

She told him about the boys. She didn't ask, but he said anyway, 'You can't do anything else and still have them trusting you.'

'I know.'

'Besides, you cook a mean breakfast, Kate. Don't worry, they'll be back.'

She was still smiling when she got out of the car. She left the windows rolled down in case Mutt wanted to grab a snack from the flocks of geese that were currently nibbling the grass around the fountain, and went directly to the third floor and the microfiche stacks. She pulled the rolls for the *Anchorage Times* for a year before Victoria's imprisonment and a year after and sat down at a machine with a notebook and a pencil.

Two hours later, she was suffering mild nausea from watching so much film scroll past and hadn't discovered much in the way of additional information either to help or hurt her investigation of Victoria's case. The facts were reported pretty much as they appeared in the police report and the trial transcript. The fire and the death of the boy, William, the discovery of the arson, and his mother's subsequent arrest and conviction were sensationalized beneath screaming banner headlines, but that was primarily due to the prominence of the family. Crimes even more heinous were reported every day; they were just bumped back to the inside of the paper because the victims were poor or unelected.

More out of guilt at the immense salary she was pulling down than from a conviction that she'd find anything, she turned to the roll of microfiche for the year following Victoria's conviction.

A year and one month after Victoria's imprisonment, Pilz Mining and Exploration declared bankruptcy.

Well now. Kate sat back in her chair and contemplated this new information. Here might be an answer as to why Victoria burned down her house for the insurance money. Maybe the Pilzes and the Bannisters really were out of money.

But if this was the case, why hadn't this information been brought forward at trial? It sure as hell provided motivation, which from the beginning had seemed to be lacking, at least in Kate's opinion.

She thought of last night's party in the Turnagain mansion. If the Bannisters had been broke, they had certainly recovered well.

She leaned forward again and began to read slowly through the story, placing the facts of the bankruptcy in chronological order. *The Anchorage Times* had been so obliging as to devote an entire business section of one Sunday issue to a history of the company, which wasn't surprising when you realized that over two hundred people would have lost their jobs if the company had just folded. Of course, they were only making ninety-three cents an hour, but the mine commissary made a point of selling goods to miners' families at or near cost. Back in 1941, the commissary made a profit of just $247 on $36,000 in sales. No, Skyscraper Mines had a history of high pay, good food, and fair dealing, and never lacked for labor.

Kate, back before the injury that left the scar on her throat and the permanent damage to her vocal cords, used to play the guitar and sing. A crowd-pleasing favorite was always 'Sixteen Tons.' She didn't think Tennessee Ernie Ford himself could have put it over at the Skyscraper Mines.

Not that this had anything to do with the matter at hand. Kate scrolled forward.

Pilz Mining and Exploration had been formed as a partnership between the scions of the houses of Pilz and Bannister, to share the expenses and profits of, primarily, the Skyscraper Valley Mines and, secondarily, additional mines outside of Fairbanks and Juneau. The first lode of the Skyscraper Valley Mine had been discovered by one Torrance Hurley in 1906 near the top of Skyscraper Mountain in the Talkeetna Mountains north of Anchorage. The gold was fine, but the ore was high grade enough to haul in a sluice box, and of course as soon as the news got out, every miner with a gold pan showed up, and pretty soon the 3,500-foot alpine valley was wall-to-wall claims. Over the years, the mines consolidated into two controlling corporations, and in 1935 along came Herman Pilz, who bought them both out, and the Pilz Mining and Exploration Company, adding to their holdings in Fairbanks and Juneau, became the largest producer of gold in the state. From 1936 to 1942, the Skyscraper Valley mines produced a total of 152,429 ounces of gold. At $35 an ounce, that was $5,335,015. At the time, that was real money.

In 1941, the Japanese attacked Pearl Harbor, the nation was at war shortly thereafter, and the U.S. War Production Board declared gold mining to be a nonessential industry. There was a brief period of fierce activity on the part of PME to extract as much gold as was humanly possible in the time before the closure, followed by a war-long hiatus. The mine didn't get back up to speed until 1947. In 1951, gold was selling at $34.72 an ounce. PME began to diversify, beginning in the 1950s with oil leases in Cook Inlet, more oil leases in Prudhoe Bay in the 1960s, coal leases near Healy in the 1970s, zinc and lead leases near Kotzebue in the 1980s, and still more oil leases in Cook Inlet and on the North Slope in the 1990s.

PME held no majority in any of these concerns except for outright title to their various gold mines, enough to exert a healthy influence over the board of directors, but not enough to concern themselves with anything except the bottom line. The gold mines were the only part of their mineral-producing empire that required them to pay salaries and benefits to employees. There had been union problems, which led to problems with the color of the bottom line, which had led to layoffs, which had led to more union problems, and then the price of gold, which had reached a high of $615 dollars an ounce, began to fall. The company had racked up a lot of zeros in legal debt. By then, the mines were, without exception, in serious need of some heavy investing in new mining technology and infrastructure. Their debtors were unwilling to wait for payment, and PME's legal staff advised declaring bankruptcy to give the corporation breathing space to get back on its financial feet.

At this point, Kate's stomach growled loudly enough to draw a condemnatory glance from the reference librarian. Kate busied herself with loading up on quarters from the change machine and printing out the relevant stories.

It was one o'clock, and Kate headed for Thai Kitchen on Tudor, where the best pad thai in town was served. She was head-down in it when her backpack started to vibrate. She jumped, dropping her chopsticks and knocking over her Coke. The backpack fell off the chair and scattered its contents across the floor and under the next table, which was, fortunately, unoccupied. One of the things that fell out was her new cell phone, which vibrated even farther across the floor, where it was scooped up by a white-haired matron in flowered polyester. 'Is this yours, dear?' she said.

'Thanks,' Kate said. She couldn't remember which button to push to answer it. The matron said, 'Need some help there, dear?' and took the phone back. 'I've got the same phone,' she said with a smile. 'Costco, right? It takes a while to figure the little devil out.'

Kate retired to her table, kicking cash, notebook, pens, an address book, pencils, Tampax, Blistex, a comb, and a roll of cherry Lifesavers toward her backpack, and said into the phone, 'Hello?'

'Kate?' Kurt said. 'Is that you?'

'Yes.' She tried to keep her voice low. She'd been around too many people who seemed to think their cell phones were bullhorns. She knelt down and restuffed her backpack. 'What's up?'

'I've got some news for you.' Kurt paused for dramatic effect.

Kate sighed. 'What?'

'I want to show you.'

'Kurt–'

'Come on, Kate, you'll love it, I promise.' He gave her directions somewhere out near Jewel Lake. 'I'll be there in thirty minutes. I'm starving, I've got to grab some lunch.'

'Kurt, wait a–' There was a click and after a moment a dial tone.

Kate pulled the phone from her ear and looked down at the keypad. She sighed again and went back to the white-haired matron, who showed her how to turn it off.

CHAPTER 12

Arriving in Jewel Lake fifteen minutes later, Kate drove through a subdivision of prepackaged cracker-board houses that all looked exactly alike and were all painted the very same shade of ash gray with the exact same white trim. The pavement ended in a forest of scrub spruce and spindly birch. A gravel road with more bumps and grinds than a stripper dodged tree-trunks as it passed by what looked like the original homesteads, which were closeted in stands of lilac and honeysuckle that had been there long enough to grow into trees thick enough to reduce the evening sunshine to an occasional dapple. Wouldn't be long before the taxes got too high and some developer showed up with a fistful of cash and the plans to another cookie-cutter subdivision, where all of the houses had exactly the same floor plan and where the neighbors could lean out of their windows to exchange a cup of sugar instead of having to walk all the way down the sidewalk and knock on the door.

She maneuvered the Subaru around an old

Pontiac someone had left parked not very close to the side of the one-lane road, and found the address on a mailbox. She turned into the driveway next to it, found a winding and rudimentary path between a thicket of birch trees, and pulled up in front of a log cabin, right behind the white Ford Escort Kate had rented for Kurt yesterday morning. She got out. 'Kurt?' she called.

Mutt took three paces forward and froze in place, one paw elevated. She raised her nose a fraction of an inch, testing the air.

Kate, about to head for the cabin, stopped. She shut the door of the Subaru and took a long stride away from the vehicle, arms held slightly out from her sides, doing a sweep of the clearing. There was nothing in it except a few dried-up flower beds and a gravel parking area where the dandelions were fighting a last-ditch battle for primacy with the horsetail. The house was a small cabin made of logs gone the dull dark gold of age. The windows had no drapes, probably because the house looked out on no neighbors.

Mutt's head drooped down beneath her shoulders, and she began a low, menacing whine. She stalked forward, nostrils twitching.

'Hold up, girl,' Kate said, and Mutt's growl changed from a whine to a snarl. 'Hold on just one damn minute, Mutt,' Kate said. She'd seen Mutt like this before, and what happened next was never pretty. She looked around for something to use as a weapon. There was nothing, not a shovel or a broom; this had to be the neatest yard she'd ever seen around a log cabin. She went back to the Subaru and found a box in the back holding a bottle of Windex, a roll of paper towels, a first-aid kit, flares, and a pair of jumper cables. She took out one of the cables and doubled it into kind of a short whip, with the clamps hanging free. She held it hip-high in her right hand, ready to swing, and kept her center of gravity over her feet in a kind of knees-bent glide, which contrasted with the sidling, stiff-legged movement of the dog shadowing her every step.

The steps up to the porch creaked. She saw no movement through the windows, but it was pretty dark inside. 'Hello,' she said, raising her voice. 'Anybody home?'

There was no answer. When she rapped on the door, it opened. Mutt's growl intensified, but Kate didn't need Mutt's nose to smell the rich coppery scent of blood. She crouched down and hit the door a sharp rap with her left palm.

She caught a confused glimpse of a lumpen mass on the floor inside. There was a muffled curse and the door came back at her hard. Her head slammed against the jamb, and in the split second granted her for reflection she saw little bluebirds flying around in a circle. She even heard them tweeting. In the next second, instinct and training kicked in and she tucked and rolled into a forward somersault. It was a move designed to have her back up on her feet, and it would have worked if she hadn't somersaulted right into the body of Kurt Pletnikoff. She scrabbled to get up and slipped in his blood.

Mutt's growl cut off and someone screamed. Someone else cursed. Kate, slipping around like Abbott and Costello as she tried to regain her footing, heard Mutt's teeth snapping together like a cleaver chopping up a chicken. There was another scream, louder this time. A gun fired and a bullet slammed into the stovepipe of the stove against the back wall of the living room.

Kate ducked and rolled behind a seedy old couch – dubious protection, but better than none – at the same moment the stovepipe came crashing down, raising a cloud of soot. There was another menacing growl and three more shots snapped off quickly. One shot thudded into the couch she was crouching behind and the other two into the wall over her head.

Mutt erupted into a fury of savage barks and snarls and there was the distinct sound of teeth tearing into flesh, and then another scream.

'Get it off me! Get it off me!' a panicked voice yelled, and then he screamed.

'MUTT!' Kate yelled.

'Let's get the fuck out of here!' someone else shouted, and there was a trample of feet through the door, down the porch steps, and across the gravel. Kate rolled to her feet and peered over the back of the couch. To her immense relief, Mutt stood in the doorway, taut, tense, lips drawn back in a fierce snarl, ears flat, up on her toes, mane stiff, tail straight out. She started to move forward, quivering in every limb.

'Mutt!' Kate said. 'Stay!'

Mutt looked at her and snarled. She had blood on her muzzle.

'Oh, good girl,' Kate said, 'good, good girl, but stay, damn it.' She went forward to check on Kurt. He'd been shot once through the chest, but high and to the right. As she stooped, his eyes fluttered open. His pulse was fast and thready and his skin was cool to the touch. A quick glance around revealed no telephone. 'Kurt,' she said urgently. 'Hang on. I'm calling for help.'

She began to rise, but his fingers plucked at her sleeve. 'It's okay, I'm just going for the phone.' She heard doors slam and an engine start in the distance. She half-rose to her feet. 'Goddamn it!'

He grasped at her with a feeble hand.

Kate swore again but let him pull her back down. 'All right, what?'

His lips moved, but she heard no sound. She bent down to put her ear next to them. 'What?'

She felt his lips move but could make no sense of the words. She straightened so she could look into his face. 'Okay, I got it, Kurt,' she said. 'I got it, I got what you said. I'm going to call for help now. Hang on, do you hear me? You hang on!'

She ran out to the Subaru and got the cell phone from her day pack. She hit every button until she got a dial tone and then punched in 911 and gave her name and location. 'Someone's been shot,' she told the dispatcher. 'Send an ambulance, and tell the cops to be on the lookout for a dark-colored Pontiac Firebird two-door hatchback coming out the same road, moving fast with two men inside, they're the shooters.' She tossed the cell phone back in the Subaru, the woman still squawking at her to stay on the line, and ran back into the cabin. Kurt had lapsed into unconsciousness and his skin was now clammy, but he was still breathing and the blood from his wound had clotted. She didn't dare move him,

215

but she yanked the worn, nobbly afghan from the back of the couch and covered him with it. 'Hang on, Kurt,' she said. 'The ambulance is on its way. Please, please just hang on. I'm right here; I won't leave. Hang on. Mutt!'

Mutt, looking mightily pissed off but mercifully less feral, came to lie against Kurt's side.

Kate soft-footed it through the rest of the small house.

The living room took up the whole front of it, the back divided into kitchen, bathroom, and bedroom. The kitchen was antique but clean, the bathroom had a pink toilet that dated back to the fifties, and the queen-size bed in the bedroom had a body in it.

Kate swore and searched for a pulse. There was none, and the body was cold and rigid. Twelve to twenty-four hours, then, which meant he'd been dead before Kurt had arrived. Kurt was laid out in the living room, though, which meant he might not have made it to the bedroom before being ambushed and so might not have known the body was there.

The body was of an old man. Kate lifted the covers and saw that he was dressed in a T-shirt and shorts, probably what he'd worn to bed the night before. There was a single bullet hole in his right temple. She stooped to peer at it. There were powder burns in the skin around the hole and the distinct smell of spent powder. The shot had been fired at very close range, so he'd been shot where he lay, probably in his sleep, given the neatness of the bed and the room.

She straightened and widened her focus from

the wound to his whole face. He was Native. She estimated his height at around five six, his weight at about 150. He was wiry, broad-shouldered, long-waisted, and his legs were short and looked slightly bowed. His hands were large and rough.

She replaced the covers and, ears on alert for the sound of approaching sirens, went swiftly and thoroughly through every cupboard and drawer in the place, as well as the pocket of every pair of pants and coat she came across. She found a checkbook showing a balance of $530.72, bills for light, gas, and phone, and a wallet with a driver's license. She compared the face in photo on the license to that of the dead man in the bed. It was the same.

There was another photo in the top drawer of the bedroom dresser, a four-by-six snapshot in a cheap wooden frame, the kind that came in a two-pack from Wal-Mart. It showed a group of three people posing on a boat on a sunshiny day, all laughing, all sunburned, all in life vests. The background looked like it might be Kachemak Bay. The stern of the boat was pointed at the camera, but only the tops of the letters of the name showed.

There was only one other picture in the entire cabin, this one in another wooden frame, the twin of the first. It was a black-and-white head shot of a young woman posed for a formal portrait. It looked like every other photo of a high school senior Kate had seen in her life.

At long last, she heard the distant wail of sirens. She stuffed both pictures into her day pack, and shut the door to the Subaru, turning to face the driveway.

The cops beat the ambulance by three minutes, but they still missed the Pontiac.

The doctor came out of the operating room. He wasn't smiling. Kate got up on shaky legs. 'How bad?'

'Bad enough,' the doc said. 'But not fatal.'

'Not?' Kate said. The relief took the strength out of her legs and she sat down again.

The doc shook his head. He was a wiry man, not much taller than Kate, and had a lined face and lively eyes. He didn't smell like he'd showered in the last twenty-four hours and he didn't look like he'd slept in longer than that. 'Missed his heart, lungs, spine, even passed between his ribs on the way out.'

'So he'll be all right?'

The doc shrugged. 'Maybe. Probably.' He rubbed his face with both hands. 'There's a lot of muscle and tissue damage. Goddamn bullets just love to turn cartwheels when they get on the inside of a human body. He'll be a while healing, that's for sure.'

'When can I talk to him?'

The doc gave her a derisive look. 'Forget about it. He's out of it for the next twelve to twenty-four. Sleep's the best thing for him. He's going to hurt like hell when he wakes up. The longer he can hold off on that, the better.'

From behind Kate, a voice said, 'I'll need to know the minute he wakes up.'

The doctor flapped his hand. 'Yeah, yeah, I

218

know the drill.' He shambled off down the hall, white coat stained with blood.

'So I'll talk to you instead, Shugak.'

Kate turned. 'O'Leary.'

'What were you doing there?'

'Kurt asked me to meet him there.'

'What was he doing there?'

Kate did a rapid mental review. 'He's working for me.'

'So you said. Doing what?'

'Finding a witness to a case I'm working.'

'What was the name of the witness?'

'I don't know,' Kate said. It was her first lie. It wouldn't be her last. 'I was coming to town, and Billy Mike asked me to look for Luba Hardt while I was here.'

'I remember.' She paused, and to her relief and somewhat to her shame, O'Leary jumped right in. 'So Kurt was looking for witnesses to the assault?'

'Yes. He called me to ask me to meet him there because he'd found something or someone. He wouldn't tell me what it was, he just asked me to meet him. Who does that cabin belong to, anyway?'

She saw his look and hoped she hadn't overdone the innocence. There was a long pause. 'Guy by the name of Gene Salamantoff. You know him?'

'Never heard of him.' That was the strict truth, so far as it went.

'Mmm.' O'Leary, big, beefy, red-faced, examined her with careful eyes, and decided for reasons best known to himself to provide further information. 'Turns out he's dead, too.'

'Salamantoff?'

O'Leary nodded. 'We found his body in his bedroom.'

'You're kidding,' Kate said, and earned herself another long look. She couldn't help it – lying just wasn't her very best thing. 'Was he shot, too?'

O'Leary nodded.

'Same gun?'

'By the entry and exit wounds, yeah. Take ballistics a few days to be sure.'

'There were two men,' Kate said.

'I read your statement,' O'Leary said.

'Did you raise any prints?'

O'Leary shrugged.

'Got this, though,' and handed her a mug shot of the dead man.

'Thanks,' she said, a little surprised.

O'Leary's middle name was not 'helpful.'

'Anybody spot the Pontiac anywhere?'

O'Leary shrugged again.

'When you find them, look for bite marks,' Kate said.

O'Leary looked down at Mutt, who was standing one pace behind Kate, and almost smiled.

Kate left the number of the town house and the one for her cell phone at the nurses' station with strict instructions to call her if Kurt showed any sign whatsoever of regaining consciousness. To be sure, she slipped into his room when the nurse's back was turned and left a note under the bedside phone to that effect, too. She stood for a moment looking down at him. Tubed and wired and bandaged. No respirator, though. Kurt was breathing on his own, always a good sign, and the heart monitor registered a reassuringly steady blip.

He seemed to be frowning, his brow puckered. Truth to tell, he looked more than a little pissed off, and for some reason this caused Kate's heart to lift a little. Pissed off was nowhere near to dying. She touched his shoulder. 'I left both my phone numbers, Kurt,' she said in a low voice. 'Call me when you wake up. In the meantime, I'll get on the trail of those sons a bitches in the Pontiac.'

Kate pulled some pork ribs out of the refrigerator and put them on to boil with salt and garlic powder, started rice in the rice cooker, and took a diet Sprite over ice with a lime twist into the upstairs bathroom. She stripped out of the clothes stained with Kurt's blood and got into the shower. She let the water, hot as she could stand it, beat down on her back and took a long, cold swallow of her drink.

She turned her face into the water, soaking her hair, breathing the steam in deep.

Kurt was going to be all right, that was the main thing. 'He's going to be all right,' she said out loud, and then she said, 'Son of a bitch. Son of a *bitch*,' and slapped the tile with her open hand hard enough to make it sting.

She soaped down, rinsed off, and toweled herself dry, then stalked into the bedroom and yanked on clean clothes. Mutt, who had followed her into the bathroom, trailed her into the bedroom. Kate took her bloodstained clothes into the laundry room and started the washer. Mutt followed her there, too, and followed her into the kitchen, where Kate boiled water for tea, got out a cup, and added a huge dollop of honey. She took the cup of tea into the living room and curled up in the easy chair, the afghan from the back of the couch tucked in around her. Mutt whined at her, so she scooched over, and Mutt climbed into the nest with her. It was a tight fit, but Kate was more than grateful for the reassurance that emanated from Mutt's warm, solid body.

Suddenly, Kate was freezing. She was shaking so hard the tea spilled over the side of the cup and her teeth chattered on the rim. She had an immediate desire to call George and tell him to come get her and Mutt out of this friggin' town at once. She had an equally immediate desire to find the two shooters in the Pontiac, cut out their livers, and feed them to Mutt as a special treat.

Kate had never had anyone working for her hurt before.

Come to that, Kate had never had anyone working for her before.

It was one thing to get hurt herself. The risk of injury, even death, was always there in her line of work. The last time she'd been in the hospital the doctor had offered her frequent flyer miles.

But Kurt was new to the job, a mercy job Kate had thrown him because she'd felt guilty about separating him from his previous profession of poaching. It wasn't like he was a professional private investigator. He'd never had any training, and other than the rare brawl at the Roadhouse, he probably had no experience in defending himself. He'd just been stumbling around in the dark, making it up as he went along.

Kate didn't have a lot of personal investment in Kurt Pletnikoff. They lived on opposite sides of the Park, they hadn't been in the same grade at school, they hadn't been friends or lovers. He was some kind of second cousin twice removed – Kate thought through Auntie Vi, or maybe Auntie Balasha – but then, that could be said of half the residents of the Park.

But she'd accepted responsibility for him when she had hired him. From that moment forward, he was one of hers. She'd thought to share a little of the Bannister wealth, maybe give Kurt a head start in the next stage of his life, since she'd been instrumental in ending the last one.

She didn't feel guilty about that. Somebody had to stand up for the Park bears, poor little defenseless creatures that they were.

She could have sent Kurt out into the PI fray with a little less insouciance and a little more preparation, though.

For the first time, Kate understood what it must be like to send a soldier out into battle, and to have to explain to his loved ones why he hadn't returned.

Mutt whined, an anxious sound, and touched her cold nose gently to Kate's cheek. Kate closed her eyes and leaned her head against Mutt's and tried to think. Charlotte had hired her to free Victoria. She had hired Kurt to help her do so. Someone had shot Kurt and had been waiting at the cabin to shoot her, too. It was just plain blind luck, and Mutt, that she hadn't charged right in the door and picked up her very own personal bullet in the chest.

She managed to down most of the tea, and the heat of the brew and the sweetness of the honey finally managed to calm her trembling. She was able to feel her feet again. She could think.

She wondered whether Victoria Pilz Bannister Muravieff might perhaps be innocent of the charge of murder that had had her incarcerated for thirty years. Perhaps whoever had really done the crime might be alarmed that someone was checking into the case again.

But if that was true, if Victoria was innocent, why had she refused to talk to Kate? What, was she nuts? Who the hell turns down a Get Out of Jail Free card? Who wants to stay in prison?

Victoria could be one of those people who had become completely institutionalized, so used to the structured life of the prison that she could not envision any other. It happened, Kate had seen prisoners released on probation re-offend and be back inside within the week. For some of them, a bed and three meals a day were worth it. Kate didn't think Victoria Pilz Bannister Muravieff, scion of Alaska's landed and moneyed gentry, was one of them. Someone who had the ability, even after being tried, convicted, and imprisoned for the with-malice-aforethought murder of her son, to finish a BA and a master's degree and who had single-handedly gone on to organize and run what amounted to a small high school and community college on the inside was not institutionalized. At this point, Victoria pretty much was the institution, only she didn't go home at night along with the rest of the staff.

Reopening a thirty-year-old case had its risks.

There were always secrets that people thought they had buried deep, but in Alaska, never deep enough. The community was too small, and the memories of the old farts too good.

When she thought her hands were steady enough, she got up and went to her day pack, where she got out the notebook she'd taken from Kurt's pocket before the police and the ambulance got there.

CHAPTER 13

It was a small spiral-bound notebook with lined paper. Kurt's sprawling handwriting was barely legible. He'd written down Eugene Muravieff's name on the first page and Henry Cowell's name about halfway through. Notes followed each name.

He'd exploited those sources Kate had given him first, and Kate had to give him points for thoroughness. An attorney in private practice who subscribed to the Motznik public records database and who was willing to allow Kate to access it for a small fee had been his first stop, as indicated by the directions to the office that Kurt had scribbled down. Neither Muravieff nor Cowell had a current driver's license, although the old ones had furnished their birth dates and Social Security numbers. The last litigation – the only – Muravieff had been involved in was his divorce from Victoria, when Victoria had been given all the property they held in common and sole custody of the children, and Eugene an admonishment from the judge to complete rehab, or detox, as it was called in those days. The last litigation Cowell had been involved in was as attorney of record for Victoria in *Victoria Bannister Muravieff vs. the State of Alaska,* one count of murder in the first degree, one count of attempted murder in the first degree, judgment found for the state.

Neither had a telephone number, listed or unlisted. Neither had a mortgage or a car payment. Neither had a vehicle with tires, wings, skis, tracks, or a hull listed in his name in the state of Alaska. Muravieff had had a commercial fishing license for a set-net site in Seldovia, which had evidently been sold at some point, because Kurt's notes indicated it had been transferred to an Ernie Gajewski. In parentheses Kurt had written 'Wanda's brother.'

Kate paused to look up Ernie Gajewski in the phone book. No joy. No Wanda Gajewski, either.

Neither Muravieff nor Cowell had applied for a hunting or sportfishing license recently, and neither had ever applied for a permanent fund dividend since the payment had begun being made to Alaskan citizens in 1981. Cowell's membership in the Alaska Bar Association had lapsed. Both men had registered for the draft their senior year in high school. Muravieff had served in Korea, risen to the rank of sergeant, and been awarded a Purple Heart and a Medal of Valor. Cowell had served his time as a legal aide with the U.S. Navy's Judge Advocate General's Office in

Washington, D.C.

All of which was no information at all. Kate wondered what happened when the Internal Revenue Service stopped getting taxes from a citizen. Did they notice? Did they follow up? Did they require proof of death? She'd had to file a final income tax statement for her grandmother when she died, so that Kate could legally give away most of Ekaterina's belongings and take possession of the rest. That had required a death certificate. It might be worth checking into in the matter of Muravieff and Cowell, if only because of the spectacular lack of other evidence of what had happened to either man.

It was information of sorts, if only in a negative way, that both men had dropped out of sight entirely.

She wondered if anyone had shot at them.

She looked at the first photo she'd taken from the old cabin earlier that day. It was black-and-white in a blue wooden frame, a group of three preadolescents, a girl between two boys, arms around one another, smiling broadly at the camera. She recognized a much younger Charlotte. The two boys with her would be her brothers, the dead William, and Oliver, whose much younger face was easily recognizable.

She looked at the second photo, the formal portrait of the girl. No clue as to her identity. She removed the back of the frame. The photographer's name was stamped on the back of the photo, Gebhart Studio. She looked in the phone book again. There were half a dozen Gebharts, but no Gebhart Studio.

Mutt had moved to the floor next to the chair the first time Kate had gotten up for the phone book, and she watched Kate's every move with alert yellow eyes.

'If Victoria didn't kill William, who did?' Kate asked her.

Mutt didn't know.

'They're still around.'

Mutt barked, a single, sharp, thoroughly pissed-off agreement. Mutt didn't care for people shooting at her human.

Quick footsteps came up the walk, a fist beat a rapid tattoo against the door, and the doorbell chimed several times. 'Kate? Kate, I saw the car through the garage windows. I know you're in there. Open up, goddamn it!'

Kate sighed. She looked at Mutt, who was on her feet, tail wagging furiously. 'Shall we let him in?'

The bark was still short and sharp, but this time it was joyous. Kate got up and opened the door.

'Are you all right?' Jim demanded. He walked in without invitation. 'I ran into somebody at the courthouse who said you'd been involved in a shooting.'

Of course. The Bush telegraph might be a shade faster than a courthouse when it came to spreading the news, but not much.

He stood her against the wall and more or less frisked her. 'You're okay? You're not hurt? Nobody shot you?'

'I'm fine,' she said, and fended him off when he showed signs of stripping her down right there to check for wounds. At least that was what she thought he was doing. 'Really. I didn't get hit.'

'Who did? They said somebody got shot.'

'Kurt.'

He stared at her. 'Kurt Pletnikoff?'

'Yes. He's working for me, helping track down some of the people connected to Victoria Muravieff's case.'

'Jesus Christ,' Jim said. 'Kurt Pletnikoff?'

'Yes.'

'Is he going to be all right?'

'Yes. The guy he found isn't.'

'What guy?'

'The guy lying dead in the bedroom with a bullet hole in his head.'

Jim stared at her for another minute and then shook his head. 'Okay. I want you to start over, at the beginning.'

'I told you most of it last night.'

'Tell me again.'

It couldn't hurt to talk it through again, especially since she was now hovering on the side of believing Victoria to be innocent. She knew how Jim, who was after all a practicing law-enforcement professional, would react to that notion, but maybe she needed a devil's advocate right about now. Getting shot at always had a tendency to screw with her head. 'Okay, but – what time is it?'

He looked at his watch. 'A little after five.'

'God, is that all? It feels like a year since this morning.' Her stomach growled and she realized she hadn't been able to finish her lunch. 'Want some dinner?'

He followed her into the kitchen, where the pork ribs were stewing. She checked the rice, and pulled a package of frozen snow peas from the freezer and set it on the drain board to thaw.

Jim sat at the kitchen table with a mug of coffee and listened to her story. When she finished, he stirred and said, 'What took Kurt to that cabin?'

'I don't know. He's unconscious and his notes don't say.'

'What did he say when he called you?'

'He said, "I've got some news for you." And when I asked him what, he said, "I want to show you."'

'Did he call you from the cabin?'

She thought. 'No. He said it would take him thirty minutes to get there because he was going to pick up some lunch on the way.'

'There're damn few places in Anchorage that are thirty minutes away from anywhere, even when you're stopping for lunch on the way,' Jim said.

'I know. Which leads me to believe he was in Muldoon, or South Anchorage, or...'

'What?'

'Or maybe up on Hillside,' she said.

'Who lives on Hillside?'

'Charlotte Muravieff.' Kate went into the living room and picked up the phone. It rang four times before the machine picked up. 'Charlotte, this is Kate Shugak. I need to speak to you or Emily immediately. Call me at this number.'

She hung up and went back into the kitchen.

'You think your client sent Kurt to that cabin?' Jim said.

'If she did, I'll rip her a new bodily orifice,' Kate said.

There followed a brief silence. No one who knew Kate Shugak would take such a threat lightly. Jim waited long enough for the sizzle to die out of the air before he said, 'Do you suppose he found the body and wanted to show it to you before he called the cops?'

She took a deep breath and blew it out. 'No. He sounded happy, like he knew he'd found something I needed. Kurt's a lot of things, but morbid isn't one of them. And I found him in the living room, so I'm not even sure he made it to the bedroom before they shot him.' She drained the ribs of all the broth but for half a cup and put the pot back on the stove. She opened a can of cream of mushroom soup and added it to the meat. Seeing Jim watching her, she said, 'Secret Filipino ingredient.'

'I beg your pardon?'

'A friend in college was Filipino. This was a dish her father taught her to make. He told her never to tell what the secret Filipino ingredient was.'

He laughed, but not for long. 'Kate. Who do you think the dead man is?'

She sighed. 'Eugene Muravieff.'

He digested this in silence for a moment. 'Really.'

'I can't be sure. I haven't seen any pictures of him. But the dead man had a picture of the three Muravieff kids on a boat in what I think is Kachemak Bay. And he's the right age.'

'Did he have any ID?'

She nodded, breaking open the pea pods and tossing them in with the ribs. 'O'Leary said his name was Gene Salamantoff.'

'So, probably Aleut. And Eugene Muravieff was Aleut.' Jim frowned. 'I don't get it. Why'd he change his name?'

'Somebody shot him today, Jim. Who knows how long they'd been looking for him?'

The rice cooker clicked off and she found two trivets and set them on the table and the pots on the trivets. He found plates and silverware while she got the soy sauce out of the refrigerator. 'I've got some phony lemonade,' she said.

'Okay,' he said, and they sat down and dished up their dinner. 'Yum,' he said after the first bite.

'Yeah,' she said, and dug in.

He cleaned his plate twice before putting down his fork. 'Had rigor subsided?'

'No. He was cold and stiff. Lividity was pronounced. They shot him while he was sleeping.'

'Sometime last night or this morning, then.' Jim thought about that. 'If they shot – we'll call him Muravieff for the duration, okay? – if they shot Muravieff hours before, what were they doing hanging around till this afternoon?'

'Waiting for Kurt,' Kate said.

'Which means they felt that Kurt was as dangerous to them as the dead man was.'

'And me,' Kate said, and got up to clear the table. She put the leftovers in a Tupperware container to take to Kurt the following day.

His mouth tightened. 'And you,' he said evenly, and went into the living room to turn on the television news.

She was putting her clothes in the dryer when she heard him call her name. She went to the living room and poked her head in the door. 'What?'

He turned up the sound on the television with the remote.

'Charlotte Bannister Muravieff, well-known local caterer, was killed by a hit-and-run driver late last night as her car was struck by a large pickup truck on O'Malley Road. A witness told Channel Two News that–'

Jim looked at Kate, whose eyes were fixed on the screen. 'That's your client, right?'

She nodded dumbly.

The witness, a woman walking her Scottish terrier on the bike trail leading to the zoo before they both turned in for the night, had little to say beyond describing the hit-and-run vehicle as a pickup, dark in color. She thought it was a man at the wheel but she couldn't be sure– 'It's hard to tell the difference nowadays, you know?' The terrier, held in her arms, yipped accompaniment until the woman took firm hold of its muzzle.

Mutt, sitting next to Jim on the couch, got down and padded over to Kate to shove her head under Kate's hand.

Charlotte had been pronounced dead on arrival at the hospital. There was a brief shot of the Cadillac Escalade, crushed like an accordion from the driver's side door over, another of Emily, described as Charlotte's good friend, weeping on her way into their house, and then Erland Bannister's face flashed on the screen, looking tight and angry. The newscaster's voice did a voice-over that said Erland Bannister was offering a $100,000 cash reward for the arrest and conviction of the driver of the vehicle that had killed his niece.

This time, the guard at the Hiland Mountain front desk welcomed Kate with a smile. 'Brendan McCord says hey.' The guard was a willowy blonde, and from the inquisitive blue eyes busily inspecting Kate for flaws, she was evidently somewhere on Brendan's list.

Kate smiled. 'Tell him hey back next time you talk to him,' she said, insinuating that the guard would be talking to Brendan long before she would.

It was the right tack. The blonde relaxed, beamed, and waved her through.

Victoria was waiting in an interview room. She wasn't happy. 'Evidently I didn't make myself clear the last time you were here,' she told Kate as Kate came through the door. 'I have nothing to say to you.'

It wasn't visiting hours, and only Brendan's prior relationship with the willowy blonde had gotten Kate in the door and Victoria into the interview room.

Victoria was just as militant as she had been the first time Kate had seen her, and Kate realized with a sinking heart that no one had told Victoria that her daughter was dead. She wanted to turn and run from the room and keep running until she got all the way home. She wanted to hunt up Erland Bannister and kick him in the balls.

'May I?' she said instead, indicating the chair opposite Victoria.

Victoria snorted. 'You don't need my permission to sit in this place.' Nevertheless, the request softened her attitude a little.

Kate pulled out a chair and sat down, slumping

234

against the chair back, hooking a foot over the edge of the table, trying to present as relaxed an attitude as possible.

Her problem was, she liked Victoria. She liked a woman in jail for life who refused to be coerced or intimidated. 'Did they threaten you to get you in the same room with me?'

Victoria snorted again. 'Like you didn't know.'

'Humor me,' Kate said.

Victoria put both hands on the table and leaned in. 'They told me they'd cancel my class for a week.'

'I'm sorry,' Kate said, and she meant it.

'Sure you are. You're so sorry, you'll walk out of this interview under protest because I was brought into it under duress.'

Kate thought about it, shook her head ruefully. 'Not that sorry,' she said.

It surprised a laugh out of Victoria. She suppressed it immediately, looking annoyed. 'What do you want?' she snapped.

'Your daughter hired me to look into your case because you have been diagnosed with uterine cancer and she doesn't want you to die in jail,' Kate said.

'Oh, for heaven's sake.' Victoria tossed up her hands and rolled her eyes. Before she could throw Kate out again, Kate said quickly, 'You said you knew my grandmother.'

Victoria gave Kate an assessing look. She knew she was being distracted, but then she took the bait anyway. 'She died recently, didn't she?'

'Going on three years ago.'

Victoria nodded. 'She was a fine woman, and a

great leader.' She frowned, and then she said abruptly, 'She visited me here.'

'You were friends?'

Victoria thought about it. 'Acquaintances,' she said at last. 'We met through my mother-in-law, Mary Muravieff. Mary worked on the land claims act with Ekaterina. When I started the school here, Ekaterina heard of it and came to offer help. There are a disproportionately higher number of Alaska Natives in jail, as you know.'

'I know,' Kate said.

'That's right, you put some of them in here.'

'I did,' Kate said without apology.

'She was proud of you,' Victoria said. 'Proud of what you have accomplished. Which reminds me. What does the Anchorage DA have to do with reopening a thirty-year-old case?'

'Nothing,' Kate said, 'I don't work for them anymore.'

'What do you do?'

'I'm a private investigator,' Kate said, 'which is where I came in. Your daughter hired me to look into your case. She doesn't think you're guilty of the crime for which you have been imprisoned. She wants me to reopen the investigation and find out who did it.'

'I did do it,' Victoria said. She met Kate's eyes squarely.

'Did you?' Kate said, hiding her surprise.

'I did,' Victoria said firmly. 'I won't say I'm innocent, because I'm not. I won't thank you for trying to get me out of here, because the judge was right to sentence me to life. I deserved it. I siphoned the gas out of my car, I splashed it all over the living room, and I set it to go off after Charlotte and I were safely at the fund-raiser at my brother's house in town.'

'Hmmm,' Kate said. 'How did you set it to go off?'

'A delayed fuse attached to a timer,' Victoria said promptly.

Exactly as had been presented by the district attorney at Victoria's trial. 'How did you learn to do that?'

'From a book,' Victoria said.

Kate gave a thoughtful nod. 'You can find anything in the library, can't you?'

Victoria blinked. 'Well, yes, I suppose you can. That's what it's for.'

'It is indeed,' Kate said. 'Why did you do it?'

'Money,' Victoria said. 'I was broke.'

Kate winced and shook her head. 'You had me going there, Victoria, I admit. But money as a motive?' She leaned forward, hands flat on the table. 'To burn your sons alive?'

For the first time, she saw Victoria flinch. She recovered immediately, though, and met Kate's eyes with a stony gaze.

Kate sat back. 'Do you ever hear from your attorney?'

Victoria's brow furrowed at this change of subject. 'Henry?'

'Yes. Do you ever hear from him?'

Victoria was wary, but she couldn't come up with a reason not to answer. 'No.'

'When was the last time you talked to him?'

'At my sentencing.'

'No further contact after that?'

Victoria shook her head.

'How about your ex-husband?'

Victoria became very still. 'Gene?'

'Yes,' Kate said, watching Victoria from beneath her eyelashes.

'I haven't heard from Gene since our divorce.'

'Didn't he try to see the children?'

'He had no visitation rights under the divorce decree. I had sole custody.'

That wasn't what I asked you, Kate thought. 'He was their father,' she said. 'Seems odd that he wouldn't try to work something out with you so he could spend at least some time with his children.'

'He didn't,' Victoria said. Her elegant shoulders were looking very tense.

'Charlotte and Oliver were both underage when you went inside,' Kate said. 'Who did they go to?'

Victoria stared at a point on the wall in back of Kate's head. 'My brother Erland took them in. It wasn't for long. Charlotte was sixteen, Oliver was seventeen. They were in college and out of his house in a very short time.'

Kate nodded. 'I see.' She folded her hands on the table in front of her and took a deep breath. 'Ms. Muravieff–' She paused. 'You kept the name,' she said.

'What?'

'You kept your husband's name. Even after the divorce.'

Victoria's eyes narrowed, as if she were really looking at Kate for the first time. 'Why are you here, Ms. Shugak?' Despite her best efforts, something of what she was feeling must have crossed

Kate's face, because Victoria sat up straight in her chair. 'Tell me at once,' she said, snapping it out like an order.

'I'm afraid I have bad news, Ms. Muravieff,' Kate said. She took another breath and said steadily, 'Your daughter, Charlotte, was killed going home yesterday evening by a hit-and-run driver.'

Victoria sat very still, frozen in place. Kate couldn't even hear her breathing.

When she spoke, her voice was frail and thready. 'Yesterday? Charlotte's been dead all day today?'

'Yes. I'm so very sorry, Ms. Muravieff.'

Victoria spoke again through stiff lips. 'Leave me.'

Kate got up at once and left the room.

CHAPTER 14

Jim was waiting for her when she got back to the town house. 'My trial was continued until tomorrow,' he said the minute he saw her.

'Oh, save it,' she snapped, and stamped upstairs to take another long hot shower. She was turning into a ritual bather. Lucky she had her own bathroom to go back to. She wished more than ever that she could go back to it right now.

She had her face turned into the spray when she heard the shower curtain being drawn back. She didn't move, and she didn't jump either when his hands slid around her waist to draw her against him. By unspoken agreement, they took their time, drawing it out to a point way past pleasure, something that was almost pain, and when they were done, she let her head fall back against the tiles and laughed out loud for the sheer joy of it.

He mumbled something into her neck.

'What?' she said.

He raised his head, and she was moved almost to pity by the look of despair on his face. 'I don't understand how it can keep getting better.'

She laughed again, low in her throat. 'Don't you?' No one, not even Kate's best friends, had ever said she was a nice person, and she proved it now. She raised his hand to her face, nuzzled into his palm, and sank her teeth into the base of his thumb.

He swore, but he didn't pull his hand away. Instead, he picked her up and carried her into the bedroom, where he tossed her onto the bed and followed her down.

'I'm going to stay in town for a while,' he said later.

'Okay,' she said.

'Maybe I could hang out here.'

'Sure.'

'It's only until this case of yours is finished.'

'Of course.'

'I mean, somebody just took out your client.'

Kate willed away the remembered fury, the images of Kurt on the floor and Eugene with the bullet hole in his head, the footage of Charlotte's crumpled car, the tears on Emily's face, Victoria's stricken expression. Not now, she told herself. Not now.

'Stands to reason whoever did it might think you know something you shouldn't.'

'They might.'

'Seems to me they might think twice about trying something if you had a trooper hanging around.'

'You're probably right.'

'And there's nothing really pressing back at the post, and Tok and Cordova have promised to cover for me if something happens.'

'Good to know.'

'And I might be recalled to the stand tomorrow.'

'You might.'

There was a brief silence. 'Oh fuck,' he said.

'Don't mind if I do,' she said, and rolled over on top of him.

'I don't want to talk to anyone.' Emily stood in the open doorway with a tear-blotched face, arms crossed, hugging herself tightly. Every line in her brow looked deeper, her eyes seemed sunken, and her hair lay lank and lifeless upon her head.

'Is anyone else here?'

Emily shook her head miserably, and Kate shoved her way in, closing the door behind her, Jim barely making it inside. She took Emily in a firm, impersonal grip and steered her into the living room. Emily sat on the couch and stared in front of her with unseeing eyes. Kate found the kitchen and made hot, sweet tea. She took it into the living room and pressed the mug into Emily's hands. 'Drink.'

'I don't want it,' Emily said.

'Drink,' Kate said firmly.

It took half an hour, another cup of tea, and a box of Kleenex to get Emily to where she could speak in more or less coherent sentences. Kate was unfailingly kind and patient, never at a loss for what word was needed next. Jim, observing from a neutral corner, was reminded of a rock battered by waves of emotion and incipient hysteria, only to emerge each time from the sea spray with the same unshakable face. Kate Shugak was the only person he'd ever met able to combine the qualities of the irresistible force and the immovable object at once. It was only a matter of time.

Evidently, Emily came to realize that, too. Lying back against the couch, she closed her eyes and said in an exhausted voice, 'What do you want?'

'Why weren't you in the car with her on the way home from the party?' Kate said.

A tear slid down Emily's cheek, but only one this time. 'I drove to Erland's from work. Charlotte had to haul the food to Erland's house, and she had to be there early to set things up.'

Kate suffered a slight feeling of déjà vu, remembering where Victoria and Charlotte had been the night William had been killed. Bad things had a habit of happening when the Bannister women were away from home, and in particular when they were helping host parties at their male relative's house.

Still, two similar occurrences thirty-one years apart didn't necessarily constitute a pattern. 'Were you behind her on the road?' Kate said.

Emily shook her head miserably. 'Ahead. I left

242

right after you did. There's only so much of that crap I can take.'

'Then why do you go?'

'Because Charlotte wants me there. Wanted.' Another tear. 'She hates all that glad-handing stuff. She isn't a public person. Wasn't.'

'Were you home yesterday?'

'What?'

'Did you stay home yesterday, or did you go into work?'

Emily, uncomprehending, said, 'I stayed home, I – I couldn't go to work.'

'Did a man come to see you?'

Emily gave a convulsive sniff. 'All kinds of men. Policemen, mostly. Knocking, knocking at the door, they wouldn't leave me alone. They kept asking questions about Charlotte, and her mother, and her father, and I just didn't see what that had to do with anything, I just couldn't, I – oh God, oh God, I can't believe she's dead.' Emily buried her face in her hands and began to rock back and forth. 'Charlotte, oh God, Charlotte.'

'Emily.' Kate grasped her hands and pulled them from her face. 'Is there someone I can call? Someone who can come and stay with you?'

Kate couldn't stand the thought of leaving her there all alone. Emily kept shaking her head – at the thought of her loss or the thought of enduring companionship, Kate couldn't tell. She looked for and found a desk, located an address book inside the top drawer, and started calling numbers. Twenty minutes later, two women showed up, so alike they were almost twins, stocky, short, cropped gray hair and piercing blue eyes.

'You Shugak?' the first one said, and walked inside without waiting for an answer. 'I'm Becky. This is Lael.'

'Hi,' Kate said.

'Where is she?'

'In the living room. She's pretty shook.'

'I don't blame her,' Becky said gruffly. 'I'd hate to think how I'd react if Lael—' And here the two women exchanged such an unexpected and naked look of emotion that Kate felt like she was intruding on something very private, and she averted her eyes.

'I tried calling her aunt and uncle,' Kate said, 'but they aren't picking up.'

'Hah!' Becky said.

'I left a message,' Kate said.

'Hah!' Becky said again.

'Oh, Becky!' Emily said from behind Kate, and rushed forward to be enfolded in an all-encompassing embrace. 'Charlotte's gone! Charlotte, oh my God, Charlotte!'

'It's okay,' Becky said, patting Emily's back soothingly. 'It's okay, Emily, Lael and I are here now. We'll take care of you.'

Lael was already producing a bottle of pills from the day pack she was carrying. 'A sedative,' she explained to Kate in a soft voice.

'You a doctor?' Kate said.

Lael nodded.

'Did you hear how Charlotte died?'

Lael's lips tightened. 'Charlotte Bannister was a good friend of mine, Ms. Shugak.'

'And she was my client, and she's just been

killed in what could be considered suspicious circumstances.'

Lael's eyes widened. 'I thought it was a hit-and-run.'

'It was.' Kate glanced over her shoulder at Becky and Emily and lowered her voice. 'Look, I can't say anymore right now, but just keep the doors and windows locked, okay? And here's my number, if you need me for anything.'

'What are you doing here anyway?'

'Charlotte hired me to get her mother out of jail,' Kate said baldly.

Jim, still sequestered in his neutral corner, noticed that discretion had just suffered a hit. Kate's favorite weapon had always been the bludgeon, and she would regard Charlotte's death as a personal affront that had to be avenged. He felt a spark of sympathy, albeit a very tiny spark, for the perp. Like Kate, like any cop worthy of the name, he didn't think much of coincidences. He was still pretty sure Victoria had committed the crime of which she had been found guilty, but he was equally certain that Kate, in ferreting around after the circumstances of that crime, had stirred up something nasty associated with that crime that had lain dormant for thirty-one years. There was nothing worse than that kind of nasty. Old nasty had a tendency to ripen. Left alone, it would eventually rot away. Exposed to the bright light of day before that happened, the stench rolled out and over everyone in sight. Considering the wealth and power connected with this case, the smell could reach all the way to Juneau and maybe even Washington, D.C.

Lael was quick. 'And you think that might have something to do with Charlotte being killed?' she asked Kate.

'I don't know. But I think it's interesting that she was killed right after she hired me to start investigating a thirty-one-year-old murder case.'

In the car on the way down O'Malley, Jim said, 'You're taking the gloves off.'

She spared him a brief glance. 'One. I hire Kurt Pletnikoff to do some legwork for me. Two, he finds a dead man – I'm guessing someone connected to this case. Three, he is shot and left for dead himself. Four, somebody tries to take me out. Five, my employer is killed.' She pulled to the side of the road, provoking an indignant honk from the Chevy Suburban that had been riding their bumper all the way down the mountain. 'And notice I'm not even mentioning the attempt to buy me off with the Niniltna VPSO job.'

He looked around. 'What are we doing? Kate, you parked right on the bike trail.'

She pointed at a shred of crime-scene tape tied to a tree branch. 'This is where Charlotte got hit.'

A narrow dirt road intersected O'Malley at right angles. The trees grew in close and closed in overhead to form a canopy. Kate walked down it, Jim pacing behind. At intervals, houses were visible through the trees, but there was a good hundred feet before the first driveway. Kate turned around and paced back, looking down. She stopped and squatted. 'Look,' she said, pointing.

Jim squatted next to her, scrutinizing the dirt track. There were tire tracks from a big vehicle, and a dark patch where the engine had leaked oil. 'Somebody was parked here.'

Kate nodded. 'Waiting.'

'And then started fast, spinning the tires, kicking dirt.'

'A big black pickup.' Kate rose to her feet and walked out to the intersection. It was 10:30, the sun well up in the sky, beating down on the backs of their heads as they looked west. 'See the way the road rises just before it gets here?'

Jim nodded. 'Yeah. Charlotte wouldn't have seen them coming until the last minute.'

'The question is, how did they know when to hit the gas?'

A brief silence. 'There were two of them,' Jim said finally. 'Jesus Christ. There were two of them, with walkie-talkies or cell phones. The one down the road called the one parked in the lane, waiting until Charlotte was about to come over the rise, and told the guy in the truck when to go.'

Kate nodded. 'Yeah.' She walked back to the Subaru and pulled her own cell phone from her day pack. Jim's jaw dropped about six inches. She ignored him and called Brendan McCord.

She dropped Jim at the state courthouse. He sat in the car for a moment. 'Two people, connected to the case you're working on, both dead within a day of each other,' he said.

'I know,' she said a little grimly. 'I'm glad I didn't bring Johnny in with me.'

'Kate,' he said, and caught her chin in one hand and pulled her face around so she had to look at him. 'It occurs to me that you could be in some danger.'

She let a slow smile spread across her face, and instead of pulling away like any normal Kate Shugak would have done, she leaned into his grip and purred, her lips touching his as they moved. 'Were you thinking I'd need my very own personal bodyguard?'

'Ah shit,' he said, and kissed her hard. 'Take care of yourself, damn it.' He opened the door and something – he didn't know what – stopped him half in and half out of the car. Over his shoulder he said gruffly, 'I should be out of here before five. You want to meet somewhere for dinner?'

She spent two hours going back over the case file, reexamining the record of the chain of events, the eyewitness testimony, the physical evidence. She reread the trial transcript, resetting her internal bullshit monitor up a notch to filter out all the extraneous information that was a part of every criminal trial (e.g., Q: 'Where were you at 8:00 P.M. the evening of the twelfth, Miss Doe?' A: 'Well, I was having dinner with my friends right after work – you know Sally is going through a really rough time with her boyfriend and Margie said we should show our support by giving her a good time – and boy I can tell you the margaritas at La Mex are the way to go, and anyway I didn't get home until 7:00 P.M. and my mother called the minute I walked in the door, and she and Dad are thinking about retiring to Flagstaff next year and they wanted to know what I thought of the area and how often I could get down there, and when she finally hung up,

Carrie – that's my dog, named for the girl on *Sex and the City*, you know? – anyway Carrie really had to go, so I took her for a walk, and then I ran into Paul, the hunk who lives two doors down, and we were talking, and gosh, "Kate could just imagine the adorable giggle" – I guess I was talking to Paul about then. We kind of, you know, hit it off?').

Unfortunately, none of the facts had changed since the last time Kate had visited them. Victoria was the one who had called in the fire, and, according to the statements of the firefighters, she was found sitting outside the burning house, crying and clutching fifteen-year-old Charlotte. Cowell had dabbled with the notion that the older, deceased brother, William, had set the fire to try to kill Oliver, the younger brother, motive determined to be an unnamed schoolgirl they were both in love with, which sounded like such a ludicrous stretch that even the judge had made fun of him. Of course, Cowell had also, in the best tradition of defense attorneys, speculated on the motives of everyone involved, up to and including the firefighters.

Only Victoria had any motive that could be supported by evidence however circumstantial. And only Victoria had not spoken in her own defense.

Why not?

'What?' Victoria said. 'You're afraid you won't be paid?'

Kate looked at the proud chin, which was trembling a little now, and forbore to answer in kind. 'I'm so sorry,' she said again.

Victoria was sitting in her usual fashion, straight-backed, head up, fixing Kate with a fierce, fearless eye. Kate felt that same reluctant admiration that she had before, but she needed answers and she needed them now. 'I've been doing some research, Ms. Muravieff. Thirty-two years ago, your father laid off over a thousand Bannister employees and replaced them with contract hires. A company isn't required to pay the same benefits to a contract employee as a union employee – health benefits, a retirement plan, workman's comp, things like that. What's more, he did it in the middle of the construction of the TransAlaska Pipeline, the biggest cost-plus contract in the history of this planet, when union members had the pipeline consortium by the short hairs and twisted them to their heart's content. Teamsters rioted at Isabel Pass when they were refused steak for lunch, seven-ninety-eighters refused to share living space with other unions, and electricians walked thirty at a time when the plumbers got Sundays off with pay and they didn't. Average union wage with overtime was something like twelve hundred dollars a week, back when twelve hundred dollars a week was real money. They were pretty much sitting up and begging to be slapped down, and your father was the first one to do so. He was hailed as a hero by every corporate owner in the state, and his action was a snowball that started a landslide, leading to the beginning of privatization of state services.'

Kate paused. Victoria's breath was coming a little faster, but her expression was graven in stone. 'You were quoted in the press as being adamantly opposed to that action. You marched with the employees. There are pictures of you holding a sign that read 'People Before Profits.' You excoriated your father in the newspapers, on radio and television, all over the state. You even made it to the Washington state papers, and I found at least one op-ed piece in the *Wall Street Journal.* They hammered you, but consider the source.'

Jolted out of her grief, Victoria said involuntarily, 'You've done your homework.'

'It's what I do,' Kate said, who was still nauseated from yet another dose of microfiche. 'Did your action against your father have something to do with the fire at your home and the death of your son?'

'No,' Victoria said. She sounded very calm, a little too calm.

'He was probably at that fundraiser you and Charlotte went to that evening. He probably knew you would be there. Maybe he didn't mean to kill anyone. Maybe it was just supposed to be a warning to you, to shut you up, to stop you organizing the peons, so he could continue to rip off the average Alaskan Joe in the best tradition of robber barons since J. P. Morgan. It's not like it's a new story in American history, after all. At least your father spent what he ripped off right here in the state, instead of retiring Outside to spend it all in Palm Springs.'

'No,' Victoria said, refusing the carrot. She wouldn't implicate her father even if it meant exonerating herself.

Kate tried very hard not to lose her temper. For one thing, it wasn't fair. Kate could walk away, Victoria couldn't. For another, it was usually unproductive of anything except fear in her target. Although Victoria did not look noticeably fearful. 'Look, Ms. Muravieff,' Kate said tightly, 'it's obvious that the death of your daughter Tuesday night is connected in some way to the death of your son William thirty-one years ago.'

'I don't see why,' Victoria said with flinty composure.

'Come now,' Kate said a little impatiently. 'I show up and start asking questions about a thirty-one-year-old homicide, moreover a closed case, a case for which someone has been convicted and imprisoned, and suddenly people related to the case start dying, including the one who hired me to ask the questions. Seems like, gosh, cause and effect.'

'I don't know what you want from me,' Victoria said, and waved a hand at her surroundings. 'It's not like I could have seen anything. I don't get out much, you know.'

'There has been another death,' Kate said, and placed on the table in front of Victoria the head shot O'Leary had given her. 'Someone killed him hours before my associate had a chance to ask him any questions, and then tried to kill my associate, as well.'

She watched Victoria, but the woman had herself well in hand. She raised her eyes to look at Kate. 'I don't know who that is,' she said in a voice like flint, but Kate heard the quaver beneath.

'Ms. Muravieff–'

'I don't know him,' Victoria repeated in a stronger voice. 'If that's all, Ms. Shugak, I have work to do.'

CHAPTER 15

Kate left Hiland Mountain ready to wash her hands of the whole damn Bannister clan.

Instead, she went to the Pioneer Home to talk to Max.

He was getting beaten at checkers by a wizened old man who cackled like a hen every time he made a double jump, and he was cackling pretty much nonstop when Kate marched up. Max greeted her with evident relief. 'Shugak!' he said. 'My girlfriend,' he explained to his opponent.

'I need to talk to you,' Kate said.

'I thought I might be seeing you.'

'You catch the news last night?'

'Don't sleep much anymore,' he said. Max noted the militant gleam in her eye, the stubborn set of her jaw, and the way her shoulders somehow resembled a battering ram. 'About time for lunch, ain't it?' he said.

She took him back to Club Paris. The staff recognized him (and Kate, who had left a very nice tip behind last time) and upon request, the maître d' seated them in the very last booth. They'd get a lot of action from the kitchen but wouldn't be seen by the other diners.

'Is this a three-martini luncheon?' Max said, settling in for the duration with a look of anticipation on his wrinkled face.

'If I drank, it would be a five-martini lunch,' Kate said, 'but I'm in kind of a hurry, Max.'

'Like that, eh?' he said, and ordered a double, 'and keep a watch, darlin', 'cause when the glass is empty, I'd like another ready to go at my elbow, okay?'

The waitress, smiling, promised to keep an eye, and when they were served, she vanished discreetly. Max took a long, continuous swallow and put the glass down with a loud smack of his lips. 'That's the stuff,' he said, and gave her a long, considering look. 'You don't drink?'

Kate shook her head.

'Recovering?'

She shook her head again.

He nodded. 'Opposed to firewater on general principles, then. You're missing out.'

Kate, who would have made all the alcohol in the world disappear with the snap of her fingers if it were in her power, said, 'I don't think so. I need your help, Max. I've got two people dead and one person wounded and I don't know what the hell is going on.'

He settled into his seat like a race car driver waiting for the flag. 'Tell me all about it, Kate my girl.'

She took a deep breath and then laid it all out, in order – the sequence of events that had begun when she drove into the clearing in front of her house and found Charlotte Muravieff waiting for her.

Max grunted. 'Who's the guy in the hospital again?'

'Kurt Pletnikoff. I hired him to look for Eugene Muravieff and Henry Cowell.'

'Did he find them?'

'He called me and told me to meet him at this cabin at Jewel Lake. I went there and two men started shooting at me. They'd already shot Kurt in the chest, and another man in the head, probably earlier that morning. I found this in the dead man's bedroom.' She produced the photo of the three kids.

Max got out a pair of reading glasses and perched them on the tip of his beaky nose. 'That would be William, Oliver, and Charlotte Bannister when they were kids, be my guess.'

She produced the head shot of the dead man.

'Eugene Muravieff,' Max said immediately.

'Victoria says she doesn't know him.'

Max's eyebrows went up. 'Doesn't know the father of her three children, does she? Interesting.'

'And now Charlotte's dead, too.'

'Yeah.' He cocked an eyebrow. 'Does that mean you're off the case?'

Kate's jaw became very much in evidence.

'I didn't think so,' he said, without his usual sparkle.

'What?' she said.

He sighed. 'Ah hell, maybe I'm getting old. I'm thinking they've already killed twice, attempted to kill twice more. Pursuing this could be hazardous to your health.'

'Not to mention the people working for me.'

'He over twenty-one?'

'What?'

'This Kurt guy. He over twenty-one?'

'He's in his thirties, what's that got to do with anything?'

She snapped out the words, and Max didn't bother hiding a grin. 'It's got to do with him being a grown man, and you not being his mom.'

She shrugged, uncomfortable.

'You didn't kill Charlotte, either,' he added, 'just in case you were feeling all-omnipotent over there. Any identification in the cabin with the dead guy?'

'There was a wallet with twenty bucks and change in it, along with a driver's license that identified him as Gene Salamantoff.'

'Salamantoff are shirttail relatives of the Mura-vieffs, as I recall. Be easy to get one of them to share his social security number for a fake license.' The waitress twitched by, and since she was a kind young woman, she put a little extra into it when she saw Max watching. He gave a sigh of pure appreciation. 'Nowadays, legs on a woman are just basic transportation, you know? Used to be a plea-sure watching them walk. Used to be they took care of their butts and walking was an art form. Now it's just a butt in a bag and they could care less how they sling it around. But that girl, I'm happy to say, is an exception.'

Kate looked at him.

With some asperity, Max said 'Well, pardon me all to hell for expressing an appreciation for one of the finer things in life.'

Kate rubbed her forehead. 'Could we just concentrate for a minute here, Max? I've two dead and one injured, and it all seems to be related to an arson murder that happened thirty-one years ago.'

'Victoria did it,' Max said.

'She might have killed her son,' Kate said, 'but her alibi for her daughter and her ex is kind of solid. Look, could we–'

'What?'

'For the sake of argument, could we imagine for a moment that Victoria didn't do it? And that if she didn't, who had the next best motive?'

She watched him take a mouthful of martini and swirl it around. The man had to have a cast-iron stomach, not to mention a worm in his gut that sucked up all the alcohol he downed and got drunk for him. She waited, patient and not entirely without hope.

In her experience, retired cops were less cynical than cops on the job because people hadn't been lying to them on a daily basis lately and they were once again willing to allow doubt into their lives. If she could get Max to speculate, maybe it would open up a line or two she could follow.

In the meantime, Max had made a decision. 'Okay,' Max said, 'maybe it wasn't meant to be murder. Maybe it was only meant to be a warning.'

'To Victoria?'

'Maybe. Maybe to Erland, or the old man. Did you see the old man at that party you went to?'

'The old man? You mean Jasper, Erland's and Victoria's father? I thought he was dead.'

'Not yet, although he must be even older than

257

me by now.'

'No, I didn't see him. Why?'

The stubble on Max's chin rasped beneath his fingers. 'Jasper had him a reputation. You ever hear the story about Richie Constantine?'

Kate shook her head.

'Before your time. You know about Jasper's wife, Erland's and Victoria's mother.' Kate shook her head, and Max snorted. 'They teaching you newbies anything these days? Jasper had a mistress. Her name was Ruby Jo, Ruby Jo Lawson. Rumor had it she was working the back rooms at the Mustang Club when they met, and he took her out of there and set her up in her own little house in Spenard, where he visited regularly. About that same time, another local businessman, Calvin Esterhaus, was going up against Jasper in some financial deal or other, had to do with oil leases somewheres, or that was the rumor. He told Jasper to back off, Jasper wouldn't, and Calvin hired Richie Constantine to make Jasper see the light.

'Richie Constantine was a small-time thug who had the single virtue of loyalty. Some people say he had some kind of a thing with Calvin.' Max shrugged and looked uncomfortable. 'I wouldn't know. Alls I know is that Calvin was one of the sicker sons a bitches to walk the streets of any town, anywhere, and Anchorage was unlucky enough for him to call it home. Richie was his button man, his bag man, his enforcer, you name it. Calvin said jump and Richie said how high.

'Calvin told him to put a scare into Jasper, and Richie watched and waited until Jasper was away

258

from home, and he went inside and raped and killed Ruby Jo.'

Max brooded for a bit. 'We knew right away, of course. We arrested Richie within twenty-four hours. We even had ourselves something of a case – physical evidence linking him to the scene, not a half-bad description from an eyewitness, who even picked his photo out of a book of head shots.' He looked at Kate. 'So we let him go.'

Kate stared at him. 'What?'

'We let him go,' Max repeated, and waved over another martini. When it came and Max had appreciated the waitress's walk enough, he said, 'It was a different time, Kate. The word came down to turn Richie loose.' He smiled, and it wasn't a nice smile. 'He didn't want to go. At one point, we had to pry his hands loose of the bars. But we tossed him out on his ear.'

Kate was beginning to understand. 'When did you find him?'

'We didn't.' He paused, enjoying Kate's expression for a moment. 'We found Calvin, though. Next morning, floating facedown in McHugh Creek. His dick was cut off and stuffed in his mouth.'

'Jesus,' she said.

Max nodded. 'Yeah.'

'And Richie?'

'Richie?' Max's mouth twisted up at one corner. 'Richie was next found on the payroll of Jasper Bannister.'

'Tell me you're kidding.'

Max shook his head. 'Oh no. Jasper appreciated loyalty and efficiency in an employee, especially when he needed somebody to get at those hard-to-reach areas.' Max paused, clearly enjoying the expression on Kate's face, and added, 'Of course, there was that whole disappearing thing Richie did during the pipeline days – oh, say a year before oil in. Richie just flat disappeared. You know that rumor that kept floating around, about somebody finding a body in the pipeline when they walked the first pig in front of the oil from Prudhoe to Valdez? I always thought that must have been Richie.'

In spite of herself, Kate couldn't repress a shiver. Seeing it, Max nodded. 'Calvin was an amateur compared to Jasper.' He saw her expression. 'What?'

'I had a case this summer. A guy got killed in the Park. Turned out he was a baby raper, on the run from the law. We had the hell of time identifying him. He didn't have a driver's license or a pilot's license or a fishing license or a hunting license. He didn't have a social security number. There was a screwup with the fingerprints, and we didn't know until way late in the game that he'd done time, let alone been in the army. Hell, he never even applied for a permanent fund dividend check. By then, I knew we had a vic who didn't want to be found. I never did know who he didn't want to be found by.'

'So?'

She met his eyes and said softly, 'One of his victims was a Bannister girl.'

Max pursed his lips in a soundless whistle. 'Yeah,' he said finally, 'I'd have run, too.'

Kate digested all this new information for a

moment. 'Like father like son, you think?'

'Erland?' It was Max's turn to think. 'I don't know. I never heard so, but I never heard different, either.'

'He could be riding on his father's reputation.'

'It would be enough for a while,' Max said, 'but not forever. Sooner or later, he'd have to make his own bones.' He drained his glass. 'You said Victoria was fighting with him and her father back then, in public, something to do with the family business.'

'They were laying off union employees and replacing them with contract hires. Victoria thought that sucked and said so, right out in front of God and everybody.'

'Reason enough to get you killed, in Jasper's book,' Max said.

'But his own grandson?'

Max looked exasperated. 'Are you deaf, girl? Have you been listening at all to what I been telling you?' He fixed Kate with a stern look. 'Two things. One, Victoria could have threatened to expose whatever shenanigans were going on over to the family firm, and her house could have been burned down as a warning, and the boy's death would've been collateral damage. After all, Victoria and Charlotte were gone, the arsonist could have thought the house was empty.'

Kate nodded.

'Two, the arson could have been either an attempt on or a warning to Eugene, not Victoria. He might have been gone, but his kids were still living there, weren't they?'

Kate's mouth opened and closed once or twice.

Max regarded her, not without satisfaction. 'Didn't think of that, did you now, missie?'

Kate rubbed her forehead. 'Fuck,' she said, and saw Max wince. Like he said, he came from another time, when women didn't use those words. 'Sorry, Max,' she said, and then she swore again. 'Sorry, Max, I almost forgot,' she said, pulling out the photograph of the young woman she'd found in Eugene Muravieff's cabin. 'Do you know who this is?'

Max picked up the photo and smacked his lips. 'Oh my yes,' he said, 'I surely do. There wasn't a red-blooded all-American boy in Anchorage at that time who didn't. Talk about a honey pot. Mmmm, mmmm.'

'Does the honey pot have a name?' Kate said.

'Sure,' Max said. 'Wanda Gajewski.'

'Wanda Gajewski,' Kate said. She took the picture back and looked at it. 'Wanda Gajewski, Ernie Gajewski's sister?'

'That's the one. She went to high school with Victoria's kids. Was a classmate of William's, I think.'

'Okay,' Kate said, 'what we have here in police-speak is a clue. Ernie Gajewski is the guy who bought Eugene Muravieff's set-net permit.'

'Really,' Max said. 'That's interesting.'

'Why?'

'Because Ernie Gajewski drowned off Augustine Island when he was just a boy, swimming from the shore to his dad's seiner.'

Kate stared at him. After a moment, she said, 'And this case just keeps on getting more and more fun. Why would Eugene have a picture of

262

Wanda, his oldest son's teenage classmate?'

Max drained his martini with the air of a man who knew that was all he was going to get, and grinned his evil grin at the woman sitting across from him. 'Because Wanda Gajewski was the straw that broke the camel's back. She was the reason Victoria divorced Eugene.'

Kate called Brendan and in five minutes had an address to go with Wanda's name. 'She's got a phone number,' Brendan told her, 'but it's unlisted.' He gave her that, too. 'Anything you want to tell me, Kate?'

'I'm wading through a pit of snakes and they all bite.'

'Okay, not loving the visual,' Brendan said.

'Not loving the reality, either,' Kate said, and hung up.

Wanda's house was in Windermere, the split-level four-bedroom, two-bathroom floor plan so dear to the hearts of developers during the sixties and seventies. Kate pulled into the driveway and knocked on the door. No answer.

She went next door, same floor plan, different paint job. No answer. Same thing with the house on the other side. It was a sad day when the women had to go to work outside the home and not be there when Kate needed answers to questions.

She went across the street to a third house, this one with the biggest Winnebago Kate had ever seen parked in the driveway, and struck gold. The door opened at the first knock. A plump woman with thick white hair cut short stood there, dressed in brightly flowered polyester trimmed with plaid braid in rainbow hues. Kate blinked involuntarily, and the woman chuckled. 'Pretty, aren't I? "Dayglo Diane," that's what my friends call me. But we need something to brighten up these long, dreary arctic winters, don't you think?'

It was only August, but Dayglo Diane wasn't really wanting an answer. 'Come in, come in,' she said, sweeping Kate irresistibly inside, 'you, too, little doggy,' and she patted Mutt on the head. Mutt didn't quite know how to take that and looked at Kate with a quizzical eye.

'I saw you knocking at Wanda's house. Are you looking for her? She's probably at work you know. Would you like some iced tea? I always think there's nothing like iced tea on a hot day, with lashings of lemon and of course simply packed with ice, don't you?'

Kate found herself ensconced on a wide couch in front of an entertainment center bristling with electronics. There were four remotes on the coffee table. Where was Bobby Clark when she needed him? Mutt was sitting next to her, one ear cocked toward the kitchen, as if to say, She's still in there. There's still time to get out of here.

But then their hostess bustled in, carrying a large and extremely well-laden tray and set it down on the coffee table. 'Sugar? No? Not even phony sugar? Imagine that. Here's a nice biscuit for you, doggy.' Mutt took the treat gingerly in her teeth, lips drawn back as far as they would go so as not to be contaminated. A snack for Mutt meant something with fur or feathers, something usually going in the opposite direction as fast as possible, something requiring pursuit. Except for Bernie's beef jerky, Mutt didn't hold with processed pasteurized anything, especially if it contained the hair and bones and hooves of any animal she had not caught and killed herself. She probably wanted Kate's case solved even more than Kate did, because when it was solved, they could both head back to the Park, where nobody yelled at you for chasing the geese or harassing the moose. She held the biscuit in her teeth, looking pained, until Kate took pity and told her hostess, who had yet to introduce herself by her full name, that Mutt was allergic to dog biscuits.

'Oh my, how simply dreadful, I've never heard of such a thing, well, what can I get her, let me just–'

'She's fine,' Kate said, staying her hostess with one hand on her arm. 'I–'

'–get you some cookies, I just got back from driving the Alcan up from Grand Junction, that's in Colorado you know, and whenever I come through Canada I lay in supplies, you know you can't get Dare cookies in this country and they are just the absolute best cookies there are, try one of these Maple Leafs, you're just going to love them–'

'–was wondering–'

'–and then of course I have to lay in a supply of two-two-two's – you know those marvelous aspirin they have there that that silly old FDA won't let us have in this country, the Canadians are so much saner about drugs than we are, I've thought about immigrating, really I have, did you know that the Yukon is actively soliciting immigrants, I've half a mind to fill out an application, the reason I know about this I came back by way of Dawson City and there were advertisements in all the papers asking for qualified people to become Canadians, and I'm sure I'd qualify, after all Mr. Hockness left me quite well off, dear man, and of course I came home by way of the Top of the World Highway, have you ever driven that road my dear, well you ought to. There is nothing between you and the sky–'

'–if you know–'

'–and though you wouldn't think to look at it my Winnebago can handle some pretty rough road, so we just turned right at the Y and went up to Eagle, what a charming little town, if you've never been you should really go, although I couldn't believe it when I saw the Holland America bus in front of me, my dear, the road, there are places when I swear if you went off it you'd fall five hundred feet before you fell into the Fortymile River–'

'–Wanda Gajewski,' Kate said loudly, because it seemed the only way to be heard.

'Of course I know Wanda, dear, I told you, I saw you knocking on Wanda's door, and then of course I saw you knocking on Genevieve's door and then Margaret's door but of course they both work during the day, all three of them do, they're never home hardly ever at night either, sometimes I wonder why they own houses at all, but Margaret owns her own flower shop and makes a good living from it, too, and you'll never guess but Genevieve is a police officer, can you imagine, how adventurous of her! And Wanda certainly is old enough to retire why she's as old as I am, although you'd never know it to look at her, she's been dyeing her hair for the last thirty years, even if she stopped dating after the trial although I must say she's kept her figure marvelously well–'

'After the trial,' Kate, desperate and her mouth full of Dare Maple Leaf Cream, said thickly. 'After the trial, she stopped dyeing her hair?'

'Oh, you know about the trial, my, what a dreadful thing, Wanda's parents were good friends of mine and they were so mortified, all those reporters all over the place and people taking your picture' – the sparkle in her hostess's eye told Kate that she hadn't minded the attention – 'of course they all wanted to know all about Wanda and I couldn't lie, could I, no, certainly not, I was raised to tell the strict truth or my mother would know the reason why and my father would get out the belt, ours was a very traditional home, my dear, you look Native, are you Native, you must be with that beautiful black hair, it just shines like coal in the sun, it was the first thing I noticed when I looked out the window and saw you on Wanda's doorstep, but why don't you let it grow, dearie, her hair is a woman's crowning glory you know, it used to be we'd keep it up during the day and then let it down at night when only our husbands would see it, that's the way it should be but you young girls nowadays have your own ideas about things and I suppose–'

'Wanda has a job?' Kate said. It was rude, but there really wasn't any other choice. She wasn't eating any more cookies, either, she didn't care if this woman stocked every one that Dare made.

'Of course she does, and a good one, too, with

267

the state, you know, down at the new courthouse, in fact I think she might be clerking for a judge now, if I understood her – wait, where are you going, but you haven't finished your tea!'

Wanda Gajewski was sitting behind a large desk in a plush foyer. 'Yes?' she said pleasantly when Kate came in.

'Wanda Gajewski?' Kate said.

'Yes. May I help you?'

'My name is Kate Shugak. I'm a private investigator, hired by Charlotte Muravieff to look into the death of her brother William.'

'But he was–'

'Killed thirty-one years ago,' Kate said, 'yes, I know.'

'And Charlotte is dead; she was killed by a hit-and-run driver–'

'Day before yesterday, yes, I know that, too.'

'And Charlotte's mother was convicted of setting the fire that killed her son,' Wanda said, her fine-skinned broad brow wrinkled.

Dayglo Diane was right, Wanda Gajewski had kept her figure marvelously well. Kate now understood completely the reverence in Max's tone when he'd spoken of her. Her spectacular breasts were displayed to advantage in a blue twin-sweater set, and her equally spectacular long legs in a pencil-slim black calf-length skirt. Their length was enhanced by the three-inch heels she wore. It made Kate's feet hurt just to look at them.

Her hair was a rich chestnut brown, which set off her pale skin. Her eyes were large and thickly lashed and carefully made up. Pearl studs in her ears matched the string of pearls around her neck. She looked like Coco Chanel must have looked on a very good day. She reminded Kate of every Doris Day movie Kate had ever seen, with or without Rock Hudson, back before everyone knew Hudson was gay.

She was enough of a knockout now. In her teens, she must have been breathtaking.

'Yes,' Kate said, 'Victoria was convicted of the crime. But Charlotte didn't think her mother did it, and she hired me to find out who did. I was doing a little research at the library, and I came across your name.'

'How did you find out where I worked?'

'Your neighbor told me you worked at the state courthouse.'

'Margaret?'

Kate shook her head. 'A woman across the street.'

'Dayglo Diane,' Wanda said with a wry smile. 'She's the only one of us home at this time of day.'

'She is colorful,' Kate said, matching Wanda's smile. 'Look, it's almost five. Could I buy you a cup of coffee, and ask you some questions? I'll try not to take up too much of your time.'

Wanda was silent for a moment.

'Please,' Kate said.

Wanda said finally, 'I suppose anyone who runs the Dayglo Diane gauntlet and survives deserves a hearing.' There was a smile in her eyes that had Kate revising the 'bimbo' label she had had ready to stick on Eugene Muravieff's mistress's file.

Kate got Mutt and they walked down past the old federal building, bought coffee from M.A., and sat on the grass. The tourists, mostly retired people bundling up against the sixty-two-degree temperature in jackets, hats, and thick socks, grazed through the carts hawking T-shirts silk-screened with the legend UNLESS YOU'RE THE LEAD DOG, THE VIEW NEVER CHANGES, tiny seals carved from ivory, and necklaces made of strands of small round garnets so hard-polished, they looked almost black. They mingled with workers from downtown offices dressed in suits and ties, many of them pausing for a moment to turn their faces up to the sun, eyes closed, determined to catch every last ray because they knew the first snow could be less than a month away.

Echoing Kate's thoughts, Wanda said, 'I wonder how many of these we have left?'

'Feels good,' Kate said, closing her own eyes briefly. Mutt, lying on the grass next to her, pulled her head back in an enormous yawn. Kate heard a clicking sound and looked up to see a woman dressed in navy polyester pants with a matching bomber jacket and a white knit cap pulled down over gray hair lowering a camera. 'Thanks so much!' the woman trilled, and trotted off toward a man of the same age who was staring yearningly toward F Street Station and the bar visible through its window.

'You're a tourist attraction,' Wanda said.

Mutt looked bored. Kate shook her head and took a sip of coffee. It was excellent, rich and strong.

Maybe it was Kate's refusal to get mad at the tourist. Maybe it was her appreciation of the sun and the coffee. Maybe Wanda thought that something that had happened over thirty years before couldn't hurt her. Whatever it was, without prompting Wanda began to talk. Her voice was low and precise, unfaltering, unembarrassed. She laid things out in chronological order, stating the facts without bias or self-pity.

'I was dating William,' she said, 'and then he brought me home, and I met Eugene. We were attracted to each other, but he was married, and I didn't do that kind of thing.'

'He was also – what – twenty years older than you.'

Wanda didn't take offense. 'It didn't matter,' she said. 'I wanted him, and I knew he wanted me.'

'You were underage,' Kate couldn't help saying.

Wanda nodded. 'When we first met, yes. I was a year older than William, you see. My parents held me back a grade when I was in second grade because I had a problem with reading. Dyslexia,' she added.

She sipped coffee. 'I wanted to see Eugene, but I stopped going out with William because it just seemed too creepy to use him to get to his father. I could see, in the brief time that I was at their house, that Victoria and Eugene's marriage was falling apart. I had an after-school job at PME, and one day we bumped into each other at a union meeting, and then we met again, outside the office.' She paused and gave a twisted smile. 'And then all of sudden, I did do that kind of thing.'

271

'How long?'

'Almost a year before the divorce.'

Kate thought about how to ask the next question without giving offense, decided there was no way, and asked it straight out. 'Did he say he was going to leave his wife for you?'

'Oh no,' Wanda said calmly. 'He told me from the beginning that however bad it got with Victoria, he would never leave his children. I believed him.'

Frowning, Kate said, 'But he did.'

'Yes, he did,' Wanda said, 'but it wasn't his choice.'

'What do you mean?'

'His father-in-law pulled all the strings in that family.'

'The old man, Jasper Bannister?'

Wanda nodded.

'Why would the old man want to split up his daughter and her husband?'

'He never liked Eugene. Eugene was a Native, and Eugene had always wanted to do serious work for PME. They gave him a job, but it was a make-work, glad-handing kind of job. He wanted to go into management. They stonewalled him. It took a while, but he got mad, and he decided if he couldn't get into the business one way, he would another.'

'Which was?' Kate said.

'He joined the union that represented the PME workers and ran for business representative.'

'Did he win?'

'Oh, yes. The Bannisters may have had little use for Eugene, but the workers liked him. They were renegotiating their contract with PME, and they figured that Eugene, being a part of the owner's family by marriage, had pull on the other side. They were wrong, but they didn't know that.'

It was right about then that Jasper would have been finalizing plans to switch from union employees to contract hires.

'You know,' Wanda said pensively, 'the older I get and the more I read, the more I think that most things that happen are personal.' She looked at Kate. 'I remember reading something that somebody wrote one time that World War Two happened because Hitler's mother didn't spank him enough, or at all, and as odd as it sounds, I think there is some kind of truth to that. Lyndon Johnson said he didn't want to be the first American president to lose a war, so instead of cutting our losses and walking away, it's "One, two, three, what are we fightin' for..." Benjamin Franklin is personally insulted on the floor of the house of Parliament and he goes home to start the American Revolution. It's all personal,' Wanda repeated, 'and this was personal, too. On both sides.'

Thinking out loud, Kate said, 'So Eugene couldn't get in the front door, and he decided to use the union to get in the back door.'

There was a brief silence. 'I felt horribly guilty when he moved out,' Wanda said. 'I've never thought of myself as a home-wrecker. I certainly wasn't raised to be one. You know that Woody Allen quote– "The heart wants what it wants," something like that? I've always hated it. Eugene married Victoria, and they had three children together. He had no business sleeping around on them. I knew it, and I did it anyway.'

'Were you still together when his son died?'

'Yes.'

'You weren't subpoenaed to testify at the trial.'

'No.'

'Were you deposed?'

'Yes.' Wanda said, and took a deep breath and let it out slowly. 'I've had a lot of time to think about it. On the face of it, I think I was deposed to establish that Eugene had been with me that night.'

'An alibi.' Which would focus attention on Victoria as the prime suspect.

'Yes,' Wanda said. She closed her eyes and shook her head. 'Someone in the district attorney's office leaked my statement, and it was all over the news the next day, and of course they had to do a little digging, and they found out that Eugene and I had had a relationship before the divorce. My parents were ... very upset.'

Kate, in her extensive search through the library's microfiche files, had somehow managed to miss this particular Bannister scandal. That would teach her to go without the help of a reference librarian in the future. 'So Eugene was with you the night of the fire, the night his son was killed.'

'Yes.'

'All night.'

'Yes.'

So Eugene hadn't altogether disappeared after the divorce. Well. Perhaps if the Bannisters considered you a non-person, you did. Kate hesitated before asking her next question. 'Had there been

274

other women?'

Wanda didn't flinch. 'He said not.'

'So you were it.'

'Yes.'

'You had a brother named Ernie.'

Wanda's eyes widened a little. 'Yes. He died very young.'

'Eugene's set-net permit was sold to an Ernie Gajewski.'

Wanda nodded. 'Yes.'

'Your brother was dead by then.'

'Yes. Eugene needed to keep his set-net site so he could fish, but he couldn't keep it in his name. So I used Ernie's Social Security number to help Eugene make it look like he'd sold his permit.'

'Why couldn't he keep it in his name?'

There was a short pause. 'He had his reasons.'

Kate put down her coffee. 'There's something I have to tell you. I'm sorry as hell to have to tell you this, but Eugene Muravieff is dead.'

'I know,' Wanda said. 'I had his body picked up from the morgue this morning.'

Kate stared at her. 'Did your relationship continue?'

'Yes.'

'For the past thirty years?'

'Yes.'

'Why didn't you live together?'

Wanda hesitated. 'He wanted a place his children felt free to come to. Charlotte and Oliver were very upset about their father and me, particularly Oliver. And Eugene couldn't stomach the thought of living off my money. He was never going to make a lot of money, not when he couldn't even own up to his own identity.'

It just wasn't good enough, Kate thought. Two people were dead and a third in the hospital because Charlotte had hired her to get Charlotte's mother out of jail. Someone was willing to commit murder to make her go away. Wanda had to know more. She had been too close to the Muravieffs for too long not to.

She opened her mouth and a new and a very unwelcome voice intruded upon their conversation. 'Kate Shugak, I thought I recognized you.' She looked up and found Erland Bannister beaming down at her.

Without knowing how she got there, Kate found herself on her feet. She registered the fact that Mutt was standing, too, her shoulder pressed to Kate's knee, not growling but hackles raised, and ready to launch on command. Mutt's character analyses, with the possible exception of Jim Chopin, were nearly infallible, but in this case, they weren't necessary. Kate knew they had both reacted instinctively to the appearance of a predator.

Erland looked at Wanda. 'And you are?'

'Wanda Gajewski,' Wanda said through stiff lips.

'Wanda Gajewski, of course,' Erland said almost fondly. 'Judge Berlin's clerk, aren't you? And how is rascally old Randy these days? Still keeping the streets safe for the rest of us?'

Wanda began to rise, and Erland took her hand and helped her to her feet. 'I've got to get back to work,' Wanda told Kate.

It was past five o'clock. 'I'll walk you back,'

Kate said.

'No, that's all right.' Wanda attempted a smile. 'Thanks for the coffee. Mr. Bannister,' she said without looking at him, and was off, giving the impression of running without quite breaking her stride.

Erland Bannister watched her move away with an appreciative eye – Max would have approved of Wanda's walk – and then looked down at Kate. 'And how do you know our Wanda?'

He was still smiling, but Kate could almost hear the big-cat snarl in it. 'A business acquaintance,' she said, and moved to a trash container to toss the coffee cups.

He kept pace next to her. 'Really? Something to do with the case you were working on for my niece?'

'That would come under the heading of confidential, Erland,' Kate said coolly.

'But why?' Erland said, spreading his hands, the very picture of sweet reason. 'My niece is dead, Kate. You no longer have an employer. Therefore you no longer have a case, and there is no longer any need to go around asking questions, particularly of people who would much rather leave the past right where it is.'

'Don't you want to know who killed your niece?' Kate said.

His smile faded and his eyes widened. 'Didn't you hear? The police have the driver in custody.'

Kate had been working on keeping her face impassive, but she couldn't help reacting to this.

Erland was watching her like a hawk, and he said, 'Oh yes, a short while ago.' He shook his head admiringly. 'It's amazing what these new police technologies can do, how swiftly miscreants can be brought to justice. We can only hope that the man who so wantonly and carelessly killed my niece will come before Judge Berlin. Randy knows what to do with people like him, although I still think it's a pity that the constitutional convention chose to omit capital punishment.' He checked his watch. 'Well, will you look at the time. Best I be getting on home.' He took Kate's hand and she let it lie limp in his. 'I probably won't be seeing you again, Kate, but let me tell you just what a pleasure it's been.' He let his eyes run appreciatively over her body and back up to her face. 'I hope we see each other again sometime soon, under better circumstances.'

'Erland,' Kate said. She knew it wasn't smart, knew it was provocative and dangerous and very probably productive of threat to life and limb, but she couldn't leave things like this, and she certainly couldn't let him have the last word.

He turned, the smile still on his face, his eyes alert, attentive, even caressing.

'Your niece, Charlotte?'

'Yes?' he said.

'She paid me in full in advance,' Kate said. She didn't wait to see his expression change, she just turned and walked away.

She didn't look back to see if he admired her walk. She only hoped the tremor in her knees didn't show.

Or that it looked like she'd rather be running.

CHAPTER 16

'It was an anonymous tip,' Brendan told her, hanging up the phone. 'A man called nine-one-one and told the dispatcher he'd heard the driver bragging in a bar about getting away with a hit-and-run. And will you please for sweet Christ's sake sit down?'

Kate was pacing back and forth with a scowl on her face. Mutt had backed herself into a corner, tucking her paws as much beneath her as she could, but it was a very small office and at every half turn, Kate's left stride would come perilously close to Mutt's toes. Mutt and Brendan wore identical wary expressions. They'd both seen Kate in this mood before, and both were experienced in the fallout.

'Who's the driver?' Kate said. 'What do we know about him?'

'Kate,' Brendan said heavily, 'do you really think Erland Bannister hired some guy to kill his niece and then take the fall for it? Erland Bannister, scion of a family that has roots in Alaska going back to before the gold rush, a family who married into the Native community' – he held up a hand, palm out '–doesn't matter how it ended or why, because those ties are there, and you better believe both families realize it. Erland Bannister, CEO and majority stockholder of a corporation whose GNP is bigger than the state of Alaska's and whose payroll is second only to RPetCo's, with a seat on the board of the Alaska Red Cross, the Humanities Forum, and the Alaska Council on the Arts – hell, I could go on, but you're a bright girl. You've got the picture. Do you really believe that Erland Bannister hired someone to take out his niece? And for crissake, why? For hiring you to look into getting her mother, *and*, may I point out, his sister, out of the clink?'

'Why would he threaten me if there wasn't something he didn't want me to find out?'

Brendan gave this the judicial consideration it deserved. 'The way I heard it, it sounded more like a bribe,' he said.

She tossed him a look of such scorn that it was only with a strong exercise of his backbone that he managed not to wilt. 'That was two nights ago. This afternoon was a threat.'

Again, Brendan considered. 'No, I'd have to say none of what you've repeated to me could come under the heading of a threat.' Kate turned on him and he shook his head. 'He didn't say anything that could be followed by an 'or else,' now, did he? No. He didn't even tell you to butt out. Near as I can figure, adjusting for the decibel level, of course, all Erland Bannister told you was goodbye.'

'He sure wasn't upset over Charlotte's death,' Kate said fiercely. 'Fucker was erring more on the side of overjoyed.'

'I'd have to check the statutes to be sure, but I don't think that's a crime, Kate.' Brendan reflected. 'Of course, I haven't seen the latest bulletin from John Ashcroft, either.'

280

Kate came to a halt, clenching the back of the chair across from Brendan's desk in both hands, as if she'd like to tear it apart. 'This situation is bent, Brendan.'

'What situation?' Brendan said. 'Look, Kate, I'm sorry, but it seems to me you're out of a job. It's closing time.' He looked at the clock. 'For both of us. Go home.'

Instead, Kate tracked down Axenia.

Axenia was her cousin, who had moved to Anchorage, married a lobbyist, and had recently had a child. Relations were cool between them for many reasons, but mostly because Kate had been born first and smarter and prettier. The expression on Axenia's face when she opened the door to her house told Kate that she would just as soon be closing it again immediately. 'Kate,' she said evenly, and shifted the drooling toddler on one hip.

'Axenia,' Kate said. 'I need a favor.'

Inside, the house boasted tastefully chosen and perfectly matched furniture ensembles, a hardwood floor polished to a painful shine, and paint that was never allowed to become smudged. Plastic toys in primary colors were carefully corralled in a toy box in one corner, a pile of glossy magazines was neatly stacked on a teak coffee table, and there were no books to be seen, but that was okay, because there were no reading lamps, either, only wrought-iron torchères in all four corners, whose job appeared to be to light the ceiling above them. While waiting for the water to boil for coffee, Axenia and the toddler took Kate on a tour of the

281

College Gate split-level house, which included four bedrooms, three baths, a wooden deck that took up most of the backyard, and a room converted into a theater that seated twenty. 'A lot of Lew's clients are pretty labor-intensive,' Axenia said. 'We entertain a great deal, cocktail parties, dinners.'

Kate managed to restrain a shudder. 'Where is Lew?'

'In D.C., doing some lobbying for UCo.'

Axenia put the baby down for a nap and served Kate coffee and Oreos on the beveled-glass table in the kitchen. 'You look good, Axenia,' Kate said.

Axenia, less defensive and more self-assured than Kate had ever seen her, inclined her head in acknowledgment. Her hair was styled in the latest do and her clothes were the latest in casual chic, no doubt fresh off the rack at Nordstrom, and this would be Nordstrom in Seattle, where Axenia would fly to do her shopping, probably half a dozen times a year. 'You look well, too,' she said. 'Have you been in town for long?'

'A few days. I'm working on a case.'

'Really? What kind?'

'A murder,' Kate said, 'thirty-one years ago.'

Axenia raised an eyebrow. 'Didn't they catch him?'

'Her,' Kate said, 'they caught her, and she's in jail, but there seem to be some unanswered questions. I was wondering if you knew anybody in the Muravieff family. They're sort of connected to this case.'

'Of course,' Axenia said, 'Nadine and I are good friends.'

'Nadine.' Kate passed in review a mental flip chart of what she knew of the Muravieff family tree. 'Would that be Celia's daughter?'

'Yes.'

Celia was Eugene's sister. Nadine was Eugene's niece. 'Could you ask Nadine to introduce me to her mother?'

Axenia didn't ask why; she just reached for the phone and dialed a number from memory. The call took less than two minutes. She hung up and said to Kate, 'Celia lives with Nadine. You can go over there right now.'

'Thanks, Axenia.'

Axenia inclined her head again. 'No problem.'

'You've got a cute baby there,' Kate said on the doorstep.

'Thank you,' Axenia said, and closed the door.

Kate stared at it for a few moments.

Nope, nothing in the way of a reconciliation going on there anytime soon.

Eugene's niece Nadine lived west of Axenia, in Roger's Park. Nadine's house wasn't as large as Axenia's and it looked a lot more user-friendly, but then Kate told herself not to be so judgmental. Axenia had been well on her way to being a drunk in the Park. In Anchorage, she was sober and a mother and one hell of a housekeeper. Kate told herself she really had to learn how to let go.

'Kate Shugak?'

Her reverie interrupted, she looked up to see a short, slight woman regarding her.

'Yes,' Kate said.

'Ekaterina's granddaughter?'

Kate stifled a sigh and nodded, wondering where her own identity had gone.

The woman had a compact, neat-featured face, well-proportioned, a face whose chief characteristic was its calm, a face it was hard to imagine angry, which would make it all that more formidable when it was. Her eyes were dark and direct and her hair a styled gray cap. She wore dark blue slacks and a white long-sleeved button-down shirt, tucked under a slim brown leather belt that exactly matched her penny loafers.

In the Park, Kate would have addressed Celia as 'Auntie,' an honorific demonstrating the respect due an elder from a younger person. The word did not rise to her lips this afternoon. Maybe it was the fact that Celia was wearing her shoes inside, not the general practice in Alaska, as it tracked in snow and mud. Whatever the reason, Kate found herself saying formally, 'Thank you for speaking with me this afternoon, Ms.–?'

'It's Herrick, and it's Mrs.' She indicated a chair. Kate sat. Celia sat opposite her and folded her hands. A younger woman came bustling in with a tray with coffee and a plate of homemade cookies. At least it wasn't Oreos again.

'My daughter, Nadine,' Celia said. 'Kate Shugak.'

Nadine filled the cups and made as if to sit next to Celia. Some signal passed between them that Kate did not see. Nadine stood back up as if she'd been attached to a wire that Celia was pulling, and said brightly, 'Those kids sound like they're killing each other. I'd better check on them.' She bustled out again.

Celia poured coffee. 'I was sorry to hear about your grandmother. She was a strong woman, a strong leader, and very wise.' Celia allowed herself a small smile. 'It doesn't always happen that the two are able to coexist in one personality.' Her diction was smooth and uninflected, with no trace of ancestral gutturals. Celia was old enough to have been sent away to school, to Mount Edgecumbe in Sitka or even as far away as Chemawa in Oregon, where in that day and time she would have been punished severely for speaking in her Native tongue.

Of course, the Muravieffs had been members of the first tribes to be impacted by the intrusion of Western civilization, as witness their Russian-derived last name. They'd had a couple of centuries to learn how to speak English. 'Thank you,' Kate said, accepting the coffee. She sipped it, scalding her tongue. 'Your own family has produced some fine leaders itself. Harold Muravieff was one of the founding members of the Alaska Native Brotherhood, was he not?' She, too, could be formal when there was need.

Celia inclined her head, accepting the implied tribute as her family's due.

Kate took a chance. 'And I believe I remember my grandmother speaking of Mary Muravieff, your mother, who worked with her on the language of the Alaska Native Claims Settlement Act.'

Celia inclined her head again. Emaa and Mary had hated each other with a fervor that had passed into legend long before either woman was dead. Kate had never known the source of that hatred. When she was younger, she had tried to find out, but when she got older, she had come to realize that some things were better left to die a natural death. She still wondered, though, and it had been a risk mentioning Mary to Celia. Still, Mary had been a well-known Alaska Native leader in her own right, and deserved mention. She also provided a neat segue into Kate's next comment. 'Eugene was her son, I believe.'

Celia's expression didn't change. 'He was.'

'And your brother.'

'Yes.'

'Ah.' Both women sipped coffee. 'I wonder,' Kate said, displaying as humble a facade as she could manufacture, 'I wonder, Mrs. Herrick, if you would mind talking to me about your brother, Eugene.'

'What do you want to know about him?' Celia said, still calm.

'I have been employed to look into the matter of his wife's criminal case.'

Celia's composed face displayed nothing but polite interest. 'Indeed. By whom, may I ask?'

'Her daughter.'

'Charlotte?'

'Yes, Charlotte.'

Celia reached for the newspaper that was sitting on the table next to the serving tray. 'Didn't I read that Charlotte had been killed by a hit-and-run driver?'

'You did, yes,' Kate said.

'And you are continuing to look into this matter?'

'Yes. Charlotte was concerned that her mother

had been wrongly imprisoned.'

'I see.' Celia put down her cup and gave Kate a kind and carefully limited smile. 'I haven't seen my brother in thirty years. I don't know what I could tell you about him.'

'Were you at Victoria's trial?'

Celia shook her head. 'I'm afraid not.'

'He did not testify at her trial.'

'He was not called.'

'Did he tell you if he thought Victoria had set that fire?'

'On the contrary. He was sure that she had not.'

'Did he, perhaps, have any thoughts as to who might have?'

'No.' Celia rose to her feet. 'I'm sorry to cut this so short, but I have an engagement this evening. Was there anything else?'

'Do you know where I might find your brother, Mrs. Herrick?'

Celia looked Kate right in the eye and lied like the trooper she was. 'No,' she said. 'As I said before, I haven't seen Eugene in over thirty years.'

And you know he's dead and can't contradict you, Kate thought.

She wondered how much of Celia's stonewalling had to do with Emaa and Mary's relationship. She wondered if perhaps it had more to do with who had really set fire to Victoria's house, and why.

As seemed to be this case's increasingly annoying habit, she had no answers to either question.

It had all seemed so simple on Monday, Kate thought as she drove back to the town house. The facts were all right there in the police report and the trial transcript. Someone, with malice aforethought, had splashed gasoline around Victoria Bannister's house and set it on fire. There, those were cold, hard facts that no one could deny.

The gasoline had come from the tank of Victoria's car, as proven by an extensive chemical analysis by the police lab and again by an independent testing lab hired by the defendant. There was another fact.

There were no signs of forced entry to the house, and Oliver and Charlotte had both testified that their mother was very conscientious about keeping the doors and windows locked. A third fact.

The fire had resulted in the death of William Muravieff, seventeen, by smoke inhalation, and in the injury of Oliver Muravieff. Fourth and fifth facts.

Victoria Bannister Muravieff had taken out substantial life-insurance policies on all three of her children just weeks before. Another fact.

Victoria Bannister Muravieff had refused to take the stand.

That, in Kate's opinion, was the most interesting fact of all. The peripheral stuff about Victoria's marriage and divorce and Eugene's whereabouts the night of the murder were just the defense trying to cast reasonable doubt. Cowell had been throwing up as much of a smoke screen as he could muster to deflect the jury's attention from the facts.

Why hadn't Victoria testified? Never mind the Fifth Amendment, juries always wanted to hear from those accused, wanted to hear them say they didn't do it, wanted to test the veracity of their testimony in person. There were gigantic traps laid for those who did, of course, and it was every criminal attorney's job to dissuade his defendant from getting up on that stand and falling into them, but with a case as weak as Cowell's had been, there would have been nothing to lose and everything to gain, especially if Victoria's testimony had been convincing.

Kate, thinking of her two interviews with Victoria Bannister Muravieff, that pillar of community rectitude, the good daughter, the good wife, the good mother (except for the little matter of filicide), and now the good inmate, thought that it would have been.

And then she thought, What if Victoria had stayed off the stand not because she didn't want to testify against herself but because she was afraid she would be asked questions about something else, something that had nothing to do with the murder?

She got back to the town house at 9:15 P.M., to find Jim Chopin pacing up and down the sidewalk. He didn't look happy. 'Where the hell have you been, Shugak? I've been checking in since I got out of court. I nearly put out an APB! Get down, damn it!' This last to Mutt, who had greeted him in her usual exuberant fashion. After being addressed in this ungentlemanly fashion, she dropped to all fours and slunk past him, the picture of dejection.

'I've been chasing my tail all day,' she said. 'Did you get him?'

'Jury was out for seven minutes, guilty on all counts, and who gives a shit? Chasing your tail how, and why the hell didn't you call? And how the hell am I supposed to watch your back when I can't find it anywhere!'

'Congratulations,' she said, leading the way into the kitchen. 'Want a beer to wet the head of the newly convicted?'

'You have beer?'

'I stopped at the store on my way home.' She uncapped a bottle of Alaskan Amber and poured herself a glass of cranberry juice.

Mutt, careful to keep herself within Jim's range of vision, sidled into the kitchen, her body language devoted to broadcasting how severely her heart had been broken by her idol.

Jim took the beer ungraciously and stamped into the living room, from whence the sound of the television soon followed, turned up probably a tad bit more than necessary. Mutt followed. After a few moments, Kate heard Jim's voice say, 'Oh for chrissake sake, dog, get your butt over here!' and there was a joyous bark, the scrabble of toenails on wood, a loud thump, and an even louder groan.

Kate's stomach growled. She sliced a ring of Polish sausage into a jambalaya mix, brought it all to a boil, reduced the heat to low, and covered it to simmer for twenty-five minutes.

She walked into the living room, to find Jim barely visible behind a lapful of Mutt. The easy chair must have been straining in every joint, but Jim seemed a little calmer. They were both watching the end of *Law and Order*. Jim looked up.

'Find out anything new today?'

She sat down on the couch and propped her feet on the coffee table. 'I don't know. I don't know what the hell's going on, Jim. Maybe Brendan's right. Maybe I should just walk away.'

'Brendan?' Jim said, shoving Mutt off his lap. Mutt gave him a look of burning reproach and padded over to sprawl out on the hearth. Made of dark green slate, it was the coolest surface in the house that Mutt could find to sleep on.

'He agrees there's something bent about Victoria's case, but he doesn't think there's any point in pursuing it. I haven't unearthed any evidence about the actual case, now, have I?'

Jim was obviously torn between a reluctance to agree to anything said by a rival for Kate's affections and his inclination that Brendan was right. After a brief inner struggle, he said, 'Were you thinking there was something else you could do? Some line of inquiry you've missed?'

'Plus, although he'd never admit it, I think Brendan is a little intimidated by Erland Bannister being involved.'

'"Involved"?' Jim said.

'Yeah, I was having coffee with Eugene Muravieff's mistress and he saw us and came over to have a little chat.'

'"A little chat"? You had a little chat with Erland Bannister?'

'What,' Kate said, amused, 'big bad Erland scares you, too?'

'Kate,' Jim said, pushing the footrest of his chair down so he could address her from an upright position, 'out of the blue Erland Bannister invites you to a party at his house, and then he just happens to run into you downtown, where the two of you have a little chat? Erland Bannister, also known as Alaska's kingmaker and all around super-duper utility political angel slash fat cat. I'd say this time Brendan's right on the money.'

Kate was grinning openly now. 'You think I should get the hell out of Dodge, do you?'

But he wasn't listening. 'Did you say Eugene Muravieff's mistress?'

But she heard a familiar name from the television and turned to look.

There was Bruce Abbott, the governor's gopher, doing a stand-up behind a podium with the state of Alaska's seal on it. On his right stood the attorney general of the state of Alaska, a large man overflowing his three-piece pinstripe, and on his left the state DA for Anchorage, a bleached blonde in a gray two-piece. Abbott wore a red tie, the attorney general a red handkerchief, and the DA a red scarf, indicating that they'd all graduated with honors from Television Spin 101.

'–due to the stellar work Ms. Muravieff has performed in achieving a level of quality education for the inmates at Hiland Mountain Correctional Facility, and because he feels she has contributed substantially to the lowest rate of recidivism for a corrections facility in the state and one of the lowest rates in the nation, because Victoria Bannister Muravieff has set a standard for community service under the most difficult of conditions, with a selfless disregard for her own situation and a commitment to the rehabilitation of people the rest of us have given up on long ago, the governor has decided to commute her sentence to time served. And now I will take just a few questions. Yes, Mike.'

'Bruce, is this action in response to the rumor that Victoria Muravieff has inoperable cancer?'

Bruce looked reproving. 'I don't know where you got that information, Mike, but certainly not. Jill?'

'Bruce, does the governor's action have anything to do with the recent death of Charlotte's daughter?'

Bruce looked grave. 'The governor's heart goes out to the Bannister family in their time of grief and mourning. Nothing can replace the life that was so randomly, so carelessly, and so criminally taken, but we want to reassure the Bannisters and the Muravieffs that the perpetrator of this most heinous act will be prosecuted to the full extent of the law. Yes, Andy?'

'Bruce, it's well known that Erland Bannister, Victoria Muravieff's brother, was a big supporter of the governor's candidacy and subsequent election. Did–'

Bruce look austere. 'I know where you're going with this, Andy, and I'm shocked that you would suggest for even a moment that this act was in the nature of a political debt paid. The governor made this decision on the merits of the case in question and on the character of the person named, nothing else. Yes, Sandy?'

The scene cut away to an interview with Erland Bannister, who answered the questions put to him with an appropriately somber (demonstrating his grief at the death of his niece) but quietly joyous (demonstrating his happiness at the release of his sister) face. He was delighted that the state finally had a governor who could show mercy where it was due. Victoria had done extraordinary work during her incarceration, and Erland thought that even the judge who had sentenced her to life without parole would have agreed with the governor's action today. Victoria had already been released and was lodged with family members, exactly where, the reporter would understand, Erland was disinclined to say.

Next up was the chief of police, who was prepared to accede that some recognition must be given to those felons convicted of even the most heinous crimes for their attempts to redeem themselves, and that on the whole the APD was behind the governor's decision.

'Back to you, John,' said the reporter, and the screen went to a commercial. Jim clicked off the remote and looked at Kate.

'The governor's been in office for almost a year,' she said. 'Why wait until now to commute her sentence?'

'Why indeed?' Jim said.

'Unless, of course,' Kate said, gathering steam, 'it had something to do not with the merits of her case but with her daughter's hiring a private investigator to take a new look at the case?'

'What are you thinking now?'

'I'm thinking,' Kate said grimly, 'that Victoria didn't set that fire. I'm thinking someone else did. I'm thinking they're still around. I'm thinking if Erland didn't do it himself, he knows who did, and I'm thinking he's determined I won't find out.'

'I'm thinking he's wrong,' Jim said. 'But then that's just me.'

CHAPTER 17

'There's always a third possibility,' Max said.

He sounded grumpy, but that might have been because Kate had gotten him out of bed. They sat alone in the cafeteria at the Pioneer Home, both of them hunched over mugs of coffee.

'What third?' Kate said, sounding a little cranky herself. 'I've got too much information going on here as it is.'

'What if Charlotte did it herself?'

Kate stared at him for so long, he began to get a little nervous. 'You're not going to cry or anything, are you?'

'Why,' Kate said finally, almost despairing, 'why on earth would you think that Charlotte had set the fire that killed her brother? And why oh why would she ever have hired me to find her out?'

'Maybe she wanted to use you as her confessor,' Max said. 'It happens.'

Kate knew that. It didn't make her any happier to hear Max say it.

'Or maybe she really did want her mom out of the clink, and she figured it had been so long that even if you did find out enough to get her mom out, you'd never find out who really committed the crime.'

'My head hurts,' Kate said. 'And I want to go home.'

'Don't blame you,' Max said. 'So do I, and I don't even have one.'

Gloom settled in over the table.

She could go home, she thought, sitting in the Subaru in the street outside. Victoria was out of jail, even if Charlotte was dead. Kurt had regained consciousness, and although he remembered little of the events leading up to the shooting and nothing at all about getting shot, the doctor, whom she'd spoken to earlier, had assured Kate that in traumas such as these, the memory often did return a little at a time. They would have to be patient.

Everyone wanted her to go home, Jim, Brendan, even Max had told her to pack it in. Mutt put her cold nose on Kate's cheek and gave an imploring whine. Nobody wanted her to stay in Anchorage.

But she couldn't let it go. She knew someone was running a scam on her, she knew she hadn't come anywhere near the truth, and she knew that if they had their way, she never would. It was, she thought, resting her forehead on the steering wheel, a combination of things – a need to know the truth that would not be denied, and a fierce disinclination to lose.

So, wearily, because she hadn't gotten a lot of sleep the night before, Kate went back to the town house to lay in supplies, and trundled back up the hillside to park inside a stand of alder down the road from Charlotte and Emily's house. It was a little after 8:30 in the morning. After two hours, she'd finished *Last Standing Woman* by Winona LaDuke and a bottle of water, watched a moose cow with two leggy calves graze on alder bark off her right front bumper, eaten a chicken sandwich, watched three magpies chase off the moose, peed in the bushes, read a quarter of *Lamb* by Christopher Moore, and seen a big brown dog trailing a leash come kiyiing out of the underbrush with a small but irritated black bear close on his trail.

'Stay,' Kate said.

Mutt, who had long since abandoned the Subaru for the shade it cast, yawned wide enough for Kate to hear it from Mutt's sprawled position beneath the car, just like she'd never given any thought to adding a new parameter to that chase.

The sun beat down on the roof of the Subaru. Kate had all the windows open, but she was still sweating into the driver's seat. In the distance, the sounds muffled by trees, mothers would call to children, men would call for dogs, car doors would slam and engines would start. Kate would peer hopefully through the foliage, only to sink back disappointed when whoever it was left from the wrong house.

At 2:30 in the afternoon, a gold two-door Eldorado came almost silently up the road and turned into Charlotte's driveway. Kate got out of the Subaru and slipped through the trees to the edge of the clearing surrounding the house. Fifteen minutes later, Erland opened the door of the Cadillac for Emily. The Cadillac purred down the driveway and vanished.

Kate didn't wait. 'Mutt,' she said, and Mutt

297

emerged from out of the bushes. 'Guard,' Kate said, and headed for the house. The front door was locked. So was the back door. A sliding glass door that opened from the master bedroom onto the upstairs deck was not, and Kate, proud that she was barely breathing hard from the climb up the crossbars, stepped inside.

The bedroom held a king-size bed with a matching suite of furniture, including a vanity and a dresser. Kate rifled through all the drawers and then the closet without discovering anything more exciting than a cutout bra that looked like it would be awfully uncomfortable. The master bath was cluttered with various oils, ointments, creams, lotions, and every brand of makeup Kate had ever seen advertised in a magazine.

The guest bedroom down the hall was neat, clean, and impersonal. The closet had a shelf full of wrapping paper, ribbon, and items marked with sticky notes reading 'Sandy for Christmas' and 'Carolyn for her birthday' and 'Cathy for her birthday' and 'CathyO for the dinner.' Downstairs, the kitchen looked like it was used, and through it, aha, an office.

There was a desk in the middle of the room and file cabinets lined all the walls except one, which had a bookcase filled floor to ceiling with cookbooks. Kate remembered that Charlotte was a caterer. She went to the desk and opened the first drawer that came to hand and found a big red book of lined pages full of writing Kate recognized from Charlotte's check. Each page was dated. Sometimes you just got lucky.

She sat down and found the date of Charlotte's

death. From there, she worked backward, slowly and methodically, one eye on the clock.

All the Monday entries began the same way: 'Went out to Eagle River, tried to see Mom.'

Kate closed the diary and looked around. There was a shelf full of similar diaries. She pulled down a few and leafed through them. Every Monday began with the very same entry: 'Went out to Eagle River, tried to see Mom.'

There were only twenty-two diaries on the shelf, so Kate couldn't confirm that Charlotte had been trying to see her mother every Monday for the past thirty years, but it was a safe bet.

She went back to the current year and began reading steadily, with critical attention to detail, from the first of January. Some of it was personal: 'Emily and I talked. She's working too much, too many late nights. I hardly ever see her anymore, and I don't like it. She's promised to cut back.' Some of it was business: 'Catered the Williams-Lujon wedding. Everyone really liked the cheese puffs, so I'm including them in the A menu from now on.' Some of it was social: 'Took the governor's wife to lunch in hopes of interesting her in establishing a culinary arts school at UAA. We could use a friend at court, and she actually admitted to cooking the occasional meal, so fingers are crossed.' Some of it was trivial. 'Shopping at Nordie's with Chris, who always makes me buy more than I should. But oh, how could I resist that little black dress! Emily will drool!'

And then, suddenly, an unexpected entry in mid-July.

'Dad called. He wanted to meet so I went out

there. He wanted Oliver to come, too, but Oliver said no. Oliver says no a lot. He's like Dad – he doesn't think Mom did it. I don't know why he won't go out there with me. Dad's all we've got left.'

Oliver didn't believe Victoria was guilty? Since when?

Well. Kate sat back. Charlotte, in spite of protestations to the contrary, had kept in contact with her father. Witnesses always lied – any cop could tell you that – but it always pissed Kate off when they did.

Only one other entry did Kate find of interest, the one the night before Erland's party, and Charlotte's last entry:

'Uncle Erland's party is tomorrow. I hate those things. I hated them when Mom used to make us help out with the ones Grandfather used to have, and I hate them now. The boys were braver than me when they told her they wouldn't go anymore. I wouldn't except for Alice. Alice needs somebody there.'

Kate replaced the diary and went out the front door, locking it behind her. 'Come on,' she told Mutt, and led the way back to the Subaru, where they waited another hour for Emily to come home. As before, the gold Cadillac hushed up the driveway, there was the sound of a car door opening, a moment of murmured conversation, the door closed, and the Cadillac purred back down the driveway and out onto the road.

Kate waited for ten minutes before starting the Subaru and driving up to the house. Emily took a long time answering the door, and when she saw Kate, she closed it again immediately. Kate put a hand up to catch it before it latched. 'Emily? I need to talk to you.'

'I don't want to talk to anyone.'

'Anyone, or just me?'

Emily tried to close the door again. Kate exerted a little muscle and Emily was forced back a step. 'Emily, what did Charlotte tell you about hiring me?'

'Nothing.' Emily refused to meet Kate's eyes.

'Driving to the Park takes at least a day. You didn't ask her where she was going, or why?'

'No.'

Before her better self could take over, Kate said, 'You and Charlotte were on the outs, weren't you?'

Emily's head jerked up. 'What? That's not true. It's a lie. Where did you hear that? I—'

'You'd been working a lot of late nights, and Charlotte was tired of never seeing you. I can understand — no point in living together if you never see each other. Did she want you to move out?'

'No! She loved me! We loved each other. She would never have asked me to move out!'

'If you loved her so much, then help me find who killed her.'

Emily's mouth opened, closed, opened again. Through stiff lips she said, 'They caught the man who was driving the truck that hit her. He's in jail.'

Kate waited until Emily looked up again, and said in a soft voice, 'But you and I both know somebody paid him to do it. Who was it, Emily? And why? Am I getting too close to the truth of

301

William Muravieff's murder? Why didn't Victoria fight harder? Why has she stayed in jail all this time without complaint?'

'She's out now,' Emily said desperately. 'It was what Charlotte wanted. That's what she always wanted. Whatever you did, it got Victoria out. The job is finished. You're done. Go home. Go home, and leave me alone.'

Kate regarded her in silence for a moment. 'You're terrified of something,' she said. 'What? Or should I say, Whom?'

Emily cast a hunted look over Kate's shoulder. 'You don't know,' she said. 'You don't understand.'

'Make me understand.'

'Go home,' Emily whispered. 'Go home now. Go home before it's too late.'

'Too late for what? Emily? Emily!'

Emily closed the door, and this time Kate let her.

Kate manhandled the Subaru into the garage and slammed into the house.

Jim looked up from the couch in the living room, marking his place in the book he was reading. 'You got up early.'

'I know.' She looked more closely. 'Are you wearing glasses?'

He whipped them off and tucked them out of sight. 'No. Well, yes. They're just reading glasses. Listen, Kate. My case is done. I don't have to go back to court. I could have gone with you this morning. Where did you go, by the way?'

She walked toward him, shedding her jacket and starting to unbuckle her belt.

He gaped at her. 'Kate?'

'Put the glasses back on,' she said.

Half an hour later, he flopped back, gasping for breath. 'Jesus,' he said, wheezing a little. 'I think you broke something.'

Kate rolled off him and waited for the ceiling to come back into focus. She was suffused with a warm glow, trembling in every limb, covered in a fine mist of perspiration. Also, her knees were smarting from carpet burn. She definitely felt better. Maybe even leaning toward immortal. Who knew glasses could be such a turn-on?

They hadn't made it out of the living room. One end of the sofa was jammed into a corner, the coffee table was tipped over, and the magazines on it lay splashed across the floor, along with the pillows from the couch and their clothes.

Jim wheezed some more. 'Maybe even every-thing.' He mustered enough energy, barely, to raise his head and look at her. 'Mind telling me what that was all about?'

'I saw, I wanted, I took,' she said, stretching lazily. 'Oh yeah.'

'It's not that I'm objecting.'

She grinned at the ceiling. 'Shower?'

He groaned a little, getting to his feet, but he followed her upstairs.

She had an epiphany in the shower, and she told Jim.

'For God's sake, I'm not a rabbit,' Jim said, but his body seemed willing to give it the old college try.

'Not that kind of epiphany,' she said, shoving him away and drawing back the curtain to reach for a towel. 'Can you get me into the Cook Inlet Pretrial Facility?'

'Who do you want to talk to?'

'The hit-and-run driver who killed Charlotte.'

Jim had to make a phone call before she'd let him get his pants on, and they arrived at the facility damp but determined.

A stocky corrections officer with a round face and a dimpled smile was waiting for them. 'Sam,' Jim said.

'Thanks for setting this up.'

'I was never here, I saw nothing, and I'm about to go off shift anyway.'

'I appreciate that.'

'Feel kind of sorry for the little bastard,' Sam said as he buzzed them inside and escorted them down the hall.

'Why is that?'

'His wife was just here. They've got a kid with cystic fibrosis. She's a waitress, and he drives a cab. They don't have any kind of insurance. She was bawling her eyes out when she left.'

Jim's eyes met Kate's for a significant moment. 'Really,' was all Kate said.

The interrogation room at CIPTF had been more recently painted than the one at Hiland Mountain. Otherwise, it looked exactly the same. A man in prison blues was already seated at the table, with a corrections officer standing against the wall, arms crossed over his chest. Sam nodded at him. 'Thanks, Al.'

'No problem.' Al left, Sam crossed his arms

over his chest and leaned up against the wall, Jim began a slow pace around the room, which took him in back of the man in the blues, and Kate pulled out a chair opposite him. 'Ralph Patton?'

'Who wants to know?' It was a pitiful attempt at pugnacity from a skinny white guy with bad teeth, lank hair, and a skimpy attempt at the unshaven look so popular nowadays with male Hollywood starlets. He was twenty-three but looked seventeen.

'I'm Kate Shugak, and this is Sergeant Jim Chopin of the Alaska State Troopers. We're here to ask you a few questions about the hit-and-run.'

'I was drunk,' Patton said immediately, as if that was some kind of excuse.

Kate opened the file she had carried in. 'So you said in your statement, but your blood-alcohol level was point-oh-four, well below the legal limit.'

He hunched his shoulders. 'I have a low tolerance for booze.'

Kate looked back at the file. 'Along with a low tolerance for booze, you've got a wife, as well as a year-old child diagnosed with cystic fibrosis.'

Patton started to get out of his chair, but Jim slammed him back into it.

'Who paid you to kill Charlotte Muravieff, Ralph?'

'I want you to leave now,' Ralph said, his face contorting.

'And who helped you do it?'

'I want to talk to my lawyer. You can't talk to me without my lawyer present.'

'Because the thing is, we went up to O'Malley to look at the crash site, Ralph, and we found the

305

driveway where you waited until your lookout told you Charlotte was coming up the road. You pulled out on the road and accelerated at just the right time, with just enough speed to cause maximum damage. That took some planning.'

'I don't know what you're talking about.'

'You got a bank account, Ralph? Because I'm guessing that when we take a look at it, we're going to find a large and recent deposit.'

'That money is mine,' Patton said, his voice rising.

'Nobody's saying it isn't,' Kate said soothingly. 'If it's in your bank account, of course it's your money. So long as you can explain where it came from, it shouldn't be a problem.'

'It's mine,' Patton said, 'it's my money, and it's going to pay the doctors for my little girl. You can't touch it!'

'Of course I can't. It's your money, just like you said. So long as the Internal Revenue Service gets their share, they don't really care. Have you reported this money as income yet, Ralph?'

'It's my money!' Patton shouted, spraying Kate with spittle. 'You can't touch it. I earned that for our baby!'

Jim slammed him back into his seat again and Kate pounced. 'Who paid you, Ralph? Who paid you to crash your pickup into Charlotte's car as she was coming home Tuesday night?'

'What the hell is going on here?' a voice said from the doorway.

Kate and Jim looked up, to see a man in a three-piece suit that screamed attorney standing in the doorway.

'Mr. Dial,' Patton said, shoving his chair over in his hurry to get to his feet, 'I didn't say anything, sir, I promise!'

'You don't have to talk to these people, Ralph,' Dial said. He looked first at Kate and then at Jim. 'I'm Joseph Dial, Mr. Patton's attorney. And you are leaving. Now.' He looked at Sam. 'I understand you're responsible for this meeting. I'll be lodging a complaint with the governor's office in the morning.'

Five minutes later, they were outside the front door. 'I'm sorry as hell, Sam,' Jim said.

Sam didn't appear to be upset. 'The worst they can do is force me into early retirement, and I've already got my thirty in. Don't sweat it, Jim. I owed you more than one.'

'Thanks,' Jim said, and they shook hands.

'Where now?' Jim said as he and Kate got into the Subaru.

'Max,' Kate said, and started the engine.

'Tell me about William,' Kate said to Max.

Max looked at Jim, standing at Kate's shoulder. 'You the boyfriend?'

'No,' Jim said.

Max surveyed him with palpable contempt. 'If you'd said yes, I'd've called you a lucky bastard. Now I'm just gonna call you a stupid one.' He looked back at Kate. 'You want to know about William Muravieff.'

'Yes,' Kate said.

'He was only seventeen, Kate.'

'I know. Tell me anyway. Everything you can remember.'

307

'Why?'

'I'll tell you when you're done.'

Max made a production out of looking at his watch. 'About lunchtime, I'm thinking.'

'You're nothing but a serial opportunist,' Kate said, and that was how Jim Chopin found himself seated at a table at Simon & Seafort's, in the middle of a gaggle of tourists in purple polyester and straw hats, with a few shysters in three-piecers mixed in and reminding him uncomfortably of Dial. The chatter was deafening, but the food was great, and the view went south all the way to Redoubt.

Max gave the drinks menu prolonged, concentrated study and then ordered a Lemon Drop. 'No martini?' Kate said, and with an airy wave, Max said, 'I like to broaden my experience from time to time,' and then he ruined the comment with his nasty old man's grin. Kate laughed, and Jim, so help him, resented the laugh – or rather, the fact that Max had elicited the laugh and not him. The man had to be ninety-three, for crissake.

Besides which, Jim knew he had no serious relationship with Kate Shugak. They were acquaintances merely. Acquaintances who were at present having most excellent sex, but that was simply a matter of propinquity, born out of the circumstances of her life being in danger because of the case she was working on. Didn't matter a damn to him who made her laugh.

He'd like to see Morris 'Max' Maxwell, Sergeant, Alaska State Troopers (Retired), protect Kate from a crazed killer.

Mercifully, at that moment his steak sandwich

308

arrived and he used it to keep his mouth full.

Max's second drink appeared as he was draining his first. 'How do you do that?' Kate said.

'Do what?' Max said, smacking his lips.

'Never mind,' she said, shaking her head. 'You're going to be this case's highest-paid informant, I'll say that for you.'

His bristly cheeks creased. 'Have to spend it on someone.'

'Okay, old man, earn your keep. Tell me about William Muravieff.'

Max shrugged. 'Okay, but it ain't going to do you no good. He was a seventeen-year-old boy. Didn't have no record, not so much as a speeding ticket. He majored in basketball and only kept his grades high enough so he could stay on the team.'

'Was he good?'

'At b-ball?' Max shrugged again. 'Nothing flashy. Had a dependable free throw. Didn't foul except when the coach told him to.'

'How do you remember all this after thirty years?' Jim said. At Max's glare, he added, 'I can barely remember my own games.'

'You played b-ball?' Kate said, diverted. 'I didn't know that.'

'I was six feet tall by the time I was twelve,' he said. 'I was recruited in grade school.'

Max, still affronted by Jim's challenging his memory, said crushingly, 'Tall ain't everything. Hell, Butch Lincoln ran rings around players twice his size when he played for UAA.'

Kate jumped in to head off the pissing contest at the pass. Testosterone didn't wane with age,

309

evidently. 'What else did William do besides play b-ball well?'

Max's eyes narrowed. 'What are you looking for?'

'She was wondering if he ever had a summer job working for his uncle,' Jim said.

Max's expression told Jim that he was not allowed to speak. Jim, whose sense of humor was strong and broad, would normally have grinned. Jim, whose sense of humor was being seriously tested, found himself getting annoyed at how Kate Shugak hung on this old fart's every word.

The old fart left off glaring at Jim long enough to look at Kate. 'What are you thinking, Shugak? That the kid worked for Erland Bannister long enough to stumble across something bent with his uncle's company?'

'It's a theory.'

'Have you talked to Victoria since she's been out?'

Kate looked glum. 'I can't find her.'

Max snorted. 'You're not much of a detective, are you, girl?'

Kate sat up. 'You know where she is?'

'I might.'

Jim started to say something. Kate shut him up with a single searing look. Max saw it and said, 'Guess we know who's top dog now, hey, boy?' He looked back at Kate. 'Why don't you go talk to his girlfriend, you want to know about William.'

CHAPTER 18

Wanda Gajewski opened the door. She looked more resigned than surprised. 'I knew you'd be back sooner or later.'

It took a little of the wind out of Kate's sails, but not all of it. She walked in without invitation, followed by Jim Chopin. It didn't help her temper that Wanda and Jim took one look at each other and formed a mutual admiration society. 'I need you to tell me about William Muravieff.'

Wanda closed the door behind her. 'Would you like some coffee?' Without waiting for an answer, she disappeared into the kitchen while Kate paced up and down.

'Relax, Kate,' Jim said.

'Relax, my ass,' she said.

Wanda's home was as architecturally un-remarkable inside as it was outside. The living room carpet was new, its color a horribly dull dusty rose. The furniture was a collection of modular units upholstered in some nubby fabric in a brown-and-gold weave that would hide dirt well. The walls were livened by large paintings of wildflowers, oil on canvas. They looked as if Wanda had bought them in bulk for a discount from the artist at a street fair, on the last day of the fair, just as the artist had been packing up to go home and long after all the best paintings had been sold. They were bright, Kate would give them that. One of them might even have looked like a lupine, if she squinted. She winced away from it and encountered the very blue eye of a Siamese cat, curled into a perfect circle in the dimpled seat of a chair. It hissed at Kate.

'Same backatcha,' Kate said, hurt. Usually animals liked her. Good thing they'd left Mutt in the car.

Wanda came into the room carrying a tray. Kate had seen more trays on this case than in the rest of her life combined. She didn't own one herself, not even before the fire. She wondered if perhaps she should buy one with which to serve guests coffee when they came to visit her brand-new home.

'I need to know everything you can tell me about William,' she said.

'I thought I already had,' Wanda said, pouring the coffee.

'No, you told me everything about Eugene, William's father, for whom you dumped William when you were in high school.'

The Siamese took exception to Kate's tone.

'Come on, you,' Wanda said, rising to scoop up the cat. 'You know you want to get hair all over my pillow anyway.' She carried the cat into another room. 'Sorry about that,' she said when she reappeared. 'Wilma's a little overprotective.'

Wanda and her cat, Wilma. Kate put the mug down on the coffee table, a rectangular wicker basket with a sheet of glass cut to fit the top. She rubbed her face and leaned forward, elbows on her knees, hands dangling. 'I'm trying to figure out who killed your lover, not to mention his son and his daughter, too. Aren't you the least bit interested in helping me do that?'

Wanda met her eyes steadily. 'William's mother was convicted of the crime. The police told me that Eugene was the victim of a home invasion. The paper said that Charlotte was killed by a hit-and-run driver. It's awful that so much tragedy has happened to one family, but it's not evidence of conspiracy to commit serial murders.'

Jim looked like he might applaud.

'They just let Victoria out,' Kate said.

'Yes.'

'They pardoned her for the crime of killing her son.'

'Yes.'

'How do you feel about that?'

'It's been thirty years. She's worked hard and made a difference during that time. She's paid for her crime.'

'That's big of you,' Kate said. 'Talk to me about William.'

There was a brief silence. Wanda took a deep breath and let it out slowly. She sat back and looked at Kate. 'He was one of the good guys,' she said, her eyes sad. 'He never said he'd do something and then didn't deliver, didn't make promises he didn't intend to keep. He was kind and honest and trustworthy. He wasn't a saint, you understand. He was just a good boy who never got to be a good man.'

'Did you believe Victoria had done it?'

Wanda shook her head again. 'I didn't know her that long or that well, but from what I did see, it seemed insane to me that anyone could possibly accuse her of such a thing. But the police seemed so sure, and then the trial... When she was convicted, I thought she must have done it, after all. How could a jury find her guilty otherwise?'

'And now?'

'And now I don't know,' Wanda said. She looked exhausted suddenly, and less beautiful. Again, Kate imagined a younger Wanda and the stir she must have created at Anchorage High School. Even Max had vivid memories of the young Wanda. What had he called her? A honey pot? 'Wanda, before you met William, did–'

'That's enough,' Victoria Bannister Muravieff said, appearing in the hallway.

Kate's mouth dropped open, and she suffered a momentary flashback to Max's smug expression. *I might,* he'd said when she asked him if he knew where Victoria was. Might, my ass, she thought to herself. 'Ms. Muravieff,' she said. 'I've been looking for you.'

Victoria came forward to take a seat next to Wanda. She took Wanda's hand in both of her own. 'Are you all right?'

'I'm fine,' Wanda said, managing a watery smile.

Victoria looked back at Kate. 'Why are you here? What else can you possibly need to know?'

Kate looked at Victoria, every regal inch the matriarch of a family whose roots went deep into Alaska's history. Truth be told, it was all that mattered to either of them. 'What if I told you,' Kate said slowly, 'what if I said I'm starting to think that the person who died in that house fire thirty-one years ago was the target all along?'

314

Victoria snorted. 'Today's big surprise. I already told you, I killed them both, or I tried to. I was broke,' she said stonily, 'and I needed the money. Now I want you to leave this house, please.'

She didn't rise to see Kate out. The last Kate saw of them was Victoria putting an arm around Wanda's shoulders, and tears running down Wanda's face as she let her head fall on Victoria's shoulder.

Jim looked back at Wanda's house as they drove away. 'How the hell did she wind up there?'

'Wanda works for Judge Berlin. She would have known about the release, and made sure she was waiting when Victoria got out.'

'That wasn't what I meant. What the hell is Victoria Bannister Muravieff doing staying in the same house with her husband's mistress? My God, thirty years ago this was an eighteen-year-old who'd had an affair with her husband. You'd think Victoria would want to scratch Wanda's eyes out.'

'They both loved William,' Kate said. 'And they both loved Eugene. I suppose it's natural that they would become–' She hesitated.

'Friends?' Jim said.

Kate shrugged. 'At least they'll both have someone to talk to about their lost men.'

'Sweet Jesus. I will never understand women.'

She summoned up a smile, but it was lacking its customary provocation. 'You're not supposed to.'

'Good to know.'

The gold nugget numerals on the Alaska map

clock read 5:00 P.M. when they walked in the door, and Jim reached for the remote and clicked on the television. He saw Kate's glance and said, 'Sorry. It's like a nervous twitch when I'm in Anchorage,' then made as if to turn it off again.

'Wait,' she said, staring at the screen.

Ralph Patton was shown leaving the court-house, his arm draped protectively around a woman holding a baby, shielding them from the television cameras. He looked angry, and immensely relieved.

'–in what the judge called a tragic and inexcusable miscarriage of justice, it appears that the arresting officer did not read Mr Patton his rights when Mr Patton was taken into custody. Further, in an exclusive interview with this reporter, Patton's attorney, Joseph Dial, inferred that there were other and multiple irregularities to do with Patton's arrest, culminating in the arraigning judge's decision this afternoon to allow Patton to go free on bail.'

A clip of Joseph Dial, talking head. 'It's hard to imagine such incompetence in this day and age,' he said into the camera. 'We have one of the finest police forces in the nation, well educated, well paid, and virtually free of corruption. But because of the victim's prominence in the community and the pressure on the Anchorage Police Department to hold someone accountable for the crime as soon as possible, there was a rush to judgment. My client is innocent, and I fully expect all charges against him to be dropped in the next twenty-four hours.'

The scene shifted back to the anchor, who

316

offered a brief recap of Charlotte's death, with a mention of Victoria's release, and moved on to the next story. Jim turned off the television.

Kate stared at the blank screen and saw Max's face as he was recounting the story of Jasper Bannister and Richie Constantine and Calvin Esterhaus: '*We even had ourselves something of a case – physical evidence linking him to the scene, not a half-bad description from an eyewitness, who even picked his photo out of a book of head shots. So we let him go.*'

She went to the phone and dialed.

'Erland Bannister, please,' she said when someone answered.

'Kate?' Jim said ominously.

'May I ask who is calling?'

'Kate Shugak.'

'One moment, please.'

'What the fuck do you think you're doing, Shugak?' Jim said.

'Kate,' Erland's voice came smoothly on the line. 'How nice to hear from you.'

'Hello, Erland. I just wanted to call and thank you for the invitation to your party. I had a lovely time.'

Kate felt the exhale of breath on the back of her neck.

'Why, thank you,' Erland said, 'it was my pleasure entirely.'

'In fact, I'd like to take you out to dinner as a way of showing my gratitude.'

He almost purred. 'You mean we will see each other again after all? How nice. When and where?'

'Are you free this evening?'

'I'll get free for you, Kate.'

Kate laughed, as low and as husky as she could make it. 'Great. 'What's your favorite restaurant?'

'It's a beautiful afternoon. Let's try the Crow's Nest for the view. Do you know it?'

'I'll find it,' Kate said.

'Seven o'clock? I'll make a reservation.'

'Perfect,' Kate said, and hung up.

'Nice outfit,' Erland said, giving her the once-over. 'I thought so the other night, too.'

'It's the only dress-up outfit I've got,' Kate said, smiling.

'Stick with what works,' Erland said.

'I generally do.'

The waiter appeared and Erland ordered wine. Kate let him pour her a glass, touched the rim to her lips, and smiled at him over it.

They were at the top of the Hotel Captain Cook, with a view all the way down Cook Inlet to Redoubt, and Kate thought she might be able to see the peak of Iliamna, too. Their table was set with white linen, silver, and fine china.

Kate let Erland order for both of them, sitting back in her chair, and thought that there wasn't a whole lot of difference between a man and a bull moose in rut. The moose had a bonus, the antlers with which he could fight off pretenders to his harem, but Erland's competence with a menu and a waiter could not be denied.

He finished and reached for his wine. 'A toast?'

She raised her glass. 'To what?'

He touched his glass to hers. 'How about to the

beginning of a beautiful relationship?'

She laughed. 'A *Casablanca* fan? Are you a closet romantic, Erland?'

'Oh, I've been out of the closet for years,' he said, and she laughed again.

'I was delighted when you called,' he said. 'I didn't know you were still in town.'

'Well, it's like I told you, Erland,' she said, allowing her smile to fade into an appropriate mixture of sadness and determination. 'Charlotte paid me in advance.'

'I understand that,' he said, leaning forward and letting his eyes drop to her neckline, 'and I honor your work ethic. But surely...' His voice trailed away artistically.

She leaned forward, arms crossed on the table. Might as well give him the full view. 'Surely?' she prompted.

'Well, certainly you have heard that my sister has been released from prison. The governor commuted her sentence to time served.'

'I had heard that,' Kate said. Their salads came. 'Why, do you think?'

Erland's eyes opened very wide. 'Why, because of the extraordinary work she did, building an education department at her facility.' He dropped his voice. 'Of course, I wouldn't want this to get around, since our governor doesn't like to appear as being soft on crime, but I think part of the reason was humanitarian.' He looked at Kate with dewy-eyed sincerity. 'Victoria has just lost a daughter. I think that played a part in his decision as well.'

'Of course,' Kate said with equal sincerity. 'The

governor has always been on the cutting edge of humanitarian concerns.'

Her voice was innocently smooth, but her words earned her a sharp look, quickly concealed. 'So you see,' Erland said, sitting back and taking up his wine to admire its color with the sun shining through it, 'really, Kate, your job is finished.'

'It would seem so,' Kate said, pretending again to sip at her wine. 'Still...'

'Still?' Erland said.

Kate gave him a smile of pretty apology. 'Charlotte did seem certain that Victoria did not set the fire that killed her son. I feel a certain...' She hesitated.

One of the better tricks in the interrogator's toolbox was to entice the subject into eliciting information himself.

'Yes?' Erland said. 'A certain what?'

'Obligation,' Kate said, and looked at Erland for reassurance.

He gave her a benevolent smile. 'Your sense of duty does you credit, Kate, but really, there is nothing left for you to do in this case.'

'But if your sister is innocent of the crime, wouldn't you like to have that innocence established beyond all doubt? And you lost a nephew, Erland. Wouldn't you like to see his real killer brought to justice?' Kate leaned forward again, all earnestness. 'I saw you on the news when you offered the reward for information leading to the arrest and apprehension of the hit-and-run driver who killed your niece.' She peered at him from beneath her eyelashes. 'I was impressed at your determination to see him brought to justice. Would

320

you want any less for the murderer of your nephew?'

He sighed heavily. 'It was all so long ago.' He paused, and asked almost casually, 'Do you have any leads?'

Not by the flicker of an eyelash did he betray that he already knew of her interview with Ralph Patton, but Kate could feel his attention focused directly and unwaveringly upon her, as if she were a bug beneath a microscope. The act of observation changes the thing observed, she thought. Obviously, Erland had skipped that class in Physics 101. 'A few,' she said dismissively. She smiled modestly. 'As you say, it has been thirty years. It's been difficult to track down the investigating officers and the witnesses who testified at your sister's trial. Many of the people involved have died or moved Outside.'

He sat back and smiled at her, an intimate smile full of intelligence, a smile that knew women inside and out, a smile of power and assurance. 'That's a shame. I wish you luck.'

'You have no objection to my proceeding with the investigation, then?' Kate said, trying to infuse her question with a hint of anxiety, as if she required permission of the great and powerful Erland Bannister before going forward.

'None at all,' Erland said, waving a hand. 'As you pointed out, if my sister is innocent of the crime for which she was convicted, certainly that is something that I want the whole world to know.'

It was a bit of a change from the 'Here's your hat. What's your hurry?' attitude the last time

321

they'd met.

'You did know that the person who killed my niece has, in a travesty of justice, been set free on bail.'

'Really?' Kate said. 'How on earth did that happen?'

Erland allowed rage to darken his eyes, just enough to be convincing. 'I don't know, but I'm going to make it my business to find out.'

'If anyone can do that, Erland, you can,' Kate said.

The waiter served their entrées, and afterward they talked of other things – local politics, the cost of a week's worth of groceries for a family of four now compared to ten years ago, the problems of shipping to Bush communities, Oliver's most recent case (Erland wincing at the thought of the family's only child of that generation in the business of turning criminals loose on the streets again, then saying, 'But I have high hopes of enticing him into Dwyer, Watson, an estate-planning firm run by a friend of mine'), the record salmon run up the Kanuyaq River and the lack of one up the Yukon. Erland was by turns witty, wise, and charming, with a large dollop of obvious attraction to his dinner companion. He was well-nigh irresistible.

For her part, Kate kept her lips parted in a constant gasp of wonder and admiration. She didn't know how much of it Erland bought, but like all great men, he had an ego that was there to be stroked, and, needs must when the devil drives, Kate could stroke a male ego with the best of them.

She permitted him to walk her to the car, where they took fond leave of one another.

On the way home, she wondered if it had worked, if he was as smart as she thought he was. Lacking his resources, all she could do was lure him out of hiding, encourage him to show his hand in some way.

'You're provoking him to attack, Kate,' Jim had said earlier, and she had replied, 'I know. At this point, it's all I can do.'

'You're going to get yourself killed, goddamm it!'

His anger was enough to have her cruise past the town house once, checking for suspicious vehicles or activity, before she pulled into the driveway.

She lowered the garage door and went into the house. 'Mutt?' she said. There was a muted, un-identifiable noise from the postage stamp-size piece of lawn that served as a backyard. Her skin prickled, and she slid along the wall to the window and looked out.

Kevin and Jordan had erected a tent and were currently occupying it with Mutt.

She opened the door. 'Hey, guys.'

'Hey, Kate.'

'Your mom know you're over here?'

'Sure,' Jordan said.

'Sure,' Kevin said.

'Wuff,' Mutt said.

Right. 'Okay, but in the morning, we really have to talk. You got enough to eat?'

'Yes.'

'Want more blankets?'

'We're using the sleeping bags from the garage.'

'Okay. I'll see you in the morning.'

'Kate?'

'What?'

'Thanks.'

Don't thank me, she thought.

She went into the kitchen and poured herself a Diet Sprite by the light of the refrigerator. When she closed the door again, Jim was standing there. Kate nearly jumped out of her skin.

'So?' he said. 'How'd it go?'

'I didn't know you were here. I didn't see your car outside.'

'The guy I borrowed it from needed it back. How'd it go?'

Kate rolled her head, and he surprised her by turning her around to put his hands on her shoulders, whereupon he began to knead them.

'Oh yeah,' she said on a quiet exhalation.

'How'd it go?' he said for the third time.

'He's pretty slick, is old Erland Bannister. Honestly? I don't know.'

'How long are you going to stick around waiting to find out?'

'I don't know that, either.' She gave the ghost of a laugh.

'What?'

'It turns out there is such a thing as too much information, and I've got it all. I just don't know what the hell to do with any of it, and I still don't know who burned down that house and killed that kid.'

'Even the governor stopped short of saying Victoria was innocent of the crime,' Jim said softly,

324

his thumbs zeroing in on the knot of tension below her shoulder blades.

'Oh God, *yes*,' she said, 'right there.' She was silent for a moment. 'Then why kill Charlotte? There's no point to her death if I wasn't looking for who really killed William Muravieff. There's no point to the murder of Eugene Muravieff and the attempted murder of Kurt Pletnikoff. Killing them was supposed to put me out of a job.'

'Those two goons were waiting to kill you, too.'

'Yeah, that would be another way of discouraging me. Someone is tying up lose ends all over town. And Erland Bannister is–'

'Is what?'

'He's just so damned smug.'

'I don't think you can arrest someone for aggravated smugness, Kate.'

'His whole attitude is – it's like he's got all his exits covered, and he knows it, and he's making sure I know it, so that there is nothing left for me to do but go home or...'

'Or?'

She thought of the party at Erland's house. 'Or stay here and join his herd.'

'"His herd"?'

'You should have seen the people at his party. Talk about suck-ups, brownnosers, and hangers-on. You should have heard how he talked about them. Guests in his house, for whom he had no liking and no respect. It was sickening.'

His hands paused. 'You turning this into some kind of class warfare, Kate?'

'What?' she said, her head whipping around. 'No! What the hell are you talking about?'

325

'The Bannisters have, you don't. Is that what this is about?'

It was so ridiculous, she laughed out loud. 'No. That is not what this is about.'

Jim resisted an urge to cover his balls. 'Well, then, how about race warfare?'

'What?'

'You heard me,' Jim said steadily, still kneading her shoulders. 'Is there possibly a little bit of "us versus them" going on here? The residue of three hundred years of white power?'

'You think this can be reduced to skin color?' Kate said hotly.

'No,' Jim said. 'I don't.'

There was another, longer silence. 'Okay,' Kate said. 'I heard you.'

Jim remained silent.

Kate glared at him. 'Why are you still here, anyway?'

'I told you.' He mustered up a lazy grin. 'I got your back on this one, Shugak.'

Never happy on the defensive, she was delighted to switch on the siren. 'You sure that's all it is?' she said, mimicking him. She leaned back against him, and smiled when she felt his erection settle into the crack of her ass.

He didn't move away, but he said, 'This has nothing to do with us.'

'Oh.' The gluteus maximus, properly employed, was a well-muscled instrument of torture.

He caught his breath. 'Because there is no us.'

'No?'

'No. This is about you pissing off one of the most powerful men in Alaska, Kate, a man with

326

his fingers tied to every Alaskan string there is. It won't be long before he starts pulling those strings. If you're determined to carry on with this, you're going to need backup. I'd do the same for any friend in this situation.'

Kate smiled.

'I've got to pee,' Jim said.

'I cannot begin to tell you how much I am enjoying this,' Kate said to his vanishing back.

She followed him up the stairs, unbuttoning the glittering red jacket. He came out of the bathroom as she walked into the bedroom.

'You know,' Kate said, 'from the beginning, this has been all about family. There's Erland and Victoria, brother and sister. Erland married Alice, and from what I picked up at the party, they had no children. Which may be a contributing factor to why she carves up her face every six months.' Remembering Alice's pale, taut skin, as firm and smooth as a Barbie doll's, if not quite so forever young, Kate shivered. There was something frightening in such a single-minded pursuit of a semblance of youth. She walked over to the dresser and peered into the mirror.

Her skin was firm and smooth and a pale brown that had turned its usual gold after a summer spent outdoors, but it was thirty-five-year-old skin, no getting around it, with at least the hint of squint lines at the corners of her eyes and laugh lines at the corners of her mouth. Her eyes were the sort of indeterminate hazel that could seem anything from gray to green, depending on where she was and what she was wearing. She examined her temples. Still black as an October night, but it wouldn't be long. She raised her chin and looked at her throat. Nope, she would never be mistaken for sixteen again.

'So what?' she told her reflection.

Jim, at first wary and then baffled, thought the best option available to him in this situation was to remain silent. Nobody ever got into trouble by keeping their mouth shut.

'Okay,' Kate said, turning from the mirror and removing the jacket to hang it in the closet. He watched her every move with close attention, his gaze lingering on the lace cups of her bra, cut almost down to her nipples.

She walked over to the bed and turned on the lamp, back to the door to turn off the overhead. Half in shadow, she slipped out of the silk slacks, leaving her dressed in the bra and a pair of matching panties. He swallowed hard. Now he understood why they called them briefs.

'Erland and Alice had no kids,' Kate said, wandering back over to the dresser. She raised her arms to run both hands through her hair. The line of her back arched and he could see in the mirror that her breasts were threatening to spill out of the bra.

She met his eyes in the mirror. Did she know what she was doing to him? Her voice was so cool, so controlled, so matter-of-fact. 'Victoria, Erland's sister, married Eugene, had three kids – William and Charlotte dead, Oliver still living. Victoria divorced Eugene – according to Max, at least in part due to family disapproval over their lily white daughter marrying an Aleut. Victoria then went to work in the family business, helping keep the books. Prior to that, though, she'd had a very public falling-out with them over their plans to lay off union workers and replace them with contract hires. In the meantime, her husband, Eugene, gets himself elected to head the employees' union. This must have been pretty annoying to a man like Jasper Bannister, not to mention his son and heir.'

She walked over and got the straight-backed chair out of the corner and carried it back to the dresser. She straddled it and rested her arms along the back and her chin on her arms. His eyes dropped to the graceful line of her leg, knees bent, toes pointed. She rolled her head one way and then another, and met Jim's eyes again in the mirror, an obvious invitation in her own. He walked over to put his hands on her shoulders again, this time with no fabric, no beads between his skin and hers.

'Is that enough, in and of itself, to cause Erland, a highly respected and greatly feared member of the community, to gallop out to the valley and torch his sister's house?' Kate closed her eyes and tipped her head back. 'Maybe my neck a little. Yeah, right there.'

Her body seemed to hum with pleasure beneath his hands.

'I could understand that,' Kate said, 'if the attempt hadn't been so clumsy. One thing you can be sure of, Erland would hire good help. If Erland had meant to burn down Victoria's house as a warning to her, he would have hired someone smart enough to check that the house was empty. Arson is one thing. Murder is quite another.'

He held her neck firmly but gently and began

working at her spine with the other.

She let her head fall forward again and moaned a little. The sound went straight to his cock, which he had thought couldn't get any harder. 'Not to mention which,' she said, gasping a little, 'Victoria and Eugene's actions on behalf of the union were fruitless. PME did in fact lay off all its union employees and replace them with contract hires, and now it's one of the top twenty business concerns in the state. It's hard to quarrel with that kind of success, and certainly Victoria's daughter, Charlotte, and her son Oliver both have had some kind of financial stake in the success of the family firm. And so does Victoria. Now that she's out.'

He had to clear his throat to speak. 'You're thinking he didn't do it, then?'

'I don't know,' she said. 'He knows who did, though. Hey.'

He was having difficulty focusing on her words. It was a minute before he said, 'What?'

'I wonder who Charlotte's heir was?'

Her skin had been steadily warming beneath his hands. He'd been angry at her for meeting Erland, for deliberately putting herself in harm's way. Now all his anger seemed to have vanished, to be replaced by a need so great it threatened to drown him.

'I said I wonder who Charlotte's heir was? Emily, do you think?'

He dragged himself back from the precipice with difficulty.

'Yeah. Probably. Why not? They were as good as married.'

'It would explain why she won't talk to me.

330

Erland could have threatened to contest Charlotte's will in court.'

'Could have.' He couldn't stop himself, his hands slipped down over her shoulders and cupped her breasts.

She leaned back against him and he looked up to see them in the mirror, her seated in front of him, straddling the chair, his hands slipping into the cups of her bra, that tiny little pair of panties barely containing the mound between her legs.

He picked her up and carried her to the bed.

CHAPTER 19

She woke up thirsty in the middle of the night and slid from the bed. Jim rolled to one side but didn't wake up. She pulled on his T-shirt and padded downstairs to get herself a glass of water.

In the cold dark before dawn, she knew Erland Bannister was never going to bite. All he had to do was wait for her to leave. She was beaten, and she hated it. She couldn't remember the last time it had happened. 'Some days you get the bear,' she said out loud, 'and some days the bear gets you.'

It was the thought of Charlotte Muravieff that bothered her most. Charlotte, that middle-aged Alaskan icon with the alternative, pampered, extremely well-funded lifestyle. Charlotte, not Victoria, very possibly the victim of a thirty-year miscarriage of justice, Charlotte, not Eugene

Muravieff, whom Kate had very probably gotten killed just by looking for him, Charlotte, not William, a seventeen-year-old boy barely on the cusp of manhood, who never had a chance at life. Kate thought of the first time she had seen Charlotte, so desperate, so determined. She thought of her at Erland's party, when Kate had scored off the phoniest person in a room full of phonies, and Charlotte had looked so pleased and grateful.

It seemed about all Kate was going to be able to do for Charlotte.

She heard a noise in the backyard and went to look out the window. The boys' tent was silent and dark. She opened the door just to be sure, and had just enough time to see two dark figures coalesce out of the gloom before something dropped over her head and everything went black.

'Hey!' she yelled stupidly, and a sledgehammer hit her face and everything went blacker.

Three different cannonballs hit Jim at once and he came awake thrashing and yelling. He slid off the bed in an ignominious heap just about the time someone switched on the overhead light. He blinked up at it. 'Kate? What the hell is going on?'

He was engulfed by a seething swarm of what looked like ten kids and sounded like twenty dogs, all yelling and barking.

'What the hell?' he said in frustration. He was rewarded by another burst of sound, and he put back his head and bellowed, *'Quiet!'*

Silence fell. The melee resolved itself into two frightened boys and one angry dog, who snarled at him in a way that reminded him of the time

332

Kate had been—

'Kate?' he said. 'Kate!' He got to his feet, scooping up his jeans as he ran. She wasn't in the bathroom, in the kitchen, watching a movie. 'Kate!' he bellowed, even though he knew it was useless. He turned to head back upstairs and had to stop before he ran over the boys and the dog, who had followed on his heels and were now staring up at him with equal anxiety over, their faces, furred and furless.

Jim felt his heart stop. Yes, he did, and it did, it simply stopped in his chest for one interminable moment. His mouth opened and closed again. With a thump that deafened him, his heart resumed beating, fast and high up in his throat. His voice, when it managed to get out around his heart, was a low croak. 'Where is she?'

Mouths opened and closed, including Mutt's. He couldn't hear anything. 'What?' he said. 'What?'

Sound returned without warning and he winced away from it. *They took her!'*

One of the boys – Kevin? Jordan? Jim couldn't remember. God help him, he couldn't remember. What kind of cop was he? This boy took Jim's arm and led him to the living room and more or less shoved him down on the couch. He put his hand on the back of Jim's head, preparatory to pushing Jim's head between his knees, when Jim raised a hand to stop him. 'It's okay, kid,' he told him. 'I'm okay. Thanks. You did good.'

'What?' the kid mouthed. Jim still couldn't hear him, but that was because the other boy was back up to one thousand decibels. He flapped his hand and it ceased. Mutt nosed beneath his arm, emitting a continual anxious whine, and that scared Jim more than any other single thing in the last five minutes. If Mutt had even a smidgeon of a clue as to where Kate was, she'd have been on her trail and long gone. Instead, Mutt crowded next to him, restless, even whimpering. He couldn't remember ever hearing Mutt whimper.

'Who took her?' he said, enunciating even these few words with extreme care, because his tongue felt inexplicably too large for his mouth.

The older kid spoke. 'Two men. They had something thrown over her, a blanket or a coat or something, and they hit her and then they threw her in the back of a van.'

'A van?'

The kid nodded.

'What color?'

The kid hesitated, and Jim's heart sank. 'It was dark,' the kid said.

'Of course it was dark; it's four in the fucking morning,' Jim said, and caught himself when he saw the kids' expressions.

The older kid swallowed and said, 'No, I meant the van was dark, dark blue, maybe, maybe even black.'

Jim's heart lifted again. 'Did you – is there a chance – can you remember one or two or any of the numbers on the license plate?'

The kid reeled off the number like an off-duty cop. Jim stared at him, mouth slightly open. 'What?' he said.

The kid did it again. 'They'd daubed mud on

the plate, but the streetlight hit it just right when they turned, and I–'

Jim lunged out of his chair and grabbed the kid up by his shoulders, the boy's feet dangling two feet from the floor, and almost kissed him. The kid was afraid he was going to, but Jim set him down on the floor and thumped him on the shoulder hard enough to knock him forward a step. 'Good job, kid,' he said fervently, 'I mean *really* good job.'

He was halfway out the door before he thought about the boys, and he paused just long enough to bellow over his shoulder, 'Don't move from this spot, do you hear? And don't open the door to anyone except me! And call your damn parents, damn it!'

Later, he wouldn't remember very much about the drive uptown, but the expression on the face of the willowy blonde who was sharing Brendan's bed that night would stay with him for a while. Mutt didn't help, prowling next to him, ears lying back, fangs slightly bared, and an expression in her great yellow eyes that was not at all human.

Brendan took one look at Jim's face and said, 'What?'

His response was not adequate to the occasion, evidently, because Mutt leapt up on his table and barked once right in his face.

'Holy Mary Mother of God,' Brendan said. The blonde screamed and slammed the bedroom door.

'They took Kate,' Jim said tightly.

'Who took her?' Brendan said, but he knew as

335

well as Jim did.

'I've got a tag number,' Jim said, and reeled it off.

A laptop sat on a crowded desk, and Brendan booted it up. 'It'll be stolen,' Brendan said over his shoulder.

Jim paced up and down in an agony of suspense. Mutt stood stiff-legged in the doorway, glowering and occasionally growling, although apparently just on general principles. Brendan cast an unfriendly eye in Jim's direction. 'And where the hell were you when she got took?'

'Asleep,' Jim said.

Brendan looked at him.

'Just find the fucking van!'

The computer beeped and a screen popped up. Brendan scrolled down. 'Your van is registered to a Paul Cassanovas. And lookie here – it has in fact been reported stolen. Let me pull up the police report.' Brendan tapped some keys, another agonizing wait, and a second screen popped up. 'Mr. Cassanovas reported it stolen yesterday when he parked it at the Dimond Fred Meyer and forgot the keys in the ignition when he went inside to buy groceries.'

'He left the car running in August?' Jim said.

'It happens, only usually it's the driveway, when they run back inside in the morning. But you're right: Usually you run across this kind of thing in the winter, when it's cold and they want to come back to a warm car. Hmmm. Let's do a search on Mr. Cassanovas in the corrections database, shall we?'

A minute later, Brendan said, 'Bingo. Mr. Cassanovas has served time for B and E, burglary, theft.'

'Has he got an address?'

'Yes, but wait.' Brendan tapped a few more keys. 'Last known address was a boarding house on Ingra. Here.' Brendan scribbled the number down. 'Call them, see if he's there.'

Jim snatched up Brendan's phone and punched in the number.

'Not only does Mr. Cassanovas have an address—' Brendan said.

A sleepy, surly voice swore at Jim but answered his questions before the receiver slammed down. 'He checked out last week,' Jim said.

'—he has known associates.'

'Who? Names, addresses.'

Brendan's lips thinned. 'The only one who matters is Ralph Patton.'

'Son of a bitch,' Jim said, 'they've got her, god-damn it, they've got her.'

'Son of a bitch,' Brendan echoed, still looking at the computer screen.

'What?'

'Guess who Mr. Cassanovas' counsel was?'

'Son of a bitch,' Jim said again.

'Well, yeah,' Brendan said, 'but he's also known as Oliver Muravieff. Wait a minute. Where are you going?'

'I'm going to talk to Oliver Muravieff about a little matter concerning his billable hours.'

Moving faster than anyone had a right to expect of a man of his size, Brendan was up and had his hand around Jim's arm. 'Wait a minute,' he said. 'Let's think about this. And after we've thought, let's call the cops.'

The next thing Brendan knew he was slammed up against the wall. 'Take it easy, Jesus, Jim,' he said. A door cracked open and the frightened face of a neighbor peeped out. 'It's okay, Mrs. Hartzberg,' he told her. 'Everything's fine. Just go on back to bed.'

It wasn't easy to be serene with two hundred pounds of pissed-off trooper in his face, not to mention the snarling, snapping half wolf next to the trooper, but, to his credit, Brendan managed it. 'Just calm down a minute,' he said. Brendan let go of Jim's wrists, where his hands weren't doing much good anyway, and raised both hands, palms out. 'Just take a beat here and think this through.'

'There's nothing to think about, Brendan. We can't call the cops.'

'Why not?'

'Because they're his family's cops,' Jim said. 'They let Patton go on command. They're not going to help us.'

'Come on, Jim, you don't really believe that. Jim. Jim!'

Jim let Brendan go and walked out, Mutt moving like the hunter she was at his side.

He was conscious enough of what he was going to do to stop at the town house to pick up shirt, jacket, and his sidearm, although the latter was too big not to attract too much of the wrong kind of notice. It would have to go in the glove compartment. His backup piece, a .38, he strapped to his ankle.

He looked in the mirror and saw a grim-eyed

civilian staring back at him. Whatever happened next, the troopers were going to come in for as little blame as possible. He looked up Oliver Muravieff in the phone book and copied down the number.

He went back downstairs and told the boys, 'Pack up your stuff. I'm taking you home.'

They were frightened and silent during the ride. As he pulled into their driveway, he said, 'Can you get in?'

'We hide a key outside,' the older one said as the younger one slid from the Subaru. 'Mister?'

'What?'

'Could you ... could you maybe call us when you find her?'

The forlorn little voice pierced Jim's self-absorption the way nothing else could have, and he looked at the kid, really looked at him for the first time since he'd gotten back from Brendan's. 'Yes,' he said. 'I will. Better, I'll bring her here so you can talk to her yourselves.'

'Thanks,' the kid said, and trudged after his brother.

Jim watched them for a second, and then he got out of the car. 'Hey,' he said.

The boys stopped and looked back at him.

'You did good, getting that license plate number,' he said. 'You're the reason I'm going to find her.'

The kids' faces lightened a little, and he climbed back in the car and drove downtown, where he found a parking space within walking distance of Oliver's building. He got out to case it. It had an underground parking garage, so he would have to do it the hard way. He went back to the Subaru and waited with hard-won patience for the clock to read 8:00 A.M.

At 8:01 A.M., Oliver Muravieff arrived, his silver Miata disappearing into the underground parking lot.

At 8:05 A.M., Jim dialed Oliver's office number from Kate's cell phone. 'Yes,' he said in a voice from which any trace of impatience or worry had been completely erased. 'I'm an old friend of Mr. Muravieff's from law school, and I've got an eight-hour layover before I head for Barrow. I just wanted to know if he was in his office. I'd like to drop in and say hello... He'll be there for the next couple of hours? Splendid, I'll see you soon.' He dropped his voice to what he'd been told was a sexy baritone. 'Listen, do me a favor. Don't tell him I'm coming. I want to surprise him. Thanks.'

He disconnected. 'Stay,' he said to Mutt.

She wasn't having any.

'I mean it, goddamn it,' he said. 'Get back in that fucking truck!'

A couple of young attorneys who hadn't been practicing long enough to take such scenes in their stride scurried by, not making eye contact.

Jim squatted down on his haunches and took Mutt's head in his hands. She was alternately whining and growling. 'She's not here,' Jim said, trying to shake some sense into her. 'She's not here, damn it, but the guy I'm going to see will know where they've got her, and that's when I'll need you. Mutt, please, get in the truck.' He stood up and held the door open. 'Get in, and stay,' he said.

She eyed him narrowly. It was her choice, and they both knew it. There was no way he was going to bundle 140 pounds of snarling, snapping half husky, half wolf unwilling back in the truck if she didn't want to go there on her own. 'I'll need backup, girl,' he told her, painfully conscious of seconds ticking away. 'Best they don't know I've got it yet. Get in. Please. Get in.'

She whined, she snarled some more, she even nipped at his calf on her way by, but she got in. He heaved a sigh of relief, and as a sign of trust, he rolled down the window halfway. 'I know you could take this out if you wanted to – hell, you could probably take out the door if you wanted to – but I'm trusting you to *stay* here and wait for me. Stay,' he repeated.

She looked at him, ears a little flattened, lips slightly drawn back, teeth gleaming in the morning sun. She did not look friendly.

'Well, for sure no one's going to steal that Subaru,' he said.

'Hello, darling,' he said to Oliver's receptionist, affecting the slow drawl he had used earlier on the phone. 'Which way is that old boy's office?'

The receptionist fluttered her eyelashes and said, 'I'm afraid Mr. Muravieff has someone with him just now – oh, no, I believe he's just leaving,' and she turned to smile as her boss came through the door behind her desk.

Oliver Muravieff's client barely registered on Jim's peripheral vision. 'Ollie!' he said in his biggest, boomiest voice. 'How the hell are you!' And he steamed forward, hand extended.

341

Oliver's hand came up either in greeting or in self-defense.

'I'm sorry?' he said, his brow creasing, 'I'm not sure I–'

Jim pushed him back into his office before he could finish the sentence. He stumbled a little over his cane, and when he got his balance back, he looked at Jim with the beginnings of a scowl. 'Who the hell are you?'

'All right, you little motherfucker, where is Kate Shugak?' Jim said.

'Who?' Oliver said. But he took just a little too long to say it.

Jim kicked the cane out of Oliver's hand. 'Where is Kate Shugak?'

Oliver fell awkwardly, and Jim heard a sound that might have been the crack of a bone. Oliver yelled.

The door started to open, but Jim slammed it shut and raised his voice. 'Ollie, old buddy, you're just as clumsy catching that ball as you were in college. It's okay, honey. He's just taken himself a tumble, but we're fine!'

Oliver stared up at him in pain and disbelief. 'Who the hell do you think you are,' he said, 'barging into my office, assaulting me verbally, assaulting me physically? Do you know what a felony is?'

Jim took a step forward. 'If I commit one, I'll hire you to get me off. Just like you got Paul Cassanovas off. It's what you do.'

'Paul Cassanovas? What's he got to do with anything?'

'He's a client of yours.'

'So? I've got a lot of clients.'

'This client hangs out with a guy name of Ralph Patton.'

Oliver was recovering a little of his sangfroid. He looked at his cane as if to pick it up. Jim took another step forward, and Oliver abandoned the idea for the moment. 'Again,' he said, 'what does any of this have to do with you barging in here and assaulting me?'

'Paul Cassanovas just had his van stolen.'

Oliver rolled his eyes. 'Look, Mr. – whoever you are – I–'

'Yesterday,' Jim said, 'about eight hours before somebody coldcocked Kate Shugak and tossed her into the back of it.'

There was a moment of silence. Oliver appeared to be thinking deeply. 'There's no way you can know that.'

'There were two eyewitnesses. How do you think I traced the van?'

'I knew nothing of this,' Oliver said. His face had paled and he was breathing a little faster.

'Yeah,' Jim said, 'you did, and you're going to take me to her.'

'Is that so?' a voice said, and Jim looked around to see Fred Gamble of the Federal Bureau of Investigation step into the room.

She woke to a dull, throbbing ache that seemed to take up the whole left side of her head. She couldn't see and she could barely breathe through the covering over her face. For a moment, she panicked, and then she forced herself into shallow respiration, one breath at a time. She tried to move her hands, her feet, couldn't.

343

She could barely feel them.

There was a narrow concave surface beneath her. She tried to roll and hit an edge. She rolled back to the center. A cot perhaps. She could smell wood smoke, or the residue of it. She was in a cabin, maybe?

She was also hearing voices.

Was there pain in heaven? Certainly there were voices. Joan of Arc had heard them; it stood to reason Kate Shugak would hear them, too. Of course, Joan had been given directions. Maybe the Woman Who Keeps the Tides or Calm Waters' Daughter would give Kate a sign.

She moved again and her head fell off. She couldn't stop a low, agonized groan.

Maybe it was hell. Definitely pain in hell, according to the preachers, lots and lots, and Kate had sinned, big-time. She wished she was sinning right now, back at the town house, upstairs in that king-size bed with Jack.

That wasn't right. Jim, that was it, Jim in that enormous bed and her having her way with him.

Was he one of the voices?

'I only hit her once,' someone said.

'You shouldn't have hit her at all,' another voice said coldly and clearly.

Nope. Not Jim, neither one of them. But the voice did sound familiar.

She went away for a little while, hiding from the pain, and when she woke up again, the stifling cover had been removed from her face. She sucked in lungfuls of clean, cool air. They hadn't gagged her, hallelujah, but of course that only meant there was no one within shouting distance.

Still, she had to try.

She gathered everything she had, took as deep a breath as she could, and produced a small croak. She waited a moment and tried again. 'Help,' she said, gaining volume. 'Can anybody hear me? Help! *Help!* HELP!'

No one replied. She heard the rustle of wind in the trees, a flock of chickadees, talking amongst themselves, and what might have been the heavy footsteps of a moose. Nothing else.

She looked around her, her restraints permitting her limited movement. The wood smoke had been a clue. She was in a cabin, a small one-room affair, studiedly rustic, filled with Adirondack furniture Kate recognized from a catalog she had read once when she'd been stuck on a long flight with no books. There was a little woodstove and a counter with a Coleman stove and a pink plastic dish tub and a matching pink plastic dish drainer on it. There was a shelf beneath holding a variety of canned goods and a cardboard box with the top cut away to form a tray, holding bottles of water.

Kate had a sudden raging thirst. She rolled towards the edge of the cot and discovered that, along with tying her hands and feet, they had tied her to the cot. She looked down and saw that she was still wearing Jim's T-shirt, which had rucked up to her waist, and she was so enraged and so thirsty that she cursed at the top of her voice for a full minute.

When she was done, she felt much better. Her head still hurt and her right eye was swollen almost shut. Her vision in that eye might even be a little foggy, but she could still see fine out of the other. She looked the room over again. She twisted around on the cot and saw that it had folding legs. She considered the possibilities.

The ropes around her hands and feet were tight, tight enough to cause her hands and feet to swell. The rope around her body, the one tying her to the cot, was a little looser. One end of it was connected to her hands, the other tied off to itself in a slipknot.

She smiled, showing all her teeth and displaying a distinct and unnerving resemblance to Mutt, had anyone been there to see it. She began rocking back and forth in the cot, back and forth, back and forth, until the cot began to rock up on its legs, an inch, two inches, three, six, twelve. It was a heavy sea and Kate was wallowing in the troughs, way up and way down, the rope cutting into her now-bare stomach as she flung her body weight at it, until finally, the cot flipped over at last and Kate splatted facefirst against the floor.

It didn't do the injury to her face any good, and she groaned again.

It was a wood floor, poorly finished and dirty. In the end, that was what got her moving again. She pulled her knees to her chest and, using her shoulders and her head, began to inch her way toward the counter, the rope attaching her to the cot really cutting into her now, and the cot on her back weighing a lot more than it looked.

She'd about given up hope of ever reaching the counter, stopped even looking up to see how far away it was, when the cot bumped into it. She looked up, and there on a shelf not a foot away loomed the bottles of water. Alaska Glacierblend. Virgin Water from the Eklutna Glacier. It might as well still be frozen in the Eklutna Glacier, for all the good it was doing her. Kate felt tears well into her eyes and forced them back by a massive effort of sheer will. She managed to get her knees beneath her again and tried to snag a bottle with her teeth, but the damn cot kept getting in the way. That gave her an idea, and she used one of the poles of the cot frame to knock one of the bottles down. It rolled beneath the shelf.

'FUCK!' she yelled. 'Mutt! Where are you, damn it! There's never a goddamn wolf around when you need one!'

Which was patently unfair, considering how many times Mutt had galloped to her rescue, but Kate wasn't in a fair frame of mind. She used the cot pole to knock another bottle to the floor and this time managed to pounce on it before it got away. She finally got the bottle in between her chin and her chest and wriggled it down to her hands, which were bound wrist to wrist. She could open them just far enough to grasp the bottle near the cap, although – sweet Jesus! – the flexing of her fingers hurt like a bastard. Her breath hissed through her teeth as her hands fumbled at the cap.

She was ready to bite it off with her teeth, but the seal broke and the cap unscrewed easily enough. She slid the bottle carefully upward through her hands and took the neck in her teeth and tilted the bottle upward. Cool, clean water flooded down her throat. She choked on it, and some got up her nose, but she drank the rest of it down, every single wonderful drop.

She let the empty bottle fall and watched it roll beneath the counter. The floor seemed to slant that way. She hoped the contractor had charged Erland Bannister an arm and a leg for extremely shoddy workmanship.

For she had no doubt as to the identity of her kidnapper. Charlotte Bannister had hired Kate Shugak to get Victoria Muravieff out of jail, and in so doing, Kate had stumbled into a can of worms, which had turned out to be a nest of vipers. Of them all, Erland's bite would be the most poisonous.

Really her only question at this point was why he hadn't killed her outright. What did she know that he needed to know before he did?

She put those thoughts behind her. Her thirst satisfied for the moment, now she had to get free.

She knelt on the floor in a sort of crouch beneath the cot, which was roped to her like an overaffectionate dog.

Mutt, Jim, wherever you are, please be on your way here. Please have seen me get tossed into the back of that vehicle; please be on the trail of that vehicle right now.

She pushed those thoughts away, too.

The cot's poles ran through two sleeves, one at either edge of the canvas that formed the bed. She couldn't look around behind her to see how the legs were attached. She tried to stand up, but the poles were longer than she was tall. She bent over, as far over as she could, and tried to stand again.

This time, she made it, although her blood pounded through to her bound feet. The aft portion of the cot's legs dragged behind her on the floor, and she could only manage the smallest hop, the poles scraping behind her. She hopped and scraped, nevertheless, until the upright ends of the poles bumped into the wall of the cabin. She hopped up and down, knocking the ends of the poles against the wall. Slowly, a fraction of an inch at a time, the poles began to slide into their canvas sleeves, until the sleeves extended beyond the poles and the canvas was flopping down in her face. Still Kate hopped, bent over, her back beginning to ache, the side of her face one enormous hammering pain, thumping the ends of the poles into the wall.

Eventually, she noticed that the rope had slid up the cot a little, too – not much, but maybe just enough. About that time, the rope around her must have caught on the cot legs, or maybe the legs had caught on the canvas, or maybe both, so it was now or never. She had one thing in her favor: The rope that bound her was half-inch polypro, plastic rope, which if improperly knotted had a tendency to lose tension and slip. These knots were at best granny knots and they were already loose. She crouched down, nose to knees, and began to wriggle.

After that, it was almost easy. She dragged the cot back to the counter, managing to collapse its legs and fold the poles together. The canvas hung down, making a nuisance of itself, but Kate managed to reach the Coleman stove with her bound hands. Heart knocking against her ribs, she turned the right knob in front of the right burner. Nothing, not a damn thing, not even so much as a hiss of fuel.

'Shit,' she said, and tried for the other knob.

This time she heard the clicking of an automatic ignition and could have shouted for joy. The burner lighted with what looked to Kate like a positively joyous flame. Without a moment of hesitation, she held her bound hands over the burner, as close as she could get. The rope began to sizzle. She lowered her hands more, careless of the heat on her wrists, and the rope began to melt. She strained with all her muscles, pulling the rope against itself, and it separated suddenly without any warning. Her left hand hit the cot and toppled it to the floor, and her right hand hit the plastic tub and sent it flying across the cabin.

The ropes binding her feet were quickly untied. She rummaged through the items on the counter and the shelves, looking for a weapon. There was a box of silverware, including a few bread knives with serrated edges. She set them aside.

She remembered the water bottles rolling beneath the counter, and dropped down to peer into the narrow space. It was dark and she couldn't see anything. She reached beneath with one hand, feeling around in the darkness, hoping a big rat wasn't waiting there to bite her. Were there rats in Alaska? She couldn't remember ever seeing one.

She shook her head angrily, concentrating. The sleeve was shoved back from her shoulder and it scraped the bottom of the shelf, picking up a splinter. She pulled out the empty water bottle, the full bottle, a church key, three metal beer caps, seven kernels of popcorn, a couple of blue plastic poker chips, a thick rubber band, a steak knife, and a handful of .22 shell casings.

The steak knife was a welcome sight. The shell casings were not.

She didn't make the mistake of running for it, not yet. She walked back and forth across the cabin, stepping carefully and opening and closing her hands. God, they hurt, like her feet, and her head. She was so tired. She wanted to set the cot back up and take a nap. She was certainly dressed for it.

That brought her back to her senses in a hurry, and she rifled through the cabin's one closet, formed by hanging a wire across a corner, where she found a pair of women's slacks cropped above the ankles. They were too tight in the hips and too loose in the waist, but she put them on and fashioned a belt from the polypro and knotted Jim's T-shirt at her waist. There was nothing in the way of shoes, which was a damned shame.

The cabin had four windows, one in every wall. Each looked out on trees standing in what looked like late-afternoon sun. Five o'clock, maybe. This time of year, maybe six. Kate went to the door and found it locked from the outside. She picked up a chair and sent it through the nearest window. The glass cracked and prismed but didn't fall.

'Safety glass?' Kate said out loud. 'I don't think so, you son of a bitch.' She took the chair to the little woodstove and used it to knock the chimney down. There was a small poof of soot, no more, someone had been burning Red Devil regularly in the little stove. Little, but heavy, it was made of cast iron. Kate stooped and got both arms around it and lifted, grunting. Later, when the adrenaline rush abated, causing her muscles to feel the strain, she would realize just how angry she had been, because she now raised that stove up off the floor, staggered over to the window, and reared back to send the stove into the window.

This time, the window gave up the ghost and the stove crashed through and fell on the ground outside. The fresh air coming in through that open window was the sweetest odor Kate had ever smelled. She fetched the chair again and used the legs to clear the window frame of glass, and then she was out and on the ground.

One single-lane road that was more of a game trail led up to the front door, which was locked with a padlock. Kate went back inside for a bread knife. The cabin had never been painted and the screws securing the hasp to the doorjamb came out easily with a small application of muscle. She threw the hasp and the padlock deep into the woods, then took a long, luxurious, and much-needed pee in the outhouse out back, which came equipped with toilet paper. Ritzy.

She walked ten minutes down the road before her feet began to feel it. She heard a jet high over head. It seemed to be descending. She didn't hear any street sounds that might indicate a road. The trees never thinned out enough to give her a view, something to tell her where she was.

She padded back up the road, went to the window of the cabin, and climbed up on the sill. She stood up, reaching for the eave of the roof. She caught it with both hands and gained the roof in a sort of scrabbling kick. It was made of corrugated metal and was warm from the day.

She stood up.

There were mountains in front and behind and all around, sharp peaks, some with snow, some without. They looked slightly familiar. Soft in the distance she thought she heard the sound of running water. A creek perhaps.

The setting sun slanted on the mountains with no snow, another jet appeared over the eastern horizon, and Kate knew where she was. The cabin was located in the Chugach Mountains, somewhere between the front and back ranges. Crow Creek Valley, maybe, reasonably accessible if you knew your way around the Anchorage bowl area. The cabin probably sat on a chunk of land subdivided from some old homesteader's claim.

Her spirits lifted. Kate liked being lost about as much as she liked getting her feet wet. She went back inside the cabin and found a can of cream of tomato soup and a can of evaporated milk. She stirred both into a pan over the working burner of the Coleman stove and had a dinner of soup and saltines spread with peanut butter, chased with another bottle of water.

They wouldn't come until dark. They were off busily establishing their alibis, but they'd waited until the wee hours to take her, and they'd wait until the wee hours to kill her, too. But they'd come earlier tonight, because she had something Erland wanted, and they would need time to question her before they killed her. Maybe he thought she knew who had really killed William. Maybe he thought she had proof that he'd had Eugene and Charlotte killed. At any rate, no plan of his would include her leaving this place alive.

She remembered again Max's story of Jasper Bannister and Richie Constantine and Calvin Esterhaus. How like his father was Erland Bannister?

The .22 casings showed that a gun had been fired in this cabin before. She wondered where the bullets from them had lodged, and in whom.

Erland might come armed tonight, too, but maybe not. He had left her pretty well trussed up. He wouldn't be expecting to find her free. But then he'd locked the door, as if guaranteeing that if she did get loose, she wouldn't get anywhere. Which she had done. But maybe he'd locked the door to keep stray hikers out. And the windows were high enough that no one smaller than a giant could look in, so he must have thought she was pretty safely shut in for the day.

She remembered the voices she'd heard the first time she'd come around. He probably wouldn't come alone, he'd need someone to clean up after him, because guys like Erland Bannister never dirtied their hands with the cleanup work. Probably he'd bring the same someone who had kidnapped her, because using the same crew meant fewer witnesses.

All she had to defend herself was a steak knife. She knew she should walk away, right now. That was the smart thing to do. Start walking, right now, start eating up some of the mileage between her and 911.

Where was her cell phone when she needed it? Back in the town house, in her day pack. Oh yeah, some of the smarter money she'd spent this year.

On the other hand, there was no guarantee that

anyone would come if she called. There were damn few Alaskans who were going to believe some wild tale about Erland Bannister murdering his nephew and contracting to murder his brother-in-law and his niece over thirty years later. Kate had some street cred, but nobody had enough to put that story over.

Although Kate was beginning to have a sneaking suspicion that she'd been wrong about who'd killed William Muravieff, and if she ran, she'd never know.

And she really, really wanted to know.

Using the steak knife, she cut rough pieces out of the canvas cot, shaped them into soles, and bored holes through which she laced the rope. The canvas was stiff and the rope was harsh against her skin. She found a man's flannel shirt in the closet and cut up the sleeves for socks. She cut off every single hanging thread, every dangling bit of rope, because when it came time to run, she didn't want anything tripping her up.

She tucked the steak knife into the rope around her waist. She situated the table to the left of the open door and placed the chair so that it was just out of eyesight of the doorway. She went outside to look over the forty-foot spruce tree that stood at just the right spot to give her a good view of what would come up the road later this evening. She broke a few dead branches, bent a few living ones, and made a reasonably comfortable seat, padded with the canvas left over from the cot and the remaining bits of rope, about twenty feet up. It was clearly visible from the cabin, but in her experience, people seldom looked up. She cleared what she hoped was a fairly unobvious path to the ground, then went from ground to seat and back again a couple of times to familiarize herself with hand and footholds. She wanted to be able to ascend and descend as quietly as possible.

Her hands were sticky with sap when she was done. She went back to the cabin and gathered up half a dozen bottles of water. She took three of them up the tree. The other three she secreted in a hollow beneath a fallen spruce about a hundred feet off the road. If she needed them, they'd be there. She hoped she wouldn't.

She went back to the cabin and cleaned up the broken glass in front of the window and hauled the stove back inside. It felt a lot heavier on the way in than it had on the way out. If she was right and they came late, chances were that with no ambient light to reflect off the glass, they'd never see that it was missing. If she was lucky, they wouldn't notice the broken stovepipe. It was amazing what people missed seeing just because they had preconceived notions of what was supposed to be in front of them.

She got another bottle of water and scrubbed the sap from her hands. She'd found a nappy fleece jacket with a broken zipper that was at least thirteen sizes too big for her, but it was heavy. She hid it in the deadfall with the water.

The sun went behind the mountains and took at least as much time to set below the horizon. The forest was filled with the sounds of the birds and the beasts going about their business, hunting, feeding, grooming. A bear sounded off in the distance, and Kate hoped he or she wasn't heading toward the cabin.

They came, as near as she could figure, around midnight. The witching hour, the hour when the blues band in your favorite neighborhood dive was just cranking it up, the hour when even Ted Koppel was ready to pack it in for the night, so it figured. They came in a nondescript pickup, a dull gray in color, plates the old blue-on-gold Alaska plates, no hubcaps, no mag wheels.

Only it wasn't *they*. It was only one man, whom Kate recognized as Erland the moment he stepped out. She couldn't believe it. She was even a little annoyed. Was she, Kate Shugak, so easily dealt with that the task required only one man, and that one man not accustomed to doing his own heavy lifting? Had no one considered the possibility that she might escape and do some heavy lifting of her own?

He saw the open door and halted, half in and half out of the vehicle. She began to descend the tree in stealth mode, glad her hair was no longer long enough to catch on spruce needles as she went.

She froze halfway down when he reached into the truck and took the keys out. Damn.

He walked up to the door. 'Kate?' he said.

She came up behind him, the canvas and fallen spruce needles masking her steps. 'Go on in,' she said.

He jumped and swore, and it did her heart all the good in the world. He sucked air in and let it out in an explosive breath 'You are one hell of a woman,' he said with what sounded like sincere regret.

'Well, don't sound so sorry about it,' she said. 'Go on, go in. Sit down.'

'How the hell did you get loose?'

'Sit,' Kate said, and leaned up against the wall next to the open door.

He sat, looking at her through the gloom. 'Can we have a light? I think there's an oil lamp around somewhere.'

One of the things Kate had learned during a five-year intensive stint with the Anchorage DA was that, contrary to popular fiction, bright lights did not make people spill their guts. On the contrary, the darker the room, the more forthcoming the secrets. 'I like it the way it is,' she said.

She sensed rather than saw him shrug. 'You're the boss.'

She didn't believe that for a New York minute. 'Who killed William Muravieff?' she asked.

'Ah,' he said.

Kate waited out the silence that followed. Erland Bannister was not the kind of man to be held accountable for his actions by anyone, from the IRS on down to Kate Shugak. Perhaps especially Kate Shugak, Alaska Native, female, two societies to which Erland had entrée but not membership and to both of which he almost certainly felt superior.

'First of all, I didn't kill him,' he said finally.

'I did sort of figure that out on my own,' Kate said. 'Was it Oliver?'

There was another, longer silence. 'Ah, Kate,' he said, and there was a world of sorrow in the words.

'Was it really that petty?' she said. 'William had

the girl Oliver wanted, and Oliver killed him for it?'

Again she sensed the shrug. 'When you're sixteen and male, girls are all you're thinking about. And Wanda was something.'

He still hadn't admitted anything, but then she wasn't wearing a wire, either. 'And you let Victoria take the fall. It was just so convenient. She was making so much noise over your decision to replace your union employees with contract hires, and then, lo and behold, she gets arrested for murdering her own son. Her trial knocks your restructuring of the family business off the front pages long enough for you to get the dirty work done and over with, and then, my god, she's found guilty. You must have thought you'd died and gone to heaven.'

'I kept hoping she'd beat the rap, right up until the verdict,' he said heavily.

'Bullshit,' Kate said. 'She wouldn't let her sons work for you after you announced what you were going to do, would she? And you didn't have any sons of your own to carry on the family business. With Victoria in jail, you naturally assumed custody of Oliver, and put him right to work. What happened, Erland? Did he figure he had you by the short ones, since you were covering up each other's dirty secrets? Is that how he could go to school and be a lawyer and start his own firm, leaving you high and dry?'

Silence.

'And then, thirty years later,' Kate said, 'certainly long enough for all the buried skeletons to have long since deteriorated, Victoria gets cancer and her daughter hires me so she doesn't have to die in jail. And you start tying up loose ends and a loose cannon. Eugene Muravieff, who was hiding in plain sight so he could stay in touch with his kids. And then Charlotte, because I wouldn't leave it alone, and the only way you could see to make that happen was to kill my employer.'

Erland must have read Disraeli. Never apologize, never explain. Arrogant but effective, especially when faced with three felony counts of murder, not to mention a felony count of kidnapping.

'You must have wished that Victoria had choked to death on a bone,' Kate said into the silence. 'She was always more trouble than she was worth anyway. Marrying that worthless Eugene. Finding out you were cooking the books.'

A stir. 'What?' he said, and his voice was no longer sorrowful.

Kate checked to see that the doorway was still clear. 'Of course you were embezzling funds, Erland,' she said. 'Victoria was working in accounts payable, where she found evidence of double billing.'

'How do you know all this?' Erland's voice was very cold and very clear, and Kate instantly remembered one of the voices she'd heard when she first came to in the cabin. 'You shouldn't have hit her at all.' Of course not, Kate thought, a fist in the face is too obvious – the ME would have had no trouble recognizing it for what it was, and it would no doubt have been inconsistent with the other injuries her corpse would have presented when it washed ashore in Turnagain Arm. A dead giveaway – pardon the expression, she thought – that foul play had been done. She was equally certain that Erland wanted it to look like an accident. Not so much like his father after all.

But who had he been talking to? 'She told me,' Kate said.

'She told you?' he said. 'You've seen her since she got out? Where is she?'

'Tell me something, Erland,' Kate said. 'Did you farm me out?'

'What?' he said.

'Did you farm out my kidnapping,' she said. 'I was just wondering. Sooner or later, you weren't going to want any witnesses. I'm figuring it was sooner, and maybe that's why you came up here alone.'

For the first time, she heard tension in his voice. 'I don't know what you're talking about.'

'Sure you do,' she said, and dived out the doorway in the same instant that he drew the gun and fired.

CHAPTER 20

She tumbled into a forward somersault to come up on her feet running. Round one to her.

She hit the trees in three strides, just as the gun cracked again. The sound of glass breaking on the truck made her laugh beneath her breath, as did the sound of Erland's curses.

She felt rather than saw her way to the water

cache. She paused, listening. There was the sound of glass breaking. He was probably kicking out the remains of his windshield. The truck's engine started.

She would have to stick close to the road. He'd know that and stay on it, waiting for her to emerge.

So she wormed her way under the deadfall, hoping that nothing had taken up residence in the hollow beneath in her absence. Nothing had. She felt for the oversized fleece jacket, snuggled into it and curled up into a ball. She wished for Mutt's warm bulk next to her, wished even for, god help her, Jim, and with that thought she dropped blessedly into a deep, dreamless oblivion.

Birdsong woke her in that pale hour before dawn, three pure descending notes, repeated and answered. Kate blinked, yawned, and stretched, and reached for one of the bottles of water to relieve her morning mouth. She got to her knees to peer out from beneath the underbrush.

The dew lay heavy on the bracken, a precursor of frost. She took a moment to be thankful it wasn't. She didn't see anyone or hear anything but animal noises, but that didn't mean that Erland wasn't sitting in his truck smack in the middle of the only road leading out, waiting for her to show up so he could shoot her dead and leave her to the bears to snack on. At this point he wouldn't care if her death looked like an accident or not. He'd risk shooting her now and coming up with an explanation later, delivered no doubt by a fine battery of expensive attorneys.

She'd been lucky so far and she knew it. Well, she thought, there's no point in not pushing your luck when it was running in your favor. She peed where she'd slept, just to underline her determination to sleep between clean sheets that night, and pushed her way through the dead branches and into the open.

The sky was light with the anticipation of sunrise. The three-note descant sounded again, sounding like an all clear, and Kate smiled. 'Thanks, Emaa,' she whispered, and began to creep forward, keeping her head at the level of the poushki while avoiding their spiked leaves. The forest floor was dense with pine needles, all the better to muffle her steps, but she watched where she placed her canvas-shod feet anyway.

She passed a cow moose with a yearling calf, so close that she could have touched them. The cow's ears went back, but she didn't get up, and Kate faded into the trees before she could.

The forest ended at the road. Kate peered out beneath a clump of wild roses. No sign of the truck. She had a choice here. She could start down the road, chancing discovery to move faster, or stick to the trees, where it would take much longer but would be much safer.

Erland Bannister wasn't the type to cut his losses and get on the next jet for Rio. He had too much property and too much money and too much power to leave it all behind. His only choice, as he would see it, would be to kill Kate before she had a chance to take that all away from him.

And it probably wouldn't hurt him to take her out. Somewhere down deep inside, the practical businessman resented the hell out of these upstart Natives, these people who hadn't done a lick of work in three hundred years' worth of Alaskan history and who had had it all handed to them on a platter thirty years before and now were a force with which to be reckoned – a political force, a social force, a governmental force – dangerous to offend, impossible to ignore. They were even marrying into the goddamn families of the power elite, bastardizing a line of entrepreneurs and visionaries going back a hundred years.

Well. One woman's merchant adventurer was another woman's pirate. Kate grinned to herself.

If she were Erland, she would have driven down to where this road intersected with the next road. There was only one way into the cabin and the same way out. Kate had to stay on or near the road to get back to Anchorage, and help. Yes, that's what she would do.

Kate stepped out into the road and stood there for a moment.

No one shot at her.

The three notes sounded from a nearby branch, and Kate looked up to catch the cocky eye of a golden-crowned sparrow. The tiny, plump brown bird launched from the bobbing branch it had been perched on and flitted down the road from tree to tree. Kate followed.

It was a long road and the sun was sliding up over the horizon when Kate rounded a corner and saw the intersection. She stepped into a thicket of alder and peered through the leaves. She didn't see the truck, or any other vehicle. But then, she wouldn't have parked in sight, either.

She would have wanted to lure her quarry into the open.

Okay. She was lurable. She soft-footed it down the little incline. The intersecting road was two lanes wide and the gravel hadn't been graded in a while. She still didn't see the truck, so she stepped out on it, and again, no one shot her. Life was good.

She put her back to the rising sun and set off down the road at a slow trot, working out the kinks of sleeping in the woods and working up some body heat while she was at it. She'd had peanut butter and crackers for breakfast, so she wasn't hungry, strictly speaking, but she would have killed for a big plate heaped with bacon and eggs over medium, with a big pile of crisp home fries on the side. She was fantasizing over the home fries – with onions and green, red, and yellow peppers and garlic mixed in – when she rounded a corner and saw the truck, parked with its nose downhill.

Without thinking about it, she dived for the side of the road and tumbled down a small bank, fetching up hard against a tree trunk.

'Shit,' she said before she could stop herself. She got to her feet and found herself looking down the barrel of a pistol held in the shaking hand of Oliver Muravieff.

He looked, if possible, even more terrified than Kate felt. 'Uncle Erland?' he called over his shoulder. 'Uncle Erland, I've got her.'

'Shoot her, you moron,' Kate heard Erland say, and that was all she needed to hear. She made a diving tackle for Oliver's bad knee. It cracked when she hit it and she knew a fierce satisfaction in the sound. Amazingly, he didn't drop the gun. He tried to point it at her, but she had his wrist in both hands. They struggled, rolling back and forth, and Kate's biggest fear at that point was the crashing of underbrush that signified Erland's approach.

'Drop it, you little weasel,' she said through her teeth, and at that moment the gun went off.

Kate's ears rang with the sound of the shot, and her nostrils stung from the smell of burnt powder. She jerked back and felt her torso, her legs, her arms. There was blood on her left hand and she stared at it, horrified, before realizing that it wasn't her blood.

She looked down at Oliver, at Oliver's belly, where a huge red bubble was growing. 'Oh fuck,' she said, and turned to meet the bull rush of Erland Bannister as he came crashing through a diamond willow. He looked past Kate to Oliver and said, 'Goddamn you, Oliver, you useless little shit!' Given that moment of distraction, Kate grabbed for an overhead branch, hoisted herself up, and kicked Erland Bannister right in the chin. His jaw clicked shut and he fell backward most fortuitously against a white birch that had grown so tall its branches were a good eight feet above the ground. His skull hit the birch's trunk with a very satisfying smack, a sound that Kate would have been happy to hear again, but there was no time. She rifled his pockets for keys and found them, and then she ran for it, flat out, right to the truck. It started at a touch and she put it in gear and floored the gas pedal.

Halfway down the hill, she met Mutt and Jim

Chopin coming up in one of those anonymous black SUVs that had government issue written all over it. Fred Gamble was driving.

'Who took out the insurance policies on the kids?' Jim said.

'Victoria did,' Kate said, 'just like everyone said she did. They were maturation policies, generating funds for when the kids got old enough to retire, or to provide financing for their burials, should that be necessary before their time.'

Brendan shook his head. 'She never denied taking them out, did she?'

'She never denied much of anything,' Kate said. 'Erland told her he'd turn Oliver in if she did.'

'Tell me that part again. I'm having a hard time with it.'

Kate sighed and let her head fall back. 'Oliver was in love with Wanda. He thought she was in love with William. Oliver drugged William with his mother's sleeping pills, took a couple himself so they'd show up in the drug scan, and siphoned some gas out of his mother's car, which he then ran from the fireplace to both sets of drapes. Then he put the gas can back in the garage, went upstairs, and climbed in bed to wait for the fire to catch and the smoke to rise to the second floor.'

'I still don't get it. He broke his leg trying to get out the window.'

'I don't think that was part of the plan.'

'Going out the window?'

'No, he meant to do that all along. It would have looked funny if he'd come down the stairs without trying to bring William with him. William's bedroom was between his and the stairs. No, Oliver had to go out the window to make it look good.'

'It looked pretty damn good,' Fred Gamble said. 'It certainly fooled an entire police force. Not to mention a jury.'

They were in Brendan's office. Kate had been giving statements continuously since nine o'clock in the morning. It was now one o'clock in the afternoon. She was sticky with tree sap, grimy with sweat and dirt, and very, very tired. Her one consolation was the shaggy gray head pressed to her knee. She knotted her fingers in Mutt's ruff and Mutt gave a comforting whine and leaned harder. She had been glued to Kate's side since they'd found Kate that morning. Sooner or later, such devotion was going to make it difficult to go to the bathroom, but right now it was equal parts relief and reassurance.

'And Victoria refused to speak to Charlotte because...'

'I'm guessing, to protect her,' Kate said. 'Victoria never told Charlotte that Oliver had killed William. Erland wouldn't tell her, either, if Victoria would refuse to talk to her. He wanted a complete rift. So long as Victoria was in jail for William's murder, no one would think to look at Oliver as a suspect. And Erland would have the heir he couldn't provide for himself.'

'And it worked,' Jim said. 'For thirty years.'

Kate nodded. 'Okay, your turn. You guys have been pumping me dry for four hours. What happened here?'

'I woke up, you were gone, the boys saw you get taken, they caught the tags, Brendan found that they were registered to a buddy of Ralph Patton's.'

'Was Ralph one of the men who took me?'

Brendan shook his head. 'I had a prowl car go out to his place. He was home with his wife and kid.'

Kate looked at Gamble. 'Not that I wasn't happy to see you, Fred, but how the hell did you get involved in this?'

Gamble looked at Brendan. Brendan brushed fruitlessly at a speck of something disgusting on his tie and said to it, 'I had reason to believe the FBI might have an interest in PME and all those who sail in her.'

Kate's eyes narrowed.

'We were watching Oliver. We followed him to the cabin,' Gamble said primly. 'And that's really all we're prepared to tell you.'

Racketeering? Money laundering? Kate wondered just what it was that had pulled PME back from the brink of bankruptcy all those years ago, and just how legal it had been.

She noticed Jim looked uncomfortable, and wondered what that was about. An enormous yawn split her face, and she decided to leave it for another day.

The phone rang. Brendan answered it, listened for a moment, said 'Thanks,' and hung up. 'Well, that was the crime-scene guys. They've been going over the cabin. Seems they found a grave.'

'What's in it?'

'What's left of what they think was a man.'

'Henry Cowell,' Kate said.

Brendan nodded at her. 'We'll have the lab put

a rush on it, but that's what I'm thinking.'

'He wouldn't stay bought.'

Brendan said, 'You think Erland paid him to throw the case?'

'Maybe not throw it,' Kate said, standing up and stretching. 'Even old hanging Judge Kiddle might have noticed that. But Henry Cowell sure didn't try very hard to get Victoria off.'

Back at the town house, she showered and changed into clean clothes and started to pack. Mutt knew what that meant and she was tiresomely happy about it.

Kate left her duffel by the door and called the cleaning service. They promised to come by the following morning. 'Oh,' Kate said, 'and there's some fresh stuff – fruit, vegetables, some meat – in the refrigerator. Tell your people to take it all.'

She drove everything she'd bought to a shipping firm that specialized in palletizing goods and shipping them into the Bush. On the way home, she detoured over to Kevin and Jordan's house.

Their mother opened the door. She looked sober, for the moment. Kate introduced herself in case the woman had been too drunk last time to remember her, and said, 'Your boys have been eating and sleeping at my house off and on for the last couple of days. I'm leaving now, so I won't be there for them. You've got two choices, ma'am. You can sober up and shape up and start taking care of them, or I can call the Division of Family and Youth Services and report you for child neglect and endangerment.'

She took Max to a late lunch to wash the taste

of that out of her mouth.

'Goddamn it,' Max said with a bitterness that not even the best mixed martini would soothe.

'Not your fault,' Kate said. 'It was a family conspiracy. There's nothing harder to crack.'

'Bullshit,' Max said. He looked like a very old and very irritated eagle, with his fierce blue eyes and his hawklike nose.

Yes, he was very like Abel. Abel Int-hout, another quintessential Alaskan old fart with an independent streak as wide as the Yukon and an attitude as convivial as a wolverine's.

'We should have figured it out,' Max said. 'It's what we're paid to do. Instead, we imprisoned the wrong perp for thirty years.'

'Well, she's out now, and pardoned. Plus, after all the hoo-ha dies down, there will be no stain on her character,' Kate said. 'She's going to take over PME, they say.'

'What about her cancer?'

'It's operable, about an eighty percent survival rate. She got a second opinion. She's going in for the operation this week.' Kate cocked an eye at him. 'I gave her your number.'

'Me?' Max didn't look so much surprised as outraged. 'Why the hell did you do that?'

'She's walking into the lion's den, Max,' Kate said. 'The FBI's running some kind of investigation of what they are calling PME's "past improprieties," and PME's board of directors were all hand picked by her brother. You think he won't be trying to pull strings from the inside?'

Max snorted. 'He's never going to see the inside. He's going to be out on bail by the end of

371

business today.'

'All the more reason Victoria could use a sharp-eyed old fart like you to watch her back. Not too many flies on you, old man.'

He smiled, albeit reluctantly.

Kate went for the jugular. 'She could use a friend about now. All three of her children are lost to her, two to death, one to jail.'

'Okay, all right, enough with the violins,' he said. 'I'll talk to her.' He denied any softening by giving her a sharp look. 'What about you?'

'Me?' Kate said. 'Well, my record on this case has not been what you might call stellar. I got my employer killed. I got my employer's father killed. I hired my first employee and almost got him killed.'

Max snorted again. 'I don't know how to break this to you, Shugak, but you're just not that powerful. You didn't make the calls. You didn't pull the triggers.'

'Maybe I could have been a little smoother,' she said. 'A little more subtle.'

'Maybe you could,' he said, 'and maybe pigs'll fly. Anybody who hires you finds out fast that your chosen instrument is the sledgehammer, not the scalpel.'

He surprised a laugh out of her at a time when she didn't feel much like laughing.

'Not much point in looking back,' Max said. 'Waste of time. Look forward.'

He leaned forward to give her knee a sharp rap. 'There's almost always tomorrow.'

She made one more stop on the way to the airport.

'Hello, Emily,' she said, when Charlotte's partner opened the door.

Emily's hand went to her mouth. There was almost nothing left of the smart, aggressive attorney Kate had met just days ago. Emily looked as if she hadn't showered since the day of Charlotte's death. She was dressed in the same gray sweats Charlotte had been wearing the first time Kate had visited this house. Her hair was lank and her face was colorless. She'd aged ten years since the last time Kate had seen her. 'Oh,' she said listlessly. 'It's you.' She walked away from the door without closing it behind her.

'Stay,' Kate said to Mutt in a soft voice, and followed Emily into the living room where she had curled up on the couch beneath a worn quilt decorated with illustrations of Holly Hobby.

'What do you want?' Emily said, still in that listless, disinterested voice.

'Has anyone told you what happened?'

Emily shook her head.

Kate told her everything.

'Oliver?' Emily said. 'Oliver killed his own brother?'

'Knock it off, Emily,' Kate said.

Frightened eyes raised to meet Kate's. 'I don't know what you mean.'

'You knew it was Oliver all along,' Kate said. 'I don't know how you figured it out, maybe it came out of being his law partner, maybe he let something slip at the office one day, but you knew.'

Emily's eyes filled with tears.

'You were Charlotte's heir,' Kate said. 'You knew about Oliver, and when Charlotte died, you confronted Erland. You threatened to expose Oliver. He threatened to contest Charlotte's will if you talked to me or anyone else about it. Stalemate.'

She waited. Emily picked at a loose thread on the afghan. 'This house is so big, so expensive, I couldn't afford it on my own. And I wanted to keep it, it's all I have left of her now—'

'Surely not all,' Kate said, looking at Emily with equal parts pity and disgust.

'You don't understand! I have to maintain a certain standard of living, I have to entertain, it's expected by my clients!'

'So you let Erland walk away from the cold-blooded murder of the person you loved most in the world. You did that for a house? For a career?'

Emily's face crumpled, 'Don't,' she said, warding off Kate with a shaking hand. 'No more.'

Her face was contorted with pain and grief, but superceding them both was an agonizing, overwhelming guilt. She had betrayed Charlotte in life by keeping her knowledge of Oliver's guilt a secret, and betrayed her again in death by bowing to Erland's blackmail, and what that meant was only now becoming clear to her.

There was nothing Kate could say that would make Emily feel any worse, and suddenly the desire to do so receded. She turned and left. Behind her she could hear Emily dissolve into helpless, racking sobs.

By the time Kate hit the door, she was running.

He saw the cab and knew it was them. He busied himself with preflighting the Cessna. He was back in full trooper regalia, from the perfectly centered set of the ball cap with the trooper insignia on his head to the glossy black of his half boots, and in between everything blue pressed to a knife-edge crease and everything gold polished to a high gleam. He was the very model of a modern major general, only in this case an Alaska State Trooper sergeant, and no apologies to either Gilbert or Sullivan, thank you very much.

It felt like armor, and he welcomed it. This was it, he told himself. No more putting it off, no more allowing her to fog his mind with sex, no more following her up the stairs of that town house and down onto that enormous bed in the master bedroom. No more losing himself in that firm muscle beneath smooth skin, those tip-tilted hazel eyes, that rich ripe mouth.

He yanked his wandering imagination back under control. They were done. There had never been a 'they.' He wouldn't even be here if it weren't for the fact that he'd spent some time with Kate Shugak, a night or two – okay, six, and he wasn't such an asshole that he couldn't say good-bye nicely when he had to. He wasn't one of those guys who just walked away when it was over. No, by God, he took his leave properly, like a gentle-man, and he would do no less with Kate Shugak.

The thing was, he didn't want a relationship. He'd never wanted one. We are what our parents make us, somebody once said, and it was true. His parents were your typical suburban couple who'd had their one token child, raised him to be a functioning, productive adult, and then agreed to coexist for the rest of their lives in the neutral zone they had made of their ranch-style home.

He'd never wanted anything that subdued, that lacking in passion, that colorless. If that was what marriage was about, and he had no evidence to the contrary – Bobby and Dinah Clark were clearly an aberration, Billy and Annie Mike the exception that broke the rule – then he wanted none of it.

He didn't want passion, either, none of that headlong, the world well lost, only for you in mine eyes nonsense. Deliberately, he willed to mind Virgil and Telma Hagberg. If passion meant you were instantly blind to all of your lover's faults, up to and including infanticide, he didn't want any part of that, either.

No. Better to pursue a more cautious middle road, a series of well, better not call them relationships. Affairs, perhaps? How about good old carnal knowledge? Scratch the itch and move on. There was nothing wrong with single, footloose, and fancy-free.

'Look at Old Sam Dementieff,' he told the gas tank. 'He must be a hundred and three, and he still scuttles down to Alaganik Bay and gets it on with Mary Balashoff every chance he gets. And that's only when she doesn't send word via Park Air to meet her in Anchorage first. He looks perfectly happy to me.'

The gas tank remained blandly nonresponsive.

The cab stopped on the tarmac and Kate got out. Mutt trotted over to greet Jim, who was on a stepladder, topping off the gas tank in the left wing.

Kate remembered Max's words. *'There's almost always tomorrow.'*

He was right. Tomorrow always came, and there was only one time when you didn't see it. William, Eugene, and Charlotte were dead. Emaa was dead. Her parents were dead.

Jack was dead.

But all that was yesterday, and yesterday was past praying for. She was alive.

She looked over at the Cessna, at Jim Chopin in glorious blue and gold, checking something beneath the cowling.

Jim was alive.

Mutt gave a distinctly feminine little yip, front paws as high as she could get on the ladder, begging for attention, and Jim dropped an absent hand to pull on her ears. Kate smiled, a long, slow, anticipatory smile.

Mutt was right. So was Max. Much better to focus on today.

She saw Jim spot her, and her smile widened at his expression.

Today, there was a chance of joining the Mile High Club.

AUTHOR'S NOTE

There is an actual Hiland Mountain Correctional Facility in Eagle River, Alaska, but it and the people who work and reside there bear no resemblance to the people in these pages. Besides, Janice does a better job of giving people a second chance at life than any imagined character ever could.

The reminiscences of my fictional character Morris Maxwell are inspired by those of Joe Rychetnik, a Renaissance man who was, among many other things, a pilot, a territorial policeman in Alaska, and a photographer for *National Geographic* magazine. He died in 2003, damn it, but you can still get to know him and prestate-hood Alaska through his books. Begin with *Bushcop*.

The publishers hope that this book has given you enjoyable reading. Large Print Books are especially designed to be as easy to see and hold as possible. If you wish a complete list of our books please ask at your local library or write directly to:

Magna Large Print Books
Magna House, Long Preston,
Skipton, North Yorkshire.
BD23 4ND

This Large Print Book for the partially sighted, who cannot read normal print, is published under the auspices of

THE ULVERSCROFT FOUNDATION

THE ULVERSCROFT FOUNDATION

... we hope that you have enjoyed this Large Print Book. Please think for a moment about those people who have worse eyesight problems than you ... and are unable to even read or enjoy Large Print, without great difficulty.

You can help them by sending a donation, large or small to:

**The Ulverscroft Foundation,
1, The Green, Bradgate Road,
Anstey, Leicestershire, LE7 7FU,
England.**
or request a copy of our brochure for more details.

The Foundation will use all your help to assist those people who are handicapped by various sight problems and need special attention.

Thank you very much for your help.